'We've got through to the ship,' said Stuart, turning on the shelf radio. The last chorus of 'Peggy Sue' faded and Bill's announcement boomed into the room.

'This is FREE Radio broadcasting on 244 metres medium wave. We'll be on the air twenty-four hours a day from April 15th with the best music in the universe and the hottest jocks in Great Britain. While we line up our bits and tweak our transmitters, here's a sample of what you're going to hear. This is FREE Radio. Bob Dylan – "The times they are a'changin'".'

Stuart hadn't felt this great since the episode of the exploding Dean's chair. Bill stared into space – it was the first time he'd heard himself on English radio. Emma watched them both. A happy, warm feeling drifted through her. She lifted her glass.

'Shall we toast, gentlemen? To the best radio station in the world.'

Dave Cash, currently presenting the Sunday morning show at London's Capital Gold, has been a DJ in the radio business for 30 years. His first novel, The Rating Game, *was a bestseller in 1992. He lives with his family in Kent.*

DAVE CASH

All Night Long

Mandarin

A Mandarin Paperback
ALL NIGHT LONG

First published in Great Britain 1993
by Mandarin Paperbacks
an imprint of Reed Consumer Books Ltd
Michelin House, 81 Fulham Road, London SW3 6RB
and Auckland, Melbourne, Singapore and Toronto

Reprinted 1993 (three times)

Copyright © Dave Cash 1993

The author has asserted his moral rights

A CIP catalogue record for this title
is available from the British Library
ISBN 0 7493 1563 6

Typeset by
Hewer Text Composition Services, Edinburgh
Printed and bound in Great Britain by
BPCC Paperbacks Ltd
Member of BPCC Ltd

FOR

Emmylou & Si-Fi

Thanks To

The folks close in for the support, understanding and coffee.

The management at Capital Radio for the most flexible contracts in media.

Garry and the crew at ADM Computers in Canterbury for the technology.

Louise, Mary, Potter, Mad Max, Jan, and all the Michelin Mob.

Robinson, Forst, McCormack, Walker, Everett, Fluff, Hamilton, Blackburn, Symonds, T.K., Raymondo, Ahern, Glass, Rosco, Burnett, Rose, Prince, Parsons, Brady, Vance, Dee, Ward, Rodigan, Sharp, Phear, Tarrant, Brown, Ashford, Gershlick, Wells, Read, Hayes, Sachs, Young, Parkinson, Double D, Wogan, Jensen, Fox, Chalker, King, Frey, Nino, Stewart, Chantler, Day, Warren Ryder, Thomsett, Taylor, Dean, Myatt, Horn, Skues, Aspel, Murray, Jacobs, Saville, Edmonds and all the others who have shared the air over the past quarter century.

And in fond memory of Tony Windsor, Paul Kazerine, Ray Moore, Roger Scott and Barry Alldis.

PROLOGUE

In the mid sixties, pirate radio changed the face of the British media and influenced a generation. It was a time of rapid change, milestone music and natural radio. For the first time in England DJs talked *to* people, not *at* them.

The radio station in this story is fictitious; the historical events are true. The characters are also fictitious, except where you recognise the name.

Chapter 1

Monday, 5 April 1965. 5 a.m.

Emma Saxby quietly closed the front door and climbed the worn stone steps to Elm Park Gardens. Her sister had kept her up 'til well past midnight telling lurid stories of her boyfriend Robert's nefarious activities with the bottle-blonde at number thirty-six. She'd actually caught them; seen them through the kitchen window – Robert's jeans around his ankles, his naked posterior tightening with every hurried stroke; Mrs Blonde Bitch gripping the edge of the breakfast table, her breasts flattened against the Formica top, shouting raucous obscenities that could be heard by at least two neighbours each way. In the end Emma managed only four hours' crumpled sleep on the living-room sofa; and this before the most important day of her life. Being the eldest of three sisters had its drawbacks.

The Mini's engine spluttered into life at the second time of asking. Adjusting the choke until the car ran smoothly, she sank into the familiar driving seat and waited for the engine to warm. She felt safe in here. She could talk to this car. As long as she let it warm up, checked the oil and didn't take too many liberties when cornering, she knew it would never let her down. When she'd broken up with her last boyfriend, she'd driven into the country and the car seemed to know where to go. It listened patiently as she told it the whole story, and it didn't laugh at her when she cried.

She loved driving this early in the morning. Fulham Road, Sydney Street, King's Road and Sloane Square were all deserted. Swinging the Mini leisurely into Lower Sloane Street she reflected on the 'Robert' scenario. A smirk of satisfaction made a brief appearance on Emma's face as she recalled her sister's revenge. The unhurried way she'd packed his suitcases, the one-line note: *I'll redirect your mail to number thirty-six*, her calmness as she prepared herself for work, and her skill in depositing two pounds of sugar into the petrol tank of his beloved 1954 MG roadster without spilling a granule.

There's more important things in life than walk-about willies, she gloated reassuringly to herself. 'I hope Robert's gets caught in his zip!'

She parked outside Bristol House in Lower Sloane Street, gathered her dry-cleaning from the carpeted boot and fairly skipped across the pavement to the glass-fronted building. The first pale ray of morning sun reflected off her car keys; she smiled up at the sky.

Her tiny third-floor bedsit felt chilly. She flicked on the fanheater and kettle. The flat was new and heated quickly; two things Emma loved about it. She'd grown up in old houses – cold, draughty places, where her mother would always be stuffing paper under the ill-fitting doors to keep out the winter wind. In Bristol House the windows fitted and the sinks were brand new. Even the overflow from the tiny plastic shower drained efficiently away across the white tiled floor. Her mother'd approved of the flat on her only visit. She'd told Emma to always keep the bed folded up in the

2

wall, for appearances. Emma always kept it down, for comfort. She appreciated her mother's ways. It hadn't been easy after the War with three young children and no husband. When the telegram arrived from the Ministry of Defence reporting her father's death at Bastogne her mother cried for days. She'd had a chance to remarry in 1948, but refused, telling the girls she didn't want anyone with dirty habits in the house. Emma pondered that statement through puberty; until Philip Davenport, a tall sixth-former, took her for a ride in Battersea Park, when she concluded her mother was probably right.

Slipping the plastic covering off the Cardin copy suit, she inspected it carefully and longed for the day when she'd be able to afford the real thing. It was a good copy and looked stunning when worn by a confident woman. Today she would not only be confident; she would be the best PA any managing director could have. Today she started work at Radio FREE.

Emma was an optimist in most things; a characteristic she shared with the great majority of her generation, which now accounted for over a third of Britain's population. The nation might be experiencing economic difficulty; Vietnam, Russia and Rhodesia were concerns, but only to people over thirty. The youth had the Beatles, Bob Dylan and, most important of all, spending money. If you didn't like your job, you simply walked across the street and got another; everything seemed to lead to something else, naturally, and with the minimum of effort.

She'd landed her new job by playing gooseberry for her friend Rachel. The Who had just finished their set at the Glenlyn, Forest Hill; one of several dimly lit basement clubs that were springing up all over London

3

in the shadow of the Marquee's success. Rachel fancied a tall, blond, Ivy League American who propped up the bar most elegantly in a slim-fitting black mohair suit, crisp white shirt and the narrowest of black knitted wool ties. It was Emma's job to engage his friend in conversation long enough to allow Rachel time to get Mr Clotheshorse on to the dance floor.

Within five minutes Emma had accepted this stranger's offer of employment. She would normally have been far more wary of such an instant invitation, but there was a directness, an honesty about this man that made her believe he really did own a pirate radio station, he was in desperate need of an assistant, and that she could be in at the start of something very special.

Physically, he was only just out of place in this dual-fashion dance house. Ninety per cent of Who fans were Mods; hooded coats and scooters with lots of lights and mirrors. The remaining elite preferred the Ivy League look – narrow tie and lapels on three-piece suits of exceptional cut and quality; far beyond the financial reach of the ninety per cent. They also tended to park their Porsches, Jaguars and Aston Martins at least two streets away from the venue. This stranger's dark blue Savile Row pin-stripe, with its tailored waist and slightly wider lapels, couldn't accurately be described as 'in'; but he wore it with such assurance and poise that any detrimental comment seemed futile, and would probably lead to the perpetrator being verbally cut off at the knees.

His eyes were the first thing Emma noticed; blue-grey, bright and intelligent. They reflected the colour of his suit in a certain light and seemed to move very deliberately from one person to another, locking his gaze and giving the subject his undivided attention before

4

moving on. She also saw sensitivity, kindness and humour. When he laughed his eyes sparkled; Emma liked that best of all. Her first impression was of a man not dissimilar to how she imagined a young Sherlock Holmes. Six foot three, brown wavy hair neatly trimmed and parted on the left, an oval face with a classic nose, slightly too big but nevertheless attractive. His boyish grin betrayed a mischievous side she could feel bubbling beneath the surface. She liked Stuart Salisbury immediately.

Emma placed the suit on the bed and squeezed into her micro-bathroom. A two-foot-square shower took up half the room, the loo and basin the other. She'd nailed a full-length mirror to the back of the louvred door and as she let her bathrobe slip to the floor she gave herself the regular morning once-over. Thick jet-black hair cut in a stylish Sassoon bob framed her rounded face. Her mouth was generous, her teeth large and straight. Her flawless Mediterranean complexion shone in the mirror. Bright brown eyes flashed from top to toe. Her body was prone to be heavy, but at five foot eight she could take it. The battle of the bulge was her never-ending nightmare. Riding a rocky path between diet and exercise, she would add five more sit-ups to her morning routine to compensate for the second helping of last night's pudding, or skip lunch in a vain attempt to equalise the absence of a morning run. Last summer she'd ballooned to ten and a half stone during the two-week family holiday in Devon, when her mother found a beautiful little bakery in Witheridge, and her sister discovered a fabulous restaurant in the neighbouring village of Washford Pyne. For the entire month of August Emma starved herself back to nine stone two.

It had been hell, but, physically and mentally, worth every hungry moment.

At thirteen she'd started to develop and by the time Philip Davenport came on the scene she filled a 'D' cup. She noted the tones of jealousy in the voices of peripheral girlfriends who said they felt sorry for her now that the fashion was all 'Twiggy'. She also noted she never got the same fashion awareness from men.

After a shower she patted herself dry and pondered the sequence of her day. Being a naturally neat person, she would have to organise her new boss from the coffee cups up. There was another reason for her determination. At her mother's insistence, her secretarial skills had been finely honed by the Pitman School, where, from Mrs Goldstein, a tiny but fiery feminist, she'd learned two lessons in life not on the curriculum: you don't need to be educated at Oxbridge out of Roedean to be successful, and you should always organise your boss better than he organises you. Another of Mrs Goldstein's sayings registered six months later when she quit her job at the insurance company: when you know more than the boss, either get his job or get out. She felt things would be different at Radio FREE. She remembered how proudly Stuart had described his radio station; how he'd shared with her his dream of seeing music radio in Great Britain, and his determination that, if the Government wouldn't allow it, he'd do it without them. She'd smiled when he explained FREE stood for the Future of Radio Entertaining Everyone and listened particularly intently when he forecast a million pound a year turnover. This was a dream worth pursuing; this was a job with a challenge. This was very Emma Saxby.

From the flying bridge of M.V. *FREE*, Bill Mason stared

6

wearily through US Navy binoculars at the empty sea stretching interminably ahead. He'd hoped by dawn they'd be in sight of Caroline and London. Three weeks out of Galveston; a pleasant crossing to North Africa and then the bitterly cold Portuguese coast and French Bite. The fur of his hood lining slapped his face. He focused again. 'There! Twenty degrees!' he shouted to an empty bridge, as his gaze sharpened on a converted mine-sweeper with a tall mast and the numbers 266 in ten-foot figures down her side. 'Radio London!! The Big "L"! The *bloody big "L"*!' He moved the binoculars thirty degrees to port where he slowly focused on M.V. *Mi Amigo* – Radio Caroline. Letting the binoculars drop around his neck, he threw off his hood, punched both arms in the air and issued a challenge to the wind. 'Hail ye titans of Radio! Know you that from this day forward FREE radio is here! *We*, I say WE, will be NUMBER ONE as sure as Cassius Clay's gonna whip Sonny Liston next month!' He paused. His only answer was the moaning wind. He punched the air again. 'YES!!'

'I thought from the sound of your voice, Mr Mason, you were in pain. I'm glad to see you are not.' The soft voice of Captain Jan Vourner made Bill jump as if it had been cannon fire. He spun around.

'Shit! You scared me!'

'I'm sorry, Mr Mason. It was not my intention.' The weathered man gestured toward the binoculars. 'May I?'

'Of course.'

The Captain set both elbows on the glass transom that ringed the flying bridge and slowly focused on the two ships. He opened the communication pipe and gave it a kick near the base. 'Bridge! You there?'

'Aye, Cap'n.'

'Ten degrees port. Engines down a third.'

'Ten degrees port. Engines down a third. Aye, Cap'n.'

'Thank you, number two.' He replaced the pipe-cap. 'You, sir, could do with a hot chocolate,' he said, swinging his arm around Bill's shoulder. 'We won't be there for an hour. May's well get warm before we get cold again.'

This was the Captain's last voyage. Sail the boat to England, a few months at anchor and he'd be replaced. He would finally take his lovely Lisa from Amsterdam to Venice, as he'd promised all those years ago. He'd told Bill his story over a bottle of Jack Daniels during a perky mid-Atlantic squall. How in thirty years of marriage he'd been home a total of five and a half years, and how he could remember each day ashore. How during the war, disguised as fishermen, he'd smuggled Lisa out of Rotterdam and across the Channel while on a five-day pass from Scapa Flow. How, after Venice, they'd sail to Portugal and live in a three-room villa overlooking the sea, where he would write his book and she would cook paella. Bill enjoyed his stories and felt very safe with Captain Jan Vourner in command.

After swirling the last swallow of liquid around his cup to gather the residue of concentrated chocolate that always seemed to deposit itself around the bottom edge of any receptacle, he drank the bitter, luke-warm mixture and placed the mug on the small table next to the shower. The table also stood next to the bunk and wardrobe, so meagre was the accommodation. He stepped into the shower and let the warm jets of healing water run over his athletic frame, washing the North Sea frost from his pores. The wetness darkened his neatly cut blond hair; the shampoo slid down his suntanned forehead, cascading over his cheeks and strong, bristled jaw, and flattening the mass of blond curly hair that covered his chest. A small trickle flowed directly down the centre of his perfectly straight nose and ski-jumped directly to the shower floor. He lathered his face with shaving soap for a good minute before stepping back from the shower, opening his steel-blue eyes, and adjusting the six-inch mirror he'd jammed behind the shower pipe. He had a tough beard; it would take at least two shaves before he'd be smooth enough for London.

Immaculately groomed and bristling with excitement, Emma Saxby switched on her portable radio and sat down at the small dining table next to the window. She looked down at the early morning bustle of people and her dark blue Mini parked tightly against the kerb. A cheerful Tony Blackburn welcomed her to the day on Radio Caroline, 199, and hit the voice-over to 'Can't Explain' perfectly.

Her new boss listened to Pete Brady on the Big 'L'.

Stuart Salisbury, hands clasped firmly behind his back, took a long, slow breath and surveyed the Thames. The river looked beautiful at this time of year. Albert Bridge to the left, Battersea Bridge to the right, connected by a row of gently shifting houseboats. He gazed down over the front-garden treetops, across the Embankment, taking a glint of sun in his eye from the flying-bridge glass of a wooden cruiser as it emerged from beneath Battersea Bridge. He watched, with some satisfaction, its unhurried progress past the houseboats and its disappearance under the Albert Bridge. The sixth-floor flat in Cheyne Walk had been a very good idea.

Being born the second son in a moneyed Northern

English family has distinct advantages. The family fortune had been founded by his great-great-grandfather, Admiral Bingham Salisbury, when he decided to reject the usual retirement offer of a hundred acres in the south-west in favour of considerably more land in the north-east, which he quickly cultivated into profitable farms. Stuart's great-grandfather built six textile mills and two factories making farm equipment, which his grandfather sold at a handsome profit. His father diversified into property development and road building which now formed the basis of the family's business. It was hoped that the next generation would move into the fast-developing world of electronics. The first born, Peter, had no option but to take up the family mantle and was subsequently groomed for business from the age of three. Stuart, on the other hand, was left pretty much to his own devices, very dangerous when a boy is prone to having ideas. He trailed around the school circuit two years behind his brother and for three ghastly terms at Bradford, a top-notch boarding school, was actually known as Salisbury Minor.

When a don from Balliol wrote to his father saying that young Stuart showed little interest in academia, even less in politics and was fast becoming a nuisance with his persistent playing of rock 'n' roll records, it was thought prudent to show young Stuart the door with three neatly packed suitcases, two hundred thousand pounds-worth of blue-chip stock and a fifty thousand pound credit note for Coutts in The Strand.

Stuart took his ideas to London.

They had not always been good ideas. The first band he promoted took him for eight hundred pounds' worth of equipment before signing with an East End manager 'Cos 'e 'ad betta con-nec-shuns!' They said they'd pay him back when they made it big: that was three years ago and he hadn't seen a penny, or the group in the charts. The E-type Jaguar was another bad idea, that nearly killed him. The R-type Bentley that replaced it reflected his style with considerably more accuracy. Comfort became Stuart's byword, be it in cars of any other aspect of life.

Luckily, the good ideas outweighed the bad. The best had occurred to him last summer while he was sitting in Hyde Park listening to Radio Caroline. He noticed that most of the people who passed him were also tuned to 199 and, if not, some other pirate station. He would have his own station!

From the off, everything fell right into place. He sold his Kensington flat at a profit and bought number twenty-five Carlyle Mansions. It had central heating, double glazing and an extra room for an office. Peter just happened to be going to Texas on business and was glad of some company, giving Stuart the opportunity to shop around for equipment and personnel without arousing suspicion within the family. He was now allowed back to the country seat at weekends in the vain hope that he might bring a suitable young lady with him; he never did. Also, the family had heard of his limited success in London property and were anxious to 'give the lad a boost', 'show him we're proud of him'. Stuart thought it more a way of controlling him than any spontaneous display of family love.

Calbraith House had supported the Salisburys for over a hundred years and they, in turn, had supported it. Great-grandfather Salisbury had it built upon receiving a considerable dowry from his marriage to great-grandmother, the former Miss Eliza Abercrombie of Mayfair. Snugly nestling in seventy acres of mixed woodland and three acres of formal gardens, the house was both grand and practical. Grand as, architecturally, it resembled a scaled-down Balmoral Castle; practical, as it stood equidistant from the family's mills and factories.

Stuart felt overwhelmed by both the house and his family. His mother, Faye, suffered the domination of his father, Gordon; she, in turn, tried to dominate the boys, unfortunately for her with little success. Stuart hoped his parents had found some happiness along their rocky marital road, although he remained convinced theirs was not so much a four-lane freeway as a two-track dirt road littered with potholes. They'd stopped arguing openly shortly after Stuart started boarding school; the relationship now moved from point to counterpoint with disinterested familiarity, punctuated by acrid comment and cynical repartee. Part of Stuart's unwillingness to settle down was based on observation of his parents joyless marriage; combined with the unlikeliness that anyone he brought home would be mutually suitable. And, to date, he'd not fallen in love: a state to which he attached far more importance than did his parents.

Alone in this arm's-length family stood his brother, the only person in the world he truly trusted. They shared a secret so terrible, it would bind them for eternity. For two years they had perpetrated some of the most imaginative and, as yet, unsolved pranks ever to have graced the halls of Bradford public school. The legendary apple scrumping of '55; the talking statue (with certain moving parts) of spring '56; and the divinely inspired exploding Dean's chair of last-term Speech Day. Each caper was planned by Peter with military precision; Stuart acting as his confidant and sounding board, often injecting a vital twist or planning a secondary escape route. They took his route once and got lost, but Stuart still managed to think on his feet. They picked two bags full of blackberries, marched boldly in to the House Master's room, and offered them for his wife to make 'one of her delicious pies'. The House Master thanked the boys for their kindness, oblivious to the pair of his wife's voluminous bloomers adorning the main flag-pole, directly opposite his study window. Maggot Cooke, Curly Browne and Cockburn Minor were involved on a 'need to know' basis for supply reasons but, save those three, nobody ever found out the identity of the villains.

Peter steered Stuart through the rigours of the last weekend in the country and, once airborne over Land's End, asked his younger sibling what this 'big deal' was all about.

'People! It's about people with radios.' Stuart reclined his seat slightly. 'There's a new generation who are listening to radios. Not the BBC, but Caroline and London. They're exciting, dynamic; the Beatles and Stones love them, millions of young people are tuning in.' He gave his brother a light tap on the shoulder. 'And I'd like to own one.'

Peter tipped his chair to the same inclination as his brother's. 'And so you shall, dear boy,' he smiled indulgently. 'And so you shall.'

The engines of M.V. *FREE* throbbed full astern for thirty seconds before grinding to a stop. Two f'ward anchors were released by four oilskin-clad seamen. The massive metal hooks crashed into the dark water, their chains paying out with frightening speed. Captain Vourner stood on the bridge and waited for the tell-tale slack that would signify contact with the bottom. He pulled the control lever to Full Astern. Once again the engines did his bidding. Within a few seconds the chains were taut. He pushed the control lever to All Stop and pressed the ship's intercom.

'Anchors secured. Gentlemen, we have arrived.' He nodded towards his number one. 'Have the antenna engineers deployed.'

'Aye, C'tain.'

'I'd like to see Mr Mason and Mr Todd in my cabin.' The Captain left the bridge.

'I've got, a six-month option on this flat and it has two bedrooms.' Bill took a deep breath. 'You can have a bedroom for four pounds a week. We'll probably be off at different times and if we clash, we compromise.'

Brian Todd knew a good deal when he heard it. Despite making several enemies along the way, he'd survived seven years in the tough world of Australian radio, the last two as a programme director in Sydney. His job had been to compile the record playlist, run the format and keep the other jocks in line, all of which he handled with remarkable dexterity. However, his ethics were not all they should have been. He didn't see the harm in taking a small amount of money or the odd piece of jewellery in return for including a record in the station climber list. The record promoters loved him; his colleagues thought a good kick in the coccyx more appropriate and promptly told the station manager.

He'd escaped with a severe reprimand and decided to try his hand at television reporting. This, too, proved disastrous, not only because his numerous offers to 'stand in front of the sign for a few dollars' got right up everyone's nose, but also because he was not photogenic; his forehead too low and his mud-coloured eyes too close together. His nose had been broken on two occasions; he said in surfing accidents, his colleagues said by pissed-off peers. Whatever the cause, his face was left sloping slightly to the left and although when suntanned at forty paces he could pass as reasonably attractive, with his long blond hair and solid muscular body, through the eye of a camera he looked a lopsided fool.

He joined the pirates two months later for the same reason that attracted many young media men in the mid sixties; a sense of newness, of starting afresh, a belief that this time everything would be different. His priorities, however, remained crystal clear: Brian Todd was number one. A chance of a flat in Knightsbridge for four pounds a week was too good to pass up.

'You've got a deal, mate.' Brian offered his hand. The ship rolled slightly to port. 'I s'pose we've gotta get used to this,' he said, slamming his hand on the table to balance himself. 'Being at anchor ain't my favourite pastime. You feel so bloody vulnerable; at the sea's beck and call, so to speak.'

'Right now we're at the Captain's beck and call, and I don't fancy keeping the old fellow waiting.' Bill stepped through the bulkhead-hatch and walked down the carpet-covered companionway that led to the top deck and Captain Vourner's cabin.

M.V. *FREE* had enjoyed an extensive refit before she'd left Galveston, mainly due to Stuart's passion for comfort. He knew he'd have to spend time on the ship and to that end he'd spent more than a little money on carpets, furnishings and heating. The accommodation on the other pirate ships was very basic, the driving force of their backers being to make as much money as quickly

15

as possible; Stuart, however, saw this as a long-term investment. *FREE* was the sister ship to M.V. *Galaxy* (Radio London), a US Navy mine-sweeper, pensioned off by the Pentagon but ideal for the job at hand. The lower stern deck, which had housed the business end of the war machine, made a perfect studio. Fifty square feet of double-skinned emptiness, divided in half to house 'on-air' and 'production' studios. Both studios were equipped identically with RCA ten-channel consoles, two Gates P12 turntables with Greys' research arms, four Spotmaster high-speed cartridge machines, two Scully multispeed tape-decks for use in bad weather, and an Ampex 500 tape machine for production work, all of which could be interchanged in case of failure. F'ward from the studio, housed in the old magazine, stood two twenty-five kilowatt RCA ampliphase transmitters. They split the studio signal on entry and fired it up what looked like two six-foot radio valves, delivering maximum output to the aerial on the deck above. The power of the radio frequency delivered to the mast was so intense that if you held a fluorescent tube in your hand next to it, it would light itself within five seconds. Many DJs, having experienced sudden hair loss, were beginning to feel concerned about things cancerous and the possibility of a nil sperm count in later life.

The galley and crew's quarters were f'ward of the transmitter room. Then came the general mess-room, stretching the full width of the ship. This was used for meals, meetings and watching the small black and white television which was the focal point of the limited social activity on board. From the mess-room to the bow, ten officers' cabins were converted into DJs quarters. Each cabin was carpeted, individually heated and furnished with a bunk, writing desk, wardrobe, sink and small box-shower.

Above decks, the ship appeared remarkably bare. The four-inch f'ward gun had been removed, as had the aft sweeping equipment. From the original ship, only the main superstructure, bridge and flying bridge remained. The Captain's cabin took up most of the space below the bridge, along with a small radio room which would be used as the only link with London and to monitor the BBC's news. Three steel structures had been built on deck to house the transmitter link and standby generators.

The cold northerly wind sliced through Bill's bulky sweater as he stood on deck and knocked politely on Captain Vourner's door.

'Come!'

The cabin felt warm and welcoming. Jan Vourner knew from years of experience how to make comfort out of chaos. His cabin boasted a private toilet, a comfortable leather settee, and a built-in kitchen unit. Pictures of his lovely Lisa adorned the walls.

'Boys, you look frozen.' He pointed towards the stove. 'Help yourselves to coffee.' He sat behind his small oak desk and watched Bill and Brian cup their hands gladly around the hot mugs. 'The tug will be here by noon, which means you should be ashore by half past one.' The men smiled at each other. 'Now I'm sure you're both anxious to get to London as fast as possible, but before you start terrorising the female population there's a delivery I must ask you to make.' He pulled a large brown envelope from the top drawer of the desk and placed it in front of him. 'I want to get to Amsterdam as soon as possible. In here is my complete list of requirements. I need the okay from

17

Stuart by tomorrow noon. He knows you're coming. He'll wait for you at the office.'

Bill picked up the envelope. 'No problem.'

At 146 Baronsmire Road, Finchley, nineteen-year-old Anna Papanicholas had a massive problem. Yesterday her father had forbidden her to apply for a job as a receptionist. He wouldn't object if it was at a doctor's surgery, a lawyer's, or even, please God, the local church office; but at a pirate radio station? That was completely out of the question!

'The Papanicholas family,' he'd shouted at her over dinner, 'is one of the most respected families both here and at home in Cyprus, and I will not allow my daughter to be involved with a bunch of drug-taking sex maniacs!'

Anna had no desire to defy her father or in any way disgrace the family name, but she did wish, with all her heart, to be involved in the most exciting thing she'd ever heard of. She stretched out on the bed and looked up at the Rolling Stones poster pinned to the ceiling. She heard Tony Windsor start his morning show on Big 'L' with his customary '*Hul-lo*' and realised that her ambitions went far beyond being a receptionist. She wanted to be the first female DJ on pirate radio. She knew in her heart she'd be good, the problem would be convincing the station. But the biggest problem would be getting a job in the first place, be it receptionist, DJ or dogsbody; and to do it without her father knowing.

Mr Papanicholas's booming voice drifted up the stairs. 'Goodbye, Anna. See you this evening.'

'Goodbye, Father.' She watched from her bedroom window as he boarded his Zephyr Six and backed carefully into Baronsmire Road. As soon as he'd disappeared from sight however she jumped to her feet and scampered to the bathroom. The rambling Victorian house was now empty – just the way Anna liked it. Some mornings she'd run naked through the thick-carpeted hallway and into the oak-panelled living-room, where she'd jump onto the ornate French settee and shout, 'Geronimo!' at the ceiling. It was a futile teenage rebellion, but it made her feel good. Today she must look good; the kind of style that befitted the front line of what was going to be the best radio station in the world. After she'd showered, brushed her teeth, combed her shoulder-length golden hair and given her dark brown eyes the Dusty Springfield treatment, she danced back into the bedroom and pulled her white mini-skirt and white Courrèges boots from the wardrobe, choosing her favourite orange ribbed top to complete the outfit.

Anna's figure was ideally suited to mini-skirt fashion. At five feet four inches she was tall enough to look leggy and small enough not to look gawky. Her ample breasts were in hourglass proportion to her body, and long, shapely legs extended her perceived height by at least three inches. Her unusual combination of blonde hair and dark eyes, together with her luminous complexion, had turned male heads from the age of seven. By the time she'd become the main topic of bawdy conversation in the fifth-form locker room at Muswell Hill Comprehensive, her father had spotted the danger and imposed a strict regime of chaperone and curfew that would have made the Kremlin proud. She never complained about the restrictions placed on her, it would do no good. Her father's word was law: end of story. But at nineteen, with school behind her and the big, bad, real world awaiting, all this over-protective repression felt outdated and unwanted.

19

This was England 1965, not Cyprus 1840, and Anna couldn't wait to escape.

'I'm sorry, Father,' she whispered as she clipped on her round black plastic earrings. 'But I want to be on the radio.'

Stuart tuned his office radio on to 244 metres medium wave. Nothing. He checked his watch; eleven-thirty. 'Damn!'

'What's the matter?' Emma stood in the office doorway, a cup of coffee in each hand.

'They should at least have the carrier signal out by now. They've been in place since nine o'clock.'

'We don't know that for sure.' Emma placed both cups on Stuart's desk. 'I'm sure they'll get on as soon as they can. I've got this morning's letters for you to sign and I want to talk to you about staffing.'

Stuart relaxed his stance and turned to face his new assistant. She read his mind with consummate ease.

'Priorities, Stuart. You must get them right. The station isn't on the air for at least two weeks, but right now I have over a hundred job applications to deal with and nearly two hundred audition tapes.' She could see she had captured his attention. 'What do you want me to do first?'

Stuart sat down at his desk and carefully studied this beautiful creature who had so effortlessly taken over his life. In a few short hours she'd organised his diary, his files, and the backlog of bills; as well as ordering new furniture, fresh ground coffee and him into his own office. She seemed totally in control of herself and Stuart admired that. He admired that very much indeed. 'Do I have any interviews?'

'Not in the diary, but there is a Anna Papa-something

outside who says she's come for the receptionist's job.'

Unbeknown to Stuart, at the Pitman school Emma had also learned to impersonate a swan perfectly; smooth and elegant on top, paddling at top speed underneath. Since her arrival just before eight this morning she'd been trying desperately to absorb all the sights and sounds of her new workplace while remaining outwardly tranquil. The office looked spacious for a mews house, and gloriously empty. In Stuart's room, a desk, sofa and drinks cabinet gave the impression of occupation, but there were no pictures, magazines, or knick-knacks that could suggest any sort of permanence. The remaining five rooms were clean, carpeted and bare, save the telephones and their connecting wires that snaked across the grey short-pile carpets and disappeared through white plastic points in the skirting board.

Her office adjoined Stuart's via a glass panelled door. She thought Philip Marlowe, Private Detective would be a more appropriate sign on the frosted glass than the present John Deacon, Solicitor. Her first task was to cover the previous tenant's advertising with a poster of the Beatles. The second problem was her desk. This ten-by three-foot monster, a thick slab of scuffed teak sitting atop a sturdy chrome frame, took up half the room. She wondered how on earth the removal men had managed to negotiate the narrow wooden stairs which were the only visible access to the office; the lower floor being taken up completely by garage space. She couldn't move the damn thing, already piled high with tapes, letters, packages and junk mail. She'd just have to live around it.

21

She'd spent her first half hour of employment clearing 'toobigski', as she'd named it, and creating eight neat piles in two straight rows across the top of the desk. Emma often gave names to inanimate objects and plants. She'd also make up nonsense words to describe everyday things; a telephone was a gangaler, a toilet a bot pot; the miniature fern that lived on her bathroom window ledge relished in the name of giant. She knew it was silly, but it gave her a sense of freedom to escape into her world of thoughts where only she and the objects spoke the language. She'd smiled to herself as she placed the gangaler on toobigski's newly polished top.

'You'd better send her in then.'

Stuart also admired initiative. He'd placed a small add in *Melody Maker* giving only the phone number. This girl had found out the address and shown up on speculation. Definitely worth a look. He took a sip of coffee. It was just how he liked it. 'You can start on the audition tapes. Get rid of the dross and let me hear the best twenty or so as soon as poss.

Emma left the room without further conversation. She returned a minute later. 'Stuart, this is Anna Papanicholas. She wants to work here.'

Something in Emma's voice told Stuart that he was being handed a fait accompli. Anna certainly looked right. Young, bright-faced and dressed in the latest fashion, she had all the right physical attributes for fronting the station. 'Where have you worked before?'

'This would be my first job.' Anna's nervousness left her as she studied Stuart carefully, almost giving the impression that it was she who would decide whether or not to work here. 'I have four A-levels.'

Stuart noted her slightly haughty tone of voice and was convinced a conspiracy involving both girls was already in play. 'Do you know my assistant, Emma Saxby?'

'We met in her office; she told me it was her first day.' Anna smiled benignly, as if she could understand fully the complete range of emotions connected with the start of such a project. 'It must be very exciting starting a radio station.'

'It's a lot of hard work. Are you willing to put in the hours?'

'I need eight hours' sleep a day; the rest of my time is yours.' She lowered her eyes for a moment before raising them slowly to meet Stuart's gaze once more. 'I also type, speak passable Greek and French, and have no personal commitments.'

Stuart formed opinions quickly, and so far he could find no downside to this attractive teenager. She had a Lauren Bacall quality – cool, perceptive, in charge of herself. As she lowered her eyes a second time, Stuart felt a slight stirring of clandestine passion. He suppressed it immediately, committing it to memory for future examination. 'Can you start today?'

Anna's face radiated joy. 'I've already started. I answered the phone while I was waiting. Peter Salisbury; he's at his office, and a Captain Vourber or Vooner said test transmission should start at noon.'

'It's Captain Vourner.' Stuart spelled the last name, 'V-O-U-R-N-E-R, and he's always a priority caller. Is there anything else you need?'

'No, thank you. I'm sure Emma can show me the ropes.'

Bill Mason sat at his cabin desk completing his first letter home in three months. He'd phoned a few times, but he knew his mother liked to receive letters, especially when they were posted from the capital cities of the world.

He'd left his home in Russell Heights, Jamaica, at the age of eleven to become a boarder at King's College, Canterbury, graduating seven years later to Oxford. He didn't feel comfortable with what he considered the snobbish fraternity at the university. They seemed far too interested in Daddy's new Roller or Mummy's weekend dinner party to feel any genuine warmth for the people responsible for their being. Bill valued his parents. As a member of the white elite in a fast-changing Caribbean society he now understood why they'd shipped him off to an English boarding school so young and kept him closeted from the events around him during his holidays at home. When he returned to Jamaica in the summer of '64 and told them he would not continue at Oxford they didn't rant and rave or try to change his mind. They just asked him quietly what was next. He'd curled up on his favourite bean-bag and answered in one word: travel. He'd visited Paris, Rome, Athens, Tokyo, Johannesburg, Amsterdam, Vancouver and Hong Kong all in the space of two hectic years.

A bar fight in Johannesburg over Bill's insistence on sitting next to his new black friend, Wadikee, added a small scar to his right cheek, but apart from that his Adonis looks had travelled well. His six foot two inch frame, kept highly tuned by daily swimming and exercise, deterred most would-be protagonists.

On a swing through the southern states of America in the autumn of '64 he'd met Stuart Salisbury in a Dallas bar. They'd liked each other immediately and when Stuart told him his plans for FREE, Bill signed up on the spot. They also shared a particular taste in evening entertainment and Bill felt sure Stuart would have made 'special arrangements' for tonight's dinner. The problem was, what to do with Brian Todd?

A strong thump on the side of the ship interrupted his concentration. The tug had arrived. He signed his letter, 'Your loving son, William' (they never called him Bill), and folded it neatly into a pre-paid airmail envelope. He put both his letter and Captain Vourner's large brown envelope into his leather Gucci travel case, surveyed the room to see that everything was in place and stepped backwards through the cabin door. It had been his claustrophobic home for nearly a month and he couldn't wait to get out. He locked the door behind him and made his way along the narrow companionway towards the upper deck.

The bitter wind blew cuttingly cold as he approached the starboard side of the ship. He could see the tug's bridgehouse rise and fall above the gunwales. Brian and the Captain seemed deep in conversation, both holding on to the railing with one hand and gesturing with the other. As Bill approached he could hear more of an argument than a discussion.

'I don't give a bloody shit, mate! I'm not fucking jumping!'

The Captain, as usual, was calm. 'Mr Todd, there is nothing to be afraid of, except fear itself. Just wait until the tug is at its highest point, and jump. There's three burly crew members on the tug to catch you. Nothing can go wrong.'

'Says bloody you! What if I fall between the ships? I'll be crushed! Why haven't we got a bosun's chair?'

Bill looked over the side. Brian had a point. At its highest, there was still a good six feet between the tug

25

deck and the *FREE*'s gunwales. The swell of the sea pulled the tug away from the ship on its downward move, leaving a good four-foot gap between the two vessels. Bill saw the DJs from Caroline and London peering through the tug-cabin portholes, laughing at his anxious antipodean colleague. He stepped between the warring factions, winked at the Captain and locked his arm around Brian's neck tightly enough to allow no escape.

'Now listen up, my frightened friend. There are half a dozen of the finest DJs in the western world on that tug, and they're all laughing their guts out because you haven't got the bottle to do what they do every day. Now, either you jump on to that fucking boat within the next ten seconds or you can stay here for the next week and kiss goodbye to the flat in Knightsbridge!'

Brian's greed won over his paranoia. He moved to the gap in the railings, his eyes clamped firmly shut. 'Just push me when it's right!'

As the tug reached the high point Bill pushed Brian with all his strength. He seemed to be airborne for ever. Bill watched as the three tug crew caught him with the ease of seasoned circus performers and placed him, right side up, on the tug's deck.

Now it was his turn. He stood on the edge. Suddenly the gap between the ships looked much wider, the six-foot drop doubled and the catchers looked totally untrustworthy. If he hesitated, even for a moment, he would meet his peers with his reputation shattered. The tug was nearing its zenith. He gritted his teeth and jumped. He reached the tug's deck just as it started its descent on the next swell, a good three feet from the intended catchers. It felt like surfing on a giant board that had just caught a wave. Bill rode it to the bottom of the swell and then stood up straight. He looked at the faces in the cabin portholes half expecting them to hold up marking boards. Definitely a five point nine. To his surprise they just smiled and turned away.

The cabin felt like a sauna after the bitter wind on deck. Six men stood around an old electric heater that stood bolted to the floor. The man nearest the door turned to face the newcomers.

'Welcome to the North Sea. I'm Johnny Walker.'

Bill extended his hand. 'Pleased to meet you. I'm Bill Mason and this is Brian Todd.'

Brian nodded, still a bit unsure of himself after the boarding manoeuvres.

Johnny grinned. 'You'll get used to it. Scares everyone shitless the first time.' He turned to face the other men. 'Let me introduce Tony Blackburn, Simon Dee from our lot, and Pete Brady, Dave Dennis and Paul Kazerine from London.'

Bill's first impressions were that Simon Dee and Dave Dennis stood head and shoulders above the rest, Tony Blackburn was shorter than he'd expected and Paul Kazerine much older than the rest. Paul dug deep into the pockets of his full-length Navy great coat and produced a half-empty bottle of Bell's whisky.

'Help yourself, both of you. You look as if you could use it.'

The others laughed. Bill recognised the voice. Paul K; Radio London News. He looked nothing like Bill imagined. Big 'L' had been piped through FREE's ring-main for the last two days of the voyage and every hour Bill would hear Paul K read the news with authority and passion. He expected him to be in his mid-twenties, tall, hair in a Beatles cut. The man before him was mid-forties, just made five foot eight and had a receding hair-line and full beard. What little showed of his face bore the scars of many years' hard journalism, at a rate of three wars and two bottles a day. Bill took the whisky and swigged a good mouthful before passing it to Brian. He felt happy. No competition or scoring points here; just the lads heading for town.

Brian took a large drink and immediately turned very pale. It was suggested that maybe some fresh air would help. He agreed, and spent the rest of the journey leaning yawningly over the railings.

Bill's trip proved much more pleasant. He took a second gulp of whisky with a beer chaser and observed the proceedings. Johnny Walker seemed the natural leader. Simon Dee didn't say much, but when he did it was usually very funny; he mostly stood there in his tallness, looking quietly confident. Tony Blackburn was expressing concern about his shore gig at the Marquee. Pete Brady had already worked the venue and coached him on the type of audience to expect, room sound and equipment available. Bill was amazed by the lack of competition between the DJs. In other radio markets DJs guarded their information jealously. 'Don't know, never worked it,' was the standard reply; usually delivered the morning after you'd seen the poster advertising that they were there every Wednesday, starting two weeks ago. Dave Dennis and Paul Kazerine seemed happy to huddle next to the heater and discuss old battle plans while drinking, in Paul's case, the rest of the whisky and, in Dave's case, a large mug of tea.

Johnny talked to Bill for most of the journey. He warned of what to expect from the customs men at Harwich, which trains to London had bars, which bars in London had girls, and which girl in Chelsea sold

marijuana. Bill was very grateful for both the information and the friendship. He would enjoy competing
against him in the years to come. Worthy adversaries
often make firm friends.

Harwich customs proved as obnoxious as Johnny
predicted. Thorough search, curt language and no
humour. Bill thought it seemed more like point-scoring
than downright dislike, a theory confirmed when a
young officer asked Tony Blackburn for a request.

The dry land moved under Bill's feet as he tried
desperately to gain his footing after a month at sea.
A few yards behind him, 'grumbling' Brian dragged
his bag along the ground.

'For fuck's sake, mate. Slow down! My gut's killing
me.'

Bill had his answer; be kind *and* get tonight off. He
went back for the Australian. 'Come on. Let's get you
to the nearest hotel. You sleep this one off and come
down to London tomorrow.' He sat Brian down beside
the case. 'Give me two secs to tell the others and I'll be
right back for you.'

Half an hour later Bill stepped out of the Pierside
Hotel and strolled happily to the Station Inn, where
they'd all agreed to meet and wait for the London train.
They were the only people in this small, tawdry public
bar, its one saving grace a real coal fire in the corner.
The battered-looking barman took his time pouring the
drinks and informed them how unusual it was to have
a fireplace in the corner of a bar, and how it shared its
chimney with the open fire in the kitchen, and would
they like some food? It was half past two; the train was
due at three-fifteen.

'Yes please, landlord,' said Johnny, in a mockingly
arrogant voice. 'Bring us soup, bread, cheese and ale,

lots of ale, landlord, and none of your Watney's Red
– it's the real stuff we want.' He looked at Bill. 'And
wenches, landlord. We'll have wenches!'

The landlord started laughing a second after his
guests.

At exactly three o'clock Stuart Salisbury's dark brown
R-type Bentley pulled up outside the Station Inn. A
bald, stocky man stepped out and carefully closed the
driver's door. He could hear the laughter from inside.
As he walked through the door a football whizzed past
him at knee height. It crashed against the toilet door
and came back to rest at his feet. He flicked the ball
on to his right foot, then his left, on to his right knee,
then left, before cradling it on his right foot where it
began. He scanned the six men at the bar. 'Now, who
wants this?'

Bill took a step to the right, clearing the main pack.
'Over here!'

The man flicked the ball. It landed perfectly on Bill's
right foot. Even the landlord applauded.

'My name's Charlie,' said the man. 'I'm here to pick
up a Bill Mason and Brian Todd.'

Bill sat in the back seat and slept most of the way to
London. As he drifted off he thought of his new friends
taking the train and how lucky he was to have such
a great boss. He woke up as the car crossed Oxford
Circus. Bond Street next; then Selfridges on the right;
left into Park Lane. He loved this city. He looked at his
watch; five forty-five. Perfect.

Emma gently reminded Stuart that there was no such
thing as perfect when he found a typing error in the
ninth letter. He concurred and offered her a glass of
champagne.

Stuart flopped into his black leather chair. 'You've been magnificent today, Emma. What did I do before you came?'

'Managed by the skin of your teeth, I would guess.'

Stuart left a slight pause. 'You're very cheeky.'

'I'm very busy,' she replied, leaving no pause at all.

'Come and sit down.' He pointed to the black leather sofa occupying most of the opposite wall and adopted an almost fatherly tone of voice. 'Take some time and reflect. Nothing like it after a hard day.'

Emma sat down slowly, placed her champagne glass on the carved oak coffee table in front of her and straighted her skirt. In one ten-hour working day she'd brought FREE's administration up to speed. Files had been opened, correspondence sorted, diaries updated. She'd shouted at City Business Supplies in order to have an IBM typewriter delivered that afternoon, and she'd complimented Johnson Interiors on their excellent designs in order to ensure delivery by Friday. 'Please don't patronise me, Mr Salisbury.'

Apart from a slight flick of his eyes, Stuart remained expressionless.

'I'm thoroughly enjoying this job,' she continued bravely, 'but I'm not interested in being the little lady next door; the one you yell at when you're having a bad time. I want to be part of what's going on here, not an appendage.' Emma dropped her shoulders a little but not her head. 'I'm sorry if that upsets you, but it's the way I feel.'

'Upsets me?' Stuart sat upright on his chair and placed both arms firmly on the desk. 'Young lady, you don't upset me. Do you know how hard it is to find young people who even give a damn?' He lifted the Dom Perignon bottle off the desk. 'Let me top you up, then tell me what you found in the way of rising radio stars.'

Emma remained unmoved. 'I'm serious.'

Stuart's face hardened. 'So am I.' He looked directly at her. 'There's no limit to where you can go in this business. We're a young and exciting industry, continuously breaking new ground. I know you'll rise at your own pace, but right now you're my PA, and I believe you have some tapes for me to hear.'

Emma met his stare and made her decision. She stood up and walked unhurriedly towards the door. As she opened it, she turned back to face him. 'They're on my desk.' She did a fairly decent David Frost impression. 'Back in a trice.'

Stuart's Bentley glided to a halt outside number two Hayes Mews. Well rested and revitalised, Bill Mason climbed from the rear door. 'I'm sorry I've not been great company,' he said to Charlie, who closed the car door gently behind him. 'I needed that sleep. I've a long night ahead.'

'That's quite all right. I can remember when I could do that.'

Bill watched the old man's eyes glaze as his memory tripped back fifty years.

'Do you work for Stuart full-time?'

Charlie flashed a four-tooth grin. 'No, sir. The guv'nor's a self-drive man. I do mainly fetchin' and deliverin', but I do look after the chariot.' He opened the boot and removed Bill's case. 'Blimey, if I didn't take care of the jellied eels, he'd 'alf kick up a pen and ink.'

'Pardon?'

'Jellied eels – wheels; pen and ink – stink.'

Bill took his bag. 'Sorry, Charlie. I need educating in rhyming slang.'

'That's all right, sir. I'll give you another lesson tonight. No doubt I'll be needed if the guv'nor wants to drink. Now you'll 'ave to excuse me, I've got to get back to me trouble.'

'And strife – wife!'

Charlie gave a second showing of the four-tooth grin. 'That's right, sir. We'll 'ave you talking proper in no time.'

The door to number two was open. Even with his case in hand, Bill managed the stairs two at a time. From the landing he could see through the reception and into one of the back offices where the most glorious body he'd seen for a long time leaned over a desk gathering things into her arms. He quietly placed his case on the floor, walked quickly across the reception and opened the door.

'Why, Stuart. You *have* changed!'

Emma sprang upright, scattering papers and several tapes on the floor. She span round to face the intruder. Bill adjusted quickly.

'I'm terribly sorry. I didn't mean to scare you.'

'Scare me! You took a year off my life!'

Bill walked towards her. 'Let me help you.' Before she could answer he started picking up the tapes that had dropped around her feet. He looked up at her, being very careful not to succumb to the temptation of looking up her skirt, a gesture that didn't go unnoticed. Emma grinned down at him.

'If you want to grovel, that's your business.' She knelt down to help him. 'My name's Emma Saxby. I work with Stuart.'

This was the first woman Bill had been close to for

a month. Her knee brushed against his; her fragrance intoxicated him. He looked directly into her face. 'I'm Bill Mason. You have lovely eyes.'

They stood up together. Bill felt sure he could see a small tinge of embarrassment colouring her face.

'Really, Mr Mason,' she said mockingly. 'I hardly know you.'

'I'm sor . . .'

'Don't you dare say sorry again,' she interrupted, taking a good look at him for the first time. She struggled to suppress the rush she felt inside. He had the kind of looks she dreamed about on cold winter nights: a Robert Mitchum quality; just off being perfectly handsome, extremely interesting and *very* sexy.

'I'm . . . thinking I should start again,' he said, offering the tapes.

Emma took them from his outstretched hand. 'No need. That was great.' She studied him briefly before turning around and walking towards Stuart's door. She couldn't possibly stare into those laughing blue eyes for any length of time without becoming seriously tongue-tied. 'I'll tell him you're here.'

Bill picked up his case from reception and started to inspect the office. The brief encounter had unnerved him enough to trigger his defences. He was sure it was just because he hadn't seen a woman in so long. It could've been anyone. The fact that he could still see her face in front of him had nothing to do with anything. Do something different! He took a wide sweep of the reception; a large, bright, empty room with a window facing the mews and another through to Emma's office, also bare of furniture, except for the over-sized desk piled high with files and tapes and a large coffee machine balanced precariously on the back

34

edge. Bill deposited his case on the floor and sat in the office's only chair; behind the desk. He watched the door opposite, the one covered with the Beatles poster.

A loud familiar voice crashed through the door. 'Are you out there, Bill?'

'Yes!'

'Then come in here! I hate shouting!'

Bill was determined not to look at Emma as he opened Stuart's door. He looked directly at his boss. Stuart came from behind his desk and held out his arms in welcome.

'Bill. At last. You've made it. I'm so pleased to see you.' The two men embraced. 'Emma's just been going through some audition tapes. We've got hundreds.' Stuart filled another glass with champagne and handed it to Bill. 'Where's Brian?'

'He'll be joining us tomorrow. A little travel sickness. I left him in a hotel at Harwich.'

'That's very useful. I've arranged a little dinner party tonight, to celebrate your arrival, so to speak, and it's limited to four.

Bill looked at Emma. He saw a faint trace of disapproval flash across her face. 'Are you coming?'

'Good gracious, no! Much too hoi-polloi for me, I would imagine. Besides I have to see my boyfriend.'

The last word entered Bill's brain in slow motion, as if it was being spelled out. Defence . . . change the subject.

'Before I forget, I've got a list of essentials from Captain Vourner. Do you want it now?'

'Yes, please. What time is it?'

'Five to six,' chirped Emma, knowing not only the time, but also that she'd impressed the hell out of one Bill Mason. There was no boyfriend in Emma's life; she'd used it for effect and was pleased at the encouraging result.

'Good.' Stuart followed Bill into Emma's office. 'I'll be two minutes with this, Emma. Lace up the first tape.'

For most of the afternoon Emma'd been listening to audition tapes on the Revox machine she'd managed to borrow from the film production company next door. She had them playing in the background as she set about her more mundane tasks. Most were crap. A John Smith from Liverpool *demanded* to be a DJ on the strength of coming from the same town as the Beatles. He sounded unhappy, uncool and unrehearsed, with an accent so thick it would be incomprehensible to anyone who lived two miles out of Bootle. Another chap, a Peter Hollaway from Portsmouth, ended a very poor audition tape with the sentence, 'If you don't like it you can all fuck off and die', followed by hysterical laughter. Emma carefully deposited Mr Hollaway into the waste bin using only her thumb and index finger, lest any of his psychotic humour should be contagious.

The up-side of listening to so many duff tapes is that the good ones stand out like a pork pie at a barmitzvah. The best of the lot came from Ilford and was labelled 'The Twins'. Emma laced in on to the machine to have another listen.

'Hi. I'm Simon.'

'And I'm Lewis.'

Together. 'We're the Street Twins.'

A jingle in perfect harmony. 'The Street Twins on F.R.E.E., crazy kids in a crazy time.'

Music begins.

Simon. 'Not released until tomorrow and already

number one in FREE's Top Forty. The Beatles. ''Ticket to Ride''.'

The voice-over fitted perfectly, both in timing and pace. Emma studied the photograph enclosed with the tape. They didn't look older than fourteen, although their biography said nineteen years and one month. Bright, keen faces, mops of sandy hair, round NHS glasses and absolutely identical. The tape's production was flawless and the sketches were hysterical. She could hear Stuart and Bill returning and rewound the tape.

'We've got through to the ship,' said Stuart, turning on the shelf radio. The last chorus of 'Peggy Sue' faded and Bill's announcement boomed into the room.

'This is FREE Radio broadcasting on 244 metres medium wave. We'll be on the air twenty-four hours a day from April 15th with the best music in the universe and the hottest jocks in Great Britain. While we line up our bits and tweak our transmitters, here's a sample of what you're going to hear. This is FREE Radio. Bob Dylan – ''The times they are a changin''''.'

Stuart hadn't felt this great since the episode of the exploding Dean's chair. Bill stared into space – it was the first time he'd heard himself on English radio. Emma watched them both. A happy, warm feeling drifted through her. She lifted her glass.

'Shall we toast, gentlemen? To the best radio station in the world.'

They toasted, they whooped, they laughed, they said 'Great!' several times and they ran back to the radio to hear the segue between Bob Dylan and Roger Miller's 'King of the Road'. It sounded (all three) 'GREAT!'

'The man who put that tape together should be given a pay rise,' enthused Stuart.

'Well, thank you, boss,' replied Bill. 'I'll just settle for a special night out.'

Emma could see the secret between them. She'd overheard snippets of telephone conversations all afternoon full of cryptic reference to 'large ones', 'maturity is of the utmost importance', 'is your friend as gifted as you?' 'Charlie will drive you. He has the keys'. But, as yet, only her imagination could supply the scenario.

'You want to come tonight, don't you?' Stuart placed his glass on the desk. 'There's curiosity in you.'

'Mr Salisbury!' She'd been caught out. She needed time to think. Bill didn't allow her any.

'Stuart tells me you want to get involved in this station, and there's no better way than a friendly social gathering to find out what we're about.'

It would be safer to stand in a pit full of cobras than stand in front of Emma Saxby when she's cornered. She'd had time to think. She slowly uncoiled her body to its full height and smiled. 'I'd love to. Where, when, and what should I wear?'

She'd delivered the line to Bill, not Stuart. She didn't know why. Bill answered her.

'Stuart's flat, nine o'clock, formal dress.'

'As in black tie?'

Bill nodded.

'I don't know if this is a good idea,' interrupted Stuart.

'You see, Emma? That's why he's a worrywart managing director and I'm a rock "n" roll disc-jockey.' Bill turned and grasped Stuart by the shoulders. 'My dear friend, we have at least two hours to get some more of anything we need.' He pushed Stuart down on the sofa. 'Relax. The ship is here, we're on the air, Emma's a lovely lady. This is *prime time, baby!*'

Emma wasn't sure what he meant by that last remark; she would give him the benefit of the doubt . . . for now. 'If I'm to be ready by nine, you'll have to excuse me, gentlemen. I have a lot to do.' She turned in the doorway. 'There's a tape on the machine that's worth a listen.'

Back home in Bristol House, Emma started having serious doubts. This could be the date too far. Bill seemed nice; all men seem nice if you get past hello, usually until just before goodbye. Stuart wouldn't let an employee get involved with him in that way. Or would he? She didn't know him that well.

The phone rang. Emma jumped. She let it ring four times before answering.

'Hello.' She flopped on to the bed, the smile returning to her face. 'Mum. Just the person. How are you?'

'I'm fine, dear. How are you? When you say "just the person", it usually means you've a problem.'

She told her mother almost all the story, carefully missing out the telephone snippets. Mother's advice was reassuring, if not predictable.

'Stuart seems such a nice man, from such a respectable family. Go and enjoy yourself.'

Emma had heard all about 'respectable families'. Her friend, Avril, had told a gruesome tale of a weekend in Derbyshire involving an apparatus room that had nothing to do with gymnastics. 'I don't want to get involved with anything that has no escape route. Maybe I should call and manufacture a headache.'

'Maybe you should stop having such a closeted attitude.' A note of anger crept into her mother's voice. 'This Stuart fellow sounds perfectly charming.'

'It's Bill Mason who interests me.'

'Don't get involved with show-business people; they

39

love themselves too much.' Her mother now sounded authoritative, planning the life of her offspring with fixity of purpose. 'A managing director is much more your style. A handsome face will grow old, a healthy bank account grows bigger with time.'

Emma chuckled despite her mother's serious tone. 'I didn't think you were that mercenary.'

'I just want what's best for you.'

'I'm going to dinner, not arranging a marriage.'

'Then just keep an open mind.'

Emma saw no point in continuing this line of conversation. Once her mother started down the road of potential marriage partners, all light and shade disappeared from her logic. How much money? What kind of family? Does he own property? These were the only subjects that mattered. Emma wanted reassurance that she'd arrive back home in one sexual piece, not a list of the top ten eligible bachelors. 'I must go, mother, I'll be late.'

'Have a nice evening, dear. I'll speak to you tomorrow.'

'Goodbye, mother,' Emma replaced the phone and stared up at the ceiling. She was probably being paranoid; this was just a dinner, not a weekend in the country. She could handle it. She thought of Bill's sculptured face, his muscular frame, and small, rounded bottom. 'Just don't be a faggot,' she whispered to herself. 'Be an egotist, be a raver, be in love with somebody else; but, please, don't be a bloody faggot.'

The mental re-run of her second serious love-affair clicked on. At eighteen she'd never encountered phrases like faggot, queen, shirtlifter and poofter, let alone gone out with anyone to whom they applied. He'd seemed so in tune with her, understanding her thoughts and outlook on life, giving compliments the way only her girlfriends had in the past. When she'd arrived at his flat early on that fateful Wednesday afternoon and caught him in bed with the man they'd both met in the pub the night before, the repulsion she felt stayed with her for months. She ran the half mile home without daring to look back, as if some demonic monster followed two paces behind. She'd stood under the shower for fifteen minutes, long after it ran cold, and scrubbed herself with a loofah until her skin was raw; then she sat on her bed and cried for an hour.

Four years later it didn't seem so bad; she now understood the ways and minds of homosexuals, she counted two as friends. Back then, it was the worst experience of her adult life. His name was also Bill, although he liked to be called Willie. In her fantasy world she'd named him Prick, always spoken in the most derogatory tone.

On board M.V. *FREE*, Captain Vourner hung up the ship-to-shore phone and smiled at his number two. 'I shall be off on tomorrow's tug. I'd like to see *that* supply officer in my cabin.'

That supply officer was Eddie Lincoln. The Captain referred to him as 'that' because he couldn't stand the man. He'd asked for a cadet or college kid to act as cabin-boy/store-man; what he got was an ex-Navy/ex-con, who'd offered his services for nothing in order to get out of Galveston without honouring his gambling debts. The cabin-boy idea went out of the porthole as the Captain didn't trust him, and within a week of sailing he'd noticed items such as cigarettes and beer, supplied by Stuart to be rationed among the men, being sold on a first-come, first-served basis.

Eddie thought he'd died and gone to heaven. He'd purloined all the good gear for his cabin, had an endless supply of booze and fags; and when he realised the possibilities of a ship permanently moored outside the three-mile limit, and therefore beyond the jurisdiction of English law, he was ready to sign on for the duration.

His outstanding physical feature was the disproportionate size of his hands and feet compared to the rest of his stocky frame. At thirteen his relations said they expected him to end up over six foot tall, but when his extremities stopped growing so did he; resulting in a five-foot-nine-inch body sporting a six-footer's hands and size eleven shoes. He spouted the 'big hands – big dick' theory at every opportunity, but his protestations usually preceded disappointment when the women didn't fancy overcoming his foul language and bad breath to find out. He'd pumped all manner of drugs and alcohol into his body from the age of fourteen, resulting in a prematurely sallow complexion, gaunt expression, and permanently red eyes.

Luck had not smiled on Eddie for most of his twenty-seven years. When he was five a stray German bomb intended for the Liverpool docks relieved him of his parents and his home. He'd lived with various relatives in and around London until he was fourteen. Only his Uncle Gordon seemed the slightest bit interested in his welfare, and he'd died of a heart attack six months after Eddie moved in. By fifteen he was running messages for the East Ends criminal fraternity; by sixteen he was running drugs on the Old Kent Road. At seventeen, a budget-conscious magistrate in Brixton gave him a choice; join the Merchant Navy or do time in jail.

So for the last ten years Eddie had bummed around the world on any tub that would sign him on. He'd crewed on oil tankers and coastal cargo ships, fishing boats and ferrys. His jobs ranged from cook to deck-hand, none of which he excelled in; all of which were a few items lighter when he'd left.

He mainly ignored the Captain. He saw no point in sucking up to a man who obviously hated him. He'd be gone within a couple of months, anyway, and Eddie could start again with the new Captain. He sat back on his ten-pillowed bunk and opened *Playboy* to the centre-fold.

A knock on the door resounded through his cabin. 'Come in!'

A black youth wearing white stepped inside. His chef's hat hit the top of the doorway. 'Hi, Eddie.'

'Hi, Mo. Whatcha want?'

'Powdered milk; and the Captain wants to see you.'

Eddie jumped off the bed and flung the magazine at Mo's chest. 'There's one of your lot in there; page thirty-nine. Have a blimp, I'll be back in a minute.'

He returned with a twenty-pound bag of powdered milk and a carton of Lucky Strike. He gave Mo the milk. 'The Lucky's are for Barry. Tell him they're here.' He looked at the boy. 'Tell him, no money, no fags. Understand?' Mo nodded. 'What's the Captain want?'

'Don't know.'

Eddie controlled the boy through cold haddock eyes. 'Nobody's been talking to the old fart, have they?'

'No, Eddie. Not a word.'

'Okay then.' He relaxed his stare. 'Keep the magazine.'

Mo backed warily out of the door. 'Thanks, Eddie. See you.'

Eddie threw the Luckys down on the desk and

followed the boy out of the cabin, being careful to lock the door securely behind him.

Captain Vourner informed Eddie that they'd both be going to Amsterdam on tomorrow's tug and would he please see all his papers were in order. His job would be to supervise the delivery and loading of supplies. It would take two days and he would have evenings off. No invitation to dinner was given, or expected.

At half past eight Eddie sat in his cabin, feeling pleased with life. He listened to Jewel Aitkin on the test transmission and contemplated which whore house to visit first.

At Bristol House. Emma was contemplating whether or not she'd meet her first hooker tonight. She viewed herself in the bathroom mirror. The choice of evening dress had been easy, there was only one. She'd bought it on a madness trip to the Harvey Nichols sale in January. She didn't know why the long black satin and lace dress had caught her eye, but it fitted beautifully, as well as flattering her tall frame and black hair. The four times she'd worn it had proved to be thoroughly enjoyable evenings. She held the one piece of real jewellery she owned with both hands and slid it around her neck. A gold necklace, with a single emerald set in a gold pendant on the front: her eighteenth-birthday present from dear, neurotic mother.

She was committed, she was determined, she was ready. She squeezed out of the bathroom and retrieved her fox-fur coat from the bed. This had not been a mad buy, more a calculated purchase. Over the past year several people had been standing up for the anti-fur lobby. She'd listened to their arguments and agreed with a lot of what they said; but while she saw the sense in not hunting ocelot to extinction for the sake of fashion, she felt there were enough foxes to go round. With the sudden drop in prices these people generated, Emma thought £47 for a three-quarter-length was too good a bargain to miss.

Charlie picked her up precisely on time. As the Bentley swung into Cheyne Walk she felt she'd reached the point of no return. She smiled at the driver as he opened the car door.

'It's flat twenty-five, madam. I'll wait here 'til you're in.'

Stuart answered the intercom. 'Emma. Dear lady. Top floor. The lift's ahead of you.' Buzzzzzz.

Emma shut the lift door, pressed five and closed her eyes. The lift ascended. She heard Bill's voice filter down the shaft. The lift stopped, Emma opened her eyes.

'You look sensational!' Bill stood, clean-shaven, before her; his black formal suit immaculately tailored and spotless.

'And you look extremely smart.' Emma offered her hand.

'Come inside. I want you to meet the girls.'

She smiled at him without a hint of embarrassment, but inside, she felt sure that her worst fears were about to be realised.

The flat was noisy. Alexis Korner sang the blues; Stuart Salisbury acted the fool. Two beautiful women, one black, the other Eurasian, stood on either side of him, snapping their fingers and repeating the chorus line as it came through. The scents of exotic herbs and spices filled the apartment.

As Emma entered the sitting room Stuart turned off the music. 'Wonderful!' he exclaimed, throwing his arms open. 'Our last guest has arrived!'

45

Bill squeezed Emma's hand and led her gently towards the female guests. 'Emma, I would like you to meet Princess Naomi Adu from the Leeward Islands.'

The black woman turned towards her. 'Very pleased to meet you,' she said in a cultured English accent.

'And Miranda Chew.'

The Eurasian lady smiled and bowed, but said nothing.

Both women looked in their late twenties. Naomi wore a stunning evening gown of gold-embroidered black silk; Miranda a red, knee-length Givenchy creation. If they were callgirls, they were very upmarket ones.

'These ladies are, without a doubt,' continued Bill, 'the most talented Caribbean chefs on our fair island.'

Stuart handed Emma a glass of Dom Perignon. 'This is the last European taste. Tonight's the night for West Indian ambrosia. The ladies have worked for hours; I'm sure you'll like it.'

Emma looked up at Bill. His mocking glance said everything. He knew what sweet anguish he'd put her through. She'd get him back; but not now.

When Emma next looked at her watch it was one o'clock in the morning. The evening had flown by. A feast had been promised and a feast was delivered. The first course consisted of curried prawns in pineapple accompanied by Rum Santas, a delicious concoction of orange juice, molasses and rum. The main course featured Condado duck; the recipe having been smuggled out of the Condado Beach Hotel in Puerto Rico three weeks previously by Princess Naomi. The duck was first basted and fast-cooked in a mixture of olive oil, paprika and onions; then simmered slowly in a

46

sauce of vegetable stock, flour and rum. Plates of steaming hot creamed callaloo, baked green paw-paw and sweet potatoes baked in orange surrounded the platter. Miranda introduced the main-course drink as 'Good Hope', describing it as a crafty little mixture of eggs, sugar, vanilla, nutmeg, and ice-cold milk. And, of course, rum. They were spared dessert, as such. Instead, strong, black coffee was served with an enormous plate of guava cheese, which looked somewhat like Turkish Delight but tasted a million times better. And one more Rum Santa.

The conversation was as enjoyable as the food. Emma listened intently to Naomi's story of how her islands were changing; how the same person was in charge, only now he called himself Prime Minister instead of Governor. Miranda's story enchanted everyone. She was part-Chinese, and had educated herself despite her father's wish that she become a seamstress. She'd cooked her way through university, sometimes working six nights a week to finance her studies.

Emma's turn came as the last remnants of the duck were cleared from the table. She was the youngest; her stories wouldn't be as colourful as the others'. Bill was closest to her in age and he'd already been around the world. She had to say something.

'I'm just starting out. This is my first Caribbean feast.' The polite laughter gave her little confidence, but she continued. 'I lost my Dad in the War. Mum and I are close and I have two sisters.' They don't want to hear this, she thought. It's so boring talking about your mum. She felt Bill's hand touch her leg and give a little squeeze. 'I started working at FREE today and so far it's not been too bad.' More laughter, this time sounding more friendly. 'Commercial radio, I don't call it pirate, is going to be the next big business in this country and I intend to be a big part of it.' She delivered the last sentence with all the conviction she could muster.

Naomi clapped her hands. 'Bravo, Emma.' She turned to Stuart. 'You've found a good one here. Your luck still holds.'

Emma had royal approval. She smiled with relief around the table, ending on Bill. He winked at her. She felt slightly more comfortable with the company but very unnerved by Bill Mason. He'd been the perfect gentleman all evening; impeccably polite, charmingly attentive, and intellectually stimulating.

This whole scene was so different from her usual social encounters. Apart from an overly ambitious young lawyer who hadn't lasted long once he'd found out she wasn't as wealthy as she looked, and Willie the Prick, her previous experience was confined to the Mitcham Maniacs, a hard core of working lads who would take turns to pick her up from her mother's terraced Victorian house in Percy Street, deposit her on a bar stool at the Bell Inn next to Gladys, Dawn and Tracy, then go off and spend the entire evening playing darts. They were the main reason she'd quit the Surrey town a year ago, at the age of twenty-three, and moved to London. She couldn't stand another smoky evening dominated by Tracy's menstrual problems, Dawn's cackling voice and Jimmy Truman's grubby hands pulling at her knickers in his futile attempts at sexual arousal while imposing the mandatory goodnight kiss at the front door. Bill achieved more by just looking in her direction that J.T. could've managed in a month. She'd named Mr Truman 'Sotfo'; short for 'Shit of the first Order'.

Cheyne Walk was a long way from Mitcham, and

not only in distance. She'd been scared when she'd first moved to London by her mother's stories of rape, robbery and high rents. She'd found high rent, but also the work to support it. One thing was certain; her ambitions lay far beyond the confines of a suburban town. She wanted to make her own mark on this exciting decade, to wear *real* Cardin and Givenchy, to attain a position in business she could be proud of, to mix with thinking people who didn't live on four pints a day and one hurried fuck a week. She was glad she'd come tonight. This was the crowd she wanted to run with; especially the tall Jamaican with the cheeky smile and those riveting blue eyes.

Chapter 2

Tuesday, April 6 1965. 9 a.m.

High above the morning hustle of Bond Street, the directors of Branford, Hedley and Stowe met in a palatial office to discuss the progress of the pirates. BHS was one of the world's most respected music publishers; wielding political clout far beyond its own sphere of business, and losing thousands of pounds every week because off-shore radio paid no performing rights royalties. Sir David Garman, chairman and major shareholder, addressed the meeting.

'I've heard the argument that if they weren't there we wouldn't be getting anything anyway but, the fact is, gentlemen, they *are* there. Not only do they cost this company and our writers a great deal of money, they also undermine our position regarding the BBC and Luxemburg.'

'They're extremely popular, that's the problem.' This, surprisingly, from Aaron Coleman, the financial director.

'Caroline and London are, but not this new outfit, Radio FREE. They're not on the air yet. We must hit them early and hard; it might panic the rest.' Sir David searched the table for any more dissenting voices. He looked towards the man on his right. 'Oscar, find out

51

everything you can – management, money, the lot. Any criminal activity would be nice.' Then further down the table: 'William. We need to find out about their PR; what they intend to major on, how big's the budget. But most of all . . .' he looked around the assembled executives, resting his gaze on each one in turn . . . 'we need someone on the inside. Any suggestions?'

'One of our writers could pose as a DJ,' offered Oscar.

Everyone laughed except the chairman. 'That's not beyond the realms of possibility. Any more?'

'I think the Government should deal with it,' said a thin, financial suit. 'Can't you get Robin Clarke to hurry along the legislation?'

'I've tried. Too much opposition. We need direct action; that's the only way we'll force Whitehall's hand.' The chairman scanned the table for the slightest glimmer of creative input, but found none. 'Let's think about this one, gentlemen. In the meantime I believe Aaron has some good news regarding the West End musical.'

Sir David sat back in his chair and let Aaron's report wash over him. He'd read the bottom line pre-meeting; the detail didn't interest him. He carefully studied the deep red petals of the single rose that stood in the miniature Ming vase in front of him. His secretary had placed a fresh flower in that vase each morning for the last fifteen years. This morning's rose was exceptionally beautiful.

For months he'd been preoccupied with the 'pesky pirates', as he called them. Based on what the BBC paid, the pirates were costing BHS at least a million a year. Even if they halved the rate, as the pirates wanted, that still represented an awful lot of money. Sir David Garman would normally go to war for a

shilling; these off-shore royalty dodgers were seriously
out of order, and he intended to have them kissing his
backside before the year's end.

Anna Papanicholas kissed her father lightly on the
cheek and thanked him for driving her into town.
She gathered her briefcase and handbag from the back
seat of the Zephyr, stepped into the chilly sunshine
of Berkeley Square and walked into the Sun Alliance
building.

The bustle of Mayfair excited her. There was an
atmosphere of optimism – people greeted each other
enthusiastically, men held doors open for women, cars
stopped for pedestrians without the revving of anxious
engines. A certain politeness prevailed on the streets
of London that was the envy of the myriad American
tourists, who seemed to spend their time wandering
from hotel to shops in brightly coloured check-patterned
trousers congratulating English policemen for not wearing guns.

Today, Anna wore a bright green Marks & Spencer's
dress under her dark green Marks & Spencer's coat.
Her mother had insisted on buying her the outfit as
a celebration of the new job. As usual she'd not been
consulted, just handed the green St Michael's bag when
she arrived home last night. She'd learned quickly how
to feign surprise and pleasure; her mother would never
know how much she hated M & S copies, or anything
green. In her briefcase a pair of Levi's and a FREE
Radio T-shirt awaited her arrival at Hayes Mews. Her
intention was to build up an alternative wardrobe at
the radio station. She knew Papa, or any self-respecting
insurance company, would never accept mod clothes
being worn at the office. For now she'd bring them

from home; from her first pay day she'd add one outfit a week.

She watched her father drive out of sight down Davies Street before walking out of the building, across the square and along Charles Street towards the London office of the best radio station in the world.

Anna had never lied to her parents before. It made her feel frightened and remorseful. This was such a big lie. She'd told them she had a job with her best friend Eva, in the personnel department of the Sun. She'd given her parents Eva's extension and made Eva promise to call her at FREE if anyone phoned. She didn't like the deceit, and she knew the penalty for getting caught would be severe; but she had to work in radio, she simply had to.

She was the first to arrive at Hayes Mews. She sat behind her desk in the empty office, between the switchboard and the entry-phone, and dreamed of driving her own radio show. She would have the best jingles, the hippest guests, the best taste in music and the coolest name. She remembered a poster she'd seen last week on the underground, advertising a double bill of *Key Largo* and *The Maltese Falcon*, late Friday at the Odeon, Leicester Square. A name as cool as Humphrey Bogart. A name like . . . Honey! That was it! Honey Bogart!

A wave of satisfaction washed over her. She could see it all. She'd find someone who could mimic his voice. Her jingles would say, 'Of all the records in all the world, you choose my favourite', 'Here's looking at you, Honey', 'Play it again, Honey', 'Anything you do is okay by me, sweetheart'. She saw a little red light flash on the switchboard.

'Hello, this is FREE. How can I help you? Mr Salisbury,

good morning, this is Anna . . . Very well, thank you . . .
Mr Walters . . . yes, I'll tell him. What time will you be
in? See you then.'

She unplugged the switchboard, picked up the case
containing her jeans and T-shirt and stepped lightly
towards the small bathroom at the top of the stairs.
The day had started well for Honey Bogart.

Emma arrived at Hayes Mews just before ten, her
face tingling, her shoes soaked. She kicked them off
and scurried to the fan heater behind Anna's desk.
'Good morning.'

'You'll get piles.'

Emma looked down at her feet. 'On my toes?'

They both laughed.

Emma rubbed her legs. 'I walked to work. The park
was beautiful. I didn't count on it being this chilly.'

'Want a coffee?'

'Oh . . . please.'

'Bill phoned ten minutes ago. Wanted to speak to
you.'

Emma glided into nonchalant. 'Did he?'

Anna wasn't fooled. 'You saw him last night, didn't
you?'

'We were at the same dinner party, that's all.'

'*What*?' Anna nearly dropped the cups. 'Stuart's party!
With the phone calls about the big ones, maturity and
the gifted friend?'

'It was a Caribbean feast!'

The girls stood motionless for a second before coll-
apsing with laughter; out of control giggles that exhausted
them.

'Good God, brother. They're laughing already. How
can we improve on that?'

The girls looked up and experienced double vision.

'I'm Simon . . .'

'And I'm Lewis . . .'

Together. 'We're the . . .'

'STREET TWINS!' shouted Emma.

'You've heard of us!'

'Which one are you?'

'I'm Lewis.'

'Yes, Lewis, I certainly have heard of you.' She offered her hand. 'I'm Emma Saxby, this is Anna, and I'm *very* glad to see you'.

Lewis shook her hand. 'We were in the neighbourhood and we thought we'd get your reaction to our tape.'

Simon ran to the desk. 'Quick! Not a second to lose. Paper! Pen! Sticky tape!' His blond Beatle-cut mop and round glasses made him look like a demented Dougal searching for Zebedee. He gathered the vital components and rapidly made four name tags; two each; which they pinned on front and back.

'Now you'll know who it is, coming or going.'

They had a comic presence that was thoroughly contagious. The phone rang. Anna tried to stop laughing. 'Damn! Business! Quiet down, *please*! You'll have us fired.'

'Never in the field of human conflict!' quoted Simon. Pause. 'Sorry, wrong Churchill.'

'Which one did you mean?'

'The Churchill two streets away; where they're got that pinball machine.'

Together. 'Let's go!' They turned to the girls.

'Back in half an hour,' said Simon.

'Cancel all calls,' finished Lewis.

Anna reached for the phone. It stopped ringing. 'Damn again!'

56

'Don't worry.' Emma straightened her blouse. 'He thinks he's dialled the wrong number. He'll call back . . . Just give him time . . . last few digits . . . now!'

The phone rang. Both girls raised their right index finger. 'Good morning, this is FREE. How can I help you?'

A high-intensity New York accent ripped through the earpiece. 'My name is Walters. John Walters. I'm just in from the States and I thought Stuart was meeting me at the airport.'

'I have a message for you, sir. Mr Salisbury has been called to an urgent meeting. He'll see you here, any time after three.'

'That's no goddamn good! What am I s'posed to do 'til then? Drink airport coffee?'

'A room is booked for you at the Washington, sir.'

'Ah . . . What's this goddamn meeting all about?'

'I don't know, sir. I'm the receptionist.' Anna gestured with two fingers in her mouth. 'Can I take a message?' The phone went dead. 'Thank you very much, sir. Up your nostril with a red-hot poker, sir!' She gently placed the phone back on its cradle and looked at Emma in astonishment. 'And that, would you believe, is our head of sales! The whizzkid from the Big Apple! The one Stuart calls genius! The salesman's salesman. Provider of revenue!' She pulled a small mirror from her handbag, checked her face for any sign of a flaw in her make-up and, having found none, returned the mirror to its side compartment with amazing speed. 'Rude bastard!'

Emma picked up her own phone and dialled. 'We'll just have to teach him some manners then, won't we? . . . Hello. Maples? Office furnishing, please.'

* * *

John Walters was short on manners and temper; long on media savvy and salesmanship. Two-thirds of FREE's finance was American, and he'd been recruited from a major New York station where, as sales director, he'd registered the highest advertising turnover on the Eastern seaboard. His father had risen from postboy to vice-president of Irving, Warner and Slade, one of the top five agencies in the world. He'd enrolled his son at IWS the moment he left Harvard and for two years taught young John the complexities of media buying and selling. Outside his work, John had few interests. Through his father, he lived in the rarefied world of creative directors, account executives and company board members. He regarded other forms of life as unworthy of much attention, hence his belligerent behaviour towards anything subordinate. His attitude to women bordered on chauvinism and his interest in them was mainly sexual. Some girlfriends found his cool disinterest attractive and regarded him almost as a Svengali figure, staying in at night on the off-chance he'd call. Others declined the second date.

John dressed Ivy League of the first order and didn't even know it. His wardrobe, hand-tailored by Warren Goldstein in New York, boasted the latest fashions and finest quality. Twice a year they'd send him cloth swatches and he'd choose the ten he liked best; once a year he'd drop into Warren's Manhattan showroom and be re-measured. Each suit arrived with three matching shirts and ties, two pairs of shoes; lace-ups, and loafers. He never asked about style. Clothes to him were either new or old, clean or dirty.

He suited the American college style. He stood five foot ten in his silk socks, hair cropped short in a crew-cut, face round and perfectly smooth-shaven. His best facial feature was the cherub-like mouth that could curl up at each corner and flash a perfect smile in a millisecond. At a recent agency dinner party a well-scotched creative director suggested that he resembled Paul McCartney without the hair.

'Is that the guy in the Beatles?' he inquired.

'Right,' came the slightly drunken reply.

'Not the ugly one behind the drums, is it?' These were his final words on the subject.

His one hobby was military history. His interest had started in high school and by the time he joined IWS he had a working knowledge extending from Hannibal to Hitler. The offer of the post of sales director for potentially the biggest radio station in Europe didn't hold half as much appeal as living in a country renowned for its military exploits, and where battle prints by Le Blond and Baxter could be found in almost every antique shop along the Portobello Road.

He threw his crocodile briefcase on to the bed in his luxurious room at the Washington and called his father in New York to say he'd arrived safely and to extract the name of his dad's counterpart at J. Walter Thomson.

The Bentley pulled up outside seven Ovington Square. From the back seat Bill and Stuart could see the estate agent waiting for them on the steps.

'Ex-Army, I would say,' commented Bill.

'Sergeant-Major, Coldstream Guards, I would venture.'

'Queen's Own,' admitted the man who introduced himself as Benson and ushered them into the hallway. 'The flat's pukka; lovely view over the Square.'

Bill stood in front of one of the two large second-floor windows and had to admit that Benson was right. He looked over the tree tops and studied the manicured gardens below before turning to face the room. It was bright and spacious; light streamed through the windows onto pale yellow walls, lime green trimmings and matching sofas. The dark green fitted carpets extended throughout the flat, the kitchen and bathroom were modern and very avocado. On the whole, the furnishings were more Harrods than Habitat and Bill felt right at home from the moment he stepped in the door.

'It's £42 per calendar month,' Benson was saying. 'And a £50 deposit.'

Bill hardly heard him. He walked into the main bedroom. The four-poster oak bed ended just where the bay window began. Fitted oak wardrobes down one wall; a dressing table and built-in wash basin on the other. He had a flash of Emma standing in her office, smiling at him over an armful of tapes and letters. Another scenario developed in his mind as he sat on the edge of the bed; not of Emma, but his previous girlfiends trying out the bed for size and comfort. Julie from Jamaica with her lithe suntanned body and magical mouth; Sara from Canada, tall, elegant, sophisticated; Chi Lo from Taiwan, the four-foot-eleven expert on the *Karma Sutra*. They had all been wonderful and he still remembered them with great affection, but something about Emma Saxby seemed to supersede them all. She made him feel vulnerable – and he didn't like that one little bit.

'I'll take it.' He shook Benson's hand. 'Send the papers around to Coutts; a Mr Cooke will deal with it. Do you have the number?'

Benson came smartly to attention as he opened his notebook and thumbed the pages. 'Mayfair 8020.'

'That's the one. When can I take possession?'

'Is it urgent?'

'Very!'

Benson snapped his notepad sheet and lifted his head smartly as if he were about to deliver an order. 'I think we can have this wrapped up by tea-time. No reason why you can't move in tonight, if it's that urgent. The electricity is on, but you'll have to arrange the phone, sir.'

Bill smiled. 'That'll be perfect. Thank you, Mr Benson, you've been most helpful.'

Aboard the ship, helpfulness was not the order of the day. The Captain sent instructions to Eddie asking him for a detailed list of suppliers, an itinerary for his two days in Amsterdam and a contact phone number. Eddie wrote a curt note in return informing the Captain that he, Eddie, was responsible for supplying the ship based on his, the Captain's, order forms. He knew what he was doing so please, go screw the shit out of Lisa and leave him to get on with his job!

Vourner's reaction could best be described as seriously hostile. He stormed into Eddie's cabin, grabbed him by the lapels and pinned him against the bulkhead.

'If you so much as mention Lisa again, I'll do you such dreadful harm you'll regret being born!'

Eddie was amazed at Vourner's strength. He thought of kicking the old boy in the nuts, but figured he wouldn't feel it. 'Hey! Hold on! It was a joke, man!'

'It's not funny!' The Captain loosened his grip on the supply man and let him slide slowly down the wall before walking determinedly from the cabin. That was the last thing he said to Eddie until they docked in Holland.

*   *   *

Lightness and laughter were the order of the day at Hayes Mews. The Street twins returned five minutes after Bill and Stuart arrived bearing good news of the flat. Simon and Lewis astounded everyone with their humour, sketches, jingles and brilliant impersonations, all delivered with expert timing. It was uncanny how they could finish each other's sentences or start singing the same song without making eye contact. Stuart concluded that they were either extremely well-rehearsed or else magic had come to Hayes Mews. He plumed for the latter; it was that kind of day. He also decided to give them a job. This led to more celebration, the booking of production studios in London for them to work in, and a take-away Chinese for lunch.

When a stern-faced John Walters arrived at half past three all that was left for him were four spare-ribs, a bowl of cold rice and a half bottle of Mateus.

'God damn!' he told the room. 'Jet lag's really hit my timing. I never arrive at the end of a party.'

Emma was glad he had at least a modicum of humour. She postponed her manners lesson for the time being. 'Let me show you your office. I haven't ordered any furniture for you yet. I thought you'd like to look at the options.'

John's smile could grease axles. 'Why, thank you . . .'

'Emma.'

'Thank you, Emma. Tell me one thing.' Then, sarcastically, 'Is there a goddamn phone that works in there?'

Emma stopped and let him walk into the office alone. 'Oh yes, sir. It's on the goddamn floor!' She turned smartly and walked with measured steps down the hall, back to the party in Stuart's room. She heard John's office door slam shut behind her.

'Where did you find him?' Emma raised her eyebrows at Stuart.

'Hear, hear,' echoed Anna.

'He came with the American money,' replied Stuart without a hint of apology. 'He's one of the best media salesmen in the States; a Madison Avenue mandarin. He'll sell over a million a year for us, and that, ladies and gentlemen, is our business. So, I suggest you do as I do. Give him: one, all the expenses he needs; two, all the space he needs; and three, all the . . .' he looked at Emma and Anna . . . 'help he needs. You might not like the man, but his track-record alone commands respect.' Emma felt awkward. She knew he was right. 'Emma. Why don't you invite him to join us?'

John Walters didn't feel comfortable with show-business people. Media buyers, agency chairman, finance directors – these were his people. A pair of twins singing bits of Beatle songs and impersonating Humphrey Bogart bored him rigid. He was polite, took two sips from a fresh glass of champagne, made his excuses and left for the safety of the J. Walter Thompson building, where he knew he'd feel at home.

Anna's interest in the Bogart impressions was total. She invited herself to the production studio that evening so she could watch the twins at work. The hidden agenda read, 'Watch them work for her'. She had her jingles!

'I've got an idea,' announced Emma, with more than a little self-interest. 'If you three are producing magic this evening, why don't Stuart and I help Bill move into Ovington Square and we could all meet up for a late supper?'

'We won't be through 'til the early hours,' answered Lewis. 'We'll have our dinner sent in.'

'I'm out,' said Stuart. 'Princess Naomi flys home tomorrow. I've promised her the Hilton tonight. Jacques Laugenie is cooking at Trader Vic's.'

'He does know how to live, our Stuart.' Bill walked across the room and stood in front of Emma. 'Looks like it's you and me, kid. If the offer's still open, I'd love a hand, and I'll buy you a hot potato at this lovely little pub I've found in Brompton Road.'

'A hot potato with prawn filling?'

'Whatever filling you want.' His tone was flirtatious.

'How can I refuse?' She liked this feeling. 'Shall I bring my Flash?'

Bill adopted the gloomy expression of most men faced with domestic decisions. 'I guess I've got to buy all that stuff.' He looked at Stuart.

'Go on, you two. Piss off and get moved in. Be here at nine tomorrow, both of you. We have a station to start.'

Emma and Bill picked up the keys from Mr Benson and spent the rest of the day in Habitat. By half past five Bill was fifty pounds poorer and richer by a Mini-full of household items. They unloaded the car, made a pot of tea and toasted the flat. Emma set to cleaning the bath, Bill descaled the toilet. Emma washed the dishes, Bill cleaned the stove. It felt so easy. They laughed, joked and squirted water at each other. Bill watched her stand on a stool and reach to wipe the top shelf in the kitchen cupboard; her jeans stretched, her blouse pulled tight over her breasts. This couldn't be just any woman. He wanted *her*. She looked down at him, sensing his gaze, and stopped her wiping.

'What's the matter?' She stepped down next to him.

'Absolutely nothing. That's the matter! Nothing's the matter; it bothers me.' He tilted his head slightly to one side, the smallest of smiles found its way past his eyes. Emma decided to be sensible and spoke brightly, breaking the spell. 'In that case, let me get on with my work, or I'll miss out on my hot potato with prawn filling, and that will make me a very unhappy budgie.'

RING! RING! RIIIINNGG!!

Emma thanked her God. 'I think someone's at your door.'

Bill kissed her lightly on the nose. 'Hold that feeling.' He walked to the entry-phone. 'Hello.'

'Hi, mate. It's Brian. I phoned the office from the station, the boss told me the address.'

Bill covered the mouthpiece. 'It's Brian Todd, from the ship. I told him he could have the other bedroom.'

Brian's voice offended his ear once more. 'Hello, mate. Can you hear me?'

'Yes, Brian. It's just that I'm not alone.'

Emma grabbed the phone from his hand. 'Brian, this is Emma Saxby from the office. Pay no attention to him. You come in right away.' She pushed the buzzer and replaced the hand-set. 'Don't you dare do that, Bill Mason.' She opened the front door.

'I didn't mean . . .'

'You didn't think,' interrupted Emma crossly.

'I'm s . . .'

'Don't!'

The service tug bumped the Dutch jetty just after six o'clock. Eddie scrambled ashore, feeling good in his flowered shirt, brown flared trousers and black leather jacket, with a month's pay in his pocket. He'd said goodbye or, more accurately, piss off to the Captain and told the tug-master he'd be back by ten tomorrow

65

morning. It was at least a two-hour drive to Amsterdam and he'd no intention of wasting a second. He gave the cab driver a five-pound note and an instruction to wake him on the outskirts of the city.

In the twenty-seven years Eddie Lincoln had survived on this earth, he'd been held at their various majesties' pleasure on four occasions, the last being a week's lock-up in New Orleans for assault. Usually a fine would have resulted from that kind of bar-room brawl, but the judge thought his excuse for using a crowbar ('He was bigger than me') didn't justify the plea of self-defence. A week to repent your actions and then leave the state of Louisiana was the judgement; hence his departure from Galveston, Texas. His cellmate in New Orleans was a Dutchman from Utrecht who told him exactly where to go should he ever find himself in Amsterdam.

Just after nine o'clock he arrived at the Canal Palace Hotel. The first thing he noticed was the no vacancy sign; second, the massive doorman. The Dutchman had also given him a name.

''Scuse me. I'd like to see Joanna.'

The doorman looked at Eddie as if he were fly shit. 'Who the fuck are you?'

'A friend of Doc Sumner. He said I should come here as soon as I hit town.'

'Where'd you meet the good Doctor then, a gutter in Utrecht?'

'A jail in New Orleans.' Eddie hadn't travelled half-way round the world to be fobbed off by some brainless neanderthal. He'd try the direct approach. 'Listen, Quasimodo, just tell Joanna I got a message from the Doc before I have your balls cut off at the knees.'

The doorman started to lumber down the steps; Eddie

66

backed away. A voice on the entrance tannoy stopped them both.

'Let him come up, Pierre.'

Joanna greeted him at the top of the first flight of stairs. Eddie had expected a middle-aged Madam wearing a black basque and stockings. What confronted him was a georgeous red-head, about twenty-five, dressed in a black full-length evening gown.

'I'm Joanna. What's your name?'

'Eddie. Eddie Lincoln.'

She swanned along the flock-papered hallway and stopped outside a set of ornate wooden doors. 'How well do you know the Doc?'

Eddie watched her cleavage as it fought to escape the dress. 'We did time together in New Orleans. He told me to tell you: "Don't use suspenders for stirrups". Does that make sense to you?'

'It tells me you know him.' She pushed open the double door. 'Come on in. Have a glass of something and tell me the news.'

The room epitomised the pleasure principle. White thick-pile carpet covered the floor. A wall-full of mock-Louis XIV wardrobes, each sporting large mirrored panels, stood opposite the biggest bed Eddie had ever seen. It measured five pillows wide with a pleated velvet headboard that gave way to a mirrored wall. Reclining on the bed were two sensational women – one in the briefest pair of black panties he'd ever seen; the other in studded leather strips and silk stockings. On the bedside table he also spotted a small mirror beside a razor blade and a rolled £5 note. Things were looking good.

'You'll have to excuse us, Eddie,' said Joanna, signalling to the girls that they should leave. 'We were just having a quiet game of Monopoly.'

'Don't leave on my account.' Eddie looked despondent as the girls filed past him, the one in leather brushing his crotch with her hand as she passed.

'Relax.' Joanna pointed to the chaise longue. 'You can fuck your brains out with as many women as you like, later. Right now, tell be about Doc. Is he well?'

'He's okay.' Eddie was getting irritable. 'What's all this about Doc? I spent a week with him in a southern lock-up, that's all. He tells me to look you up. Who the fuck is he to you?'

'He's my husband.'

Eddie wished he'd kept his mouth shut. 'I'm sorry,' he muttered awkwardly. 'I didn't mean any disrespect.'

Joanna sat beside him. 'Tell you what. Why don't you have a bath?' She pointed to the right side of the bed. 'There's some joints in the top drawer and some coke beside the mirror. I'll send a couple of girls in to rub your back. We'll meet later in the restaurant. How does that sound?'

'Like cloud nine, baby.' He couldn't decipher whether her smile was genuine or patronising; basically, though, he didn't give a shit either way. Before Joanna had cleared the room he was lighting his first joint. 'Where's the bathroom?' he shouted after her.

'Go through the end wardrobe!' she shouted back.

The bathroom proved even more mind-blowing than the bedroom. A huge, round sunken bath dominated the room; the carpet carried through from the bedroom and was dotted with large, comfortable cushions. A brightly embroidered Swiss banquette added a splash of colour to the predominantly white room; in the corner nearest the door, gymnasium equipment and an exercise bike reflected in the mirrored wall. The bath was already full. Though not normally a great fan of bathing, he shed his clothes and slid into the warm, perfumed water.

He heard movement to his left. He opened his eyes and marvelled at the sight before him. Two women, one a tall buxom blonde dressed in a full-length black negligée covering a red basque and black stockings; the other a short chinese girl, totally naked, stood side by side in the doorway.

'Jesus! The Laurel and Hardy of the brothels!' Eddie tried to look composed. 'Are you here to wash my back?'

'We're here to do anything you like,' replied the blonde, walking slowly to the bath, then kneeling down so her breast rested on his shoulder.

The Chinese girl slid straight into the water and fell against him, her right hand sliding up his leg. She caressed his penis and brushed her lips across his ear. 'Push your bum up, I want to taste you.'

He did as he was told. She took him in her mouth; the blonde buried his face in her generous cleavage. It took him thirty seconds to reach orgasm.

By the time he'd stopped shaking, the blonde had stripped and was sitting beside him in the tub. He felt embarrassed by his prematurity.

'Hey, ladies, I'm sorry. A month on a ship comes out in a hurry.'

'It's okay by us, sweetheart. We get paid by the body, not the hour.' She plucked a large cake of soap from the wooden dish beside the bath and rubbed it on his chest. 'Joanna wants you squeaky clean for dinner. Be a doll and stand up for me.'

Once again, Eddie did as he was told. The Chinese girl silently took the soap from her colleague and started to rub him where his body left the water; just above the knee.

Joanna flowed through the door as the naked blonde was drying Eddie's hair. 'Dinner in fifteen minutes. Will he be ready?'

'Just needs dressing.'

'Wait a minute!' Eddie flipped the towel off his head. 'I didn't sign up for no bloody fancy dress.'

Joanna eyed him from atop her £100-plus Paris creation. 'Mr Lincoln! We have a tradition here.' She let her voice drop. 'We dress for dinner. You'll find a complete size range of tuxedos in the second wardrobe; shirts, ties, studs and cufflinks in the top drawer of the tallboy; shoes, the drawer under the tuxedos. Come, girls. Let's leave Mr Lincoln to gather himself.'

It took him a couple of minutes to adjust to the scenario. The two girls disappeared as quickly as they'd arrived. He sat alone in this ornate whorehouse with an invitation to a formal dinner and a choice of cufflinks. He walked back into the bedroom and opened the second wardrobe. Tuxedos, sizes thirty-six short to forty-four long, graduated along the rail. He turned in search of the tallboy.

Joanna watched him cross the room, open the top drawer and pick up a set of gold cufflinks. She watched him stand, thinking, then walk into the bathroom and place the cufflinks in his trouser pocket. She turned away from the television monitor and looked at the blonde.

'What'cha think, Dolly?'

'I think he's an asshole of the first order. Perfect for what we want.' She lit a cigarette. 'Any word from Doc?'

'He's fine. This guy hasn't said diddly squat; I'll coax

the news out of him over dinner. The trouble in New Orleans is all sorted, I know that much. Doc phoned from Parrot Key. Says there's good business on the islands; sends his love.'

Dolly sighed. 'It'll be good to have him back.'

'I must call London!' Joanna picked up the phone and started dialling the number written in lipstick on the glass table top. 'Doc says this guy's perfect for handling the English end. He runs clubs and hookers all over the East End, has countrywide distribution and a boat big enough to import. This Eddie is the supply officer for a pirate radio ship moored three miles off Frinton. Doc reckons it's a perfect springboard for the English market but we need Eddie "Cufflinks" Lincoln to help us. We are . . . Hello. Is that the Ragamuffin Club . . .? I have a call from Amsterdam for a Mick Tasker . . . Thank you, I'll hold on.'

She turned back to the monitor. Eddie was struggling with the studs on his shirt. 'I think we should show him a wild night, dangle some money in front of him and send him back with a couple of kilos of grass to spread around the ship.'

'Sounds right to me.'

'Who do you think?'

'As long as it's not me again, I don't see it makes much difference. Any right hand could make him come in a minute.'

'Dolly! I'm surprised at you.' Joanna studied the image on the screen. 'I could make him last an hour.'

Dolly laughed. 'Be my guest!'

'Not on your . . . Hello. Mr Tasker? My name is Joanna. Doc Sumner asked me to give you a call.'

Chapter 3

Monday, April 12 1965.

Hayes Mews was now fully furnished, and a hive of activity. Brian Todd occupied a small desk in Emma's office from which he phoned record companies, interviewed DJs and worked on the first 'FREE Forty'. The chart must be at least two weeks ahead of the 'nationals', and the climbers needed to reflect the sound of the station. The station was due on air Thursday; the national chart came out tomorrow. He'd make it – just.

Bill Mason spent Friday touring the record companies in search of the next pirate-made hit. The established acts of the day could rely on BBC plays to promote their records, albeit only on two shows a week. But new artists such as Georgie Fame, Tom Jones, Unit Four Plus Two and The Who courted pirate play, as the BBC were slow to play them, if at all, and the off-shores offered three plays a day as opposed to two plays a week.

Philips Records had proved most productive. They were offering a two-week exclusive on a new trio they'd signed from America who were being produced in London. Bill thought 'Love Her' would be a minor hit, but he was convinced the Walker Brothers would be world-wide stars in the very near future.

The DJ line-up had come together with relative ease.

Bill Mason would do breakfast, Brian nine 'til noon. A public-school reject named Nigel Hinckley sent the best audition tape, probably as a result of his two years' experience with British Forces Broadcasting; he was awarded noon 'til three. An ex-BBC-er, Peter Robinson, who'd applied to FREE having been fired from the Light Programme for allegedly smoking pot in the studio, pulled drive time, and the Street twins landed six 'til ten in the evening. The overnights would be split between Johnny Dark, Howlin' Thomas and Prince Mikie, three London club jocks who never got up before noon, rhymed most of their presentation, and would present a problem to daytime radio no matter where they broadcast.

The late fifties and early sixties had seen the beginnings of the rhyming technique in America with DJs like Murray the 'K', Rosco and, to a lesser extent, Alan Freed. A couple of jive-talk rhyming couplets fitted perfectly between records, sounded totally distinctive compared to anything else on radio and served to separate the generations. 'This is the station that rocks the nation', 'Fill my soul with rock 'n' roll', 'Keep havin' fun 'til the music's done': all born in the small back-street radio stations of American cities. By the mid sixties, some hip London club-jocks had adopted the style but, as yet, nothing on the radio.

'Check us out and hear our range, the rad-i-o's about to change,' was the quote attributed to Prince Mikie in the radio FREE press release.

The only slots still to be filled were the daytime replacements for times when the regular DJs were ashore. Stuart was confident he'd find somebody; Brian grumbled a lot about professionalism and last-minute decisions.

74

Anna Papanicholas watched and waited. She'd charmed the twins into making her some ace jingles, at the same time swearing them to secrecy. She would have one chance to impress Stuart and she needed to be in charge of the timing. So far, the deception of her parents had gone smoothly. They'd grown somewhat suspicious when she stayed out 'til past midnight three nights running; she told them she was helping her friend, Patricia, through a rough time following the break-up with her boyfriend. She felt terrible when they praised her kindness and compassion. She also felt a strong desire to tell them the truth. This covert charade cut into the very fabric of her family. Every time she told them a lie, she'd remember all the good times they'd had; the boating holidays on the Norfolk Broads, Christmases at home with the seven-foot tree and the twenty-pound turkey. All this deception was so unnecessary and so sad. If only her father would stop living in eighteenth-century Greece where virginity was to be sold to the highest bidder, and see how life really was in twentieth-century England. If only. But he wouldn't, and she had to: and so the die was cast.

She'd confided in Emma not only as a friend, but also to stop any unwanted phone calls at her home. To her surprise, Emma had not been totally on her side, saying that it could put the radio station at risk should her father decide to go to the press. Anna assured her it would only be for a few weeks, and anyway, what about her and Bill?

'What about me and Bill? We're just spending some time together, that's all.'

'Come on, Emma, most people call it having an affair.'

'We are not!' Emma said indignantly.

Strictly speaking, this was true. Since that first

evening at Ovington Square Emma hadn't been alone with Bill. There was much to be done at work and, although they'd seen each other every day, it was always in the company of others. On Saturday night he'd taken her to dinner at the small Italian bistro in Walton Street. She'd thanked him with a goodnight kiss; nothing passionate, just pressing her lips gently on his while holding his face in her hands. She liked him and fancied him like crazy, but she knew he'd be away three weeks in every month and, most importantly, the next time she got involved it was going to be on her terms.

Anna didn't believe her. 'Why hide it? You two are made for each other.'

'In my own time,' Emma said, with just a touch of sadness in her voice. 'He'll be on the ship most of the time, and when he's not he'll be promoting the hell out of himself. I don't want that. Anyway, you should talk; at least I'm not lying to my parents.'

'No, you're not. You're lying to yourself, which in my book is much worse.'

Before Emma could frame a curt reply, they heard Stuart shout, 'Good morning,' from the top of the stairs, and the conversation was suspended.

'Ladies do I detect a certain dissent among the troops?'

'Just a slight disagreement about the blend of coffee,' lied Emma, offering Stuart her best smile. 'Nothing we can't work out.'

'Two-thirds Colombian, one-third Costa Rican. Problem solved,' said Stuart in his best executive voice. 'Now, the boys go back to the ship tomorrow, so we have some arrangements to make. Emma, in my office if you please.'

*   *   *

Bill lay in the bath at Ovington Square convinced that any arrangements he made regarding Emma would draw a blank. He hadn't tried to force her; he felt he'd been more than understanding. Maybe she'd had a bad experience, maybe she loved someone else, maybe she didn't like sex? That first evening at the flat had been so good, so easy, yet since then she'd kept him at arm's length. He was going back to the ship tomorrow; he must find out tonight.

'You gonna be all day, mate?' Brian's antipodean tones thundered through the door.

'Five minutes,' answered Bill, pulling the plug with a disgruntled jerk. He dried, shaved and wrapped himself in one of the towels they'd bought from Habitat. He passed Brian's door. 'All yours, Aussie!'

He phoned the office from his bedroom. Emma answered.

'It's my last night in town. Any chance of a quiet dinner?'

'Stuart may want me to work late.' Her voice sounded detached, distant.

'Emma,' Bill persisted. 'It's my last night!'

A moment's silence. 'What did you have in mind?'

'Trader Vic's, or I can cook here. Brian's got a hot date in Chelsea. We'll have the flat.'

Another moment's silence. 'Trader Vic's would be lovely. Are you coming to the office?'

'In about an hour.'

'See you then. I must go, Stuart's calling me.' The phone went dead.

Bill replaced the hand-set, not sure whether to feel encouraged or not. He could hear Brian singing his own version of 'Ticket To Ride'.

'I think I'm going to get laid, I think it's today,

77

yeh. The girl that's driving me mad is coming my way, yeh!'

Bill finished dressing, called Trader Vic's and reserved a quiet table, the one by the Chinese ovens, for nine o'clock.

At six o'clock Emma decided she'd done enough for one day. The afternoon had flown by. Bill dropped in briefly just after four; Emma turned to her sixth page of dictation and managed only a quick wave through the office window. He'd held up eight fingers and mouthed 'Eight o'clock'; she'd nodded and returned to Stuart's speech on the cost-effectiveness of radio advertising that he and John Walters would deliver to the media buyers at J. Walter Thompson, after tonight's formal dinner at the Savoy.

At half past seven, back home in Bristol House, she finished off her make-up with a touch more mascara and studied the overall effect in the round, two-sided mirror she kept on the windowsill. What she saw in the mirror pleased her; what she saw in her eyes did not.

She remembered her last boyfriend, Steven Sangster, the ambitious stockbroker from Sunningdale. He was physically attractive, his career ensured financial security; but whenever she stated her point of view or voiced an opinion that did not match his, she'd detect a resentment in his tone that set all her alarm bells ringing.

She'd tackled him as to his motives one autumn afternoon when he'd called her comments on the closure of the Windmill Theatre ill-informed and feminist. She'd argued that as the venue had been a starting point for such great comedians as Tony Hancock and Peter Sellers, there was no reason why it couldn't continue as a comedy revue and dispense with the girls altogether. He'd countered by saying that nobody would pay money unless the tits stayed in full view. She replied that good marketing could change the image. He then called her a silly cow who couldn't tell a financial disaster from a frigging dildo, and she decided in a split second that she'd not be changing her name to Sangster after all.

There was no denying she fancied Bill. Physically, he compared favourably with anyone currently on offer. His presence in the same room disturbed her equilibrium; words came out wrong, she'd bump into furniture. She once answered her phone saying Bill Mason instead of Emma Saxby; it was all very embarrassing.

She'd vowed to herself after the *faux pas* at last Saturday's dinner that she'd forget him altogether. It wasn't his fault, he was the perfect gentleman throughout—damn him! A man Emma'd dated six months ago came to their table to say hello. Very straightforward and normal, one would think; a quick introduction, a little small-talk, a smiled goodbye and back to the meal. Emma forgot the man's name, introduced Bill as a dish-jockey and, while trying to correct herself, managed to send a bowl of lobster bisque crashing loudly on to the Spanish-tiled floor. But something Bill did at that precise moment had made her say yes to him tonight. He'd knocked his glass of water in the same direction as the lobster bisque, offered his hand to the stranger and said, 'It looks as if everyone's got dropsy tonight. My name is Bill Mason, glad to meet you.'

The thing that really bothered Emma, the little nagging doubt that wouldn't let go, was the thought of getting involved with another man who pigeon-holed women into sex, service and subservience. Her optimistic nature, however, told her that whatever the outcome she'd at least have a slap-up meal, and her determination reassured her she'd always be in charge of any situation.

He arrived exactly on time bearing a dozen red roses. She'd done a hurried tidy-up and folded the bed into the wall, so for once her flat looked like non-sleeping living area. She thanked him for the flowers with a lingering kiss on his cheek and deposited them in the only vase she owned.

The cab ride to the restaurant was relaxed and friendly. They chatted about Nixon's visit to Russia, the attempt on the Shah of Iran's life, and the amazing back-beat in Chuck Berry's music. Maybe she'd read too much into this, maybe it was just a pleasant way for him to spend his last night ashore.

As always, the meal was superb. Trader Vic's reflected perfectly the taste of the affluent sixties. Its prices were high, as was the quality of food and service. Politicians and pop stars mingled in a mixture of pin-stripe suits and pop art; each giving the other room to manoeuvre while respecting the money needed to support regular dining at such a soulfully deferential watering hole. The restaurant had a South Seas decor. Blow-fish and outrigger canoes hung from the roof; green leather chairs slid under highly polished tables hewn from single slabs of redwood. Concealed lighting illuminated the native works of art scattered liberally around the walls before dispersing on the wickiup ceiling. The long leather-edged bar, surrounded by imitation thatch, gave the impression of a beach cabana without the sand or water. Two six-foot Chinese ovens stood on a tiled floor at the rear of the restaurant, surrounded by glass and tended by junior kitchen staff.

Emma ate her spare-ribs in a most provocative manner; she dissected her Indonesian lamb roast with the skill of a surgeon, savouring every mouthful. Bill watched her every move.

'You are, without a doubt, the sexiest lady when it comes to food. So why do you turn into an after-dinner nun?'

Emma stabbed a slice of peach with her fork. 'I don't.'

'You certainly do where I'm concerned.'

She offered him the peach. He cupped her hand and slowly sucked the warm fruit into his mouth. Emma experienced that floating feeling she'd tried all week to suppress.

'You should talk! Can I have my hand back?'

'No, you can't.' He kissed her fingers. 'I want you, Emma. I have since we first met.' He let go of her hand and sat back into the leather banquette, keeping his eyes pinned on hers. 'Tomorrow I begin the most important three weeks of my life. I just want to know if you'll be waiting when I get back.'

That was the phrase that paid. Emma could've coped with, 'I want to know you before I go', 'I'm going to be three weeks without a woman', or even if he'd called her a prick teaser and asked her outright if she'd fuck him. She could've seen him off with any one of the twenty put-down lines she held in her carnal thesaurus. But 'Will you wait for me' got to where she lived. She kicked off her right shoe, moved her foot up between his knees, and fixed her eyes challengingly on his. 'What time is your train tomorrow?'

From that moment she was entirely lost in him. All her principles, all the promises and vows went straight out of the window. She wanted him and she wanted him now. Coffee and brandy became a sensual feast of anticipatory lust. It was as if the gods had flicked a switch, turning off all her powers of reason, leaving her a woman on heat, desperate to explore his body and achieve total sexual ecstasy. Their eyes explored each other across the dimly lit table.

Emma refused to succumb completely. She had to employ humour to ensure at least a modicum of self-control. For some inexplicable reason she adopted an American accent. 'Your place or mine?' she drawled, not knowing or caring about the answer.

It was her place in the end. They sat entwined in the back of the cab, Emma still feeling somewhat awkward with him, not allowing herself to let go completely, but drifting in and out of ecstasy in short, intense waves as the streets of London flashed by the cab window like a movie backdrop. Bill could sense her nervousness and restricted his caresses to her hands, arms and shoulders, while constantly engaging her eyes with his; searching, laughing, desiring, and communicating the happiness he felt. They held each other tightly in the small, mirrored lift at Bristol House. Bill studied every curve of her body as she searched her handbag for the front-door key. Emma opened the door and walked into the security of her welcoming bedsit. She turned to face him, her arms open. Bill kicked the front door shut behind him.

Her awkwardness with him disappeared completely with their first private kiss. They blended into each other with consummate ease; arousing, soothing, stroking, exploring, kissing, undressing each other, joining and climaxing in one naturally flowing sequence.

In the small hours of morning they lay exhausted in each other's arms; Bill savouring a feeling of happiness he'd never experienced before, Emma basking in his contentment and light-heartedly trying to find a word to describe her feelings this evening that would fit alongside gangaler, toobigski and Sotfo in her mind's alternative world. But the only word she could come up with was 'wonderful'.

Liverpool Street looked deserted except for a dust-cart and an old man passed out on a pavement bench. Emma stopped her Mini fifty yards from the rail station. She switched the engine off and put her arms around Bill's neck.

'It was a glorious night and I'll miss you.' She kissed him briefly, then pulled away. 'Now get out of here before I do something silly.'

He drew her to him and kissed her tenderly. She remembered every detail of last night. The way he'd held her, the way he'd made every part of her come to life. His kisses powerful, his touch so gentle. The way he'd come inside her and filled her so completely. She would wait for him. She would love him.

'You must go,' she whispered. 'If you stay any longer I'll make you miss the train.'

He reached into the back seat for his bag, opened the door and stepped out into the crisp morning air. 'Take care, sweetheart. I love you.'

He'd walked fifty feet down the road before the remark registered. She opened the driver's door and leaped from the car.

'I love you, too,' she called after him.

He turned and waved, then he was gone. She stepped back into the Mini, and felt the tears well up inside her. The tears of missing him already.

Harwich was cold, windy and bleak. Bill, Brian, Nigel,

Peter, the Street twins and the night boys huddled around the small heater in the cramped bridge-cabin of the tug *Offshore One* and swapped stories of their last night in town. Brian recounted every sordid detail of the two Chelsea ladies who had 'sucked and fucked him to oblivion'. Nigel's story was similar, but delivered with more panache and more imaginative use of adjectives. Peter said he was sorry to disappoint, but he'd spent his last night at home with his Mum, Dad and three sisters. Brian asked how old they were with a leer; Peter told him to piss off. The twins had spent their time at the production studio and proudly showed off the four boxes of tape containing jingles for everyone. Bill admitted to the meal with Emma at Trader Vic's, but would not be drawn on what happened afterwards. 'We both had early starts and the meal went on 'til one,' was his official line. No-one believed him, but short of calling him a liar there wasn't a lot they could say.

Johnny, Thomas and the Prince 'checked out the scene' in silence.

The tug cleared the harbour shortly before noon. The easterly wind and North Sea currents battered the little boat and made life uncomfortable and very wet. The twins loved it. They stood on deck, held on to the lifelines and pretended to be on a roller-coaster. Nigel was sick within five minutes; Peter followed ten minutes later.

'Get rid of it now, mates,' shouted Brian smugly from the bridge. 'We don't want you barfing all over our nice new carpets.'

Bill spent the trip pretending to read this morning's *Daily Mirror*. He stared at the pages and thought of Emma, the joys of last night constantly replaying in his mind. He found himself thinking years ahead, about

Emma's weight problem and if she'd end up fat and forty. Most unusual, given that his curiosity about the future of girlfriends normally spanned a couple of weeks at most.

By one o'clock they could see the ships; all three in line. London first, with her tall radio mast and the numbers 266 along her side. Then FREE, painted all white and shining in her newness. Lastly Caroline, much lower in the water and disappearing intermittently in the swell.

'Jesus Christ! This is it, me ol' mates!' There was fear in Brian's voice.

'Don't worry,' reassured Bill. 'I had a word with Stuart. They've got a platform ladder rigged. You won't have to jump.'

'Thank fuck!' Brian pulled a bottle of Jack Daniel's from his bag and swigged a mouthful. 'Want some?'

For the first time since he'd signed on, Bill didn't want to be here. He wanted to be making love in Emma's bed. Thoughts of the silky texture of her olive skin, the shape of her breasts, the soft curve of her neck flashed vividly through his mind before dissolving into cherished memories. He looked at Brian and then the bottle. 'Why not!'

Captain Vourner watched from the bridge as the tug pulled alongside. With the exception of Eddie Lincoln's presence on both journeys, the trip to Amsterdam had been quality time. Lisa had welcomed him with open arms, as usual. They'd walked the canal paths and stopped at Sven's for a meal, as usual. He'd held her ageing body that still felt like a teenager to him, as usual. They talked of Venice, Portugal and retirement, as usual; only this time it was within their grasp and they knew it.

Eddie knew nothing of the tug's arrival until it bumped the side of the ship. He was in his cabin, stoned out of his socks and relating the joys of the Canal Palace Hotel to three disbelieving crew.

'And after that, I had a go at the bucking bronco position.'

'What's that?' inquired Svenson, one of the stone-head Dutch seamen, and one of Eddie's best customers.

'It's like the doggy position, only when you get set, you call her a silly, fat cow, and hold on for all you're fuckin' worth!'

They all laughed except Eddie; he gloated in his stoned euphoria, feeling like king of the world.

Using the inside pockets of his sou'wester, he'd smuggled the kilo of top-grade Durban Poison, generously donated by Joanna, back to the ship. Dutch customs didn't even ask for his passport. He'd put half the stash in the lock-up under his bunk for his own use and quickly proceeded to sell the remainder to the bored shitless crew at £2.10s.6d an ounce.

'You'll have to excuse me, gentlemen,' he said, trying desperately to stand still on the moving deck. 'New customers on the port bow.'

Bill was first aboard. He unlocked his cabin, deposited his bag on the bunk and retrieved the photograph of Emma he'd stealthily stolen from Bristol House the night before. He placed it carefully in the centre of his desk.

By the time they'd all boarded FREE, Brian had finished most of the whisky and was in no condition to stand, let alone show the new boys around the ship. Bill accepted the task willingly and waited in the mess-room until they'd all assembled.

'Welcome to the world of FREE radio. I'm your bunny Bill and I'm here to pamper your every whim.'

Nigel and Peter were still recovering from their first encounter with the sea and were not responsive to Bill's attempted humour. The twins thought it hysterical and burst into song.

'It's not unusual to get sick on everyone . . . Da da da da da da.'

Bill laughed; Brian fell over; Nigel and Peter remained expressionless.

'One question,' stated Bill, getting down to business. 'Simon and Lewis. Do you want to share a cabin?'

'Indeed!' came the dual reply.

'Nigel and Peter, stay where you are. The Streets, follow me.'

Bill strode off to the cabin nearest the bow, the twins in hot pursuit.

'This is the only cabin with double bunks. It's bigger than the rest so you should have enough room.'

Simon and Lewis smiled at Bill and then at each other.

'This will do nicely,' said Simon.

'When can we see the studio?' asked Lewis.

Bill had never encountered the likes of the Street twins. They seemed to be in perfect mental harmony. It was unnerving; unreal. 'Let me get the other two settled in. I'll come back for you.'

He walked back to the mess-room and found Brian, Nigel and Peter stretched out on the leather sofa. Brian was snoring, Nigel and Peter staring blankly at the television their pale grey faces matching the screen.

'Come on, you two,' he said, tapping them on the foot. 'Let me show you to your beds.'

Bill carried their bags to cabins three and four and

watched them flop limply on to the bunks. He remembered the first time he'd set foot on FREE and how sick he'd felt, a nausea that wouldn't stay down or come up; how all equilibrium disappeared and his stomach had felt as if it was floating independently inside his body. He shuddered at the memory. 'Okay, lads, don't try to talk. Just sleep. You'll feel much better, when you wake up.' He left them to their misery and walked to the twins' cabin, number six. He heard the tail-end of a joke echo through the door.

'Wilson to Benn . . . stop these pirates or I'll have your title!'

He knocked on the door.

'Come in, come in, whatever you are.'

Bill opened the door. The twins were lying on their bunks, Simon upper; Lewis lower, already looking relaxed and at home. Although this was the biggest cabin, it still required a careful living plan to prevent overcrowding. The tiered bunks, double wardrobe and second chair ate up the extra space, leaving only a two-by four-foot piece of carpeted floor. For guests, it would always be standing room only.

'Have you come to show us the ship?' Simon couldn't wait to get going.

'The deluxe twenty-minute tour to include studio and all moving parts.'

The twins together. 'You got it!'

'They were shown along the narrow carpeted corridor with shiny silver fire extinguishers spaced at intervals between the bulkheads, through the mess-room with its large, wooden table and small black and white television, to the galley, then up on deck, past the steel generator and aeriel housings and on to the bridge. They finally scampered down the aft hatchway to the business end of the operation, the only bit they were really interested in.

Simon and Lewis went potty in the studio. To have two tape machines was a luxury they'd only ever dreamed about. To have the use of this electronic wonderland twenty-four hours a day made them feel shore leave was irrelevant. They looked at each other and instinctively did a high five.

It had always been that way with the twins, since they first became aware of each other at the age of three. Their teachers in primary school were the first to notice what their parents had, for years, taken for granted; almost identical test results, even when they sat a room apart; picking out the same picture from a choice of ten when shown separately; and the fascinating way they'd play with the other children, taking over from each other in perfect harmony. The teachers called in psychologists, the psychologists called in psychiatrists. Months of tests proved nothing. As soon as the boys felt under pressure, the telepathy would leave them.

They were academically bright at school, cruising through O levels on a 'B' average. By fourteen, their rapidly developing sense of humour gained them peer respect and popularity; by fifteen they were producing a very funny school paper as part of their English literature course. The headmaster at Ilford Secondary was disturbed by the harshness of some of the caricatures, understood little of the humour or the style of presentation, but was thoroughly impressed by the quality of writing and artwork, especially the strip cartoon depicting Rudolf Nureyev in full ballet costume, dancing on the heads of Russian KGB men shouting 'Catch me! Catch me!', instead of running to the French police and shouting 'Protect me! Protect me!'

as reported in the world press when Rudolf did 'Le Bunk at Le Bourget airport'.

Their only real separation had been mutually agreed during puberty. They'd joked about marrying identical twin girls and producing identical quads, but finally resolved to keep their romantic lives on an individual basis to avoid any clash of interest. To date they'd managed well under this plan, both losing their virginity within a week of each other to girls who lived twenty miles apart and were in no way related. They talked to each other of their conquests and learned from each other's experiences, while treating their fleeting partners with the consideration and respect drummed into them during their mother's friendly chats around the dinner tables of their formative years.

Their real love was radio. They'd grown up with great comedy programmes at the flick of a button. 'The Goons', 'Round The Horn' and 'Take it From Here' all contributed to their desire to be funny. The first sketch they wrote, at the age of eleven, featured Neddy Seegoon and Min from 'The Goons', only set in Ilford High Street.

The twins themselves cared little for all the fuss. The primary-school tests had hardened them against outside intrusion. They were perfectly capable of living separate lives, and did from time to time, but they enjoyed each other's company so much and shared so many interests that time apart seemed more like an endurance test than time spent being happily productive.

For the past two years they'd collected a haphazard assortment of microphones, record players, tape recorders, and a small four-channel sound mixer, mainly from second-hand shops, school friends and jumble sales. They got it all working and, given their limitations, produced excellent jingles and sketches. To be set down in the middle of a brand new, state-of-the-art broadcast studio was a dream come true for Simon and Lewis Street from Mansell Road, Ilford, Essex.

Preparation to get a new station to air is a twenty-four hour a day roller-coaster of writing, production and administration. The twins would need every available minute to produce the promotion spots, commercials and jingles needed to feed this gluttonous monster. The lifespan of a commercial campaign can be as short as three days, station promotions even less. With an average of nine commercial minutes an hour, twenty-four hours a day, the turnover is chaotic. The national clients and multinational conglomerates such as Coca-Cola and Lever, who accounted for over seventy per cent of total revenue, would be dealt with by the big London advertising agencies, delivering the finished production to the ship ready for air. The remaining thirty per cent was split between the ship and small hired-by-the-hour production studios in Soho. Stuart's policy of encouraging new advertisers in the medium-sized business and local market field meant production of demo commercials had to be added to the already bursting schedule.

Simon sat down at the ten-channel mixing board and switched on the power. He watched the volume meter twitch as the first surge of electricity lit the machines. Vary-speed tape recorders, individual tone settings, tape or plate echo facility, things he'd only read about in magazines, hummed to life. This was truly a wondrous place.

'Lesson number one, Min,' he gooned. 'Get to know your machinery!'

Lewis chose the pair of headphones with the longest lead from the four pairs hanging from the coat hook on the studio door. 'Any chance of a ten-foot lead so's I can walk anywhere?'

Bill snapped out of his dream. 'Pardon?'

Lewis pointed at the wire. 'Longer leads on the cans?'

'You'll meet Stanley in the fullness of time. He's radio engineer first-class. Anything to do with wires, tapes or turntables, he's your man.' Bill felt in need of his own cabin and a bottle of cold beer. He also wanted to write to Emma telling her it wasn't a one-night stand, that he'd meant what he said. For once in his life some *one* was more important than some *thing*. 'Can you guys manage down here? I'll have the first-day running orders finished by tomorrow. Okay?'

They both turned to face him. 'No problem!'

Emma Saxby returned home to find her favourite photograph, the one taken by her youngest sister on holiday last year, missing. She hunted around the flat for fifteen minutes before reaching the conclusion that Bill had nicked it. At first she was angry; then she sat on the bed and hugged herself.

Chapter 4

Thursday, April 15. 5 a.m.

Stuart Salisbury parked his Bentley outside two Hayes Mews and carefully locked the driver's door. No parking problems until half past eight; by then he'd be long gone. He stood for a moment outside the office door and inhaled the chill morning air. The first light of day cast elongated shadows down the empty mews. Another fine, clear spring day in prospect; just the weather to herald the beginning of the Future of Radio Entertaining Everyone.

The nervousness he felt about the station never showed on the outside; but inside it ate away at him continuously, sowing doubt and reaping inner torment. He worried about financial success, political pressure, programme content, the seaworthiness of the ship . . . Just about everything that could go wrong had passed through his mind at one stage or another, clipping hours off his nightly rest and haunting his days with grim visions.

This tendency to bottle up his fears had a lot to do with his lack of a real social life. Besides his brother, nobody shared his life or his thoughts on a regular basis. His ladyfriends divided naturally into three categories: dinner partners, riding partners and bed partners.

Sometimes a woman would fit two, or rarely, all three sections, but Stuart never talked business with any of them, preferring to suppress his anxiety and carry the burden of leadership alone.

The closest he'd come to a non-family confidante was Lucinda Taylor-Hampton. She was everything her name suggested, and perfectly acceptable to the inmates at Calbraith House. He'd dated her for most of last year and although the regularity (about twice a month) didn't give the impression that they were potential life partners, the intensity of their time together did hold up hope of real compatibility. She was a well-endowed, well-educated, and well-bred filly, whose family owned large chunks of Hampshire and a very profitable stud farm. Last November, as they lay post-coitally in the hayloft above stable seven, he'd confided his worries regarding the conversion of FREE taking place all those miles away in Galveston, and how he should really go over there and supervise the work personally.

'Why don't you take me for a Pimm's at Lottie's place and forget about those beastly American workmen?' she'd answered.

He did as requested, but from then on his visits to the hayloft became less frequent and his conversations with her decidedly one-track.

As he padded up the carpeted stairs towards reception he reflected on how lucky he'd been to find such a central office at such a reasonable price. Since, officially, FREE Radio didn't exist, Stuart had found it difficult renting office space, especially on a six-month base. During a quiet evening walk by the river it suddenly dawned on him that, although broadcasting itself was illegal, the supply of goods and revenue was not. He registered a company named Marine Supply and Sales

(London) Ltd, and, bingo, estate agents were coming out of his ears. In the end he'd decided to buy the mews outright; it was spacious, had parking on the ground floor and was a snip at fifteen thousand pounds. He was sure London property prices would rise considerably within the next few years, so even if the station folded he could always realise some profit from its sale.

Emma greeted him at the top of the stairs, her arms wrapped around a black china vase full of brilliant red tulips.

'I thought I'd be first here,' he grumbled. 'Some time to reflect before the big push.'

'I was up at three,' chirped Emma, her voice high with excitement, her face radiant. 'No time to reflect. Time to make history!'

Stuart smiled warmly at his assistant, suddenly aware of how much he relied on her. He dropped his briefcase and his shoulders. 'We wouldn't be here without you, Emma. You've been our rock, our supporter, our last line of defence.'

Emma placed the flowers on a small table to the right of the stairs. She smiled, making light of the pride and pleasure she felt at his words. 'I shall ask for a pay rise if you keep this up.' She stepped back to admire her arrangement. 'I've got another two dozen tulips. I thought they'd look nice in your office, next to the bar.'

'I think you're right.' Stuart put his arm around her waist and guided her back to her own office. 'This is a historic day. I only hope the station lives up to expectations.'

'With Bill Mason and the terrible twins leading the way, how can it fail?'

Stuart flopped into her chair, letting his guard slip

95

for once. 'Just the insecurities of a worried man. Take no notice.'

'Stuart Salisbury!' She stood before him, hands on hips, her bright eyes dancing. 'Don't you dare doubt the capabilities of this team! We're here to be number one, and nothing less will do.'

He stood up, the customary confidence returning to, his face. 'Thank you, Emma Saxby. Thank you very much.' He placed his hand lightly on her shoulder as he walked by. 'So where are these tulips?'

5:30 a.m.

Bill stood on the flying bridge, his back braced against the wind, watching the first glimmer of daylight break on the eastern horizon. In an hour and a half FREE would be on the air. His would be the first programme. The thought filled him with pride, and a little apprehension.

It had been very much a no-lose game until now. All the press ballyhoo had been hype. No-one had actually played as yet; all that would change today.

This was Bill's tenth radio station. The previous nine were scattered over as many countries. He'd won his first job, in Paris, by being passably bilingual, and because he happened to be visiting a friend in a radio studio on August 5, 1962, when half a world away Marilyn Monroe was dying. They asked him if he was American; he said Jamaican; they said close enough. From that interview sprang a few commercial voice-overs; from the success of the voice-overs he was offered some holiday relief radio shows. He met an agent at a Paris pop party who said he, Bill, had a great voice and that he, top-class agent, had contacts world-wide. Bill signed with him and, true to his word, the agent found him work in almost every city he visited, with the notable exception of Johannesburg, where the radio stations weren't keen to hire anyone who had friends named Wadiki.

He heard a door slam shut behind him.

'Ready for the off?' Brian's voice sounded tired and laboured. 'I've been up all night with those fucking twins. I don't think they ever sleep.'

'Is everything done?'

'Sure is. Jingles are ready, records in the studio and I've just finished the first chart.'

Bill turned to face him. 'Where is it?'

'In my cabin. Wanna blimp?'

They strolled down the companionway to the empty mess-room. 'You stay here,' said Brian. 'I'll get it.'

He might be a pain in the neck, but Brian was an excellent chart man. He'd worked long and hard to get it just right for the station sound. FREE's music must represent the young sound of the sixties; be the vanguard of the British sound. Out went Tony Bennett, Ronnie Hilton and Shirley Bassey; in came The Who, the Ivy League and Marianne Faithfull. 'Ticket to Ride' was number one both nationally and on the FREE Forty. Number two – 'Stop In The Name Of Love', the Supremes; three – 'Bring It On Home To Me', the Animals; four – 'Oh No, Not My Baby', Manfred Mann; five – 'King Of The Road', Roger Miller.

The secret of a chart that isn't based on record sales is to outguess the national chart by at least two weeks. Bill studied Brian's work with great interest. The top five were spot-on and the climbers, which included Dylan, the Seekers, Shirley Ellis and the exclusive Walker Brothers track, matched the station sound perfectly.

'I think you've got it nailed, Brian. Can I buy you a coffee?'

'Jees, mate, you sound like Eddie. Selling me shit you get for free!'

'Who's using my name in vain?' A stoned face appeared in the doorway. 'Everything's free today. Booze, grass, fags; I've even got a little excellent Charlie from Amsterdam. What's your pleasure, gents?'

Bill rounded on him. 'My pleasure would be to see you chucked overboard.'

Eddie stepped into the room. 'Come on, guys, it's start-up day. Get loose. Come down to my cabin. A little something for the nose will keep you going 'til noon. It's not too often old Eddie gives it away – take advantage while you can.'

Bill stood up slowly, his six-foot plus frame towering over his puny adversary. 'Eddie, I don't give a shit if you spend your entire life out of your head, and I couldn't care less if you get the crew so smashed they can't tie a slip knot, but if I catch you peddling dope to any of the on-air boys I'll use your balls for bookends. Do I make myself clear?'

Eddie lifted both arms in mock surrender. 'Okay., boss. I'm only trying to be friendly.'

Bill itched to wipe that ugly grin off his face once and for all. 'Go be friendly on the lower deck. We've got work to do.'

Eddie beat a hasty retreat, closing the door smartly behind him.

Brian collected his chart from the table. 'That's a bit strong, mate. Each to his own, don't you agree?' He patted Bill on the back. 'I'm going for a quick kip. See you in an hour.' He walked along the corridor, pausing to make sure Bill wasn't behind him, then descended the ladder to the lower deck and knocked three times on Eddie's door.

'Come!'

The cabin smelled of marijuana. Eddie sat at his desk skinning up another joint. 'Changed your mind?'

'We're not all as goodie as our breakfast jock,' sneered Brian. 'I could sure use a pick-me-up. I've been working all night.'

Eddie reached into the top drawer of his desk and produced a small paper package. He opened it carefully and scooped a small amount of fine white powder on to the desk top. Taking a one-sided razor-blade from his bits tray he proceeded to chop and spread the powder into a long, thin line. 'Roll a note and get your nose around that lot,' he said, with cocky pride. 'Pure Peruvian!'

No stimulants were needed at Hayes Mews. Emma, Anna, Stuart and John were frantically making last-minute preparations for a breakfast party which they hoped would put FREE on the media map. All the national press had been invited, along with clients, pop stars and various sympathetic members of parliament. Stuart had made sure some of his more influential friends would be present and John Walters had secured all the major advertising agencies. Emma was finally coming to terms with John Walters. It had been hard going, but she'd made a special effort and it was beginning to pay off. He was still aloof and cynical but now at least he smiled at her and said thank you when she brought him coffee. His salesmanship was unrivalled. He'd booked over £300,000 of advertising for the first three months of broadcasting without so much as a programme tape to help him. Emma looked forward to watching him with the agency people. He must treat them differently to the way he treated his staff; she was sure of that.

The office was unrecognisable. Bunches of red, white and blue balloons tied with Union Jack ribbon adorned any place Emma found room for a thumbtack. Tables were piled high with snackable goodies from smoked salmon squares to sausage rolls; silver ice buckets stood on wooden stands waiting for their fridge-chilled bottles of champagne.

Stuart sat in his office listening to the six o'clock news on the Home Service. They led with the Dakota Airlines crash which claimed twenty-six lives in Jersey and followed with Nixon's visit to the USSR. John Walters, immaculate in grey flannel suit and crocodile shoes, strode into the office and laid the final sales chart on Stuart's desk.

'Three hundred and sixty-five thousand; a quarter prepaid,' he said, as if he delivered these kind of figures every day.

'That's wonderful, John. Just the start we needed.' He paused, and looked quizzically at his sales director.

'What?'

'Could you sell news?'

'I can sell sand to the Arabs. Why?'

Stuart sat back in his chair. 'I know we're not even on air yet, but I've been looking ahead. I'd like to put our own news team in the field instead of ripping off the BBC.'

John pondered the point before replying. 'How much? Starting when?'

'About two thousand a week to do a good job and starting as soon as possible.'

'Leave it with me.' He turned and left the office as abruptly as he'd entered.

Stuart was also getting used to John's mannerisms. There was no softness in the man, he had no time for pleasantries. Stuart wouldn't want him as a friend, but as a sales director he was unbeatable.

Disinterest would best sum up John's attitude towards Stuart and the rest of the staff. He didn't share their enthusiasm for the music, the radio or the lifestyle. He looked upon FREE as nine one-minute commercial spots an hour; all to be sold at the best possible price. His social life consisted of squash at least twice a week, an occasional evening with an occasional lady, and frequent dinners with various friends of his father, who were always 'glad to do anything' for Irving Walters' boy.

In his own time he would spend hours rummaging through markets all over London in search of obscure military memorabilia and nineteenth-century prints. He really didn't have time for people below the rank of managing director, and they always expected him to remember their names, which John considered totally irrelevant and a complete waste of memory space.

Bill sat in the studio aboard FREE and reached for the number one record. He would start with the top five, then an oldie, Elvis – 'Don't Be Cruel'. Fifty minutes to go. The time seemed to crawl by. Captain Vourner peered through the double glass window and mimed a phone with his right hand. Bill ran upstairs and into the radio room. He clamped on the headphones and flicked the transmission switch.

'FREE to London, FREE to London. Come in London. Over.'

'Bill. It's Emma. Over.'

Her voice turned a great day into the best day of his life. 'Oh, baby, I've missed you so much. How are you? Over.'

'Missing you, too. Stuart wants to wish you luck. He'll be here any moment. I just wanted a quick word in private. Is everything okay out there? Over.'

Bill looked through the porthole. The sun was full on the horizon, the wind had eased and the sea was calm. 'It's a beautiful morning. Even better now. Over.'

'Stuart's here. I'll pass you over.' She had switched into efficient personal assistant mode. She'd risked discovery by speaking to him first and he loved her the more for it.

'Bill! Hello. This is Stuart. How goes it? Over.'

'Very well, sir. Everything's ready for seven o'clock. Over.'

'Splendid. One thing, Bill. Can you say hello to all the staff and guests at the London office? We're having a bit of a shindig, lots of press and agency people. Over.'

'Sure thing. Anyone in particular? Over.'

'The list would be endless. Just make it general.' Stuart looked at his copy of the first-day running order. 'Say after "King of the Road". Over.'

'You got it, boss. Anything else? Over.'

'Just to wish you all the very best of luck. We're all rooting for you. Over.'

'Thank you, Stuart. Good luck to you, too. Over and out.'

Bill stepped out on deck and fulled his lungs with fresh sea air. The morning sun had burned off the remaining traces of sea mist, the weather already developing into a bright but chilly spring day. He could hear the hum of the antenna as it delivered twenty-five kilowatts of power to the mast. He could feel the throb of the generator a deck below him, as it supplied the power for the studio. He could see Radio Caroline rise and fall in the gentle swell off the starboard quarter. This was a time to remember; a time of history; a time of change. He smiled to himself. A time to rock an' roll!

'Time to meet and greet the great British press.' Stuart hung up his phone. 'How many are out there?'

'About forty.' Emma peeked through the window blind in a vain attempt at a more accurate head count. 'I'm surprised we've got this big a turnout.'

'Proves my point.' Stuart picked a Havana cigar from the box on his desk and rolled it between his fingers. 'Hacks can smell free booze five hundred miles away.'

'They're also known for sleeping 'til noon. I think it's wonderful so many have got up this early.' Emma straightened her dress. 'And I think we should tell them so.'

Stuart decided against lighting the cigar. 'You start from the right, I'll start left and meet you at the water cooler.'

The twins labelled the last of the jingles. Simon looked at the clock.

'Six fifty-eight. Where's Bill?'

'About to make a dramatic entrance would be my guess,' said Lewis.

'How right you are!' Bill stood framed in the studio door. 'And bloody nervous, I don't mind saying.'

The twins stood on either side of the studio chair.

'Just sit ye down!' commanded Simon

'And get this show on the road!' completed Lewis.

Bill loaded the main jingle and cued 'Ticket to Ride'. This was it. All the preparation, auditions, late-night production work and even later dinners in London, the trip from Galveston; they all added up to this moment. From now on the radio station would be alive; succeeding or failing on its ability to broadcast good programmes and to attract sales revenue. From now on the public would decide the future of FREE.

At 6:59:30 he started the main theme. Staring blankly ahead at the studio console he trained his mind on the task before him. His last non-radio thought was of Emma, bringing an inner smile to his spirit that can so often make the difference between good and bloody brilliant. At seven o'clock precisely he turned on the microphone.

'This is the Future of Radio Entertaining Everyone, FREE for short, broadcasting twenty-four hours a day on 244 metres medium wave. My name is Bill Mason and these are the Beatles.'

A huge cheer erupted at two Hayes Mews. A small tear appeared in the corner of Stuart's eye as he, too, recalled the sequence of events leading to this moment. The afternoon in Hyde Park when he'd thought of the idea, the unquestioning support of his brother as he'd crossed the unmarked minefield of venture finance in Texas, emerging victorious with the ship and enough money to support it for two years. Finding people like Bill, Emma, Anna and the Captain, who believed in what he was doing and helped him to realise his dream. His old school chum Gerald Copeland, who'd advised him politically and invested a small amount of his own money to 'support his dialogue'. All these people would live in Stuart's heart for ever, regardless of the eventual fate of off-shore radio.

Even steely John Walters, seemed moved by the moment. For a split second he let his defences fall, and for the first time Emma thought she'd seen a real person behind those cold, grey eyes. The Beatles hadn't finished the second verse before he was back behind his wall of cynicism. She watched him chat with his contacts from the agencies. Coldly polite, overtly charming, he moved among them with the ease of a wolf in a dark forest; a smile here, a compliment there; he had them eating from his hand. She wondered how they'd react if they knew what a shit he was to his subordinates.

The press wanted to know everything. Where did the DJs come from? Where did the ship come from? Most of all, where did the money come from? The press was Stuart's forte. He answered all their questions and told them practically nothing, especially about the money. Anna had put together a press-pack consisting of biographies and photographs of the DJs, a brief history and diagrams of the ship, details of programmes, shows on shore, and lots of car stickers. She handed them out, carefully noting names and newspapers for future reference.

Stuart heard 'King of the Road' on the radio and prayed his timing wouldn't desert him. He banged an empty champagne bottle on his desk to get everyone's attention. 'I'd like to thank you all for coming here at this ungodly hour to help us celebrate the opening of FREE Radio. We believe this is the future of broadcasting in the UK. The BBC has had its own way far too long and we, and others like us, intend to change it.' Applause all round. 'Britain is leading the world in popular music; this week four out of the top five in America are British acts, and our first priority will be to promote the British sound around the world.' More applause. 'We have a highly trained and dedicated team both here and on the ship. I hope you'll spend many a happy hour listening to us on the radio and coming to see us at our land-based shows in London and the Home Counties.' He heard the record start to fade. 'Now a little thank you from the lads.'

Roger Miller faded. Stuart turned up the volume. Bill's voice boomed into the room.

'Roger Miller on the road and on FREE Radio. You get lots more on 244. In London, a lot of champagne is being drunk right now at Hayes Mews. Hello to all our hard-working staff and a special thank you to all the ladies and gentlemen of the press and advertising agencies who have gone without sleep to be with us this morning. My lords, ladies and gentlemen, the King.'

The start of 'Don't Be Cruel' was drowned by applause. Stuart knew he had them. There would be great press tomorrow.

Emma felt a wave of warmth rush over her. Bill had such a lovely voice; in tune, in command.

'Just good friends, is it?' Anna placed her hands on Emma's face. 'You're in love, girl, even if you don't know it.'

Emma smiled at her friend. 'Yes I am, and it feels wonderful.' She grabbed Anna's wrists. 'If you say a word I'll tell your father.'

'About what?' Stuart's voice drifted between them.

'About her managing director who cuts into conversations that don't concern him.' Emma produced her sweetest smile, knowing the ice beneath her was paper-thin. She gambled that he'd be in such a good mood he wouldn't take offence.

Stuart studied the two girls who had been so instrumental in getting the station on the air. At times like this the many years of maternal earbashing about

106

gentlemanly behaviour paid a dividend. 'I'm very sorry. I didn't realise it was personal. Please forgive me.'

Emma kissed him on the cheek. 'You're a grand boss, Mr Salisbury. Can we get you anything?'

He moved closer to them and lowered his voice. 'I want to have a quiet word with the chap from *The Times*.' He pointed out a tall man with curly hair who was deep in conversation with a voluptuous brunette from McCann's. 'Do you think you could prise him away from Cruella de Vil and show him into John's office in about five minutes' time?'

'Well, I'll be buggered by a barge pole if this isn't the best radio station I've ever heard!'

Stuart spun around. 'Copey! You made it. Well done!' The two men embraced. 'It's so good to see you! It's been bloody months!' Stuart turned back to face Emma. 'Ladies, may I introduce Gerald Copeland, member of parliament for Cheltenham North, great believer in independent radio and my very best friend since the bad old days at Bradford. Copey, this is Emma Saxby, my right-hand lady, and Anna Papanicholas who runs reception and PR.'

They all shook hands. Although the two men looked very different physically, they reminded Emma of peas from the same pod. The newcomer stood five foot ten compared with Stuart's six foot three. Gerald had a stocky build, a round face with flat features and receding hair, while Stuart sported a mass of wavy hair and his features were classic. Their clothes betrayed the link; both men wore suits unmistakably tailored within a hundred-yard radius of Savile Row and Clifford Street.

Stuart leaned close to Emma. 'Make that fifteen minutes, unless he tries to leave; then call me right away.' He turned to his friend. 'Come on, Copey. I've saved a special bottle for us.'

Anna eyed the man from *The Times* with coital interest. His thick, black curly hair and rugged Latin features performed wonders for her libido. She couldn't stop staring at him, watching his body moves and feeling very jealous of whoever Cruella de Vil really was.

'Now who's in lust?' whispered Emma.

'Too right! He's georgeous!' Anna did her impression of 'uncle' Humphrey. 'You dump the doll in the river, sweetheart, and I'll take the guy back to my place.'

Emma watched Stuart and his old friend disappear into the sales director's office. 'Fifteen minutes, Snuggles. We'll make our move in fifteen minutes.'

At BHS House, Sir David Garman was making his first move against the new pirate. For over a decade his company had been the premier music publishing house in Britain. The day Simon Dee welcomed listeners to Radio Caroline on 199 the phones started ringing in his West End office, and they hadn't stopped since. The anti-pirate brigade, political and commercial, looked to him for guidance. If anyone could stop these thieves of copyright, these eroders of the establishment, it was him. After all, he already had the legitimate media dancing to his tune; he'd been the prime negotiator in deals concerning how many records the BBC could play, how much performing rights would cost, the controlled price of sheet music – in fact, damn near everything that moved in the music world had something to do with BHS.

At first he tried the direct approach by releasing a

statement forbiding any of his employees to supply the pirates with BHS material; but smaller companies quickly filled the gap. He issued another statement saying his company wouldn't contract acts wanting pirate promotion; new signings fell dramatically. Next he tried the political approach, lobbying cabinet ministers and high-flying friends; he found large support but nobody actually did anything. The past year had produced one frustration after another, and it was getting right up Sir David's aristocratic nose.

He'd studied several options for his attack on this latest pilferer, from wavelength jamming to transmitter sabotage, but as his inside man was not yet in place he'd have to settle for revenue loss. A station can sell a million pounds-worth of space, but if it doesn't go on air, the station won't get paid. Yesterday, forty commercials bound for FREE were accidentally passed through a magnetic field at Harwich Docks, wiping them clean. The workmen responsible apologised. Sir David payed a bonus.

It wasn't a pretty scheme, far less dignified than his usual realms of activity, and would only put a minute dent in the station's yearly revenue, but it was a little something to alleviate his feelings of total frustration and would serve to remind this privateering outfit that life was not going to be plain sailing.

Stuart opened a bottle of Dom Perignon 1961 and poured a fizzy measure into two crystal glasses. 'To FREE Radio.'

'To free enterprise!'

Stuart made sure the door was firmly shut. 'How goes it in the corridors of power?'

'A lot of stink about what you're doing, dear boy. Sir

Robin Clarke says you're an unruly rabble broadcasting renegade radio; says you're corrupting the youth of this great country and threatening the very life blood of responsible media.'

'Can he do anything?'

Gerald took another sip. 'Not yet, and let me also tell you this – a good deal of the Labour party agree with Clarke, but for every one who stands behind him there are two Tories shouting Foul!'

'Where are you in this pantomine?'

'Leading the Foul chorus, dear boy.'

Stuart poured more champagne. 'Who're the main players against us?'

'Clarke, first and foremost. Tony Benn's Postmaster General, so he must be seen to toe the line, but I feel Wilson's coasting and taking advice.'

'Who's on our side?'

'Duxbury, Horton, Harry Johnson; they're the most vocal apart from me. James Denton, old Percy, Jackson and, if it came to it, I would say most of the Shadow Cabinet.'

Stuart pondered the names and did some quick mental sums. 'What about Caroline and London? Do they have a good lobby?'

Gerald laughed. 'Dear boy, they *are* the lobby. I'm the only friend you have so far. You've only been on the air for a couple of hours; you'll need a lot more ground work to even catch up.' He patted Stuart on the back. 'Don't look so glum. Even if they tabled legislation tomorrow, which they won't, it would still take two years to become law. How much money can you make in two years?'

'How much can *we* make, don't you mean? You've got a chunk of this as well.'

'That reminds me; the holding company, Hystar? Plystar?'

'Plystar.'

'Yes. It has to be moved to Switzerland. It's almost guaranteed they'll hit all English companies for big corporation tax in the next budget. You can move out legally now and I strongly advise you to do so.'

Stuart poured more champagne into Gerald's glass, thinking how useful it was to have friends in high places.

Gerald lifted his glass in salute, emptied it with one swallow and placed it on the desk. 'What else is new in the land of FREE?'

'I'm thinking of starting my own news service.'

The member for Cheltenham North looked at Stuart in stunned disbelief. 'You have to be kidding me!'

'Not at all. The other ships are ripping off the BBC. If I put a team in the field and gather our own news, that's got to be another first, and that's what I'm after. First for music, first for news.'

Gerald flopped down on the sofa and held his hands to his head. 'Short of a murder on the ship or being busted for fifty kilos of cocaine, your own news team is the fastest way of forcing the Government to get serious.'

'Why?'

'Because, dear boy, despite their public rantings, they don't really give a damn if you play rock and roll to the people and make a few quid in the process. Christ, the Beatles are big business and everyone needs young votes; but you put a news team out there they can't control and they'll cut you off at the knees!'

Stuart let the logic sink in. He'd never considered the havoc a rogue news outfit could cause in the Commons.

The idea appealed to him enormously. 'What if I were to hire a news director who was acceptable to the establishment?'

'No such animal! As soon as he joins you, he's an outcast.'

'What about Caesar's wife?'

Gerald studied his friend. 'You mean beyond reproach?'

'Precisely.'

'Like who?'

Stuart opened the office door. He caught Emma's eye and nodded, then closed the door. 'Two minutes.' He pointed to the right side of the desk. 'There's another bottle in the fridge.'

It took five minutes for Emma and Anna to cajole the man from *The Times* into John's office. Anna held his arm as Stuart opened the door. 'When you've finished with him can I have him back?' she asked, more with hope than conviction.

'Jonathan Gilby, as I live and breathe.' Stuart extended his hand. 'Are you enjoying our little breakfast bash?'

A few glasses of good champagne may have dented Jonathan's concentration, but only superficially. A double first from Queens and six years at *The Times* had armed him well. 'What do you chaps want? It's not an interview, so it must be a job.'

'News director at FREE,' said Stuart, deciding on the direct approach.

There was no perceptible reaction from Gilby, just a slight flicker of his left eye. 'Budget?'

'We haven't sold it yet, but we're looking at about two grand a week.'

'I'd be cutting my throat with Fleet Street.'

Stuart wanted his own news, he wanted to stick two fingers up at the establishment, and most of all he wanted Jonathan Gilby to run it. 'I'll give you five thousand signing-on fee; tax-free in Switzerland.'

This was a fortuitous moment in the life of Jonathan Gilby. For months he'd been having a running row with his editor over content. He felt the whole of Fleet Street was becoming politically polarised, each faction more interested in digging dirt on the opposition than reporting hard news stories with skilful, unbiased journalism. This could be the ideal time to jack the whole thing in. He'd often dreamed of telling his bosses to orally caress his posterior; the only thing stopping him had been money.

Jonathan offered his hand. 'You have a deal, Mr Salisbury.'

Gerald Copeland sank deeper into the sofa. 'Shit,' he said softly.

8:55 a.m.

On the ship, Bill Mason looked forward to joining the first-day celebrations. People had been coming into the studio since seven o'clock offering champagne, cocaine and coffee. Bill refused all three in favour of the two large bottles of Perrier that now stood empty on the console. The up-side of being first on is that you're first off. Barring a surprise voice-over, no more work was required of him until tomorrow morning. This would be a good time to party. He cued up 'Concrete and Clay', checked the Coca-Cola commercial and opened the microphone. 'Four minutes away from nine o'clock on FREE. Between nine and noon you'll be royally entertained by Brian Todd. Features include the morning recipe, three from one at ten – this morning it's Bob Dylan, and the coffee break at eleven. I'm Bill Mason, have a

FREE day, I'll see you for breakfast tomorrow. Unit Four Plus Two follows this.' He started the Coke commercial, slipped off his headphones and slumped into the chair.

Brian bounced through the studio door, arms full of albums and pupils dilated. Bill could smell the sweet scent of alkaloid on his breath.

'C_{17}-H_{21}-NO_4,' said Bill as he signed his commercial log-sheet and stood to let Brian take the chair.

'What the hell is that, mate?' Brian adjusted the microphone.

'The chemical formula for cocaine. It would make a good quiz question, don't you think?'

Brian was admitting nothing. 'I don't do quizzes. Have you done the Marquee promo?'

It would be a mistake to upset him just before airtime. 'No. You'll need to run it before nine-fifteen. See you at lunch.'

The party in the mess-room was in full swing. For Nigel Hinckley and Peter Robinson it was the first time they'd not felt nauseous since boarding the tug. Of all the bonding experiences, being seasick together is one of the strongest. Nigel and Peter hadn't met a week ago and already they were sharing secrets, sign language, and a bottle of imported Russian vodka. The Captain was also feeling jolly, largely on account of the half-empty bottle of Jack Daniel's by his side; the twins looked thoroughly wiped out.

'I think you two should get some sleep,' Bill said to Simon. 'You've been awake forever. You both need to be on the case by six tonight.'

Lewis nodded and looked at his brother. 'He's right. I can hardly keep my eyes open.'

'Put the No Entry sign outside your door,' offered Bill. 'I'll wake you at five.'

The young production geniuses excused themselves from the festivities and sloped away for a well-deserved rest.

'Now, Mr Mason,' said the Captain, slamming his bottle on the table. 'Will you join me in a toast to this magnificent radio station?'

'One magnificent screw-up is the way I'd describe it!' John Walters threw his sales sheets in the air. 'I bust my ass selling this goddamn station and you let them wipe the fuckin' tape!'

Emma had no idea what had gone wrong. She'd followed the commercial transfer procedure exactly as John had directed. She said nothing.

'How'd you send it? Pony goddamn Express?'

'As directed; rail, and then the shipping agent picks it up and delivers to the tug.'

'The Harwich agents?! Christ, those bozos would take new Beatle tapes on the underground.' He shoved his hands deep in his trouser pockets and stiffened his body and face in frustrated tension. 'Five thousand goddamn pounds of first-day revenue up the Swannee! Shit!'

Chapter 5

Thursday, April 29. 4:30 p.m.

Anna Papanicholas had been working on average twelve hours a day in her determination to achieve her ambition. She'd quickly mastered the operating technique of the small production studio the twins were using in Soho. She'd spent two exhausting nights putting together an audition tape that could rival anything produced by an experienced engineer. Her voice sounded mature, her production tight, her delivery crisp and upbeat. She'd pushed Emma into asking Stuart if he had any objection to female DJs. He said he didn't, but he doubted there'd be anyone good enough to match up to requirements. The next day Anna walked into his office and played her tape.

Stuart's first reaction was total disbelief. He asked if the twins were trying to wind him up.

'This is all my own work!' she shouted indignantly over the music. 'And I could handle it live!'

He listened again. She had a quality, a natural awareness in her voice that made her sound believable. The jingles were funny, the music correct.

'It's never been done before.' He looked at her from under his eyebrows and saw the excitement in her face. This really was important to her, and she sounded more than good. 'What the hell! FREE's never been done before! Why not? Replace Bill Mason for a week and we'll go from there.'

Anna maintained her composure until she reached Emma's office, where she dropped the tape and her purse in the centre of the room, pulled Emma out of her chair and proceeded to dance her around in small circles.

'You got the job, then?' asked Emma at the start of the third turn.

The euphoria died down somewhat that evening when it came to breaking the news to her parents. She felt sure they'd understand now that she had a chance to actually be on the radio. No mere receptionist or secretary; a real DJ, on a prime-time show. She just knew they'd be proud of her.

Her father's reaction was more violent than she could have imagined. He called her an ungrateful, lying slut and ordered her to leave the house that night and never return. Anna felt mortified, even betrayed by her father who, not even for one second, gave any acknowledgement of her achievement. The moment he called her a slut she hated him and wished him dead. The hatred didn't last, but it fired her determination. The time had come to leave for good. Her mother just sat in the large, friendly kitchen and cried.

Anna spent the first night with Emma, then made arrangements to use Ovington Square until Bill came off the ship.

Emma had picked her up in the Mini at six this morning and driven to Harwich. Both girls were so excited they could hardly contain themselves – Anna because she was starting a brand-new life doing the one thing she knew would make her happy, and

Emma because tonight she would be with her lover.

They'd stopped for breakfast at a greasy spoon on the A12, just before Colchester. A long-distance trucker asked them if they fancied a threesome in the back of his Volvo eighteen-wheeler.

'We'd love to see the inside of your truck,' Emma had said, staring directly at the front of his trousers. 'Why don't you go tidy up your little bed compartment and we'll be along in five minutes.'

'I wonder if he's still waiting?' asked Anna as they pulled into Harwich dock.

Four hours later a wonderfully happy Emma Saxby parked her Mini outside seven Ovington Square. She looked across at Bill, snoring quietly in the passenger seat, and contemplated how to best wake him up. The last two weeks had been hectic for both of them. Nigel Hinkley had gone down with a stomach-bug last Monday, so Bill had been doing double shifts. Jonathan Gilby had somehow adopted Emma as his 'go-getter' for the fledgling news department. She didn't mind, but combined with her duties for Stuart it meant a minimum twelve-hour day.

Emma decided on the method of waking. She gently rubbed the inside of Bill's leg, just above the knee; moving her hand a little further upwards with every stroke. She smiled as she watched the bulge in his pants grow to meet her hand. She leaned over and brushed his cheek with her lips. Still he quietly snored. A woman pushing a pram strolled past the car. Emma looked to see who else was in the square; save the woman, it was deserted. She gently undid his belt and top button, pulling the zip down in one flowing movement. She slid her hand slowly inside his trousers until she felt the start of his pubic hair, then further down to his penis. She held it firmly, before sliding it upwards so it cleared his clothing and stood erect before her. She wanted him inside her, to feel him enter her as he had that first night. She looked around the square again; still deserted. She bent over and guided his warm, beautiful member into her mouth. Almost instantly she felt her head being cupped by two strong hands, moving it faster on the phallus. She responded to his wish.

'I want you.' His voice was deep and husky, vibrating her senses and soaking her with anticipation. She had to have him inside her, this instant.

She slowly removed her mouth and, holding him with her right hand, slid her face over his stomach and chest and kissed him full on the mouth; searching with her tongue, then biting his lip, eating his face, nipping his neck.

'Right now!' She pulled her knickers to one side and sat across him, facing the windscreen. The cramped conditions and fear of detection added to the urgency. Emma scanned the square as she arched her back, guiding his penis to the opening. She saw a man leave number ten and walk away from the car toward Walton Street. She could feel Bill rubbing blissfully against her vulva. Slowly closing her eyes, she inhaled deeply before sitting back and taking him inside.

The minutes seemed like an eternity. They reached orgasm together, an inquisitive sparrow the only witness to their covert coupling.

Anna Papanicholas watched the seagulls circle the ship and heard their mournful cries as she stood by the port bow railing and quietly wept. It had taken this long for her emotions to come to the surface. She thought of her warm bedroom in the large, cosy house in north London; of her mother waking her in the morning with a hot cup of tea; of her father hugging her when she came home with a good report card. None of these things would ever happen again. She remembered the vicious, hurtful words he'd fired at her, each one penetrating her mind like a bullet. Why couldn't he understand? Why didn't he see that she loved them dearly and would give anything to have their approval? She wasn't ungrateful, she wasn't a slut; she'd only lied because there was no other way. She had achieved her goal and become the first female DJ on pirate radio, about to launch her career on the hottest station in the world. She wanted them to be proud of her, to share in her victory.

She removed the gold heart necklace they'd given her for her sixteenth birthday, kissed it, then threw it overboard. Anna Papanicholas was no more. She was still the same brown-eyed blonde from north London, she would still need to use medicated soap twice a day to control her teenage blemishes, she would still be fiercely proud of her Greek ancestry; but from now on she'd be known as Honey Bogart.

'Are you feeling ill?' The Captain's soothing voice reminded her of her father in better times. She tried to compose herself before turning to face him.

'Just a little homesick,' she replied

Captain Vourner could see sorrow in her face. He held his arms open. She fell into them, his solid comfortable body providing a resting place for her anxiety. He held her until her crying eased.

'Come now,' he said, gently releasing her. 'A beautiful lady like you should not cry so. You'll quickly make friends here.' He smiled; his face wrinkling with laugh lines, his eyes shining. 'I'll be your first. Come to my cabin, I'll make you a nice hot cup of cocoa.'

She felt the sadness begin to ebb. This was her family now; this was her new beginning. 'Thank you, Captain, I'd love that.'

Emma snoozed peacefully on the oak four-poster bed as Bill sat naked astride her legs and rubbed jasmine oil on her back. The fragrance filled her with contentment; his touch filled her with desire. His hands slid under her arms and caressed the sides of her breasts. She lifted her hips as they continued down her side and on to the flat of her stomach. She wanted him again.

The phone rang.

'Get that, sweetheart,' sighed Bill, stopping an inch from her delta. 'My hands are all oily.'

'As long as you promise to remember *exactly* where you are!'

'I promise.'

Emma reached languidly for the phone and dragged it on to the bed. 'Hello.'

A hesitant voice she recognised immediately answered her. 'Have I the right number? I'm looking for Bill Mason.'

'Yes, you've got the right number, Stuart. This is Emma.' She flipped over on to her back so she could see Bill's face. She handed him the phone then slipped her hand between his legs. 'You promised,' she mouthed as he put the phone to his ear.

'Stuart, hi. I was just about to call you.'

'Liar,' mouthed Emma, giving him a gentle squeeze.

'What are you doing for dinner?' Stuart's voice was still unsure.

'Emma and I were going to cook here. Why?'

The suspicions Stuart had had since the opening party were now confirmed. He chuckled down the phone. 'If you two could bear to be separated for a couple of hours, I'd like you to meet Gerald Copeland. He's a very important politician and very much on our side. On second thoughts, bring Emma along. She met him at the opening.'

Bill lifted the phone from his ear so Emma could hear the conversation. He looked at her and shrugged his shoulders. She squeezed him again and smiled.

'That would be lovely. Where and when?'

'Say eight o'clock, my place; we'll go on from here.' Stuart left a slight pause. 'By the way, I'm very pleased for both of you.'

A flood of relief washed over Bill's face. Being in love with his boss's secretary felt akin to being in love with his wife or girlfriend; a sense of stealing something that belonged to another. 'Thank you, Stuart. See you later.' He handed the phone back to Emma who replaced it on its cradle. 'Well, he knows now, and he says okay.'

'Tough titty if he didn't. I don't need his approval.' Emma felt him begin to wilt in her hand. 'Mr Mason! A promise is a promise.'

He gently lowered himself on top of her. The silken texture of her oiled skin re-aroused him immediately, her unhurried hand guided him as he entered her slowly and deliberately. 'So it is, my love.'

Her eyes and mouth opened wide as she relaxed her muscles, allowing him to penetrate completely, then tightening again, holding his erection deep inside her and drifting off to plains of ecstasy she'd only dreamed about before they'd met.

*　　*　　*

Honey Bogart flopped on to her bunk and stared at the ceiling. After the Captain's cocoa she'd felt much better. He'd made her feel very welcome and had taken time to explain to her the do's and don'ts of shipboard life. Some things she found fascinating, such as the rule of never walking through the galley without first announcing your presence. He'd told her the story of a former first mate who was scalded horribly when the cook, unaware of his preserve, turned into him while carrying a pot of boiling water. The other admonitions included: never leave cutlery or any sharp object on a table during bad weather; never leave your porthole open when not in the cabin; always wear a lifejacket on deck after dark – they all seemed common sense to her.

Her cabin was carpeted and cosy but, as yet, devoid of character. She'd announced her presence to the cook, then sweet-talked him into donating an old gingham tablecloth; which she cut up into curtains for her porthole. There were no curtain rails so she stuck them to the bulkhead with two strips of gaffer tape.

She'd made a list of things to get next time she went ashore: make-up mirror, laundry bag, a pair of non-slip rubber-soled shoes and, most importantly, a small collapsible clothesline. There was no way she was going to give the crew sight of her underwear draping over the communal line on the upper deck. She noticed that everyone had signs on their cabin doors to advise visitors whether or not they were sleeping. They ranged from 'Do not disturb' to 'Piss off'. She thought 'Please go away – I could have a man in here' might create the wrong impression, so she settled for a card with 'Yes' on one side and 'No' on the other.

Emma had marked her card regarding Eddie Lincoln,

so when he came calling with his greasy smile and hair to match, she told him that any intrusion into her life by him, or any of his dope-head friends, would be viewed as an act of war and would result in the removal of both his testicles by means of a rusty saw. The rest of the lads seemed cool enough and in no need of such a caustic warning; at least they didn't welcome her aboard with sleazy innuendo or physical harassment. They were helpful and friendly and not the least bit patronising. She hoped they'd show the same courtesy six weeks from now.

She turned off her monitor speaker and started drifting towards sleep. A polite, rhythmic tapping disturbed her slumber. 'Who is it?'

'Batman and Robin,' came the reply. 'We've come to grease your pole.'

She jumped from the bunk and stood by the door. 'I always send my pole out to be greased!'

'In that case, can we come in and hang from your ceiling?'

She opened the door and greeted Simon and Lewis with a twin hug. The last pangs of homesickness faded at the sight of their familiar faces. 'Come in. It's so good to see you again. I'd thought you'd have been round sooner.'

'We've been in the studio,' said Simon, handing her a stack of six Letraset-labeled cartridges. 'We've made some more Humphries for your breakfast show.'

'Oh, bless you both. You're so good to me.'

'We can be bad for you too,' said Lewis, producing a bottle of chilled champagne and three paper cups from behind his back. 'Welcome to the ship.'

Honey's firm rebuff had made Eddie's depressed mood

plummet to even greater depths. He was bored, horny, and nearly out of smoke. The one option left: phone Amsterdam. Joanna would cheer him up and he could place an order at the same time. He tried her number four times – busy. The radio room was so cold Eddie could see his breath; he didn't try again.

In Amsterdam, Joanna and the Doc were not taking calls. His arrival home early that morning had been greeted with much celebration by the inhabitants of the Canal Palace Hotel. His three-month absence had caused certain ambitions to come to the fore in a few of his subordinates. Doc was well aware of the 'cat's away' syndrome, and the 'mice that played' were about to feel his paw descend on them with fierce finality.

Doc controlled twenty per cent of Amsterdam's notorious red-light district, fifty per cent of its high-class prostitutes, and turned over another two million pounds a year in narcotics and porn. He'd changed his name so many times in thirty-five years that even he had a hard time remembering Franz Hengler, the name that appeared on his German birth certificate.

The Second World War started when he was nine years old and living with his parents in Berlin and ended when he was fifteen, homeless and alone in Amsterdam. Crime seemed the natural career for this tough street kid with the Aryan looks and war-scarred mind, who'd already killed fourteen people in order to survive.

He rose rapidly through the lower echelons of the criminal fraternity, buying his first whorehouse at the age of twenty with profit from his second heroin deal. Now, being one of the city's top players, he enjoyed all the trappings of wealth and power, and although the New Orleans fiasco had landed him behind bars for a couple of weeks, he knew it would've been a couple of years if he hadn't had the best lawyers money could buy. Anyway, he'd met Eddie Lincoln, and that was bound to prove profitable.

Stretching his steely body in the huge bathtub he let his muscles relax in the liquid warmth and listened to Joanna relate the various stories about who was pissed at who, and which of his 'trusty' henchmen were getting ideas above their station. He listened carefully to all she said, making mental plans to return the system to its rightful status quo; plans he would start implementing tomorrow.

He dried himself with a spotless white bath towel and walked through to the bedroom. Flopping on to the bed, he viewed his wife with lecherous desire, sharpened by his absence. She looked ravishing, standing next to the bed, a black, full-length silk negligée hugging the well-defined curves of her body.

'God, I've missed you, Joanna.'

She knelt on the bed beside him. 'We should put the phone back on the hook. I'll bet Tasker's been trying to get us for hours.'

'And I've been away for months. He can fuckin' wait!' Doc slipped his hand inside Joanna's negligée and gently rubbed the inside of her thigh. 'One more go round then we'll do business.'

Joanna slid her hand between her legs and stopped his progress. 'Call him, Doc. Let's get business over with.'

'Will you relax!' He flipped her with practised ease across his body and on to her back, pulling himself on top of her; his body weight and arm strength pinning her to the bed. 'I did the deal in London. He's only phoning to confirm he's found a way on board the ship. He tells me tonight or tomorrow, what the fuck's the difference?'

She slowly turned her hand over and encircled his penis, gently squeezing the base and pulling it towards her. Clamping her free arm around his neck, she dragged his head down beside hers and nipped at his neck just below the ear. 'In that case, good doctor, please fuck me within an inch of my life.'

Stuart poured himself a large scotch and watched Emma's Mini pull up outside. Tonight he'd advance the cause of commercial radio; tonight he'd show off his star to the people who counted; tonight he'd dine at the House of Commons. The successful lobby of parliament would prove crucial to the advancement of independent radio and Stuart knew he must make the right impression. His political acumen failed to impress even himself, as his interest in politics rated just below train-spotting on his list of worthwhile activities. He relied on Gerald Copeland to plan his strategy, and tonight Gerald had marked as 'very important'.

He welcomed Bill with a firm handshake and Emma with a peck on both cheeks. 'I'm so pleased you two are an item,' he said, beaming at them both like a proud parent. 'At least I'll have Emma's full attention while you're on the ship.'

'Please don't mention going back,' said Emma. 'He only arrived home today.'

'Not another word, I promise.' Stuart grabbed his coat. 'We must go. Gerald's meeting us in fifteen minutes.'

Charlie drove the Bentley skilfully through the evening traffic as Stuart explained the game-plan.

'We're dining with George McIntire, a hard-line Scots

Tory with a liking for enterprise as long as it's traditional; James Slattery, nicknamed 'Educated of Ilford', who needs some convincing as to the business opportunities; and Lady Heath, who's not related to Ted but is related to David, who's very powerful in the broadcast lobby. They're all bluer than blue Tories, but still unsure about the merits of our cause. I want to show them we're responsible, professional people who believe in free enterprise, not drug-crazed pop freaks hell-bent on the destruction of our society.'

'Sounds easy,' quipped Bill. 'Got any acid?'

'That's just the kind of remark that'll land us in trouble,' said Stuart angrily.

'What's the matter? No sense of humour?'

'They're politicians,' interrupted Emma. 'Of course they've no sense of humour.'

Stuart dropped his shoulders. 'This is very important. Please! No smart remarks. Promise me?'

Bill nodded.

'Are you sure?'

Emma squeezed Bill's hand. 'He always keeps his promises, don't you, Bill?'

Gerald met them at the entrance to Westminster Hall. He always looked so correct; his suit dark grey and double breasted, with immaculately creased trousers; his shirt Egyptian cotton and impeccably white. Shoes by Gucci and tie by St Laurent completed the image of the perfect Tory of 1965. As one of the party's rising stars, (some said cabinet material), he had access to policy information and trend barometers usual kept well away from members under thirty. The buzz word from his overlords this year had been 'privatise'.

Commercial radio dovetailed with the Conservative

world view for several reasons. It embodied their primary policy of free enterprise, it appealed to their cavalier attitude in opposition, and it was something the Government was trying to suppress that was extremely popular with the voters the party needed. Word from the constituencies said Mr and Miss under-twenty-five would be seriously miffed should anything untoward happen to spoil their radio. This might not win them the election, but it would narrow the margin dramatically.

Emma paused to take in the sights of history. The hall had stood since the fourteenth century. She could feel the sense of permanence radiate from the vast wooden beams and uneven stone floor. She followed behind the main party, admiring the statues of bygone political giants that lined St Stephen's Hall. She studied the stained glass windows encircling the central lobby. Once again, Emma had worn her long black evening gown; once again, it would be a night to remember.

The dining room was small and very private. Oak panelling rose half-way up the wall, giving way to striped dark green wallpaper. The highly polished wooden table surrounded by highbacked leather chairs stretched the length of the room. Everything, from napkins to chair-backs, carried the portcullis symbol emblazonned in gold.

Emma thought the food quite ordinary considering the venue – avocado with prawns followed by roast beef, Yorkshire pudding, roast potatoes and two veg. A bit like Auntie Jean's, she mused as she stabbed the last roast potato with her silver fork and mopped up the remainder of the gravy.

Conversation over dinner had been varied and interesting. Gerald acted as unelected chairman as the

Rhodesian trade embargo, Liverpool's chances of winning the cup, Wilson's visit to the Pope, Reggie Kray's wedding and the death of Edward R. Murrow were debated. Invisible points were awarded to whoever gained the upper hand. Stuart proved astute enough to back down in all the right places, a tactic not lost on Lady 'do call me Penny' Heath, who, Emma thought, really fancied her chances with the boss of the pirates. George McIntire was aggressive and very loud; James Slattery charming and mild-mannered. Bill seemed at home in this company, tiptoeing his way through all the subjects, careful to avoid expressing any strong political opinion. Emma thanked God for good timing when asked what she thought of the proposed name change from Rhodesia to Zimbabwe. She answered 'Zimbabwe – eventually'; a remark which drew applause from everyone except McIntire, whom, she deduced, wouldn't give a woman credit for anything that didn't occur in the bedroom or the kitchen.

As the brandy was left and the coffee cleared, James Slattery lit a large Cuban cigar with his small Dunhill lighter. 'Now, Stuart, what's all this talk of you putting a news team in the field?'

Stuart scanned the table while framing his reply; all remained expressionless, save Gerald who gave a small I-told-you-so smile. 'A very small operation, to cover mainly south-eastern news. Can't let the BBC have it all their own way.'

'That's what we have ITN for,' thundered McIntire. Lady Heath nodded her approval.

'That covers television. Are you saying radio's not important enough?'

'I'm saying entertain the people and leave it at that.'

'I think what Stuart is trying to say,' interrupted Gerald, 'is that FREE's news will be more of a magazine approach, with more interest stories than hard news.'

'With Jonathan Gilby heading the show?' laughed McIntire. 'That'll be the day!'

Stuart held his line. 'If we did cover anything political, why assume we'd be hostile towards you?'

'Because we don't know that you wouldn't be.' James took a sip of brandy and a long puff on his cigar.

'I would think it self-evident.' Stuart had to play an ace. 'If we took sides at all, we're not likely to back the people who're trying to put us out of business.'

'That's not my worry,' interjected Lady Heath. 'My worry is irresponsibility, incitement. In short, Mr Salisbury, anarchy.'

Luckily Stuart had a pair of aces. 'You all know Jonathan. He's one of your staunchest supporters and tonight you've talked to Bill and Emma. Do they sound like anarchists?'

McIntire grunted. Lady Heath turned to Emma. 'What do you see as the objectives of pirate radio?'

'They're of my generation,' Emma answered proudly. 'I think there's a massive commercial market for independent radio in this country and if your party makes it happen, I can't see the industry biting the hand that gave it birth.' There was silence from the table so Emma continued. 'Twenty million people already listen to the off-shore stations. At our present rate card the cost per thousand is under sixpence. If we were legal and national, the tax revenue alone would be millions every year; to say nothing of support industries and jobs created. No, Lady Heath, I can't see anarchy playing a big part in the scheme of things.'

Stuart could have kissed her; Bill did, lightly on the hand before picking up the bottle of Remy Martin, Louis XIII, that adorned the centre of the table. 'Anyone for more brandy?'

On the way back to Stuart's place, Emma sat cuddled up to Bill in the back seat of the Bentley feeling very pleased indeed.

'Tomorrow's a busy day for both of you,' said Stuart from the front seat. 'I've got two interviews for you, Bill, one morning and one afternoon. And I think Emma should take us to lunch to celebrate.'

'Celebrate what?' quizzed Emma.

'Your five pound a week pay rise.'

Emma looked at Bill and then at Stuart. 'I'm so depressed I think I'll go home and shoot myself.'

They all laughed. Emma added two more words to her secret vocabulary. Poopaloop, describing ninety per cent of political conversation, and nefagat, describing her feelings towards FREE's star breakfast man.

'Love you,' whispered Bill, gently squeezing her hand. 'Everything Okay?'

'Never, ever felt as good as this,' she smiled in return.

'No trial and tribulation on the twenty-four hour station. Dis is Prince Mikie after midnight.

> Let this station fill the hole,
> all night long with solid soul.
> For night-shift workers makin' Fords
> and nurses checkin' on the wards.
> For all you lovers into beddin',
> let's check out some Otis Redding.

133

Mikie hummed along to the first verse of 'My Girl'.

Elation, anticipation and some serious first-day nerves greeted Honey Bogart as the five o'clock alarm shattered her dreamless sleep. This was her big day. Though she'd been learning as much as she could from Simon and Lewis, today she'd be entirely on her own. She showered and dressed hurriedly in her best pair of Levi's and brand-new FREE T-shirt featuring a picture of the ship bursting bow-first through Broadcasting House with the words 'I'm FREE' at the top and 'there's more on 244' along the bottom. She completed her grooming by sweeping her shining blonde hair into a ponytail.

The ship was uncannily quiet; the sea kindly calm. Walking into the mess-room she noticed four boxes of cereal, six bowls and assorted cutlery placed neatly on the table. Propped against the bowls was a note addressed to her; it read 'Break a leg – love, Simon and Lewis.'

Smiling to herself she walked through to the empty galley, switched on the kettle and started to scramble three eggs over the shiny steel gas cooker.

'Coming through!' The voice of Stan Beacher, the chief engineer made her jump. 'Sorry about that,' he said.

'That's all right. Can I fix you some eggs?'

'Brilliant! I don't get this service from Bill.'

Stan was a twenty-four-year-old Mancunian, an ex-BBC whizzkid with a large nose and a long mane of bright red shoulder-length hair. He was in charge of all radio equipment on the ship, from turntables to transmitters, and executed his duties with the pride and thoroughness of someone immaculately trained by, technically, the best broadcasting outfit in the world. He attracted a certain amount of low-key stick from the DJs, who accused him of preferring trans-mitters to tits, but on the whole he was well liked and well respected for his expertise in all things electric.

Honey added two more eggs to the pot and continued stirring. 'Anything I should know about the morning routine?'

'Pretty straightforward really. If you don't see me by half past five, wake me up; I'm in cabin six. I'll do the same for you. I reset the limiter every morning between six and quarter past, so watch your levels; nothing in the red.'

'What does it do, this limiter?' She felt silly, standing in a ship's galley, cooking eggs for a stranger and asking him a question to which every DJ in the land would know the answer.

Stan was a kindly boffin, not one to score unnecessary points on hapless victims. 'It's a safety valve, really. Too strong a studio signal delivered to the transmitter can trip it off. If you've got everything going in there and decide to scream unholy abuse down the microphone at the same time you could deliver a nasty jolt to my sensitive tubes.'

She liked him already. 'I cook with salt. Do you mind?'

'Not at all.'

She added two pinches to the pot. 'How will I know when the limiter's set?'

'I'll buzz you.'

'Is it that crucial?'

'Oh yes.' He smiled. 'Kenny Everett ran without a limiter last week. Played the blast from the Atomic Basie album and inverted the phases in the transmitter. London was off the air for three days.'

135

Honey served the eggs equally on to two plates. 'I see your point.'

Stan drowned his in tomato sauce. 'I'll eat in the tranny room.'

'I'll bring you coffee.'

'Groovy.' He smiled at her. 'Better service and better looking. Bill can stay ashore for a month for all I care.'

At five-fifty, Honey stood behind Prince Mikie in studio one and tried to control her fear; concentration was her only weapon. She thought through her opening sequence. Main theme, twins' jingle 'If you're having breakfast with my Honey, you'd better behave yourself'; first record, Marianne Faithfull – 'This Little Bird'; segue to Beatles – 'Ticket To Ride'; early bird competition – write in with the complete lyric to 'Subterranean Homesick Blues', followed by the record.

The radio alarm at Ovington Square woke Emma with the last chorus of Bob Dylan. She listened to Honey back announce, read the weather forecast, give a time check and hit the voice-over to 'The Last Time' as if she'd been doing it for years. She slid her arm over to the other side of the bed. Empty!

'Breakfast in bed for the lady with the pay rise.' Bill stood naked beside the bed holding a tray of orange juice, coffee and cornflakes.

'Now that, dear man, is what I call room service!'

'I set the alarm so you could hear Honey. She's damn good for a first-timer.'

'She certainly is. She's a natural.' Emma studied the muscular frame before her. If she'd conjured up her fantasy man, he wouldn't be much different from Bill. Long, strong legs, flat, tight stomach, broad, sculptured shoulders. 'I suppose it's doing the breakfast show that gets you up so early?'

Bill put the tray on the table. 'Define getting up.'

Emma held out her arms. 'Come here and I'll show you.'

Bill stepped back from the bed beyond her reach. 'Before you have your wicked way with me, there's something you should have.' He reached under the bed and produced an expensive looking green cardboard box, which he placed on the bed in front of her. 'Happy birthday, sweetheart.'

'My birthday's not 'til July,' corrected Emma, thrilled nonetheless. She loved presents no matter what the occasion.

'I like to be early,' fawned Bill, sliding into bed beside her.

Emma pulled at the dark green ribbon that surrounded the box. As she removed the lid, the tissue paper inside flipped open to reveal a coat collar of Siberian mink. With one tug she pulled the garment from the box, her eyes widening with every inch of fur that appeared. 'My God! Is this real?'

'I do hope so,' replied Bill, smiling at her excitement.

She hugged the fur against her body, running her hands down the length and burying her face in the lining. 'How can you afford . . .?'

'Aside from the exorbitant fee Stuart pays me, I'm independently wealthy. Do you like it?'

'I love it! Real mink! I can't believe it.' Emma spread the coat fur-side up on the bed beside her and rolled on to it, her face pouting sensually. 'It's always been my wildest fantasy,' she said, snaking her body along the length of the coat. 'Make love to me.'

Chapter 6

Emma sat in the back seat of the Bentley and held Bill tightly for the last time for at least two weeks. Charlie had walked to the dock, leaving the lovers alone to say their goodbyes, at the same time hoping to intercept the twins, who were due off the ship, and prevent them from storming the car.

The week had been heavenly for Emma, with the notable exception of last Saturday. Stuart had managed to secure four passes to the Wembley press gallery for the F.A. Cup Final between Liverpool and Leeds. He would go with Jonathan and Bill; Emma had been invited to make up the four. Football to Emma was like human rights to Hitler. She thought it a silly game with no obvious grace or skill and no guaranteed result. The supporters' chants frightened her, the Wembley wind chilled her, and the conversation made her feel like a foreigner in her own land. The only palatable part was the drink in the press lounge at half-time. She'd drunk a large brandy to combat the cold and spent the second half swaying back and forth on her uncomfortable wooden seat. When extra time was announced, she excused herself, found her way back to the press lounge and added another three brandies to her tally.

139

With the game finally over and all the journalists desperately busy fighting each other for the ten available phones, screaming reports of how Ian St John had won Liverpool the cup for the first time with a goal nine minutes from time, Emma could barely stand. When Stuart told her Bill and Jonathan had gone to the dressing room to get an interview with Bill Shankly she asked 'Who the hell is Bill Shankley?' in a very loud voice. The room fell silent, Stuart turned beetroot red and Emma went to the ladies' and was quietly ill.

On the up-side, she'd found a new receptionist; a black girl from Peckham with a beautiful smile and a great sense of humour. She'd helped Jonathan set up the news department and received a lovely letter from Lady Heath saying how nice it had been to meet her and enclosing a private phone number. She'd also scanned the audition tapes again and come up with two more promising DJs, for which Stuart had rewarded her with a last-night dinner for two at Tiberio in Queen Street, the flagship of Mario and Franco's four Italian restaurants that were fast becoming the in places to eat for any style-conscious young Londoner.

Bill gathered his bags from the car boot and waved her goodbye. She watched him cross the concrete dock and disappear into the customs shed.

A few minutes later Jonathan Gilby arrived in a taxi. This was his first trip to the ship, and he'd chosen to travel alone. He took his time unloading his two suit-cases and favourite portable typewriter from the taxi.

The last few weeks had seen his world change completely. Six years ago he'd slipped from first-class degree to second-class reporter on *The Times* without noticing the join. His professional life consisted of toeing the editor's line by presenting the paper's view of a balanced account of the workings of the mother of all parliaments. Once in a while he'd pen a satirical piece on some minor issue, for which he'd never received a by-line. Until now home had been a first-floor, two-bedroomed flat above Giovanni's Italian Restaurant on Hammersmith Broadway. Because the police and fire service were in close proximity, the flat was somewhat noisy; but it was a Tube ride from anywhere, boasted an untarnished security record, and good pasta on credit waited only a flight of stairs away.

He was a quiet man who preferred staying home of an evening, tuning his Marconi short-wave to far-off corners of the world and listening in on other people's wars. He was more stocky than stout, would occasionally stand up straight to achieve his full five-foot-ten-inch height, but most of the time could be found slumped over the latest *Newsweek* or that battered typewriter. His two distinguishing features were his deep-set brown eyes and the black curly hair that covered not only his head but most of his body. Owing to his lack of disco-chat expertise and abundance of body hair, his love-life often suffered to a point of concern. Some women adored his teddy-bear body and would spend hours twirling his chest hair around their fingers, but none of them fancied life with a man more interested in Marconis than mammaries.

He carried his bags over to the side of the Bentley. 'Where's Bill?'

Emma didn't answer.

'He'll be back in a couple of weeks, sweet pea. It's not for ever.'

Emma took a deep breath and conjured her best smile. 'It just seems it.'

'Time for a PARTY!' The twins made them both jump.

'Move your butt,' said Simon to Jonathan. 'We're late for a date.'

'We're wasting time but we make it rhyme,' said Lewis.

'Thank God I don't have to put up with them on the ship,' said Jonathan.

'You will, so take a pill,' said Simon, playfully slapping him on the back.

'We'll soon be back and that's a fact,' completed Lewis.

'You've got them all the way to London,' said Jonathan sympathetically.

'I don't mind,' answered Emma, opening the back door and feeling glad of some light relief. 'Come on, lads, the champagne's cold and the company's hot.'

The trip to London was hysterical. One-line jokes and two-page stories of life on the medium wave flowed from the twins faster than Emma could pour the bubbly. They were finally picked up by their parents at Hayes Mews and driven home to Ilford in a modest Ford Prefect.

The Streets were a close family. Tom and Lil had been married twenty-five years and were very proud of their talented offspring as, it seemed, were half their home town. A reception had been planned for that night at the local school.

'Do you guys feel up to it?' asked Tom as he parked the car outside thirty-six Mansell Road, the small, three-bedroomed terraced house that had been home to the Street family for the last twenty years.

'No problem,' Lewis confirmed after glancing at his brother. 'As long as we can have a bucket of Mum's rice pudding for tea.'

*   *   *

A sick-bucket was the order of the day on board FREE as Jonathan came to grips with the North Sea. With Bill back on breakfast, Honey moved to cover the twins: six 'til ten in the evening. She also moved to cover Jonathan from the embarrassment being heaped on him by Nigel and Peter.

'From what I've heard, a few of weeks ago you two were barfing every five minutes,' she hissed. 'Come on deck, Jonathan, and leave the boys to their toys.'

The fresh sea breeze made Jonathan's stomach feel marginally less tortured, but did very little to alleviate the problem of being unsteady on his feet. Honey helped him to the railing.

'Look at the horizon, not the sea,' she said, propping him up with her shoulder. Even in his *mal-de-mer* state, she still found him a very attractive man. His dark eyes and shock of black hair turned her on and his intelligence counted as a welcome bonus. She slid her arm around his waist. 'If you feel sick, just chunder over the side. I'll hold on to you.'

'How come this doesn't bother you?' he asked, hoping to take his mind off his own predicament.

'I'm Greek. We're brought up on the sea.'

'I feel so foolish. It's not even rough.'

'If it were gale force, you'd be much too busy staying alive to be sick. This gentle swell is the worst kind of sea if you're not used to it.'

Jonathan put his arm around her shoulder. 'You're so kind to help me like this. How long does it take to get used to it?'

'You should be okay tomorrow.' Honey shivered in the wind. 'Let's go below. You should lie down and try to sleep.' She manoeuvred him off the deck and into his cabin, stretching him out on the bed and covering

143

him with a thick woollen blanket. She couldn't resist placing a light kiss on his cheek. 'I'll look in on you before my show. Sleep well.' He gave no response.

Ilford's response to the twins was remarkable. As they arrived at the school hall, in one of the two limousines provided by a local firm, a gaggle of girls stood on the other side of the road waving and shouting their names.

'They must think we're the Walker Brothers,' said Simon.

They turned to face the group and burst into song. 'Hold her and tell her that you care and love her. Love her for me.'

Five of the girls started running across the street.

'Shit! Let's get inside!' Simon slapped his brother on the back and ran for the safety of the building.

The hall was packed. Relations, friends, people they hadn't seen in years, people they'd never met, greeted them with rapturous applause. Tom and Lil, who'd arrived five minutes earlier in the first limousine, stood on the small stage at the end of the hall and beckoned their sons forward.

At first, the boys felt overwhelmed by the reception. They were only pirate DJs, not Olympic gold medallists or cup-winning footballers. As they mounted the podium the volume increased. They looked at each other, wide grins spreading across their faces. This was for them and it felt wonderful. They turned their smiles to the audience and waved all four hands in the air.

The headmaster, Mr Lampton, welcomed them on stage and signalled for quiet.

'Ladies and gentlemen, we've known the Street family in this community for over twenty years. For five of those years I taught Simon and Lewis at this very school. We're extremely pleased to welcome them back from their exploits on the high seas and to tell them they've achieved in a few short weeks what I've been trying to do for fifteen years; get everyone to listen to every word I say.' Applause. 'Ladies and gentlemen, Simon and Lewis Street!'

The twins took it in their stride; not cocky, just confident.

'Thank you all very much,' said Simon. 'We never expected anything like this. It's a bit like winning an Oscar.'

'The Ilford Oscar,' said Lewis. 'It has a certain ring.'

'I did notice,' injected Simon, as the laughter died down. 'There's a whole pile of excellent food and drink in the hall tonight. Now, on the ship there's no such thing as excellent food and drink, so I for one am going to have a feast. I hope you will all join us.'

Tom and Lil watched with pride as their sons moved around the hall, greeting old friends and making new.

'You've done a great job, Lil. They've turned out real good.'

The white-haired lady squeezed his arm.

The twins were busy polishing off the last few salmon sarnies when they spotted a stocky man wearing a cream-coloured suit, dark brown shirt and sporting enough gold to start a jewellery shop. He was flanked by two large bodyguards who made him look even shorter than his five and a half foot frame. He stopped in front of them and stuck his hand out to Lewis.

'Lads, a pleasure to meet you. I'm Mick Tasker.'

'Mr Tasker,' smiled Lewis, shaking his hand, 'I'm Lewis.'

'Please, call me Mick.' He turned his attention and

handshake to Simon. 'And you're Simon.' His grip was vice-like, Simon retrieved his hand as soon as possible. 'These are my associates, Benny and Pete.' The twins nodded to the mountains of muscle, not wishing to have their hands crushed completely. 'I own the Ragamuffin club in Brixton. I want to talk to you boys about working for me.'

Work is a magic word, but caution was instinctive to the twins. 'We'll have to check with our boss. I don't know if we're allowed to do outside work.'

Mick Tasker never took no for an answer; he didn't have to. Over twenty years he'd built up a network of pubs, nightclubs and betting shops which, in turn, supported his secondary businesses of talent agencies and supply companies which, in turn, were financed by companies only he and his wife knew the names of, based in countries as far afield as Spain, South Africa and the Cayman Islands. A far cry from his humble beginnings in a one-up, one-down Victorian worker's terrace in Peckham.

'Stu Salisbury's an old mate of mine.' He produced a business card from his top pocket. 'Check him out and give me a call. Do two hours for me next Tuesday and I'll pay twenty quid each in Nelsons, no Gregorys.' He placed a jewelled finger beside his nose. 'No tax.' He motioned to the two guards. 'Gotta go now. Gotta couple of right darlins waiting at the club.' He moved in close to the twins and lowered his voice. 'Birds are included. Anything you want. Know what I mean?'

The twins watched him disappear into the crowd.

'Watcha think?'

Simon studied the card. 'Sounds like getting paid and getting laid, as Mason would say.'

146

The next morning they sat in Stuart's office and relayed the story.

'He's one of the biggest rogues in London,' was Stuart's opening remark. 'He's got fingers in every mud pie east of Catford but as long as you know that, he's good to work for. He always pays.' Stuart dunked a shortbread finger into his coffee. 'Listen, lads, if you can make some extra money and promote the station, I'm happy. Just be careful who's taking pictures. Mick's a good-hearted villain. He won't harm you as long as you don't try to buy his club.'

'How do you know him?' inquired Lewis.

'He stole a band and, by proxy, eight hundred pounds off me once; then sent me a crate of Dom Perignon.'

Brian Todd sat in Eddie's cabin and concluded a deal for a carton of Senior Service, an ounce of grass and a small packet of Peruvian cocaine.

'Let's say five quid the lot,' bargained Eddie. 'And I'll give you ten per cent on anything you move upstairs.'

'I daren't! Mason would have me fired if he even knew I was doing it, let alone pushin' the jocks.'

'Mason's an asshole. What else can you do all day? Three hours on the fucking air, then sit around thinking about slippin' one to Honey Bogart?' Eddie lit a joint took a deep drag and passed it to Brian. 'Three hits on this and even Jim Reeves sounds good.'

'I don't know, Eddie. Taking dope upstairs is like frying eggs on the transmitter, down here it's safe.'

'For how long? You keep coming down here every ten minutes and going back upstairs with your eyes on stalks, he's gonna sus you anyway,' Eddie cut two small lines of coke on the glass desk top. 'Give it a

147

month and there'll be nobody left up there. My cabin'll be so fucking crowded you won't be able to move for DJs killing time.

Brian rolled a ten-bob note and snorted the smaller of the two lines. 'Jees, mate, that's nice!'

Upstairs a very straight Honey Bogart was having exactly the same thought as she stood in the cabin doorway and watched Jonathan shave. 'You look a lot healthier today, Mr Gilby.'

'I feel it, thank you. Come in.'

Honey squeezed passed him and sat on his bunk. His naked hair-covered torso and the smell of shaving cream triggered her libido. She stared at him as he scraped his neck with deliberate upward strokes; then rinsed the razor in the sink and scraped smoothly down his right cheek, the cream gathering on the blade like snow before a shovel.

'I want to thank you again for yesterday,' he said, splashing his face with water. 'Is there any way I can pay you back?'

'You could kiss me.' She couldn't believe she'd said that! It just popped out. She could feel her face turning red with embarrassment and she lowered her eyes. She felt two hands cup her face and gently lift it up. Looking straight into those dark brown eyes, she smelled his sweet fragrance drifting over her.

'It would be my pleasure,' he whispered.

All the pent-up emotions of the last week flooded out of Honey like a damburst. She didn't make love to him, or even screw him. She attacked him, sinking her nails into his back, biting his neck, sliding down his body and sucking his penis with such ferocity he nearly lost his erection. He responded to her wildness by imposing his strength, stopping her oral endeavours,

148

pulling her up his body, turning her on to her back and gripping her wrists. He entered her harshly, pumping with even, aggressive strokes. Her pain dissolved into focused bliss, beginning in the pit of her stomach, engulfing her body, and emerging as guttural groans from the back of her throat. It was over in a minute: he lying beside her, spent and panting for breath; she staring at the ceiling, wondering what on earth had come over her.

'Are you always this violent?' he asked, turning to face her.

'Not now I've got your attention,' she replied hoping he'd buy her explanation. 'I can be a little mouse if you prefer.'

He cupped her face with his right hand and chuckled. 'If there are teeth marks on my dick, I'm suing.'

'If you bruise that easily, I'm finding another lover.'

They folded into each other arms, laughing loud enough to be heard in the mess-room, where Brian Todd and Mo the cook sat drinking coffee. Brian scribed a chalk mark on the wall.

'I'll bet this panel fills up before she goes ashore,' said Brian. 'Lucky bastard!'

Emma sat at her desk in Hayes Mews and dreamily relived the recent pleasures of Ovington Square. Everyone at the office poured compliments on her new coat, telling her how lucky she was to have a boyfriend like Bill. She smiled at them all, happy with herself, the coat, and the fulfilment she felt inside.

The morning had been extremely hectic even by her standards. Through his American connections John Walters had obtained an interview with Jackie Kennedy, who was in England to dedicate the J.F.K. memorial at

Runnymede. He'd sent the interview to the ship first thing this morning via ship-to-shore and Jonathan had led the breakfast news with the story, scooping the BBC by a good six hours. The phones had gone mad. Martha, the new receptionist, tried her best to cope but in the end Emma had to deal with most of the calls. The worst was from Sir Robin Clarke, insisting on knowing how this travesty of protocol had been allowed to happen. Emma had said the only travesty was the BBC monopoly and thanked him for listening.

The newest recruits, Dave Mitchum and Charlie Beranowitz (known as 'Charlie Bare on the Air' for obvious reasons), reported for duty just after ten o'clock and were quickly dispatched to record interviews with Donovan and Marianne Faithfull. Dave and Charlie were two Canadians from Toronto with eight years' experience of first-class radio, and were hired primarily to replace regular DJs on shore leave. Emma was impressed by how mature they sounded on their audition tape, and was pleasantly surprised when they offered to work part-time and non-exclusive – just the ticket for cover-jocks. They were slightly older than the other DJs; a fact that comforted Emma, who persuaded Stuart they would add stability to the station sound and had the experience to handle any slot in the day.

Emma looked up from her daydream and noticed two dark grey suits talking to Martha. She braced herself for the next onslaught.

'Gentlemen. How can I help you?' They walked to her desk.

'My name is Simpson,' said the man in the darker of the suits. 'We're from Her Majesty's Customs. We want to see Stuart Salisbury.'

They looked to Emma like George McIntire clones with English accents. 'Please take a seat, I'll see if he's available.' She walked into Stuart's office, carefully closing the door behind her. 'Two men from H.M. Customs. Looks like trouble.'

Stuart felt buoyant in the wake of the Kennedy interview and was not about to let any Queen's cop spoil his day. 'Show them in.'

Emma listened on the intercom as the suits tackled Stuart about the illegality of his radio station. They informed him that from now on anyone coming ashore would be subject to the most rigorous search, of their luggage and person, and that any supplies reaching the ship from foreign countries would be classified under English law. They also warned him that if any contraband, from opium to oranges, was found on any of his people they, and he, would be prosecuted to the full limit of the law. Stuart countered by saying that while the ship was in international waters there was bugger all they could do about anything and please would they stop wasting his valuable time. The men left Hayes Mews without saying goodbye to either Emma or the broad-smiling Martha.

'Gerald Copeland, please. It's Stuart Salisbury.' He doodled sharp-angled drawings on his blotting pad as he waited to be connected. 'Gerald, hello. I've just had two H.M. goons in here threatening castration. Can they do that?'

'Customs?'

'Yes.'

'I'm afraid so, old chap. They can go where ever they like. Hold on a minute.' Gerald studied his desk diary. 'Can we meet for drinks, say half past five? Bit awkward to talk at present.'

'Will you come here?'

'Yes. Is anyone coming ashore today?'

'No.'

'Good. See you later.' The phone went dead.

Stuart continued doodling sharp triangles with arrows through them. His thoughts were of Bill, Brian and the others, especially Honey, having to face the humiliation of a strip search. At least the thought of Eddie undergoing the same trial encouraged a small smile.

Eddie sat at his desk reading a letter from Amsterdam, a stoned smile slithering from ear to ear. Doc was back in town and wanted to see him. He cut another line of coke, deposited it deftly up his right nostril and reached for his pen.

Dear Doc and Joanna,

Good to hear from you and great news that Doc is out of nick. I can make Amsterdam in two weeks. Things here are cool but supply running low. Can you send some emergency rations via private mail?

See you soon,

Love and sex,

Eddie.

Brian sat in his cabin in roughly the same stoned state and wrote begging letters to record companies. He would normally ask for three advance copies of all releases, full biographies of the artists and any promotional material, to be sent to either the ship or the London office; sometimes both. As the chart man he was entitled to all these things, indeed the first two items were essential to do a good job. It was his definition of 'promotional material' that raised a few eyebrows around the corridors of EMI, Decca and

Philips. The record companies would sometimes promote their artists by having a party at the Cromwellian Club; Brian's idea was a weekend for two in Paris. The record companies would sometimes hand out plastic key rings with the name of the record embossed on one side; Brian thought a gold bracelet with his name engraved on one side much more appropriate. His latest request was considered by some to be a bribe too far.

Last night, on his way back from Eddie's cabin, he'd bumped into Bill Mason. The ensuing conversation was, to say the least, fairly curt. Somehow he'd manage to salvage the proceedings by saying that now Bill and Emma were a 'thing', it might be better if he found a place of his own. And anyway, if Bill objected to the occasional puff, it would be better if it wasn't around his flat.

This morning he'd got cracking on the ship-to-shore asking all his 'mates' in the record companies to put him up for a few nights, preferably at a good hotel where we could *all* have a party; look around for a flat, preferably in Chelsea or Knightsbridge; donate any old furniture, preferably over a hundred years old and from Harrods; most of all, to organise the best house-warming in London. He regarded his present work as letters of confirmation.

'I've nothing but admiration for what you're trying to do,' said Gerald, placing his briefcase beside Stuart's desk. 'But you're upsetting too many people for the overall good.'

'Explain.'

'If you sit in the North Sea playing music, talking to pop stars and keeping your nose clean, there's a chance – a very slim one, but a chance – that you could, at best, come ashore in a couple of years, or at worst, make a million quid. But you keep scooping the BBC, my friend, and you'll feel the full weight of the corporate structure descending upon you from a very high place.'

Stuart stared at the afternoon's doodles on his blotting pad. 'The Kennedy thing is no big deal. We just had a connection with Walters and we used it. The chances of it happening again is very slight.'

'It's not what you did, it's what you're capable of doing that bothers Westminster. If you scoop the established media on what are basically political stories, people with an axe to grind will start feeding you leaked memos and documents. Before you know it you'll be reporting sensitive material, probably prematurely, in order to "get it on air first" and, in so doing, upset the proverbial apple cart all over the people who don't want you here in the first place. Of course they're going to send in the troops; you would do exactly the same in their place.'

'I thought we conveyed our intentions the other night,' said Stuart, somewhat sulkily.

'My dear boy, no wonder they booted you from Balliol. Your politics are atrocious. To achieve a result in a lobby, you'd have to turn two hundred Heaths and McIntires, and then keep them on your side despite constant pressure from the people you nicked them off. What we did at the Commons was add a cup of water to the vat of opinion, with no guarantee that some sod wasn't emptying a jug-full from the bottom of the barrel.'

'Balliols to the lot of them!' Stuart wanted to change the subject. He walked slowly to the drinks cabinet. 'The first one of the night. What will it be Copey? G and T?'

'Orange juice, please. I have a busy dinner.' He joined Stuart at the cabinet. 'What you *could* do is get together with Caroline, London, City, and maybe some of the northern stations, and form a strong lobby. Call it the Independent Radio Association.'

Stuart turned to face his friend, schoolboy mischief dancing in his eyes. 'What, the IRA?'

Both men chuckled discreetly as they sipped their drinks.

'Maybe Committee would be better,' conceded Gerald.

'Is this private or can an overworked PA get a look in?' Emma stood in the doorway, her arms full of files.

Stuart beckoned her over. 'Have a tipple. Gerald's trying to make me politically aware. Failing miserably, I fear.'

'Thank you. Some of your freshly squeezed orange juice, if you please.' She deposited the files on Stuart's desk.

'Good God! Not another one. Has somebody poisoned the whisky? Gerald's pleading a dinner party. What's your excuse?'

'I'm Bill-less.'

'You're what-less?'

Emma took her drink. 'Bill-less. When Bill's on the ship I don't drink before dinner. Makes up a bit for the week he's off.'

'Very wise.' Stuart sat down at his desk. 'Gerald thinks we should stop being a radio station, just shut up and play the music . . .'

'. . . That's a bit simplistic!' protested Gerald.

'In essence, you said just that, Gerald.' Then to Emma, 'Do you think we should just play the music and wait for the good people of Whitehall to maybe let us play indoors? Or should we stick two fingers up at them in the loudest possible manner?'

Emma saw the politician and the businessman; each with his own view, both wanting her support. She decided on a public relations approach. 'If you want people to listen you've got to tell them you're here; so make as much noise as possible. What you say could determine your political stance, so say it with music. They're so out of touch with young people they'll never understand it.'

'Exactly my point.' Gerald toasted Emma, then turned to Stuart. 'Politicians only care where you get your news. If you must have a pop, do it with a Bob Dylan record they'll never interpret. Anyway, your listeners, who should be your first consideration, don't give a stuff about politics. I'll bet ninety per cent of your letters read, please play the Beatles and send my love to Alice Brown!'

'That's not the point!'

'It is!'

'I think we should hire Alice Brown for the morning show,' interjected Emma.

For a moment both men took her seriously. It was just long enough to break the fast-building tension.

'Call me old-fashioned but I think we should make friends with them,' she continued. 'Did they make a fuss about Bill Blankly and that silly F.A. Cup?'

Both men. 'Shankly!'

'Whatever. Did they?'

'No!'

'Well then. Scoop stuff they don't mind and stay away from what they do.'

Stuart threw his arms up. 'And who's going to decide? You? Me? Gerald? Jonathan bloody Gilby?'

'Right last time! Jonathan Gilby.' She placed her empty glass on Stuart's desk. 'At least you'd have someone to blame for the wrong ones.'

Gerald placed his empty glass next to Emma's. 'You know, Stuart, she'd make a fabulous spokesperson for the IRC.'

'Just a minute!' Emma put her hands on her hips faster than most of Bill Shankly's star players could kick a ball. 'I'm working flat out. There's no way I can take on more.'

A broad smile formed on Stuart's face as he tilted backwards in his chair. 'You're so right,' he said to Gerald; then to Emma, 'How would your own secretary sound? No! On second thoughts, how would your own department sound?'

The one thing Emma had learned in her short time with Stuart was that things move extremely fast in off-shore radio. She'd seen a girl from north London and twins from Ilford become radio stars within weeks; she'd help set up a complete news department within days; she'd changed the mind of a member of parliament within hours; and she'd fallen in love in a minute. Her natural cunning told her to move slowly.

'I think I should sit down with another glass of orange juice and hear the story from the top, don't you?'

Stuart had also learned a lot about 'speed in our times'. His gut feeling said she'd be perfect, but he'd had no time to think it out. Time to fly!

'We've been talking about setting up a multi-partisan organisation that would represent all the off-shore interests and seek to further our cause both politically and commercially. We think you're the right person to run that organisation.'

Emma watched Gerald's expressionless face as he

placed a tall glass of fresh orange juice on the table in front of her. This sounded far too good to be true. 'Does this mean "run" as in open another file, or "run" as in do nothing else?'

'As in do nothing else,' Stuart heard himself say.

Emma remained silent; there had to be more. Stuart tilted his chair forward to the upright position. She remembered he'd done that with the customs men, just before he'd told them to bugger off.

'It's time to restructure. We've been running on start-up long enough.' Stuart had the floor. 'The only department up to speed is sales. It's time programming and promotions caught up.'

'Hear, hear,' said Emma quickly. Then sheepishly, 'Sorry.'

'Don't ever be sorry. One of your own, straight back to you.' Stuart tasted victory. He walked to the drinks cabinet. 'Give me a hand, Copey. Take the mirror off first then slide it towards you. Slowly.'

The two men lifted the large ornate mirror carefully from the back of the cabinet and, struggling with the weight, lowered it to the carpet. It revealed the top half of a white wooden door. The cabinet stood on small squeaky wheels and, apart from the strident noise that offended everyone's ears, proved easy to move. Emma looked understandably amazed; she'd never known anything lurked beyond the 'Tea-Time Tipple Bar', as she'd labelled it. Stuart retrieved a long, old-fashioned key from the beam above the door and put an end to their curiosity.

'My dear friends – the house next door.'

Emma could see three carpeted steps leading to a hall with a sloping roof; half a skylight beamed sun through the dust.

Stuart was already in the hall. 'Mind your heads!'

Emma noted, with relief, that she could clear the door without bending. The carpets were much thicker than those in Stuart's office; as if a new set had been laid on top of the last. Three white wooden doors with latch handles were evenly spaced along the corridor; at the end, three steps dropped to a natural wood door with brass latch handles and matching hinges. Emma opened the first door. The room was small with a partially sloping ceiling supporting two small skylights. Its freshly painted white walls and beige carpet made it appear much larger than its actual fourteen square feet. Electric and telephone points peppered the skirting board.

'The other two rooms are the same,' said Stuart, motioning them down the hall. 'Come look at this.'

The end room was vast, measuring a good twenty-five feet by twenty. The far-side wall was dominated by a large traditional brick fireplace and hearth; crooked oak beams slashed white rendering on the other three walls. There was no ceiling, just black oak roof beams. Two large windows overlooked the mews; in front of them a flight of stairs dropped down to the floor below. The room was immaculately furnished. Three dark red buttoned-leather sofas edged a decorative Persian carpet; the fireplace completing the square. To the right of the door an eighteenth-century Sheraton mahogany dining table and eight chairs; to the left, facing away from the wall, a mahogany knee-hole desk of the same period. Assorted period cabinets and standard lamps, oil paintings and charcoal sketches lent a lived-in feeling to the room. The beige fitted carpets gave it light.

'I was extremely lucky,' said Stuart to his astonished friends. 'Most mews houses have been carved up. This one's as it should be, with one big room above the stables. The previous owner built the three-roomed bridge. I bought it mainly for the garage space underneath, but when I saw this room, I just had to restore it.'

'When?' asked Emma.

'It was finished the day you started work here.' Stuart opened a small wooden hatch to the left of the door. 'This goes through to the other room. Your secretary can sit in there.'

'My secretary! You mean this is my office?'

'Of course it's your office; and the next room. The one nearest me I want for accounts, the middle room for press and PR. We'll all use this room for meetings, and with its own entrance, it's perfect for entertaining and committee activities.'

Emma stood dumbstruck, trying to take everything in. Stuart was right, the room had been restored, not redecorated. Gerald eyed the furniture covetously at close range.

'I can see you two are lost for words. Why don't I get some wood? We'll start a fire; be cosy in no time.' Stuart disappeared down the stairs.

Gerald stopped his inspection and joined Emma. 'I'm so glad he's given you the job. Lady Heath's a great fan of yours and I feel she won't be the last.' He squeezed her shoulders. 'I'll get some drink from Stu's office. What would you like?'

'A gin and tonic, please.' She watched him walk down the corridor then turned slowly full circle in the room. It was so beautiful, so spacious, so . . . her! She sat behind the desk. In front of her, the sofas ranged around the fire; beyond the sofas the antique table and chairs; to the right of her the hatch. Even without a fire, the room had a warm glow from the richness of the furniture and carpet.

Stuart carried an arm full of presto-logs up the stairs. 'There's also real wood and coal, but these are easier to start with.'

Within five minutes the fire was blazing, Gerald had moved in practically the entire drinks cabinet and Emma set the lighting using the new-fangled dimmer switch Stuart had installed.

'Now, we need to look at staffing.' Stuart placed another log on the fire. 'You'll need a secretary, so will I. Two juniors for promotion and PR one – should be a strong young man to hump equipment for the gigs, the other a dolly bird who can double as promotion girl; and I think maybe a general office bod to service all departments and do the post.'

With the exception of equipment handling, all of these had been part of Emma's job. As she heard them being reallocated it finally sank in that she really was no longer a personal assistant to the managing director; she was in charge of her own department with at least four staff to help her and an office she could quite happily live in. What she couldn't believe was how quickly it all seemed to have happened – though it was typical of Stuart.

'I'll leave the furniture to you,' she heard him say from outside her dream. 'And the telephones. You always know what to get.'

And I'll leave it to my secretary, she thought, with a great deal of satisfaction.

Sir David Garman's secretary interrupted his meeting with news of a phone call on his private line. He excused himself and left the boardroom, returning five minutes later, a wry smile on his Stonehenge face. 'Gentlemen, we have a result.' He took his place at the head of the table. 'Our friends have moved into the new part of their offices.'

Chapter 7

The last place the twins had expected to be on this bright spring morning was on board an eighty-foot luxury cruiser heading out of Southend. They'd worked the Ragamuffin on Tuesday with great success and spent the night in the company of Danielle and her friend Cathy at Mick's 'London office'; a lavishly decorated three-floor Victorian house off Acre Lane with six bedrooms, one reception, five bathrooms and not a typewriter in sight. The girls were attentive, polite and very professional; even asking the boys if they'd like a foursome in the master bedroom to round off the evening.

'Everything's paid for,' assured Cathy. 'Your host says nothing's too good for the Street twins.'

They remembered Stuart's advice regarding compromising photographs and refused the carnal feast in favour of a high-class Chinese takeaway and a lively game of Monopoly which continued until four in the morning. When collecting the second and third bottle of champagne from the kitchen fridge, Simon indulged in a little lighthearted slap and tickle with Danielle over the oak dining table but, apart from that, an asexual evening was enjoyed by all.

Mick took the boys for a slap-up lunch at Guys & Dolls on Wednesday before sending them back to Ilford in the back of his new Cloud One Rolls Royce. Over lunch, he'd persuaded them that catching a tug from Harwich didn't suit their new-found station in life and only a sail on his private cruiser *Taskforce Two* with Danielle and Cathy for company could round off their week in a satisfactory manner. The twins saw no reason to argue and, when the Roller was offered as transportation from Ilford to Southend, the deal was clinched.

Taskforce Two proved infinitely preferable to the cold, cramped cabin of *Offshore One*. She was an American-built Chris Craft, packed with every extra in the catalogue from sonar to sauna. She carried a crew of five (more accurately, a captain and four excons), and cut the swell off Maplin Sands so smoothly, hardly a ripple could be felt in the stateroom as the guests sat down to their second breakfast.

'We've had a couple of great days, boys and girls, and let's pray the good Lord will see fit to keep the skies blue for the rest of the voyage.' Mick sat at the head of the table and surveyed the company; then turned to one of the crew. 'Straight up, Danny, this younger generation – no stamina!'

Danielle, Cathy and the twins were quiet more through embarrassment than tiredness. Tuesday night had been fun; party moods, party time. When they'd met this morning, the twins exhausted from last night's partying at home, the girls hung-over from last night's new dates, they all knew this was a bad idea.

'We had a great time,' offered Lewis apologetically. 'It's been a long week.'

'Like I said, no stamina! Still, after breakfast the girls can sort you out in the hot room – that's what

I call the sauna. Soon 'ave you two cookin' with gas.'

'Leave it out, Mick, we're knackered.' These were the first words from Cathy since they'd left harbour.

Mick's rodent eyes narrowed on the girl his bonhomie suddenly vanished. 'These are our guests. They don't want to know you're bloody knackered!'

'Mick! It's cool,' intervened Simon. 'Man, we've had a great time, really. A good breakfast and a walk on the deck would go down a treat. Anyway, me and him gotta get our first show together.' He pulled a small tape recorder from his suitcase. 'The new office portable found its way into my hands. Why don't we get the girls to do us some jingles?'

Mick was well pleased – this was a definite bonus. An entry into show-business was not part of his deal with Danielle and Cathy. The guests could now enjoy the morning sun without further harassment from the Ilford hustler.

Emma caught the morning sun as it streamed through the mews windows and warmed her back while she cleared the ashes from last night's fire. Her first seven days in charge of a department had been very successful. She'd hired a secretary, a twenty-year-old Pitman graduate from Harrow, with serious shorthand and sensible shoes. She'd had lunch at the Savoy with Lady Heath, who seemed very pleased to see her, and she'd rounded off the week on a shopping spree with her friend Avril.

She always serious-shopped with Avril. They'd been friends since those awkward adolescent days at Edgware Comprehensive. It was Avril who'd consoled Emma when she broke up with the first love of her life, a slimy sixth-former named Rodney Quzak who preferred breast-fondling to serious relationships, and after two months didn't care whose breasts he was fondling. Emma returned the favour when Sebastian Cookson did roughly the same to Avril. They always greeted each other with the same phrase, lest they ever forget.

'Sebastian and Rodney are assholes, Yes . . . they . . . are!'

This time they performed this ritual outside Marble Arch Tube station, much to the chagrin of a Rodney who happened to be passing by. They'd shopped mainly in Bond Street. Emma spent a lot of money on two gorgeous wool suits in the Cardin sale, and a pair of black patent-leather shoes and matching handbag that weren't on sale, but complemented the outfits perfectly. Avril treated herself to three Hermes scarves.

She walked to her desk, carefully flicking a piece of ash that had dared to deposit itself on her royal blue Cardin skirt. Today she'd interview for the PR job, starting with a Mr Ben Fairchild at noon. Charlie the driver popped his head round the door.

'Shall I build a fire for you, Miss Saxby? Nasty wind this morning.'

'Thank you, Charlie. There should be some smokeless coal downstairs. I'd love a coal fire.' She thought briefly of Bill on the North Sea, probably wrapped in three sweaters to keep warm and fighting to keep upright. She picked up her phone and dialled the Harwich number that would link her ship-to-shore.

They chatted non-stop for twenty minutes. She could tell him nothing of her lunches and meetings over an open two-way phone, but she did fill him in on every detail of her office and how she'd spent last night putting up the most beautiful yellow curtains in the drawing room at Ovington Square. He told her Honey was sleeping with Jonathan, Brian was sleeping downstairs and he wasn't sleeping that good without her. She said she was glad, and told him she missed him too. He also told her he'd just talked to the twins on *Taskforce Two* and they would be arriving at FREE in about an hour.

Sure enough, an hour later *Taskforce Two* moored gently beside M.V. *FREE*. No jumping on and off here. Her top deck was level with *FREE*'s gunwales, – and Mick carried a twenty-foot gangplank for just such an occasion.

The presence of the two girls ensured invitations for all to come aboard. Mick met the Captain, Bill, Honey and Jonathan. When he was introduced to Brian and noticed the tell-tale white ring around his left nostril, he knew he'd found what he was looking for. The girls thought Peter Robinson quite charming and went to his cabin to inspect his record collection, leaving Mick and the chartman alone.

'Tell me, Brian, where would I find Eddie Lincoln?'

'The supply officer?'

'The very same.'

'Downstairs. Wanna introduction?'

Mick and Eddie were firm friends within a minute; kindred spirits in the pursuit of illicit wealth. Eddie took less than a second to accept an invitation to come aboard *Taskforce*. Mick showed him the sauna and sent one of his crew to fetch Danielle or Cathy; or both.

Cathy had two new boyfriends for lunch.

Emma had lunch with Stuart.

'I've got an idea.' She sipped her Perrier. 'Why don't

we spend a bit on a survey? Get a small outfit to do us a couple of thousand sample; see what happens.'

Stuart ate the last of his lamb chop from the bone. 'What do you expect to happen?'

'I expect us to come crashing in at number one!'

He let the clean chop-bone drop on to his plate and studied Emma carefully. 'Can you guarantee that?'

'No, but I've a good plan.'

'Go on!'

'We send press, PR, and half a dozen promotion girls out to say Ilford, Wednesday lunch; give away stickers, photos, tuning information. Lots of pictures for local press, lots of re-tuning radios in local shops, lots of awareness generally. Then, on Friday, we do the survey in the same place.'

Stuart pondered the logic. 'It could work. How much?'

'Under a thousand, the lot.'

'How long?'

Emma folded her napkin neatly and placed it on the table. 'We shouldn't release anything for a month, maybe two. It'll look too rigged if we do. Let's consult sales. Walters is good at this sort of thing.'

'How're you getting on with the Satan of Sales these days?'

'A totally changed man towards me,' she replied proudly, although she had no reason to be. John Walters put everyone in pigeon-holes. Emma had just risen from MD's junior shit to department head and so progressed in his rankings from 'Hey you' to 'Miss Saxby'. It was second nature to John Walters, like blackmail and bribery.

Contraband and prostitution were being discussed on

board *Taskforce*. Eddie was surprised when Mick asked him how his trip to Amsterdam had been. He was even more surprised to learn that Mick not only knew Doc, but was his British partner. He offered Eddie a deal too good to pass. Eddie would receive various sealed parcels from Doc via the Dutch supply boat; he would hold them, unopened, until *Taskforce* came to collect. The down-side was that *Taskforce* could arrive anytime, day or night, and Eddie would have to keep the Captain, crew and radio people cool. The up-side was that Cathy and/or some of her friends would always accompany the boat, and for each transaction Eddie would receive two hundred pounds in cash.

He sat on the couch outside the sauna and let Cathy's scented hands rub oil on the top of his chest while her nipples gently brushed his back. She moved slowly around his body, her hands exploring every muscle, her mouth sliding round his neck, her tongue gently probing his ear. All this and money too, he thought as he leaned backwards, letting his towel slip to the floor.

Honey opened one eye as she felt Jonathan's tongue explore her earlobe. 'Yes, please, and good morning.'

'It's afternoon,' he whispered. 'You're on the air in an hour.'

'Lots of time.' She squirmed inside the bed. 'I feel the need to be ravished. Be a darling and give me a little ravish before I go to work.'

Jonathan stood up. 'Can't! Massive news story, mustn't leave it.'

'Are we sinking?'

He was already half-way to the door. 'West Germany

169

and Israel have established relations; nine Arab states have broken diplomatic ties with Bonn.'

Honey sat up in bed and watched him disappear down the companionway. She was disappointed that a story he'd have to pirate from the BBC took precedence over her, but it did tell her the price of lust as far as Mr Gilby was concerned.

Honey was becoming more disenchanted with the head of news with each passing day. For the first week he'd been charming and attentive; feeding her new-found freedom with constant sensual passion. They made love at least twice a day, and she explored his body in a way she'd never allowed herself with any other man.

Half-way through the second week he'd started making excuses, in week three they made love twice. She was disappointed, but realistic. They still got on well together, she still liked him as a friend; most importantly, it kept the rest of the men from bothering her and that alone made his lack of attention bearable.

Peter Robinson was going ashore so Honey was on the air at three o'clock. She switched on her monitor and heard Nigel Hinkley promo the two o'clock news. An hour and a bit, she thought as she sat on her bunk gently rubbing the insides of her thighs.

Damn you, Jonathan Gilby!

Chapter 8

Tuesday June 15, 1965.

This was an important week for several reasons. First, 'I'm Alive' by the Hollies replaced Elvis and 'Crying in the Chapel' at the top of the FREE forty chart, two weeks ahead of the nationals. Secondly, Bill was off the ship, so very little work was being done for the Independent Radio Committee. Thirdly, John Lennon's book, *A Spaniard in the Works*, was becoming a huge success and fourthly, the Beatles were awarded the MBE.

Within hours of the announcement, several people sent their awards back to the Palace as a protest against 'cheapening' the honour. The first, Hector Dupuis, a Canadian MP, said that the awards placed him on the same level as 'vulgar nincompoops'. Not surprisingly the attitude of the British press was firmly in support of the Liverpool side; the reaction from the lads was one of dignified indifference.

At Hayes Mews they enjoyed a double celebration. An MBE for the Beatles; a John Lennon interview for Bill Mason. Jonathan Gilby and Brian Todd combined to persuade EMI that an interview with John would not only produce programme material, but also guarantee news coverage. Bill's handling of the conversation was sharp and intelligent; John's readings from the book, including a swipe-back at the *Daily Mirror*'s Cassandra, were hilarious.

OffShore One made a late trip to FREE carrying a ten-inch reel of priceless tape. Jonathan led the six o'clock news with the story; the twins ran the full interview at five past six. At half past six Kenny and Cash radioed from Big 'L' saying 'Congratulations, you bastards!' It was the first real scoop for the twins and they decided it merited an on-board party.

The weather at sea was beautiful; a warm southerly breeze dispersed the accumulated heat of the sun from the metal decks of the radio ship and filled the evening with sweet summer scent. Simon promised a bottle of champagne to the first boat alongside. By nine o'clock there were at least twenty surrounding the ship.

Eddie watched from the flying bridge as the last rays of daylight bounced off the shiny flotilla of small craft. He'd spotted at least fifteen females, some clad in only their bikini bottoms, ready and willing to party. Tonight would be good for business.

'Charlie Bare on the Air' took over from the twins at nine with a promise to 'rock the boat 'til midnight'. Captain Vourner locked the transmitter room, engine room, galley and radio shack before retiring to his cabin to write to Lisa, leaving FREE to the mercy of the masses.

With Bill off the ship and the Captain in his cabin, Eddie had no worries about plying his trade. He rolled thirty joints and proceeded to sell them to the partygoers at five bob a throw. He talked a busty redhead called Janice into coming to his cabin, where he proceeded to cut several lines of cocaine from his private stock. He persuaded her to lick the second line off his cock; a feat she performed with remarkable dexterity borne, he was sure, from years of experience. He was returning the favour by licking a large crystal of the drug into her clitoris when a heavy bump on the side of the boat made him swallow the rock whole. He felt the back of his mouth freeze as the narcotic slipped down his throat.

'Damn those day-trip skippers!' he rasped, gazing up the curve of her stomach and ogling her oversized, flattened-down breasts. 'I'll just get some more Charlie, stay put!'

Janice decided she'd had enough. 'I've got to get back to my boyfriend; he'll wonder where I am.'

Eddie decided she hadn't. 'Fuck him. Nobody'll find you down here.' He slid his hands around her bottom and roughly inserted three fingers inside her. Her protests gradually withered as the cocaine, grass and occasion combined to produce an orgasm louder than any Eddie had ever previously witnessed. Ten minutes later he deposited Janice back with her boyfriend, offering the lame excuse of an elongated ship's tour, before returning to his cabin and rolling another dozen money-makers.

The twins were more hosting than partying. They greeted everyone on board, signed autographs and gave tours of the studios and living area. They also noted Eddie's comings and goings and guessed what he was up to, consequently limiting their tours to the upper deck. A large man with two equally large daughters offered them a bottle of Glenross in exchange for three signed photos. By two o'clock in the morning the man and his daughters were gone; so was most of the whisky.

In Knightsbridge, the last of the dinner guests stepped

173

into the warm night air and bade his hosts farewell. A small group of press had been gathered by Emma to listen to a tape of the Lennon interview in the comfort of Ovington Square. She'd also used the opportunity to show off her new curtains and impress upon the doyens of Fleet Street that she and Bill were now a pair, should they ever need a couple's quote on music, atomic warfare, or the state of the nation in general.

Spicy spare-ribs, hot cocktail sausages, ten kinds of cheese and a dozen sticks of French bread had been ordered from Franco's, the latest in a long line of catering firms springing up in Knightsbridge and specialising in swinging soirées for the rich and famous. The food arrived with a crate of champagne and matching waiters; all paid for by Emma's new and already well-used expense account. Bill switched to mineral water after nine o'clock, more for the salvation of his sex life than from any desire to score points on the paparazzi. Emma looked gorgeous in her new mini-dress with matching belt and shoes. Bill noticed how closely the cut resembled a school uniform, and how skilfully the couturier had plied his craft to ensure only someone deeply in love or lust with the model would ever notice the similarity. As Bill was both, he'd spotted it immediately.

They made love for hours that night-warm, tender love, punctuated by bursts of raunchy sex. The kind of lovemaking reserved for those blessed with complete compatability; sensual pleasure given and received in an atmosphere of shared emotion. They learned more about each other with every passing hour. Emma loved his strength and honesty, he loved her sense of humour.

'I do love you,' she'd whispered in his ear. 'I'd love you even more if you'd stay inside me 'til Christmas.'

Unlike by brother Mikie,
my rhymes are very spiky.
James Brown supplies the song,
I'm groovin' all night long.
This is Howlin' "T" on FREE,
shake it, nasty brother "B".

Stan Beacher unlocked the galley just after 5 a.m. He wasn't much of a party animal; he'd declined the twins' party invitation in favour of an evening in his cabin reading the new *Electronic Monthly*. As he waited for the kettle to boil, he became aware of a slow, rhythmic thumping on each side of the ship. He made a strong cup of instant coffee, added a dash of milk and shuffled along the companionway to the upper deck.

He loved going topside at this time of day. No crewmen shouting Dutch, no rock 'n' roll music pounding from the deck speakers. With the weather fair and the seas calm, standing on deck watching the morning sun eclipse the beach lights at Frinton, a much needed piece of nature's beauty to penetrate the electronic world of FREE's chief engineer.

His eyes focused on two small masts bobbing slowly off the aft quarters. He walked to the port side and looked over the railings. Ten feet below a thirty-foot single-mast motor-sailor lay neatly alongside, protected by large red bumpers and secured with white nylon rope. Through the cabin skylight he could see Eddie Lincoln's naked back. He seemed to be holding something round in his hands. A dark-haired woman entered the frame, stood beside Eddie and started removing her clothes. As he looked up to watch her, Stan saw that the round object Eddie held so carefully was a blonde female head.

175

Stan deliberately dropped some coffee on to the skylight. Eddie looked up in time to see the engineer disappear from the railings on his way to inspect the other craft.

Within a minute Eddie had dressed and climbed back aboard FREE. 'Christ! What a party!' he shouted across the deck. 'Come on, transmitter-brain, join in!'

No visible signs of life emanated from the small boat on the starboard side. Stan watched FREE's steel plating sand down more of the small cruiser's wooden gun-wales with every swell and contemplated his answer. He could hear Eddie clattering noisily across the deck towards him.

'Why on earth, Mr Lincoln, would I want to go within a mile of anything you've been an inch inside?' he asked without removing his gaze from boat below. 'I'll be waking the Captain in ten minutes, so I suggest you tell your friends to get the fuck away from the side of the ship, lest he feels like shooting twenty-five kilowatts up their jacksy. Any idea where this lot are?'

Eddie looked over the side, and then with arrogant indifference at Stan. 'How should I know? I've been off the fucking planet for the past six hours!' He walked towards the small ladder hatch in the centre of the deck. 'I'll find them. You go tell the *Busy Bee* they've got to leave. You never know, a sighting of real tits might even get *your* dick hard.'

From half-way down FREE's hatch ladder Eddie could see the full length of the crew's quarters. All the doors were shut. No use checking his cabin, he'd locked it. Svenson was the best bet; he spoke English and liked the girls. He quietly tried Svenson's door: locked. He heard a thump from the cabin next door. Number eight was empty; he'd earmarked it only yesterday as another

176

possible lock-up. The door opened easily, he stepped inside. On the top bunk, two naked women slept in each other's arms; on the bottom bunk, a man, covered by a large fur coat, quietly snored. The cause of the thump was trying sit upright on the floor.

'Where are we?' he said, feeling his limbs gingerly for possible damage.

'On the good ship fucking Lollipop!' Eddie flicked on the light. 'Are you people from the boat astern?'

The women woke up and both tried to scramble under the sheet at the same time, in a badly synchronised attempt to protect what little modesty they had left.

'Yes, we are,' answered the man on the floor. 'What's happening?

'You'd better wake your friend and get your shit together. The Captain's on duty in ten minutes and, believe me, you don't want to be on board.'

The phone disturbed Emma's blissful rest. 'I'm feeling post-coital, I know it's my foible, but if it isn't important then please go away.' She wasn't prone to spontaneous poetry, especially this early in the morning; it pleased her. She hooked one leg over Bill and waited for the answer.

'Emma. Is that you?'

She tried to focus. 'Stuart? What time is it?'

'A little after eight. I need your help.'

An urgency in his voice made Emma's mind leap to attention. 'What's wrong?'

'I'm at Chelsea police station charged with supplying contraband. I can't raise Gerald, this is my last phone call.'

'What happened?'

'They stopped a boat, the *Busy Bee*, coming ashore at six this morning. They found marijuana.'

'Coming from us?'

'Apparently.'

'Stay where you are . . . Sorry, you don't have much choice.' Emma nudged Bill in the back. 'I'll be there in half an hour.' She hung up and rolled out of bed in a single movement. 'Bill! Wake up! Stuart's in jail!' She'd put on her underwear and was already tugging at her jeans as Bill poked his head out from under the covers.

'Jail?! As in police?'

'Yes! Now please! Let's go!'

They both finished dressing at the same time; Bill grabbed a few of last night's sausage rolls as they hurried from the flat. He also had the presence of mind to pick up the portable tape-recorder from the hall table, just in case.

At Chelsea police station nobody seemed in a hurry. One hour, a desk sergeant and a detective constable later, Emma finally talked to the arresting officer, a detective-sergeant Blackwell, who informed them any and all employees could be charged with aiding after the fact.

'And just what are the facts?' demanded Emma defiantly, hands on hips, eyes blazing.

D.S. Blackwell spoke as if he were giving evidence. 'H.M. Customs intercepted a light cruiser, the *Busy Bee*, as it entered Harwich harbour at approximately 06:30 this morning. One of the passengers, a Miss Holly Stevens, was found to be in possession of 0.5 grams of a substance believed to be marijuana. She has since been charged under Section Ten of the Import Code of Practice Act 1953 and under Section Twenty-two of the Criminal Code.'

'For how much?'

'0.5 grams, madam.'

Bill looked away in disgust. Emma went on the attack. 'I'm not a user, detective sergeant, but from what I understand 0.5 grams is about two joints' worth. Am I right?'

Blackwell looked slightly unnerved. 'I can't say, madam.'

'I'm close enough.' She fixed the policeman with a rivetting stare which allowed no escape. 'Doesn't it seem foolish that you're charging a leading London businessman with supplying two joints of grass to a person he's never met, on a boat he's never seen, with no real proof that the *Busy Bee* was anywhere near M.V. *FREE*? Maybe it came from London or Caroline, maybe the girl was lying.' She saw uncertainty creep into his eyes; she was on a roll. 'I'm the press officer for FREE, and in five minutes I'm calling every national paper in this country to tell them how all you big, strong policemen harassed a poor pop fan into making a statement, then arrested a perfectly innocent man because he happens to own a boat anchored in the same ocean. I think the column inches will be worth any fine the British courts see fit to impose; that is if they don't rule that this whole charade is a blatant waste of public money.' She softened her voice. 'If you really think the radio ships are running dope, catch someone who works for us with 0.5 tons; *then* you have a case.'

Fifteen minutes later, Stuart took a deep breath of King's Road air before stepping into the back seat of the Bentley. 'Can I offer you two a lift home?'

'We've got the Mini around the corner,' said Emma, holding on tightly to Bill's waist. 'There's a committee meeting at noon. Do you think you can stay out of trouble 'til then?'

Chapter 9

Friday, December 10th 1965.

Winter in the North Sea is as far removed from small boats bobbing gently at your side as a camp fire is from Hiroshima. The seas can become viciously cruel remarkably quickly. Summer had been short but sweet; the weather closed in by early September and had stayed more or less rough ever since. A spell of relative calm the previous day had allowed the tug to run a service trip with much-needed food plus Bill and Honey to replace Charlie Bare and the twins.

Today's weather was back on form – heavy rain and a fifty mile an hour north-easterly wind, producing a ten- to fifteen-foot swell. With the ship anchored at the bow and the studios in the stern, Jonathan was rising and falling some thirty feet as he stood in the production studio trying to finish the one o'clock news.

'Reports are now confirmed that Nikolai Podgorny has replaced Anastas Mikoyan as Soviet head of state. There are no plans as yet for the prime minister, Harold Wilson, or the new leader of the opposition, Edward Heath, to visit the Russian capital. Nearer to home, customs men are clamping down on rising hemlines. Until now length determined whether a dress was a woman's, and liable to ten per cent purchase tax, or a child's and so tax-free. From January first dresses will be taxed by bust size; anything above thirty-two inches will be classed as a woman's dress. Bad news for fast-developing teenagers; good news for flat-chested forties. This is Jonathan Gilby, FREE news.'

Captain Vourner stood in the radio room and broadcast his news to London on the ship-to-shore.

'I'm very concerned about some of the ship's plating. Over.'

Stuart didn't share his worry. 'What can happen? She was built to withstand mines blowing up around her. What can a bit of bad weather do? Over.'

'She was built twenty years ago. I see signs of metal fatigue on the bow sections. I think we should reinforce with an inner skin. Over.'

'I can't possibly get plating out to you in this weather. Let's put it down as a spring job. Did the food arrive? Over.'

'Thank you, yes. So did Mr Mason and Miss Bogart. Over.'

'Well, all I can suggest is that you batten down the hatches and ride it out. Over.'

The Captain glared at the receiver, wishing he could get those fair-weather sailors in London to 'ride' a force nine. They wouldn't be so damn flippant after a week. He steadied himself as the ship lurched to port. 'Thank you for the advice,' he said curtly. 'Over and out.'

Stuart replaced the phone, walked across the roof corridor to Emma's office and joined her and Gerald on the sofa in front of a raging log fire. 'My word, it's cosy in here,' he said, rubbing his hands as if the coldness of the ship had somehow reached him through the phone. 'What news on the political front?'

'Best news since Ted Heath,' replied Gerald. 'I quote

from *The Times*! Under the headline "Pirate Radio – Cabinet Relents". They say the Government has apparently comes to the conclusion that it will be difficult to legislate to put the pirate stations off the air, and that it may be better, after all, to introduce a system of licensing local commercial radio transmitters.'

'That's fabulous!' exclaimed Stuart.

'There's more! And this is where Emma's earned her Christmas bonus. The survey she did in the summer has just paid for itself in this paragraph. Quote: their soundings of public opinion have shown conclusively that if the Government were to force the pirate stations out of business and leave nothing in their place, it would do the Labour Party a lot of harm electorally. They find that large numbers of Labour Party supporters, particularly younger people, are devoted to the non-stop pop music provided by the pirates and would object strongly if these programmes were to disappear; unquote!'

Stuart looked at Emma. 'This was your survey?'

'In essence. I met this very nice member of the Labour Party last week . . .'

'. . . No such thing!' interrupted Stuart.

Emma's look left him in no doubt that such juvenile humour was not appreciated. 'A very nice member of the Labour Party said he'd be interested in what I'd gathered, so I sent him a copy. Not everyone left of centre is against us, you know.'

'Point taken.' Then to Gerald. 'Can we expect legislation by summer?'

'Good God, no! This is one newspaper article, not a bill before the House. What it does show is that the IRC is working and that Emma is one smart lady.'

Emma would have blushed six months ago; not

any more. She was rapidly becoming a national spokes-woman for the younger generation. She'd appeared on television, been interviewed by most of the tab-loids, and expanded her contacts both politically and commercially. She'd conducted herself with poise and confidence at public functions and proved herself a keen and cunning negotiator. Cathy McGowan was the queen of Pop; Emma Saxby, in six short and hectic months, had become the princess royal of pirates.

On a few occasions the tabloids questioned her experi-ence when dealing with such matters as the Wireless Telegraphy Act and copyright laws. She'd replied by quoting several passages from the Act relevant to her cause and stating that the copyright laws should now be changed to accommodate the new media. Most of her press had been excellent. The dailies saw her as a 'new woman of the sixties', independent, successful, stylish, with a celebrity boyfriend; the music press saw her as Bill Mason's busy bird. A line in *Melody Maker's* Raver column read 'We notice definite lack of IRC activity when Bill Mason's off the boat!' She'd cut it from the paper, enlarged it and stuck it to the front of her desk.

She'd also continued to build a good working rela-tionship with John Walters, learning rapidly about sales technique and advertising budgeting from the master of media marketing. What impressed her most was that *The Times* never quoted her or even admitted her exist-ence, yet all her best work had gone through them.

'I want to do another survey in the spring; this time nationally.' Silence from the men. 'Caroline, London and, if they get to air, Scotland have agreed in principle, subject to cost.'

'The inevitable question,' commented Gerald.

'About six thousand to do a good job, plus PR expenses.'

Stuart doodled triangles on his memo pad. 'What kind of split on costs?'

'Caroline has two ships so should pay more, but I'll settle for an equal split. I don't want them running the show because they're the highest contributor – subject to your approval, of course, gentlemen,' she added carefully. Her frequent lunches with Lady Heath had taught her a lot about women succeeding in a man's world. She watched Stuart doodle and Gerald think. 'Come on, you two. Contribute!'

'I think it's dead on,' said Gerald, with conviction. 'A favourable opinion in, say, April or May could be politically useful. If they try legislation, it will be June, I would guess.'

Stuart stopped doodling. 'How much control will we have?'

'It'll be run by the IRC; everything will come through this office.' Emma smiled warmly at Stuart. She loved the look of concern that crossed his face when he thought someone was threatening her. She could handle Caroline, London, Uncle Tom Cobbley and all, but it was nice to feel protected. 'One of your better ideas; having the IRC based here.' She leaned forward and touched his knee. 'You're a clever little bar steward.'

'Agreed, and agreed to the survey.' Stuart felt pleased with the compliment and smiled at them both in recognition before changing the subject. 'Now, about the Christmas bash at McCann's. It's on the sixteenth and I've accepted for all of us plus Brian Todd and Peter Robinson who should be off the boat. Sorry, Emma, Bill's not off 'til the twenty-second.'

'Tell me,' said Emma, pointing to her desk. 'Read the sign!'

Reading the *Melody Maker* seemed damn near impossible to Bill Mason as the ship spiral-turned down and then to port. A ship underway can fight back in a storm, a ship anchored at the bow is like an empty anti-aircraft gun: big, bulky and useless. The storm had steadily worsened since early morning, by lunch it was a full-blown gale. By tea-time Brian resorted to playing continuous music from the tape machine punctuated with the standard station jingles. Bill wanted to watch nature's revenge from the bridge. He staggered to the mess-room, trying desperately to go with the flow of the ship, holding on to anything that was bolted down and avoiding the odd fire extinguisher that wasn't. Honey sat at one end of the table, her white-knuckled hands gripping the edges.

'I thought I could handle this. I'm not so sure now.'

Bill fell on to the bench beside her as the next wave rolled FREE to starboard. 'I'm going to the bridge. I want to look out. I don't like it below deck either.'

She nodded to him.

'Let's use the bridge-ladder behind the galley.'

Being inside the bridge-ladder was like being inside a vertical torpedo tube. It rose two decks with no escape except at top and bottom. In summer the Dutch crew entertained themselves by placing a mattress at the base and sliding down the ladder-rail to see who could clock the fastest time. In winter it was continuously moving and extremely dangerous. Bill clung tightly to the metal rungs and prayed Honey wouldn't fall back on top of him.

From the bridge the storm looked spectacular. Sheets of spray flew off cresting waves and crashed against the glass. Honey ducked when the first breaker hit, but stood up for the rest. The bow would disappear under the sea as a wave started to travel the length of the ship, rolling her in two directions before flipping the aft like whale's fluke. Forked lightning danced on the horizon, violently illuminating the sky; and everywhere, the sound of howling wind.

Another huge wave smashed into the port bow. The sound of scraping metal reverberated through the ship.

''Scuse me,' said the Captain as he bumped against Bill on his way to the communication pipe. 'Engine room! I need power!'

All on the bridge heard the reply. 'No can do, Skipper, we've got water down here! We're trying to find where it's coming from. Looks like an aft plate's sprung. Can you get me some pumps?'

'Right away!' Then to the crew, 'Svenson! Kurt!' The two seamen were down the ladder in a new record time.

'How bad is this, Captain?' Honey's voice was trembling.

'Nothing we can't handle.' The Captain sounded much calmer than he felt.

Another wave hit the port bow; more metallic noises, then a loud bang just below the bridge. Bill watched the anchor chain rise from the water, swing in an almost perfect arc around the bow and smash into ship's port side. Vourner handed him a walkie-talkie.

'I need your help, Mr Mason. Please go f'ward and report any damage.'

'I'll go, too,' offered Honey.

'You should go to my cabin, Miss Bogart, you'll be safe there.'

'I know more about the sea than he does, Captain,' she replied in an indignant tone. 'I'm going with Bill.'

They struggled down the bridge-ladder, through the mess-room, along the companionway and down the hatch to the lower deck. Approaching the f'ward hatch, they could see water sloshing around in the compartment in front of them.

'I'm going to look,' said Bill.

'Not 'till I tie you off!'

'What?'

Honey unravelled a fire hose from the bulkhead and tied one end around Bill's waist. 'In case anything happens, I can pull you back. And leave me the walkie-talkie.'

Bill handed her the communicator and kissed her cheek. 'Thank you.'

Once inside the empty compartment Bill could see the damage clearly. The broken anchor chain had fractured a join in the plating, leaving a two-foot gash just above the waterline. The intake was intermittent for the time being, but with every wave the ship took aboard another twenty gallons through the fracture. The ship lurched to port. Bill leaned forward into the water as it rushed against him and somehow kept his balance.

Honey tugged on the fire hose; Bill backed out of the compartment, slamming the door behind him and turning the lock-wheel to ensure the room would be isolated. He reported his findings to the Captain who told them to move aft to the engine room immediately, closing all the watertight doors behind them.

Svenson found the aft leak and sealed the damaged area. The Captain sent him to the transmitter room next, as Stan had reported damage to the aeriel lead.

'This is getting too hot to handle,' said Stan. 'I'm going to shut it down.'

'No need,' boasted Svenson. 'Just isolate the wire for a minute and I'll straighten it.'

'I'd rather shut it down.'

'Bollocks! Waste of time!' Svenson grabbed the heavy-rubber gloves from the workbench and walked to the transmitter. The ship lurched to starboard, then seemed to stop in mid roll as another wave smashed into the port side. The jolt sprang open the door guarding the left side of the transmitter at the same time as Svenson lost his footing and tumbled head first into the electronic field.

Stan grabbed his flashlight and shone it into the petrified face of Marik Svenson. The shock killed the seaman within seconds and shorted the ship's electrical supply instantaniously. Stan had never seen a dead man before. The total stillness, the frozen look of terror on his face, the vacant, empty eyes; he studied it all in unemotional silence. He knew he should feel shock and remorse at the sight before him, but he felt nothing; just the sensation of capturing mental pictures that would no doubt stay with him for ever. He turned his flashlight towards the door and began his perilous journey to the bridge, where Captain Vourner stood in darkness and contemplated his next move. His walkie-talkie crackled a message.

'Captain, this is Bill. What's happened?'

'Where are you?'

'Engine room.'

'Are Svenson and Kurt with you?' The Captain's mind plotted the next sequence of events with mercurial speed.

'Kurt is.'

'Let me speak to him.'

'Kurt here!'

'You'll have to start the standby generator topside. There's a lifeline rigged from hatch eight. Go that way.'

'Aye, Captain, right away!'

'How long for engine power?'

'A few hours yet, sir. Still two feet of water here.'

'Very well, Kurt. Let me speak to Bill.'

'Captain?'

'Go with Kurt to hatch eight and run a second lifeline for him. Do not, I repeat, do not go on deck. You'll find flashlights and flares in the bulkhead locker, Kurt will show you. Give a light to Honey and send her back to the bridge.'

'I'm okay here,' shouted Honey at the communicator.

'That's an order, Miss Bogart.'

Irritation was the order of the day in Eddie Lincoln's cabin. Last week he'd bolted an eight-millimetre projector to the top of his dresser and had been charging the crew five shillings a go to watch hardcore Dutch porn films. He'd just settled down to watch two stocking-clad women do disgusting things to a black man sporting a ten-inch shlong when the power died. He'd heard various bumps and thumps over the last few hours, none of which he considered his business. The storm would blow over by tomorrow. He drank the last third of a bottle of whisky in one go, turned face-down on his bunk and prayed he'd pass out.

Honey clung to a heating pipe on the lower deck, catching her breath before the final assault on the bridge-ladder.

'Honey! That you?'

Jonathan's voice reached out from the darkness. She shone her flashlight towards the source, picking up his silhouette framed in galley door.

'Yes! Over here!'

'Thank God you're safe. I went to your cabin.' His voice was filled with relief.

Their relationship had cooled even more over the last few months. Honey liked her new-found fame and the social whirl that accompanied it, Jonathan liked to stay at home and scan the short-wave band. Honey wanted to climb the tree of carnal knowledge, exploring each branch with youthful curiosity; Jonathan was becaming a one-way lover with ever-decreasing frequency. In September, he'd stayed ashore an extra week to cover the death of Albert Schweitzer; putting their shifts out of synchronisation and giving them only one week together in three. By November they were sleeping alone. But his concern today was touching and very much appreciated. They hugged each other in the shifting darkness.

Stan relayed the details of Svenson's death to the Captain with monotoned accuracy, the shock still evident on his face. The Captain gripped his shoulders.

'You'll be okay, I'll look after you. Now, you must answer me this. Was there any water in the transmitter room?'

'No.'

'Did you see any damage on the way here?'

'No. Yes! Some water's coming in through a smashed porthole in the mess-room.'

'Go to store room seven, just aft of the galley; you'll find steel porthole covers there. Take one to the mess and clamp it over the glass. I'll send Bill to help as soon as he's free.' Stan didn't move; Vourner shook him gently. 'It's us who must survive.'

Stan started down the ladder. 'Store room seven, yes, sir.'

Captain Jan Vourner had lived through countless storms and many dangerous moments during his thirty years at sea, but none compared with being powerless, holed and anchored in a North Sea gale with one dead man, three amateurs and four crew.

At hatch eight, Kurt strapped on his safety harness and tied one end of the nylon rope around his waist. 'I'll hook the harness on to the lifeline, so I should be okay, but if it breaks you pull me in on this.' He handed Bill the coil of rope. 'Wrap it round the hatch-handle a couple of times and pay me out.' As he opened the hatch a blast of wind nearly knocked both men off their feet. Kurt crossed himself. 'Tell the Captain I'm on the way.'

Vourner received the message and stared through the bridge window searching for his crewman. The standby generator was housed in a purpose-built steel casing roughly where the forward gun used to be. It would be dry and should start easily; the problem was crossing the thirty feet of open deck to get to it. Kurt made it to within ten feet when a huge wave crashed over the bow and sent him flying backwards to the hatch door. Bill caught him and the wave at the same time, sweeping them both through the hatch. Bill landed back-first against the bulkhead, temporarily winding himself but sustaining no real damage.

The second attempt succeeded. Kurt opened the small metal door and crawled inside. He primed the motor and pulled the starter cord; it fired first time.

The Captain watched the Dutchman slide back along

the rope to safety as the bridge lights slowly flickered back to life. He also watched the second anchor chain go slack, taut, then slack again. Honey and Jonathan joined him, followed closely by a drenched second officer.

'Number Two, you look decidedly damp.' For a few seconds laughter filled the bridge. 'We're dragging the second anchor.' The laughter stopped abruptly. 'I need power, Kurt. How much longer?'

Another loud bang on the port side. The ship lurched with the next wave but instead of crashing down into the trough, she rode the crest for a few seconds before rolling to starboard.

'We're drifting!' shouted the captain. 'I need power!' Then to Kurt, 'Get everyone in the engine room, move the forward pumps down there. If the engine room floods, we'll sink; if we can pump it dry and start the engines we have a chance.'

Honey struggled the length of both decks banging on cabin doors and relaying the Captain's order. There was no answer from Eddie, but she was past caring. Vourner radioed a Mayday giving damage and position before taking his place at the pumps.

In a warm, wooden-walled office in Admiralty House, Commander Willstead stopped sipping his brandy and studied the note his secretary had just placed on his desk. He lifted his internal phone.

'Get me the Postmaster General, failing that, his under-secretary. Quite urgent. Thank you.' He read the note again. His phone rang. 'Good evening, sir. Sorry to trouble you at this hour, but we've picked up a Mayday call. One of your pirates is in trouble; holed and drifting off Frinton. Should be well inside the limit by now.' Pause. 'Yes, sir. I can send a ship from Chatham first thing in the morning.' Pause. 'Thank you, sir. Goodnight.'

Stan was the only person excused pump duty. Kurt and Jonathan removed Svenson's body from the transmitter, allowing Stan to begin repairs; his goal was the breakfast show tomorrow. As he pieced together the broken circuits and bypassed damaged relays he felt a scraping sensation from the bottom of the ship; with the next wave it sounded louder, then came an almighty crash as the third wave deposited M.V. *FREE* on to the Gunfleet Sandbank.

In the engine room, the Captain signalled for quiet. The impact had thrown Honey against Bill, who fell roughly against the bulkhead. They both heard his left arm snap like a match.

'Captain! Bill's hurt! Quick!'

'One moment!' Jan Vourner closed his eyes and seemed to rock gently on his feet. The ship had stopped its wild pitching and now rolled amidships to port and back almost gently, like a piece of driftwood on the edge of a beach. 'We're aground,' he said. 'I would guess on either Buxy or Gunfleet sands.' He turned his attention to Bill. 'Let me see.' There was a large bulge on Bill's arm between his wrist and elbow. The Captain gripped his wrist tightly and pulled. The gruesome bulge disappeared and so did Bill, from the land of the conscious. 'Kurt! Todd! Splint the arm and get him to his cabin!' He turned to Honey who sat crumpled against the bulkhead supporting Bill's good shoulder, a look of anguished disbelief on her face. 'I had to do it. He'll thank me when it's healed.' Then to everyone in the room, 'We shouldn't move so much now, so it'll be easier to get around. Please continue pumping. To get off the bank I need the engines.'

*　　*　　*

As the twins were off the ship Emma didn't bother tuning in when she got home to Bristol House. She sat cross-legged on the bed listening to 'Rubber Soul' through headphones to stop the sounds of driving rain and roaring thunder from penetrating her world. The go-ahead for the spring survey had prompted a hectic afternoon followed by tea with Lady Heath at the Savoy. She was delighted to hear Emma's news and applauded her 'subject to your approval' line.

'One peg down in their estimation; ten pegs up in mine,' she'd said, smiling at Emma over the edge of a large and sticky Danish pastry.

The album side finished; Emma tuned in the Home Service for the nine o'clock news. Stories of the Soviet leadership, American space programme and Nobel Prize winners registered briefly in her mind as she scanned this week's Raver column for bits of gossip and possible mentions.

'Finally, there are reports tonight that FREE, the pirate radio station moored three miles off Frinton, has broken her anchorage and is drifting towards the coast. The Coast Guards say they cannot attempt to reach the stricken vessel until the weather improves; possibly tomorrow morning. The Navy has issued a statement saying if the ship is found in territorial water, she will be impounded and her crew face possible arrest for contravening the Wireless and Telegraphy Act.'

Emma's first thought was of Bill in jail; her second of him being hurt. Her third, of Stuart, fired her into action. She called his flat: busy! She threw her fox fur over her shoulders, her plastic see-through mac on top, and hurried outside into the storm. The Mini's windscreen wipers fought bravely against the torrent of wind and rain that buffeted the little car unmercifully all the way to Cheyne Walk. Emma's concentration on driving spared her the anguish of thinking about conditions on the helpless ship. She parked the car behind Stuart's Bentley outside Carlyle Mansions and leaned continuously on the entry-phone until he answered.

'I don't know any more than you,' he said as he opened the front door, his face drawn. 'I've got Gerald on one phone and Harwich on the other. I can't raise the ship. Nobody can!'

'Is anyone hurt?'

'I don't know. All we can do is wait.' He gave her a hug. 'Come in, have a warm drink. It'll be all right.'

Honey cupped a mug of hot chocolate in her hands as she sat in Bill's cabin and watched him sleep. It had been the longest night of her life. She, too, desperately wanted sleep, but, Stan had promised power by breakfast and there was no way Bill would be up to it.

The Captain had quietly told her of Svenson's death an hour ago and the full horror of what had happened was just beginning to hit her. She'd only been on nodding terms with the Dutchman, but the manner and proximity of his demise made her feel as if she'd lost a friend, regardless of the real relationship between them.

She walked through the mess-room and placed the empty cup carefully into the galley sink before making her way to the bridge. Kurt and Eddie Lincoln stood in the corner trying to ignite the first splif of the day. She ignored them. Outside, the last remnants of the storm fought for supremacy with the first light of morning. She could see the ship was listing badly to port, her bow gunwales only a few feet from the water. In front of her, spreading out like a huge balloon, the sands of Gunfleet lightened the dark sea. FREE had settled bow first on the edge of the sandbank. Honey looked astern; it looked to her like deep water.

'Can you get us off here?' she asked Kurt, ignoring Eddie completely.

'I think so, Miss. I'm just waiting for the Captain to give the word.'

Eddie seemed nervous and agitated. 'For fuck's sake, man, get us off this *now*! The fucking Navy's going to send at least a frigate if not a fucking fleet! We're inside the fucking limit!'

'Have you only the one adjective in your vocabulary?' inquired Honey, her voice dripping with sarcasm.

Eddie rounded on her furiously. 'Why don't you get on the fucking air and tell the world what's fucking happening instead of rubbing your tits and making fucking wisecracks?!'

She was about to destroy him with a line comparing his prick size to that of his brain when his logic struck home. That's exactly what she should do. This time *they* were the news. She smiled at the supply officer. 'Thank you, Mr Lincoln. That's the first useful thing I've ever heard you say.' She didn't hear him shout 'silly bitch' after her as she hurried down the ladder in search of Jonathan Gilby.

'We've got to get outside the limit!' Eddie grabbed Kurt by the collar. 'I've got drugs and porn on this ship belonging to some very heavy people. If we get busted I'm a fucking dead man!'

'You're a dead man if you don't let go of me!'

197

'EDDIE LINCOLN! Get off my bridge!' The Captain stood in the doorway, his eyes blazing with anger. 'Where were you last night?'

'Passed out in my cabin,' he replied with an air of cocky arrogance

Vourner realised the futility of retaliation when dealing with the likes of Eddie Lincoln. 'Just leave the bridge!'

Honey heard the transmitter hum into life as she gingerly crossed the slippery deck towards the f'ward hatch and Jonathan's cabin. That little genius Stanley, she thought, and broke into her first real smile in twenty-four hours. Jonathan's 'off-duty' sign hung lopsidedly from his cabin door. She knocked twice before going in.

'Go away,' came a muffled voice from under the covers.

'You've got to get up,' she said, sitting on the bed and gently shaking his shoulders. 'You've got to write me the best news story in the universe.'

Jonathan emerged from the covers, the magic word 'news' jolting him awake. 'What?'

'We're back on the air and we're big news this morning.'

They heard the throb of engines and the scrape of metal on sand as FREE slipped off the bank into deep water.

'Pass me my trousers!!'

Ten minutes later Honey sat in studio one and back-announced 'Day Tripper'. 'We went on an unexpected trip last night. Here with the details is Jonathan Gilby.'

'Good morning. One crewman died and Bill Mason was seriously injured last night when, during the worst storm in five years, Radio FREE broke its mooring and drifted on to the Gunfleet Sandbank two miles off Frinton. The ship sustained considerable damage when a broken anchor chain ripped a two-foot gash in her port bow. The vessel was refloated this morning and is now heading back outside the three-mile limit. We call on *Offshore One* to reach us as soon as possible as Bill Mason needs urgent medical attention. The name of the dead seaman is being withheld until next of kin have been notified. Stay tuned to 244, more details in half an hour. This is Jonathan Gilby, FREE news.'

Honey started 'Keep On Running' by Spencer Davis. She declined the voice-over.

Emma finally fell into a troubled sleep on Stuart's sofa at four in the morning after a night of anxiety. It took five rings before she pulled herself upright and answered the phone.

'We're back on the air!' Simon Street's voice resounded in her head. 'Lewis and I are coming to town, we'll meet you in Hayes Mews.'

'Give me an hour,' yawned Emma.

'We got through to the ship ten minutes ago.' Simon's voice sounded hesitant.

Emma sat bolt upright. 'What's wrong?'

'Bill's okay, but he's broken his arm. I wanted to tell you before you heard it on the news. He's asleep now. Honey's doing breakfast. One of the crew got electrocuted.'

'Badly?'

'Badly enough, he's dead.'

Emma knew what had to be done. 'I must go! See you later. Thanks for the call.' She replaced the receiver,

199

ran across the room, turned on the radio and scurried down the hall to wake Stuart. He was already awake and tuning his bedside transistor. Emma sat beside him as they listened to Jonathan's eight o'clock bulletin. The phone rang.

'Stuart Salisbury.'

'Gerald here. You've heard?'

'Yes.'

'The Navy's sent a frigate out from Chatham. It left an hour ago. It's going to be a close thing. Oh, listen to the Home Service; they might tail their news with it. I made sure they had the story.'

'You're a brick, old chap. Speak to you later.'

Stuart returned the radio to the BBC.

'. . . damage to the port bow. The ship, which broadcasts under the name Radio Free on 244 metres medium wave, is believed to be underway and steaming towards international waters. The Royal Navy has dispatched a frigate from Chatham Naval Base to intercept the vessel.'

Stuart retuned to 244 metres. Honey Bogart was flying.

'We've just heard the Navy are after us. Well, boys, you better hurry. According to our Captain we'll be over the limit in twenty minutes. Long live FREE!' She played 'Get Off My Cloud'.

The phone rang again, this time the *Daily Mirror*. Stuart dealt with it calmly. 'Our tug is on the way . . . All we know is Bill has broken his arm . . . Of course you can send somebody, Harwich dock around noon . . . If the Navy catch us we will surrender . . . Definitely no resistance . . . Thank you.'

No sooner had he put the phone down than it rang again. 'You get that. I'm getting dressed.'

'Emma Saxby. Please hold on.' Then to Stuart, 'I want to go to Harwich.'

Stuart hesitated, then saw her anxious expression. 'Charlie can drive you. Don't worry, it's only his arm.'

Emma smiled at him. 'Will you tell the twins where I've gone?' His answering smile made her feel much better; she picked up the phone. 'Sorry to keep you. How can I help?'

Captain Vourner stood on the bridge, trained his binoculars on the smoke stack closing on him from the south-west and prayed for God's help. FREE was listing badly to port, her starboard screw breaking the surface as it thrashed the sea. London and Caroline were still a good way off. He had to get in line with them to ensure he was outside the limit. 'Engine room!' he yelled down the communication pipe. 'I need more power!'

'We're giving you all we've got, Cap'n. Port engine's damn near off its mountings!'

'Very well, thank you.' He went back to his binoculars.

The Naval ship came within a thousand yards of FREE as she crossed the line. Massive cheers rang through the decks. Honey's blow-by-blow account was being heard by five million listeners, all the national press, a few disgruntled politicians and a very relieved Emma Saxby. When Bill came on the air and praised the crew for their efforts, thanked the listeners for their understanding and sent a message to Emma saying he was all right and he loved her lots, she indulged in a little cry of relief before answering the next phone call.

By noon, *Offshore One* was moored alongside FREE

and Emma was just north of Chelmsford happily dreaming in the back seat of the Bentley. She would make Harwich in time to see Bill to the hospital then, with any luck, be back in London by six o'clock in time for an interview she'd set up for him with the *Evening Standard*. Best of all, she'd sleep with him tonight.

Bill sat in Captain Vourner's warm cabin sipping a hot coffee. His roughly splinted arm throbbed continuously. 'A little more pain killer, if you please.'

The Captain poured a generous measure of whisky into his coffee before treating himself to a small swig from the bottle. His weathered face had gained a few more lines in the course of the night. 'I need those plates and an arc welder out here double quick. If the weather closes in again I can't guarantee she'll stay afloat. I also need another anchor; the little hook that's holding us at the moment won't survive a heavy bow wave, let alone a serious swell.'

'I'll see to it before the hospital. How's that for important?'

'Very good,' said the Captain, repeating the pain-killing exercise.

'What about Svenson's body?'

'A boat left Hoek Van Holland two hours ago. I've put him in the cold-store 'til they arrive. Not very respectful hanging him up next to a side of beef, I know, but it's the only cold place on the ship. I'll send him back to Amsterdam, he has family there. I've already spoken to his mother; not the most pleasant thing I've ever done.' Sadness crossed over his weary face.

'I'll leave my things here.' Bill tried to cheer him up, a small chuckle entered his voice. 'I should be back in a couple of days.'

The Captain put the top on the whisky bottle; his

mood remained sombre. 'I've got a feeling this is just a gap between storms, you might not make it back in time.' He sealed the order forms in a large brown envelope and handed it to Bill. 'That's why the repairs are so urgent. We may only have two, three days at most.'

Twenty reporters, three television crews and an extremely relieved, Emma Saxby watched from the dock as *Offshore One* entered Harwich harbour. Bill waited until the tug was secured before venturing out of the wheelhouse.

Emma scrambled down the ladder on to the deck, her joy at seeing him clearly evident on her face. 'Where can't I touch?'

'Left side.'

She cupped her hands around his face and kissed him tenderly on the mouth. TV lights went on, cameras clicked, questions were shouted. They were oblivious to everything save their own whispers.

The press followed them to the supply company, the hospital, even into the back of the Bentley where one reporter asked for a ride to London.

'Certainly not,' said Emma determinedly. 'He's been through enough. You people have been taking pictures and asking questions for over two hours. He's mine now, so you can all go home!' She shut the door politely but firmly. 'Let's get going, Charlie. We've got business in London.'

The *Evening Standard* interview led inevitably to drinks at Hayes Mews then dinner at Cheyne Walk. By midnight, Bill finally came to rest in his comfortable bed at Ovington Square. He was starting to drift towards sleep when he heard Emma giggling at the side of the bed. He opened his eyes to see her standing in front of him wearing a devastating black silk nightdress, her black hair and olive skin shining in the reflected street light through the window.

'I was just thinking. Now I've watched the nurse make a plastercast, I could have a permanent reminder of you for when you're on the ship.' She gave him a slow, deliberate wink.

'Emma Saxby! You're a wanton hussy with a groupie mentality! Injured or not, I shall have to punish you severely for your wicked thoughts.'

In one flowing movement Emma slid into the bed. 'Oh, jolly good!'

> *This is one from Johnny Dark,*
> *For all you lovers that come and park.*
> *The lights of Frinton twinkle on,*
> *Merry Christmas, everyone.*

Chapter 10

Friday, December 24, 1965.

Honey Bogart sat in the mess-room and relayed her disgust to anyone who'd listen; in this case a Dutch seaman who spoke no English and John Silver, the ship's mange-ridden parrot who sported a two-word vocabulary, the second being 'off'.

'I've been on this tub four bloody weeks, I'm going to be stuck here over Christmas, the boat's leaking and the heating in my cabin's packed up. Where's all the glamour they promised?'

'On dry land!' said Brian, misjudging the sea swell and stumbling into the room.

Eddie Lincoln followed close behind. 'You could make our Christmas a bit merrier by throwing a gang bang in your cabin.'

'And you can rotate on the first sharp object you see!'

Eddie knew she hated his swearing, so continued unabated. 'We could make a fucking fortune, you know that? I'll get them fucking stoned and you hook 'em for a fiver a fucking time.'

Honey's aim was uncannily accurate; the ashtray hit Eddie just below his belt.

'Bitch!' he shouted, taking one step forward.

Brian's outstretched arm stopped any more forward movement Eddie might have anticipated. 'We don't hit ladies, even if they are stuck up and straight.'

'Thank you, Brian,' she said, standing up with great dignity and leaving the mess-room feeling at least partly reconciled.

The decorations at Ovington Square made Emma feel distinctly Christmassy as she stood in the kitchen waiting for the kettle to boil. She'd spent more than she'd intended, but then Harrods was so close and their selection so much better. She'd bought a small live tree, which she'd placed between the two windows in the drawing room. Twenty silver icicle ornaments, an oversized silver star and a string of white fairy lights made it look slightly avant-garde in this traditionally furnished room. Emma redressed the balance by putting holly rings and Edwardian bunting around the walls.

She intended to plant the tree in the country after the holiday and looked forward to visiting it in years to come as a reminder of their first Christmas together. In the hallway, she'd pinned all their cards on to the wall opposite the front door, made a fir-branch and pine-cone centre piece for the hall table and placed the four-foot-high Santa, which she'd carried home with much laughter and a little help from Mrs Van Couman downstairs, beside the bunting-wrapped hat-stand to the left of the door. The bedroom she'd left bare with the exception of four massive sprigs of mistletoe that she'd sewn to the top of the headboard.

She poured boiling water into the log-shaped teapot and placed it next to the Father Christmas mugs on the tray – she'd stopped at nothing to make this a Christmas to remember. It was nearly noon and even on Christmas Eve Emma couldn't help feeling a little guilty for sleeping so late.

The last ten days had seemed an endless stream of parties, press and politics. Everyone wanted to talk to the survivor of the storm. Bill handled it all with humour and patience, but at last night's celebrity dinner in aid of the British Heart Foundation, Emma could see he was reaching the end of his tolerance. A plum-mouthed lady from Stowmarket asked him how he could *possibly* manage to stay on that *ghastly* boat when the BBC were *desperately* looking for handsome young men like him for the Light Programme. Emma sensed a scathing remark was a millisecond away. She squeezed his arm.

'I think the Light Programme is just desperate,' she'd said, smiling sweetly and giving his arm a slight tug. 'You must excuse us, Lady Cosgrave. We must see Stuart before he leaves.'

She carried the tray into the bedroom, the tea now complemented by a plate piled high with Scottish shortbread. Bill slept facing her, his plastercasted left arm outside the covers. She placed the tray on the bedside table and slid into bed.

'Tea's ready,' she whispered in his ear before letting her lips slide down his neck. He rolled on to his back. She kissed his chin. 'It's nearly afternoon, I've got a bit of shopping to do.' Nothing. 'Bill, sweetheart, wake up.'

'I'm awake where it counts.' Bill opened one eye, then closed it.

Emma moved her hand down his body. 'Well, so you are. Nurse Saxby here, Mr Mason, now this won't hurt a bit.'

Bill's cast knocked her head as he tried to put his arms around her. 'Sorry.'

'Just lie still!' Emma eased him into her, sitting back and placing both hands on his chest. She flicked her head backwards as the first sensations of entry surged through her body, then forward with her mouth open as the head of his penis searched deep inside. 'Oh, God,' she whispered. 'Just stay still, I'll do everything.'

He did as requested, closed his eyes, and allowed her to take total control. She rode him slowly and deliberately, taking more of him inside her with every movement. He felt too tired and uncomfortable to reach orgasm, preferring to let her thunder towards hers in her own time and enjoying the unselfish delight of giving pleasure to the woman he loved.

The decorations on FREE consisted of a few cards Scotch-taped to the cabin walls and a foot-high silver tree on top of the television. Since the storm Captain Vourner had fought a hard battle against the weather, the repairs and Her Majesty's Customs. It took two days for the pumping equipment, anchor and metal plates to clear customs and a further day to clear the workmen. The weather was always a threat but, luckily, didn't totally close in for six days. By that time repairs were completed, FREE had been stocked with Christmas supplies including a crate of whisky donated by Stuart and all manner of festive food sent by the nice folk at Hayes Mews.

Bill didn't make it back due to serious pressure from Emma, Stuart and the press department to keep him in town. On the boat he was one of the team; on land, he and Emma became London's Darlings. Parties, press calls and pub crawls; many pictures, quotable comments, mega-coverage. They were in the dailies daily and the weeklies weekly. Stuart wanted him on shore until January, Emma wanted him on shore for good.

The twins and Brian made it back to the ship, making it almost the full first team back on over Christmas. Honey would do breakfast, Brian the morning, Nigel and Peter the afternoon, and the twins from six until midnight; Howlin' Thomas and Prince Mikie would go through the night.

Nigel Hinkley pre-recorded his first half hour so he could sit in on Brian's 'name of the game' meeting. He sat between Honey and Peter at the mess-room table and watched Brian hold court.

'There's a million reasons why we're pissed off with this place, but that's not the point.' Brian placed both hands firmly on the table, commanding attention 'The point is we are here to entertain the British people over the holiday. The up-side is we have more listeners than the BBC, we have more talent than the BBC and you have the best chart in the world to work with.' Brian paused for any applause that might be coming his way. Nothing. 'However bad you feel off the air, when you're on I want nothing but happy budgies, okay?' Nodded agreement all round. 'The bitch-box is now empty, so let's have your Christmas woes and wanton thoughts and, as usual, I'll be awarding a bottle of whisky for the best line in profanity using over twenty words. This week's winner is Peter Robinson who thinks Winifred Atwell's 'Snow Bells' should be tied to her tits and launched over the side while her ankles are tethered to the anchor chain. Nice touch Peter. And you might like to know, boys and girls, that 'Snow Bells' has entered the national chart at number forty-two after extensive play on the Light Programme and no help from us whatsoever. Our featured album by The Who has debuted at number ten; so the BBC can f-f-f-fade away!'

Nigel didn't like Brian very much; he didn't know anybody besides Eddie who did, but he couldn't help but respect the way he could hold the jocks together in the face of extreme adversity and coax a performance out of them that was, in most cases, better than his own.

'By this time next year,' Brian was continuing, 'we'll all be on land, at the Ritz, boogieing 'til Boxing Day, *and* FREE will be legal.'

The DJs showed their reluctant support in several half-hearted ways, from a half-second smile from Honey to a whispered 'right on' from Prince Mikie. Given the choice, no-one would spend Christmas on this floating jukebox. There would be a brave attempt at Christmas dinner although it would cut across most of the jocks' on-air or sleep time. The ship stocked lots of extra booze, but no family or close friends to drink it with. Each of them around the table had somewhere better to go.

Brian hated the dismal cold weather and longed for cool, bikini-clad girls cooking hot barbie food on even hotter Australian beaches. The twins wished they were going down to the Wellington in Ilford for a Christmas jar with the folks and the lads before getting home as close to twelve o'clock as possible, because the Street family always opened their presents at midnight on Christmas Eve. It had been their tradition since the boys were five. Simon and Lewis had graduated from Coca-Cola to wine spritzers to sipping whisky on successive Christmas Eves at the Wellington.

Tonight they'd be on the air, but were determinded to keep the tradition going; tonight's show would come live from the Wellington Bar. Not the Wellington Bar,

Ilford, unfortunately, but the Wellington Bar, North Sea; consisting of a round tray loaded with two bottles of brown ale and three packets of crisps. Still, this was radio: a crowd effects tape, a few clinking glasses and who could tell the difference?

Nigel Hinckley and Peter Robinson had worked every Christmas for the last four years, so they didn't miss anything specific. They just had a general feeling that they could be having a much better time elsewhere. As junior members of the Light Programme and World Service respectively, they always landed the shit-shifts over Christmas and other public holidays: it was all part of paying the dues. At least this time they'd have some fun, a rare commodity within the walls of Broadcasting House.

Howlin' Thomas and Prince Mikie regarded themselves as vanguards of the new frontier, so each hour of radio time spelled music, message and culture to the lads from the West End. But before his show was through, Mikie offered a silent prayer for his mother and father, cruelly taken by cholera in 1952; while Howlin' Thomas spent an hour alone in his cabin, meditating on and missing his younger sister, his favourite in the family, who was currently living on an Indian reservation near Seattle, Washington.

Honey dreamed of the family home in Finchley and Christmas celebrations going on there without her. She remembered her mother's hugs of love two years ago, after she'd opened her present and held up a framed copy of the twenty-third psalm, which Honey had spent many happy hours embroidering. When she was seven, her father bought her a Labrador puppy called Sam for Christmas; and she recalled how she'd chased it around the house for days. Sam had died on Boxing

Day two years ago. Of all the jocks Honey would find it hardest to 'keep a smile on the dial' this Christmas.

Stuart drove the Bentley along the tree-lined driveway towards his parents' house. He could see his brother's Rover being unloaded at the front door.

'When you've finished that, James,' he shouted at the ageing servant while bounding up the thirty-one steps to the immense carved doors of Calbraith House. His mother greeted him in the entrance hall with the usual polite peck on both cheeks and an inquiry regarding any female guests he might have invited over the next three days. She didn't actually say female, but they both knew that was what she meant.

'I'm far too busy for girlfriends, mother. I'm married to the radio station for the foreseeable future.'

'You're never too busy to find a nice girl to share your life.' His mother frowned with disappointment.

Many years of subtle maternal interrogation had honed Stuart's responses to perfection. He considered it a game, to be played with the utmost finesse so as not to hurt her feelings and still come out the winner. Although the vast hall was totally empty, he whispered close to his mother's ear; 'There is a lady in London but she has her own family to go to.' He watched the sunshine return to her familiar wrinkled face. He would continue telling her his whispered fantasies for as long as she lived; or until there was a lady in his life who could take her place.

'Hail the Pirate King, returned at last from the sea!' His brother stood at the top of the wide oak stairs, his arms outstretched. 'Come to my study. I'm just about to open my present from dear Colonel Bradbury; excellent cognac, I expect!'

Stuart held his mother's hand. In a rare moment, he saw her at peace.

'Go to him,' she said. 'But don't you dare get drunk; your father will be home in an hour.'

Peter's study overlooked the maze and occupied the end section of the east wing. It embodied the breadth of his interests, incorporating a library, a film projection room, a small science lab and a large snooker table. The brothers embraced warmly and sampled the first generous glass of the dear Colonel's cognac.

'Superb, as usual,' said Peter. 'God bless the Bradburys, present and future!' He splashed another measure into both goblets. 'By the way, I'm getting married.'

Stuart spilled extremely expensive brandy over an equally expensive suit. 'WHAT?'

'With brandy this good, how can I refuse?'

'Camilla Bradbury?'

'Of course Camilla Bradbury.'

Stuart hugged his brother in genuine delight. 'Congratulations! You lucky bugger! When did you ask her?'

'I didn't.'

'You mean she . . .?'

'No. Father and the Colonel cornered me at the RAC; said I should think about settling down and how about Camilla?'

'They *what*?'

'That's what I thought at first, but the more I mulled it over, the more I liked the idea. They arranged a dinner for us and as we talked I realised she was thinking the same.'

Stuart was flabbergasted. His dear, honest brother talking of marriage as if it were a business deal. 'Do you love her? Do you even *like* her?'

213

'Dear, naive Stuart, it's not like you think.' Peter replenished his drink. 'Camilla and I have known each other since we were children. She has a lovely nature and shall make me an excellent wife. I venture we're far more sensible going into this sort of union than the majority of star-struck lovers who can't see past next week.'

'I'm sorry, Peter, but give me that star-struck week any time.'

'You are so lucky!'

Stuart turned slowly to face his brother, trying to place his luck in the same frame as Peter's wedding.

'You can afford to be romantic. I can't. The survival of your pirate radio ships and pop stars depends entirely on the success and stability of our base companies, you know. Peter spoke in a matter of fact tone, with no trace of bitterness.

For the first time Stuart heard the chairman of the board, not just his ever-supportive brother. The reality of Peter's position struck him suddenly; for a brief second he walked in his brother's shoes, and saw how much he'd taken for granted over the years. 'Are you going to be happy?'

'Another romantic question, but one worthy of an answer if I'm to gain the support of my best man.'

'Best man?'

'Of course! Now, listen. I've known Camilla all my life.'

'Me too.'

'Not like me.' He motioned to his brother to sit down before flopping into the green leather captain's chair behind his desk. 'When we were in our early teens we, shall we say, experimented with each other.' Stuart was about to interrupt. 'No, let me finish! We shared a

214

lot in our growing up and now we've spent ten years testing other waters. I think Camilla will make me very happy and I will try my best to reciprocate; furthermore, it leaves you to pursue the path of romantic endeavour free from the constraints of procreational duties.'

Stuart looked surprised for the second time. 'She's pregnant?'

'No, but I'm working on it.'

Stuart lifted his glass. 'You crafty toad. How long have you been "working on it"?'

'About a week!'

The King of the Pirates laughed with his brother, convinced that Peter was making, for him, the right decision. He felt at peace with the world. The Christmas spirit filled his soul as well as his glass. He looked forward with childlike relish to opening the pile of gifts waiting under the lavishly decorated fifteen-foot tree in the living room. He would enjoy the familiar ritual Christmas dinner, when frock-coated servants attended them in the ornate dining room with its massive crystal chandeliers and roaring log fire. He would even be able to cope with his father's muted sarcasm, his mother's timid restraint, and his own self-imposed loneliness. Christmas at the Salisbury's would always be an enforced obligation, but at least this year there was something real to celebrate; this year his beloved brother would find at least a modicum of happiness in the closeted world of Calbraith House.

Chapter 11

Thursday, April 14, 1966.

Emma adored the luxury of Stuart's Bentley, but nothing could compete with the zip and pace of her Mini when it came to sorting out London traffic. She changed into second gear and powered around Hyde Park Corner towards Park Lane. After three months of endless meetings, area promotional days and business dinner nights, her audience survey had been published yesterday; today the press would give their verdict. Up into third for Park Lane, down to second for the Curzon Gate lights. Getting agreement with the other stations had been an uphill struggle. Her relationship with Bill gave her a certain credence at the beginning, but she soon learned that hard-nosed businessmen talk hard-nosed business, and political pressure's fine as long as it's relatively cheap. Her argument had been, 'define cheap when compared with the money to be made legally'. When Reg Calvert, the new managing director of Radio City, finally agreed terms on the understanding that the stations would be listed in alphabetical order, she lost the battle to have FREE at the top of the list, but won the war of agreement. Third all the way down Charles Street, then second into the garage at Hayes Mews.

'I'm glad you're in, Miss Saxby. I can close the door

now; it's still a little parky in the morning.' Charlie's head appeared from under the Bentley. 'Mr Salisbury's in your office. Good news about the survey!'

'I haven't seen the paper yet.' She stopped half-way up the stairs. 'Charlie?'

Charlie was ahead of her request. 'Wood or coal?'

Emma smiled. 'Coal would be lovely. Thank you.'

'Well, young lady,' Stuart beamed from behind her desk. 'Ten out of ten!'

Emma took off her coat as she rushed across the office. 'Is it good? Let me see.' 'Pirate Radio Claims Huge Audience'. She read the headline twice before continuing out loud. '"Radio FREE, the new pirate radio station operating off Frinton, Essex, has a weekly audience of 10,500,000, according to a survey conducted by National Opinion Polls and published yesterday. Of the 2,360 people who replied to questions on day-time commercial radio, 23.8 per cent had tuned into Radio London compared with 20.9 per cent to Radio FREE, 15.6 per cent to Radio Caroline, 6.1 per cent to Radio Scotland and 4.2 per cent to Radio City." That's fantastic!'

'Did you give them Phil Birch's bit?'

'No. I knew he'd quote. Where is he?'

'Half-way down.'

Emma scanned the article. 'Here we are. "Asked about Government intervention against pirate radio, Mr Philip Birch, managing director of Radio London's sales organisation, said the Government was not likely to interfere with the supply of food and staff to the stations. If advertising on pirate radio was made illegal for British residents, he would seek advertisers from abroad."' She read the last line quickly. '"He would not state Radio London's present revenue, believed to be in excess of one million pounds a year."' She smiled at Stuart. 'This is brilliant! Philip's very clever. Just the right thing to say.'

'Read further down; the bit about BBC Scotland.'

'"The BBC Scottish service said yesterday it would be surprising if so many people had not heard Radio Scotland as their transmissions were very close to the Light Programme's wavelength and that some-times confused listeners. They do not intend to alter their programmes."' Emma roared with laughter. 'More fool them!'

'You've done a sterling job, Emma. First-class.' Stuart opened the hatch to the secretary's office. 'Too early for champagne?'

'Oh yes. I'm Bill-less 'til next week. A cup of tea would go down a treat.'

Eddie Lincoln sat on his bunk and treated himself to a new Swedish blue film. Mick Tasker was due out today and that meant his three favourite things; money, drugs and sex. The movie was in the way of a warm-up for the day ahead. He stretched out on his bunk and played with himself and the slow-motion switch. He heard the bump of *Taskforce Two* against the ship's side. He really hoped they'd brought the Japanese girl; she could keep him up for hours.

Mick Tasker stood at the helm of *Taskforce* and watched Eddie secure the gangplank to FREE's deck cleat. He made sure the bridge was empty and the decks clear before signalling Eddie to come aboard. 'Go see to Karen,' he said to a large stomach with small head attached. 'Make sure she's in full tackle. He likes all that stocking stuff.' He waited patiently for his guest to clamber aboard. 'Eddie, my old son, lovely to see you.' He put his arm jovially around Lincoln's shoulder and ushered him into the stateroom, pointing to the door at the far end. 'Through there is the best blow-job this side of New York City.' He handed Eddie a joint. 'Get this down you, then go and party. I'll see you in an hour. Let me have your keys; the boys and I will restock you while Karen sucks you dry.' They both laughed; Eddie in happy anticipation, Mick to disguise his real motives.

Making sure the coast was absolutely clear, Mick went on board FREE with four men, three large cardboard cartons and a briefcase containing five thousand pounds. He left twenty minutes later with three men and three different cartons.

Karen wasn't as good as the Japanese woman. Eddie din't get turned on until she posed in front of him and played with herself; opening her vagina and sliding two, then three fingers inside. She dropped to her knees before him. 'Put your big cock in my mouth. Watch me come on my fingers.'

He did as requested, his excitement quickening as he watched her wriggle and moan. She grabbed the base of his penis with her free hand and masturbated it vigorously. He closed his eyes as he reached orgasm so he didn't see her calculated finale. Mick Tasker did, along with the two crewmen he had working the camera equipment.

'A little word in your shell-like,' said Mick, offering the exhausted supply officer a cold tube of Carlsberg. 'I've got to leave a friend of mine with you for a few days. He's no trouble; just feed him. A boat will be along from France within a couple of days. I've put him in your cabin.'

Packets of anything that looked vaguely like supplies

were easy to deal with, but an extra person was another matter entirely. 'If the captain spots him I'll be in big trouble. Christ, Mick, this could ruin a great business!'

'It's not going to ruin anything. He knows to stay in your cabin, he goes nowhere; he can piss in your sink.'

The thought of that appealed to Eddie even less. 'I can't do it, Mick.'

Tasker's face darkened with lightning speed. He grasped Eddie's shoulder-length hair in his hand, holding it not tightly enough to hurt, but firmly enough to allow no escape. His voice was slow and menacing. 'You fucking can, old son, otherwise I'll make him the supply officer and relegate you to the fucking North Sea.' He tugged the hair. 'Understand?'

One on one, Eddie would probably lose. One on five was hopeless. 'All right! . . . All right.'

'That's better.' Mick let go of his hair. 'His name's Billy the Squid.' He handed Eddie a small white package. 'Some uncut flake for the two of you to get acquainted on. Now, be a good boy and fuck off.' Mick felt satisfied that he'd established his supremacy.

Eddie's bravery returned as he cast off the last nylon rope that kept *Taskforce* connected to FREE. He had a desperate urge to scream abuse at the short-assed cockney, put him in his place, teach him a lesson. Instead he waved to Karen, who sat, framed in the stateroom doorway, depositing a huge line of cocaine directly in the back of her throat. She didn't wave back. Eddie walked to his cabin to confront his lodger.

'Well fuckin' pokey, init?' greeted Billy as Eddie entered the cabin. 'I've seen bigger cells in Pentonville.'

'You'll be back there if you don't shut the fuck

up!' Eddie was a second away from losing his rag. 'What's the game? What kind of name is Billy the Squid?'

Billy swung his legs off the bunk and stood squarely in front of Eddie. He was just five foot one; in terrier terms, definitely more pit-bull than West Highland, his face scarred, his legs stumpy but muscular. 'The name of the game is a bank job that went wrong.' His eyes softened, a smirk cracked on his face. 'The name's fuckin' self-evident.'

The choice was Eddie's – be friends, or start a scrap he had no guarantee of winning. Eddie was a natural coward.

'What's in it for me.'

Billy opened the briefcase, extracted a wad of five-pound notes and tossed them at Eddie. 'Five hundred; half now, half when I leave.'

From that moment Billy the Squid could've been Jack the Ripper for all Eddie cared. He produced the packet of cocaine Mick had given him and tossed it at his new cabin-mate. 'Exchange is no robbery.'

At BHS House, Sir David Garman was exchanging roughly the same amount of money in expectation of some very privileged information. The land-based unit of FREE news produced most of its work at Centre Sound, a small facility off Oxford Street. Sir David's surreptitious meeting involved one of its part-time engineers.

'I want to be kept informed of all the major news stories they cover. Don't bother with pop or interest; just hard news, especially political pieces.'

The young man nodded his agreement and took the brown envelope.

Sir David had waited a long time for this development. He'd applied political pressure, he'd eavesdropped on FREE's business, he'd even tried stealing their clients by offering ridiculous discounts in the national press: nothing worked. Then, out of the blue, his finance director's son knew a school chum whose friend recorded things for FREE. The lad had been easy to bribe; an almost willing lamb to the slaughter. 'There's a phone number inside; use only that number, don't *ever* call me at the office. Do you understand?'

'Yes,' mumbled his informant, overwhelmed by the money and by what he was letting himself in for.

Garman dismissed the young man as he would swat a fly. 'My secretary will see you out.'

Emma dismissed her secretary to lunch with considerably more politeness. She sat at her desk, perusing *The Times* article and feeling very proud of herself indeed. This afternoon she'd meet representatives from the other stations to discuss the survey. The co-operative nature of the poll had not allowed her to fiddle FREE's position or in any way influence the areas covered. FREE's showing at number two, behind London but already eclipsing Caroline, was genuine proof that the format and the station were working. Most twenty-four-hour stations used the catch-phrase, 'we never close'; Emma came up with 'we're never going to close'. The twins made up jingles, the press played it up, and some politicians, notably Sir Robin Clarke, became extremely annoyed.

As there was no worthwhile land-based competition after midnight, Johnny, Thomas and Prince Mikie had cornered ninety per cent of the available audience.

223

Their on-shore shows at the Marquee and various suburban palais had increased awareness dramatically; their rhyming delivery served to disguise a lot of their real meaning, which confused Westminster and delighted their rapidly increasing army of young, under-the-bedcover fans.

Another press clipping from a local Essex paper caught Emma's eye. A Mr Sullivan from the education authority was complaining about the lack of homework being handed in at local schools because students were spending all evening listening to pirate radio programmes like the Street twins'. She cut the article out and placed it on the side of her desk. The twins would be in this afternoon; they'd know what to do. The phone rang.

'Independent Radio Committee; Emma Saxby speaking.'

'Hello, Emma, my name's Catherine and I've just got back from the ship.'

Emma didn't recognise the voice or the name. 'Are you from the agents'?'

'No, I'm just a fan. I went out on Daddy's boat for an over-nighter.'

'How did you get this number?'

'Your friend Bill gave it to me.' Her voice sounded haughty, almost mocking.

Emma was nonplussed. She suddenly felt detached from this conversation. 'Excuse me?'

'He also gave me a good seeing-to; your boyfriend's really quite hot.'

Disbelief was Emma's first reaction. 'What did you say?'

'You heard me,' answered Catherine, her tone bordering on hostility. 'Billy played rumpy-pumpy, rubbed my belly from the inside.' Then, with malevolence, 'Fucked me rigid all night!'

Anger swept over Emma. 'You're a crackpot! You've never even been to the ship! Now bugger off and leave me alone!'

'Wrong, Miss I'm-so-pretty Saxby. He's got a birthmark just above his pubic hair. How would I know that unless I'd had him in my mouth?'

Emma felt sick. She slammed the phone down. This could not be happening. She'd watched Bill closely in the company of other women. He'd always been polite and courteous, but he never flirted. She knew there had been opportunities for him to stray, none of which he'd taken. She had really believed he was different; but now this. It didn't make any sense.

The phone rang again. She answered in a daze. 'Hello.'

'Hi, you, it's Simon. We're ashore!'

'Oh, yes, ah, I'll see you later, then.'

'Are you all right?'

The thought of Bill with another woman had shattered all the logical processes in her mind. This woman had to be a crank. There was no way Bill would. . . . She must pull herself together. 'I'm fine, thank you; just busy. What time will you get here?'

'About two hours, as usual. Are you sure you're okay?'

'I could do with another six staff and an extra twelve hours a day. I must go, see you later.' She replaced the phone. It rang again. She flicked on the answerphone; the caller hung up.

The feeling of triumph that accompanied the *Times* article had vanished. She sat at her desk, angry, hurt; unable to grasp any truth, either in Catherine's story or

Bill's infidelity. Her mind was racing. Tomorrow she'd go to the ship, see him face to face, then she'd know.

Her meeting with the other independents passed like a dream. She tried to wipe Catherine's call from her mind but it kept surfacing, spoiling her timing and denting her concentration. Everyone seemed more than pleased with the survey; even Radio City, who came out worst, sang its praises and put forward a motion to repeat it on a regular basis.

The twins arrived at Hayes Mews shortly before three o'clock and brought the meeting to a premature close. Emma noticed, with some alarm, that the representative from Caroline was more than a little interested in what kind of contract the twins had with FREE, and for how long. Simon told them it was for ever; Emma made a mental note to inform Stuart.

'Any chance of me using the second bedroom at Ovington Square tonight?' asked Lewis.

'We've a couple of hot dates,' continued Simon. 'Lewis's date doesn't have her own flat.'

Emma had toyed with the idea of staying with her mother in north London tonight; the twins' request made up her mind. 'Have the whole flat. I'll be out tonight and I'm going to the ship first thing in the morning.'

'Brilliant!' exclaimed Simon. 'We could both stay at the Square!'

'Who are these hot dates?'

'Mine's called Beth,' said Simon. 'She has a flat in Fulham, at least we'll have a choice.'

'I've no choice,' said Lewis. 'Catherine lives in Ipswich.'

Emma refused to register the name. It could be a different person. If it was her mysterious caller, it only proved she was a groupie. She felt a change of subject was the only safe course. 'What do you think of this?' She passed them the Essex clipping.

The twins read the article. 'Fabulous!' exclaimed Simon. 'Let's do a revision spot and help the poor blighters through the term.'

'Great idea.' Emma tried hard to inject real enthusiasm into her voice.

'I'll work on it tomorrow,' said Lewis. 'Can we offer you a lift to Knightsbridge? We have a car downstairs.'

Emma showed the twins the ins and outs of Ovington Square. She was tempted to wait and meet Catherine but decided that could be a bad and very embarrassing move. She drove her Mini through the rush-hour traffic to her mother's place in Southgate. She hoped she'd made the right decision. She'd usually talk to Avril about any trouble in her love life or, failing that, one of her sisters. Her mother tended to be more critical than helpful; a trait Emma had learned to sidestep when searching for the truth. By midnight she'd finally plucked up the courage to tell her the story.

'It's probably a different woman,' concluded Mrs Saxby. 'There are thousands of Catherines in England. This Bill Mason, has he got nasty habits?'

'Nothing I can't deal with.' Emma laughed for the first time since the phone call.

> This is Prince Mikie on 244.
> We jive you less and give you more.
> If somethings buggin' you tonight,
> I've got the sounds to put it right.
> Love is love, and that's a fact.
> Here's Uncle Otis. Can you dig that?

By nine the next morning, after a restless night, Emma was driving out of London against the traffic on her way to Harwich. She listened with detached professionalism as Bill handed over to Brian Todd. She didn't want to hear his sexy voice, his lies, his excuses. She turned the radio off.

The sea remained glassy calm as the tug gently touched the aft-quarter of FREE. Emma looked for Bill on deck; only Captain Vourner was visible at the railing. He welcomed her on board with a broad smile and a firm handshake. She hadn't been aboard since last autumn. The fresh coat of paint made the ship look almost new.

'How nice to see you, Miss Saxby. Please, come to my cabin, I have something to discuss with you.'

The Captain never gave anything away in front of the crew; the years of diplomacy had developed into an art form. 'Is Stuart coming out to the ship in the near future?' he asked, handing her a welcome cup of strong, hot coffee.

'I don't believe he has any immediate plans,' she answered.

'I must ask you to take him a message.'

Emma's thoughts were so wrapped up with the Catherine and Bill scenario that she'd failed to notice the tension in the Captain's voice. Only when he'd delivered his next statement did she tune into his concern.

'I'm worried that we may have a problem on this ship which could lead to major intervention by the authorities.'

'What problem?'

'I've known from the start that Eddie Lincoln was the type of character who would get involved with, shall we say, contraband activities. I've turned a blind eye to his selling of ship's stores to the crew, because, in spite of that, he actually does a decent job. But I also suspect him of running drugs through that Mick Tasker fellow, although I can't prove it. Things have now moved up a peg; I think he's using the ship to harbour criminals on the run from the British police. Again, I have no proof, but if I'm right in my suspicions, we have a potentially explosive situation which could endanger not only myself but also the future of the station.'

Emma was shocked. 'How do you know?'

'I don't, for sure. Yesterday, four men from *Taskforce Two* came on board and I only saw three depart. They always watch to see the bridge is empty before their comings and goings; they don't realise I can see most of the upper deck from my cabin. If I do a search and find the man, he'll only say he's a visitor from Frinton who's missed his ride home. Even if I could prove the lie, I can do very little about it unless I have full back-up from Stuart.'

'What kind of back-up?'

'Either through Interpol or striking a deal with the British Customs. I'll also need an independent witness on board to corroborate the findings. The only two people I'd trust are Mr Mason and Miss Bogart; the rest are either part of the plot or too nervous to speak.'

'This is outrageous. I had no idea this was happening here.'

'I quite understand. There's no reason you should unless you're involved.' The Captain refilled her coffee. 'There's very little I can do when Stuart's policy is to have an open ship. I realize he wants the station to be welcoming to legitimate visitors, but we must do something about Tasker before it gets out of hand.'

Emma sipped her drink. 'I'll tell Stuart as soon I get back to London.'

'Thank you. Now on to nicer things. Congratulations on the survey.' A knock on the door. 'Come!'

''Scuse me, Captain. Would you like your cabin cleaned today?'

'No thank you, Mo. It would be a great help if you could escort Miss Saxby below to Mr Mason's cabin.' He smiled at Emma. 'I'm sure she's anxious to see him.' Emma couldn't help feeling amused by the understatement.

Bill lay on his bunk chuckling over a piece in the Raver Column. '"Tony Windsor to take over as head of programmes at Radio London." Got you guys worried,' he mused to himself.

'Worried about what?'

He looked up and saw Emma standing in the door-way. 'Baby! What a great surprise!' He covered the cabin in three strides and held her before she could utter a word. He looked over her shoulder at her escort. 'Thank you, Mo, that will be all.' He kicked the door shut and began manoeuvring Emma towards the bed.

'Just a minute, Mr Mason.' She wanted him so badly; she wanted him to tell her he loved her, to hold her, to make her forget the Captain, the radio station, the phone call. She pulled away from him.

'What's the matter, baby?' He held her hands. 'You didn't say you were coming out. What a wonderful surprise! How long can you stay? Overnight, I hope.'

'I would have thought you'd had enough overnights for one week!' She felt totally divided. Unproven jealousy battled with sweet, unconditional love, but jealousy was winning. 'Catherine called me at work yesterday.'

'Catherine! Catherine who?'

'Catherine with her daddy's boat, who stayed here two nights ago. Catherine who does blow-jobs! Catherine who knows about your birthmark!'

'I don't know any Catherine!'

His eyes dropped away from her gaze. To Emma that was proof of his guilt; her right hand caught him square on the cheek. 'Liar!!'

The shock left Bill speechless. He stared at her in disbelief.

'Men are all the same!' Emma felt generalisation was the best defence. 'None of you can pass up a piece of skirt with size fourteen lips!'

'I don't know any Catherine!' insisted Bill. 'I don't know what the hell you're talking about!'

The ship's tannoy broke through their argument. 'Tug leaves in five minutes.'

'And I don't believe you!' shouted Emma, completely taken over by her conviction of his guilt. The thought of another woman having sex with him, however brief and mechanical it may have been, made her feel dirty. She wanted to be away from the ship, from him, from this whole seedy business. 'I'll have my things out of your flat by tomorrow. Please have the courtesy not to compromise our business relationship by making a scene. I'm leaving now.' She walked into the hall, turned, and saw him standing by the bunk; his face a picture of surprise and remorse. 'Goodbye, William.'

She remained falsely jolly on the return trip to Harwich, joking with the tug's crew and brewing endless cups of tea. She drove the Mini blindly down the A12, pulling off the road just north of Kelvedon to let her tears take control.

*   *   *

'What's wrong with you?'

Honey's voice pierced Bill's misery as he sat on his bunk staring blankly into the sink. Memories of the stinging slap, the bitter finality of her words, her unstoppable fury, flashed through his mind in a confused whirl. In the past, before Emma, he'd been caught once or twice by women who thought they had an exclusive claim on his time; somehow he'd always managed to say goodbye with a modicum of panache and style. This time he was innocent; this time it hurt like hell.

'She's left me.' His voice was flat.

'Emma?'

'Yes.'

Honey sat down next to him on the bunk. 'Oh, Bill, I am sorry. Why? Another man?'

'Another woman.'

'Mason! You asshole! How could you do that?!'

'I don't think I did.'

'Get real!'

'Straight up, Honey. Do you remember a woman called Catherine? Apparently came on board two nights ago?'

'Was that her name?'

'You do remember her?'

'I remember a crazy, long-haired groupie with big eyes, who came into the studio, half naked, and asked me to come on her boat to make up a foursome with Brian and Eddie. I told her to piss off.'

'That must've been her. She called Emma in London and said she'd spent the night with me; even told her about my birthmark.'

'Sounds interesting. Want to tell me about it?' Honey saw no humour in his face. 'I'm sorry. Go on.'

'Prince Mikie and I sawed a bottle of Jack in half that afternoon. I don't remember anything past tea-time. I was out for the count in my cabin. She must have come in and had a good look at me – and God knows what else she did. He groaned.

'My professional opinion is,' she said, slapping both hands on his knees, 'that you're probably the only jock who didn't spike her. At one in the morning she had Charlie Bare across the mess room table. I walked straight through; pretended not to see.'

Bill kissed her full on the mouth. 'You lovely lady. You must tell Emma; call tonight, ship-to-shore.'

'Tell her what? A groupie worked the ship but missed the star? She'll never believe it; I'm not sure I do.' His expression reminded her of an injured puppy, helpless, lost, homeless. She had to take pity on him. 'I'll try; as long as you show me your birthmark.' Bill stood up and undid his belt. 'Only kidding, sweetheart.' She walked to the door, then turned and smiled mockingly at him. 'Men!'

'Bureaucrats!' shouted Simon, as he slammed the phone down and gazed despairingly at his brother. 'We offer to cover all the subjects *and* make them fun to learn; they say they can't help us because we don't exist.'

Lewis disconnected the recording device from the telephone. 'I'll bet our listeners get a laugh out of it, though.'

'Out of what?' Stuart asked, as he strode through the office on the well-worn route to the drinks cabinet.

'The conversation we've just had with a lesser-spotted pin-stripe from the education ministry.'

Stuart plunked two ice cubes and splashed a goodly

measure of single malt into a crystal tumbler. 'More material for the Saga?'

'This is for real,' said Simon. 'Pour us one of those and we'll tell you.'

He did; they talked. All three agreed that the phone call should go out unedited; then it should be cut for the Saga.

'The Never-Ending Saga of the Universe and Mother's Recipe for Apple Pie' was a daily satire produced by the twins from news stories, interviews, film sound-track; anything they could lay their hands on. It had nothing to do with the universe or apple pie, but everything to do with off-the-wall radio and taking pot-shots at the establishment. Stuart loved it and encouraged the twins to push the boundaries of acceptability ever outward. The characters included Harold Winsome-Losesome, Edward Teeth, Anthony Wedgewood Cupandsaucer, the Archbishop of Thurrock and the narrator, Ivor Plumbinmymouth. The ratings were sky-high; John Walters charged a twenty per cent premium for the middle commercial break.

'I feel a new character coming on,' said Lewis. 'Cuthbert Scrotum, the scourge of Whitehall. His main purpose is to fail as many students as possible.'

'And place the blame on somebody else,' continued Simon. 'We could cut the line "you don't exist" out; that's all he says, the rest is narrative.'

'Wonderful!' Stuart raised his glass. 'To Cuthbert Scrotum, long may he tickle the armpit of establishment!'

Chapter 12

> *Howlin' Thomas is back from town,*
> *fillin' you in with what's going down.*
> *Check out the news with Jonathan G,*
> *the Parliament's open to radio FREE.*

Emma sat on her now unfamiliar bed at Bristol House and listened to the phone's insistent ring. She knew it was Bill. He'd come off the boat today and would have arrived at Ovington Square around tea-time. The phone calls started just after seven.

Bill replaced his phone and read her letter for the twentieth time.

Dearest William,

I've moved my things back to Lower Sloane Street. Honey told me the story and I'm sorry I jumped to what seems to be the wrong conclusion; at the moment I can't live with the fact that I jumped at all. I need time to work this out. Please try and understand.

Love, Emma.

He folded the letter with a sigh and placed it on the bedside table. Tomorrow he would deal with this. Tonight he must sleep; he knew that would take at least a bottle of whisky.

The news department didn't get much sleep as they toiled late into the night preparing what they hoped would turn out to be the best hoax of the year.

'And as the state coach leaves Buckingham Palace and slowly makes its way down the Mall towards Horseguards Parade, Her Majesty, accompanied by the Duke Of Edinburgh, waves to the hundreds of people lining the pavement between the Mall and the beautifully kept gardens of St James Park.'

The next morning Jonathan Gilby listened to the taped report with great satisfaction. The state opening of parliament was being televised for the first time and he was determined that FREE would have radio coverage to compete with the BBC, by fair means or foul. George Cunningham, his London reporter, had done an excellent job voicing and producing the report, complete with sound effects of horse-drawn carriages and cheering crowds. It was a cheat, but it was a good one. He would defy anyone to say it wasn't live. All that remained was to get the timing right. He would watch the procession on television and put his piece out synchronised to the pictures. He fast-forwarded the cartridge until it cued itself to the beginning, ejected it from the machine and walked to the on-air studio where Brian Todd was talking up the scoop of the week.

'Another first for FREE. This morning we bring you live coverage from the House of Commons where the Queen will shortly be opening the new session of Parliament; but first, the new number one on the FREE forty, The Who and "Substitute".'

As the record ended Jonathan signalled he was ready. He'd moved the television from the mess-room to studio one and, although the reception wasn't the best, it was good enough to do the job.

'Following Labour's victory at the polls with a ninety-six seat majority, the new Government has promised sweeping changes for Great Britain. We'll hear some of those changes in about an hour when the Queen delivers her speech to the House of Commons. As she leaves Buckingham Palace we go over to George Cunningham in the Mall.'

'Fuck the Queen! Fuck the monarchy! F . . .'

Brian ejected the cartridge with a lightning reflex. 'We seem to have the wrong report! Here are the Beach Boys.' As the music started the two men stared at each other in disbelief. 'Jeez. Jono! What was that?'

Jonathan snatched the cartridge from Brian's hand. 'Don't say another word; it never happened. Okay?'

'Sure, boss, whatever you say.'

At Hayes Mews the phones went mad. Stuart shouted at everyone from his office. 'Just apologize and say we're looking into it! All press calls to myself or Emma!' He ran across the roof corridor to her office.

'I heard it!' she shouted over the sound of all three phones. 'I think we shouldn't answer anything 'til we know what happened.'

'We can't just let them ring!'

'Why not? Only three people are getting ringing tones, the rest are getting engaged. Get Jonathan on ship-to-shore!'

Stuart saw the sense of her plan. He ran back to his office, where his private phone was ringing 'Stuart Salisbury.'

'Becket here, from *The Times*. Can you comment on what's just happened on your station?'

'Mr Becket, I will be more than happy to comment as soon as I find out myself. Thank you for calling.' He held the line-button down for five seconds, let go and, to his immense relief, heard a dial tone. It took five minutes to raise the ship.

'We've been nobbled!' yelled a frantic Jonathan Gilby. 'There's a second track on the tape. It didn't cue in production; well, it did, but I thought we were at the front of our report. Over.'

'Whose voice is it? Over.'

'No-one I've heard before. My guess is it's some joker at Centre Sound. Over.'

'Send the tape to London on the afternoon tug and say nothing and I mean nothing. We're being swamped by press; I'll try to hold them off but this doesn't look good for us unless we can find out the name of this asshole and feed him to the papers. Over.'

'I don't think we should talk on this link. I'll write you a note with the tape. Good luck, Stuart. Over and out.'

Stuart walked back to Emma's office quietly cursing the timing of this whole affair. His one political ally was in the House for the Queen's speech; he'd get no help from Gerald until early evening. Emma sat behind her desk, phones off the hook, staring at the empty fireplace.

'This is a deliberate act of sabotage,' she said, without shifting her gaze.

'Emma's secretary poked her head through the wall-hatch. 'I've got the *Express*, *Evening Standard* and *The Times* holding on for you.'

'Names?'

'Gerald Harmer from the *Express*, Barbara Pollard from the *Standard* and John Becket from *The Times*.'

'Thank you, Jeanette. Tell them I'm out.'

The girl nodded and disappeared through the hatch, closing it behind her.

Emma was thinking furiously. 'Too many people knew about this too quickly. Why should top political journalists be listening to a pop pirate during the state opening of Parliament?'

'They were tipped off!'

'Exactly. I smell Sir Robin Clarke.'

'He wouldn't dare!'

'One of his minions would, and what's more, they're inside our production team.'

Stuart pondered the scenario. 'We must get out of Centre Sound.'

'Immediately!' She opened her phone book at 'L'. 'Radio London has a small production facility in Curzon Street. We can rent that for a few days.'

'Are you sure they're not behind this?'

'Emma closed her book and caught the managing director in her serious gaze. She could see his concern developing into paranoia. 'If we could, we'd kick the stuffing out of each other in programming terms, but I don't believe London, Caroline or any of them would resort to dirty tricks against another independent.'

Stuart's face relaxed, and he managed a faint smile. 'I hope you're right. Go on, make your call.'

Bill dragged himself through the haze of whisky induced unconsciousness to answer his phone. He pulled the hand-set under the bedcovers and grunted into the mouthpiece.

'Bill, this is Emma. You sound drunk.'

'I've got woman trouble. What do you want?'

'I've got station trouble. I need your help.'

He felt a sudden surge of anger. To be falsely accused

of infidelity had been bad enough; to be cut off by the woman he loved with a three-line letter even worse, and now this same woman was calling to ask his help without so much as a how are you. No, thank you very much. 'This is my time off!' he shouted, his head pounding with every syllable. 'Get someone else to do your dirty work. I'm sure you can find some sucker among your army of admirers.' He slammed the handset down on the cradle, turned over in the bed and held his throbbing cranium with both hands.

He drifted in and out of sleep for at least an hour. He kept waking with thoughts of the station scratching at his mind; pictures of Emma laughing and loving him in this very bed, making love in the Mini, feeding him shortbread at Christmas. As he entered the next soporific drift he became aware of a presence in the room; a thief, a murderer perhaps, either way he didn't care.

'I'm sorry. Can you forgive me?'

He flipped the covers from his face. Emma stood beside the bed, her deep brown eyes full of remorse; a shaft of daylight from the half-drawn curtains catching the tear running down her cheek.

'You'll have to marry me,' she whispered.

Bill watched the tear fall from her chin and land on the curve of her breast. He felt he should prolong the agony; make her pay for not trusting him. But his overwhelming feeling was relief. Relief and love. 'I guess I will,' he answered, opening the covers.

Within seconds it was as if they'd never been apart. All the unhappiness and guilt of the previous week melted away as they made love slowly, passionately and uninterrupted for three hours. They were reunited in sexual harmony; holding, stroking, caressing, their eyes never leaving the other. By mid afternoon Bill had lost his hangover; Emma, all idea of time.

Bill ran his hand down the curve of her back. 'So what's all this trouble at the station?'

Emma moved closer into him; she wanted to mould herself to his body, be totally close. 'Let someone else worry about it for a change.'

'That's very unprofessional.'

She buried her face under his chin. 'Yes it is, and you know what? I don't care.'

'Tell me,' he begged mockingly.

She squeezed him. 'You're terrible.'

'Tell me.'

Bill's position in the bed changed as the story unfolded. By the time she'd relayed the tale of her last interview with John Becket he was sitting bolt upright. 'What now?'

'There's nothing more I can do 'til tomorrow. I've stopped the *Standard* tonight, but that's only postponing the inevitable.' She clipped him lightly behind the ear. 'We've been set up. Time to grin and bear it.'

He pushed her shoulders flat on the bed. 'In that case we'd better get a takeaway.'

Emma put on her best business-like tone of voice. 'Harrods, sweetheart. I'm starving!'

They ate their spare-ribs, roast lamb and profiteroles in bed, washed them down with a bottle of Nuits-St-Georges and listened to the twins take unmerciful mickey out of the educational bureaucracy.

'That's the way it happened, we haven't changed a word, have we Simon?'

'Not a word. We tried to help, kids, but they won't let us.' Lewis switched into his Captain America voice. 'The only thing that can save this grievous situation is for us to obtain the exam papers and give each and every one of you the answers.'

Simon in his BBC voice. 'And as that is highly unlikely, here is another selection of recorded music featuring that popular vocal group from Liverpool, the Beatles.'

Stuart Salisbury ordered Creole roast lamb and another bottle of vintage Château Cos D'Estournel from the evening-suited waiter at Tiberio and finished off his account of the day's events. 'The whole thing's a mystery, Gerald. Emma thinks Sir Robin's behind it.'

'Highly unlikely, old chap. Far too dangerous for him to be involved. I think you should look to the commercial side; maybe another pirate.'

'Emma says no and I tend to agree. This reflects badly on all of us.'

'Gerald, dear fellow! How are you?' The resounding voice belonged to a tall, grey-haired, sombre-suited, middle-aged man standing beside the table.

'David, how nice to see you. May I introduce Stuart Salisbury, managing director of Radio FREE. Stuart, this is Sir David Garman, chairman of Branford, Hedley and Stowe, one of our leading publishing houses.'

The two men shook hands. 'Pleased to meet you, Stuart. I've heard a lot about your enterprise, most of it good. I gather a small hiccup today with the Queen, but then, the road to success is often peppered with a few potholes of bad luck; serves to keep us on our toes.'

Something about the man made Stuart feel uneasy. He was arrogant; that was to be expected from a middle-aged company chairman. He was opinionated; another senior management trait. This was more a gut feeling that told him to be very careful of what he said to Sir David Garman. 'It seems the whole world and his sister knows about our little mishap. I had no idea we were that popular.'

'Dear chap, it's the talk of Whitehall. It's not every day some one demands intercourse with the Sovereign. I wouldn't be surprised if questions are asked.'

Gerald gestured towards the spare seat at the table. 'Surely it doesn't rate House time; anyone can see it's simply a sick joke, a prank too far, nothing to do with the station itself.'

The BBC builds its studios underground and employs several layers of security to ensure pranks like that are not perpetrated on subjects of the realm.' He signalled rejection of the offered seat. 'I'm dining with the Montgomerys; maybe another time.' Then to Stuart, with a patronising smile, 'Let's hope the press is kind to you tomorrow morning.'

Both men watched him walk away and sit down with seven people at the far end of the room.

'I wouldn't like to cross him,' said Stuart, sipping his claret.

'You may be too late with that wish. If anyone would like to see the pirates sunk, it's him. He's a traditionalist Tory, not many of them around, thank God; believes in free enterprise as long as it lines his coffers. Doubt if he takes too kindly to young upstarts like you making a million a year tax free.'

The food arrived; succulent meat arranged in line down the centre of the plate and covered with a spicy garlic, thyme and tabasco sauce; perfectly cooked vegetables served over warmers in the centre of the table.

Stuart helped himself to glazed carrots and peppered peas. 'Do you think he could be behind this plot?'

'Perm any one from ten.' Gerald spooned a hefty

243

portion of Pommes Anna on to his plate. 'He's definitely not your friend.'

'I think it's time for my brother to enter the game.'

'Can he compete with the likes of Garman and Clarke?'

'On a good day he can compete with the Queen.' Stuart's expression left no room for doubt. 'Pass the potatoes.'

> *Johnny Dark with the quality rap,*
> *It looks like the news staff are getting the sack.*
> *First I'm playing the number-one song,*
> *then I'll groove witcha all night long.*

Emma awoke just before eight o'clock and reached over to find the other side of the bed empty. She heard comforting noises from the kitchen. Breakfast soon, she thought as she drifted back into contented sleep.

'Good morning, campers! It's good news and bad news time here at Camp Ovington.'

Bill stood fully dressed beside the bed holding a tray brimming with scrambled eggs and smoked salmon, hot buttered toast, and a large pot of fresh coffee. Tucked under his right arm were the morning papers.

Emma sat up slowly. 'Is it ghastly?'

He smiled at her. 'They're only newspaper articles.'

'That bad, eh?' She held out her hand. 'Let me see.'

'Radio Pirate Insults the Nation' – the *Express*; 'Obscenity on Pirate Insults the Queen' – the *Sketch*; 'Pirate Fiasco as Wrong Tape Goes to Air' – the *Mirror*. The most damaging of all from *The Times*: 'Lack of Government Control Allows Pirate Station to Broadcast Obscenity'. Emma dropped the papers on the bed and looked up at

Bill as if believing he could make them disappear. 'This is terrible.'

'Look at the cartoon in the *Mirror*.'

'Tell me.'

'A picture of the Queen on the bridge of a warship that has just blown FREE out of the water. The captions reads, "No-one speaks to One in that manner".'

'God, what a mess.' Emma sipped her coffee. 'I should phone Stuart.'

'Already have. He's on his way over, so you'd better get dressed.'

Stuart's temper was approaching white hot as he parked the Bentley in Ovington Square. He felt ashamed to be part of the station that had let loose such profanity, bitterly disappointed that his professionals had allowed it to happen, and most of all, furious at himself for not spotting it a mile off. His only hope now was that the Gods would spare him the humiliation of meeting anyone he knew.

He made it to the sanctuary of the sitting room; Emma served him coffee with a sympathetic smile, Bill hung his coat up in the hall.

'I wouldn't get that upset.' Bill sat beside him and tried the brave front approach. 'It'll blow over in a few days.'

'Not for me.' Stuart clasped both hands behind his head and stretched upwards; he let his breath out slowly as if in an effort to release tension. 'Anything else I could ride, but not this. I have to fight to clear my name.'

'I never realised it meant that much to you.' Emma looked at Bill. 'Did you?'

'Not at all.' Then to Stuart. 'If I were to say it's only a radio station, would that help?'

'It would make me smile, for which I thank you, but whoever did this came into my home; shot me in the study, so to speak. The main reason I wanted that story featured was to keep Mother happy. She would've loved to hear the tapes, gone off to all her friends and told them what good chappies we are; the friends would tell their husbands, and FREE gets a better image in the House of Lords. Now, the reverse has happened. My family will regard this as highly offensive, and I agree with them.'

Emma walked behind Bill and leaned on him, her arms sliding round his waist. 'What can we do to help?'

'Just being here is help enough for the time being. My brother is scrounging round his pals to see what he can find out; I'll wait to hear from him. I've given him this number.'

'Fancy some good news?'

'Only a printers' strike would be good news.'

'Bill and I are getting married.'

'Good God!! Congratulations! That's wonderful!'

The phone rang. Emma was nearest. 'Emma Saxby . . . Just a moment. It's your brother.'

Stuart took the phone, placing a soft kiss on her cheek as he passed. 'Well done, you.' Then into the phone, 'Peter, hello. . . . I see . . . Are you sure . . .? When. . . .? You're a brick, Peter. I thank you most sincerely . . . I will. Goodbye.' The usual confident expression returned to Stuart's face. 'I have him! And, what's more, I have a face to put to the name, I've met this villainous peculater at Tiberio.'

'Who?' cried Emma and Bill in unison.

'Sir David Garman.'

'As in BHS?' from Bill.

'The same! In cahoots with Clarke and the rest of the Westminster die-hards to discredit the new boys. Peter has a friend in the Treasury who told him the whole story over breakfast this morning.' He clenched his fists in front of his face, pleased to have a target for his anger. 'But I'm on to you, my little beauties.'

A charge of optimism electrified the room. 'That's more like it! Come on, Bill, another pot of tea is required. Let's give the boss time to think.' Emma tugged Bill firmly by the arm and led him into the kitchen, kicking the door shut behind her.

She kissed him full on the mouth and hooked her right leg around his waist. Sliding both hands through his hair, she grabbed hold at the back and held his face inches from hers. 'Remember this feeling, Bill Mason, and promise me you'll take me to bed the moment he leaves.'

Bill closed his eyes and registered every touch of her body; the slight movement of her leg against his waist, her breasts resting gently on his chest, her hands clasped firmly in his hair. 'I promise.'

'A plan is formulating,' said Stuart, taking the cup from Emma. 'I'll need you to co-ordinate the other stations; MDs only let's meet tomorrow. Bill, do you have any friends at Centre Sound?'

'Not that I'd trust with this. I get on with Ziggy quite well, but only because he's another Jamaican.'

'I will have this treacherous villain brought before me,' informed Stuart in his best theatrical voice, at the same time removing twenty pounds from his wallet. 'Take Ziggy to lunch.' He held on to Bill's hand as he passed the money. 'I need the foot-soldier before I can topple the General.' Then to Emma, 'I want Gerald at this meeting. Can you call him now?' Back to Bill.

'I'll pay for this information if I must.' His expression softened. 'You're not planning to get married within the next week, are you?'

'With all this going on I doubt we'll get to bed for a week, let alone get married,' laughed Bill.

Emma liked Stuart in this mood. The fervent desire to win that coursed through his veins uplifted her spirit. She stood and straightened her full-length velvet skirt. The sensation of the fabric rubbing against her stockings made her think briefly of Bill's promise. She'd dressed for him this morning; now she needed to be decidedly more Dior than Biba.

'Please excuse me, gentlemen. I need to be near three phone lines.'

Stuart offered a ride to Hayes Mews.

'Bless you, but no. I want to get changed. I'll be along in half an hour.'

Bill closed the front door behind Stuart, turned and confronted his fiancée who stood challengingly before him, hands on hips and feet apart.

'Half an hour, Emma? Are you sure?'

Emma walked backwards in the direction of the bedroom, flicking her skirt in a can-can motion in front of her. 'Takes ten minutes door to door!'

Honey struggled to get her suitcase through the cabin door. The greasy voice of Eddie Lincoln slid down the corridor.

'Keep bending over like that and me and my hard-on won't be able to get down the stairs. Wanna hand?'

Honey spun around to avoid the touch up she knew was coming. Her hand grabbed Eddie between his legs. He winced with pain, and she let go.

'You call that a hard-on?' She took great delight in

248

watching the pain twisting his face despite his efforts to hide it. The ship jolted as the tug bumped its side. 'I'd love to stop and chat but I've got a real man waiting in London.' She removed the case and herself from his presence as quickly as possible.

The ship had not been a happy place over the past few days and Honey longed for the relative sanity of London to restore her spirits. She didn't keep a flat in town, preferring to stay with friends or scrounge a few nights at Ovington Square or Bristol House. Tonight she'd arranged to stay with an old school chum, Debbie Cookson, who'd promised not only the double-bedded spare room but also dinner with the very handsome young doctor from number twenty-three. Those plans, however, changed very rapidly once she arrived at Hayes Mews. Secretaries scurried, phones rang continuously, orders were barked from Stuart's office. The sales team reminded her of shadow puppets as they flitted from desk to desk behind their tightly shut frosted glass door. Emma charged through reception, pausing momentarily to knock on Stuart's door before striding through his office on her way to the welcoming fire and frantic phones in the headquarters of the IRC. Honey followed her; nodding to Stuart in passing and wondering if the two phones would soon be grafted to the side of his head.

'Who's killed who?' Honey plunked another log on the fire.

Emma relayed the morning's convoluted events in between phone conversations with John Walters, Lady Heath and Peter Salisbury. Honey listened to the story and the phone calls and wanted very much to get in the game. Jeanette's stoical face appeared in the connecting hatch.

'It's Bill on line two; says it's urgent.'

Emma picked up the middle phone. 'Bill . . . Go ahead.' She wrote a name and address on her jotting pad. 'Come back to the Mews and we'll tell Stuart . . . I love you too, goodbye.'

'I see the cracks in the love nest have been replastered.' Honey's cynicism was only just under control.

'Better than that, snuggles, we're getting married.'

'Oh . . . my . . . God!' Honey threw her arms and mouth open.

'Not now!' Emma reached for the *A to Z*. 'We'll all have dinner tonight, okay? Right now I've got to track down a Mr Grant Davies of Coborn Road, Mile End.'

Honey sat back on the sofa, impressed by Emma's cool efficiency. 'What are you planning to do with him?'

'Try to persuade him to change sides.'

'Let me do it! He won't even know where he's going until it's too late.'

Emma grinned at her friend. 'What dastardly plan have you hatched in that devious little mind?'

Honey improvised madly. 'I'll tell him he's won a big prize. A night out with me. I'll pick him up and bring him here. Easy as that!'

'This guy's the voice on the tape. He won't fall for that.'

'He will if he thinks his mate Ziggy put him up for it.'

Emma stared at the name and address on her notepad. 'Let's wait for Bill, then take the whole thing to Stuart.'

Eddie Lincoln waited for Mick Tasker to count the small brown bundles inside the cardboard box.

'Ninety-nine, one hundred.' He winked at Eddie. 'Well done, my son.'

'You always act as if it's a fucking miracle they're all there! I've never short-changed you; not ever!'

Mick placed a playful slap on Eddie's cheek. ''Course not, 'cause if you did I'd 'ave you dragged along the bottom dick first. 'Sides, you get well paid for your services. What's the sense of fucking up regular money for a few packets of hash?'

Eddie grinned lasciviously. 'Speaking of fucking, who've you brought out today? The Italian tits or the Japanese mouth expert?'

Mick signalled to his minder to pick up the boxes. 'Bit of a rush this time, old son; gotta meet someone off Jersey in a couple of hours, so, sorry, no time for crumpet.'

'Wait a minute, Tasker whined Eddie. 'Our deal includes a bird each time you come out.'

'Our deal depends on this consignment getting to Jersey. I'll bring two out next time; now get your mind weather-side of your zip and help us get this shit on board the Taskforce.'

Eddie did as requested, then slipped the ropes holding *Taskforce* to FREE. He trotted back to his cabin and retrieved five small brown bundles from his bottom drawer, a look of smug satisfaction crossing his weasely, unshaven face.

Stuart pondered three possible plans regarding the abduction of Grant Davies. Plan one, put forward by Bill: to overpower Davies the moment he answered the door and bring him, cuffed and blindfolded, to Hayes Mews. Plan two, his own: go to Grant's house, persuade him of the error of his ways and, if need be, offer him money to admit publicly that Sir David Garman had hired him. Plan three was Honey's.

'Plan one's risky in that there could be violence at Mile End and his neighbours could become hostile witnesses. I don't like my idea because it's wrong to tackle him where he lives; I want him in this office. So, Honey, it's down to your idea. Take the Bentley; Charlie and Bill will ride shotgun in case he turns nasty.'

Grant Davies didn't turn a hair when Honey stood on the doorstep of number thirty-five Coborn Road and informed him of his good luck. He also remained expressionless when Stuart confronted him at Hayes Mews.

'I knew I 'adn't won nothin'. Ziggy hates my guts.' His eyes turned slowly on everyone in the room. 'I did it 'cause I hate the bloody monarchy, and the bloody Government, and the likes of you lot and Sir David bleedin' Garman.'

'In that case, let me appeal to your sense of commerce.' Stuart met his stare. 'You sign a letter, admitting what you've done and who employed you, and I'll send you on holiday for three weeks, anywhere you like, plus five hundred spending money.'

Davies replied in a clipped monotone, keeping his eyes locked on to Stuart's. 'The Hilton, Acapulco; and my girlfriend goes with me. She lives in Amsterdam.'

'Done!' Stuart broke his stare and looked at Emma. 'Please book a room for Mr Davies at the Washington and have his lady flown in to join him there.' Then to Grant, 'Charlie will drive you home to pack and then take you to the hotel. You must talk to no one, nor leave any notes. Is that clear?' Davies nodded. 'From now on you're a material witness; you'll do exactly what I say before you leave and if you goof up in

Mexico, my friends there will see that you and your girlfriend spend a less than comfortable five years in one of their world-renowned lock-ups. Is *that* clear?'

'Perfectly, *Mister* Salisbury.'

For one of the rare moments in his life, Stuart itched to be violent; to hit this man with all his might, to wipe that impertinent smugness off his face, punish him for defaming his radio station. He sank into the comfort of his black leather chair. 'The letter will be at the Washington by six o'clock. Goodbye, *Mister* Davies.' His heart felt lighter as he watched Charlie hustle the man down the stairs. 'Emma, I want you to arrange total security on Davies until he gets on the plane. I'll take care of Mexico. How's tomorrow going?'

'Everyone's okay for eleven o'clock.'

'Excellent!' He started to feel quietly confident that this whole nightmare would eventually work out in his favour. He watched Honey sitting cross-legged on the sofa touching up her nail polish. She looked so different from Anna Papanicholas, the shy unsophisticated girl who'd applied for the position of receptionist only a year ago. She now looked sure of herself, brimming with the self-confidence borne of success. He felt justifiably proud of her for realising her potential, and of himself for spotting it.

'Ladies and gentlemen, I believe we have an engagement to celebrate.'

Chapter 13

'Of course I don't mind you calling on a Saturday.' Sir David Garman looked sheepishly at his wife who tapped her foot impatiently at the front door. 'How can I help you?'

'They're having some kind of meeting at Hayes Mews,' came the urgent reply. 'They've taken to playing the radio in the background so I'm finding it difficult to get good sound, but I'm picking up something about Centre Sound and Davies. I thought you should know.'

'Thank you, Kevin. We're just heading out for a spot of lunch. Could you transcribe whatever's audible and send in to the flat, say, four o'clock?'

'No problem, Guv.'

'Hear from you later, then.' Sir David hung up the phone and smiled broadly at his wife. 'I think we have those damn pirates on the run. Saturday meetings are unheard of in their circles.'

She hooked his arm and steered him out of the door. 'As one who is all too familiar with weekend work, I'm not letting you wriggle out of lunch today for pirates, prime ministers, or anyone else.'

'My darling lady, nothing is more important to me

255

on this salubrious spring day than our culinary pleasure.'

She squeezed his arm. 'A good thing, too.'

Carnal pleasure was uppermost in John Walters' mind as he stood on his balcony overlooking Regents Park and waited while Felicity collected the next bottle of Bollinger from the kitchen. His commissions and bonus payments for one and a half million pounds-worth of sales had made him a rich man. He now spent three-day weekends indulging in the little luxuries that money brings. One of these luxuries was Felicity Bryant, part-time model, part-time actress, full-time party girl. They'd met two months ago at the Marquee, when he'd been forced, to his annoyance, to take a client to one of FREE's 'swinging evenings'. She'd been dating Brian Todd at the time; he was to change all that.

John mulled over this afternoon's hidden agenda. Felicity's links with Brian Todd could supply vital information to fill the gap in John's understanding of the ship's covert activities. He knew something illegal was going on but, as he didn't enjoy the confidence of either Stuart or the Captain in these matters, his knowledge of the details remained sadly inadequate.

'It's a bit cold out here dressed the way I am.' Felicity stepped back inside the bedroom and dropped the cold champagne bottle in the ice bucket next to the bed. 'Come back inside. I need you to warm me up.'

John paused, watching the Asian servants walking their masters' pets around the permitted areas of the park, and let the fresh air stimulate his mind. All this business with the Queen had damaged his monthly figures; two clients had pulled their campaigns altogether, another three threatened the same unless a satisfactory explanation was forthcoming. He was powerless to change the situation. He must trust Stuart to find a way out. That remained his primary concern; he didn't trust anyone, let alone a managing director who'd gained his position through family connections and inherited money. John was New York born and bred; the English class system was as foreign to him as Wimpy hamburgers to a man raised on McDonald's and Burger King.

'Are you coming back to bed or do I drink this champagne by myself?' came a muffled voice from inside.

He watched her through the patio doors. Her long honey-blonde hair flowed over her shoulders and a curled softly over the top of her red silk négligé. He followed the lines of her nightdress as it hugged her generous curves, ending just above the knee where she'd balanced her glass precariously with two fingers. He walked into the bedroom, sliding the door shut behind him.

'Tell me something about Brian Todd.'

'Don't spoil a great day by mentioning that creep.' Felicity pushed her arms together, accentuating her cleavage. 'Come to bed.'

John dismissed her advance with a blink. 'How much dope does he smoke?'

She knew him well enough to realise all further lovemaking would depend on the answers she gave. 'Loads. All the time. That's the trouble with him; a joint in one hand and a freebie in the other.' She ran her hand down the inside of her leg. 'Come to bed.'

'Do you know who supplied him?' John was not to be swayed.

'He kept talking about some guy on the ship. Eddie something.'

'Lincoln?'

'Yes, Eddie Lincoln, that's him.'

John sat on the bed, a sly smirk crossing his unctuous face. 'Has anyone ever told you you've got the best body this side of Hoboken?'

'Where the hell is Hoboken?' she giggled, quickly placing her glass on the bedside table.

John's sexual technique mirrored his business dealings. His only real concern was his own reward, but he knew that to achieve this required sensitive foreplay, which he classed alongside business dinners as a tedious but necessary prerequisite. He always remained in control, never allowing his partner to dominate any part of the proceedings; performed oral sex and massaged erogenous zones with textbook precision, and always showered before and after each session.

Felicity understood him and serviced his desires with measured professionalism. Her real reason for being with him was to persuade the exacting Mr Walters to invest some of his hard-earned bonus in a television pilot starring herself and written by David Belzec, an up-and-coming playwright from Highbury, with whom she'd spent the previous three nights.

All things considered, they probably deserved each other.

Emma cleared the last of the coffee cups from the Sheraton table and stacked the coasters on the windowsill. 'I'd say that went fairly well.'

'I think most of those bastards just protect their own ass at all costs,' spat Stuart angrily.

'Calm down,' interjected Gerald. 'You've got to expect them to guard their own first. Several good points were raised this morning and no-one walked away without giving their support.'

'I didn't notice any cheque books on the table when we said we'd go to court. Are we suppose to swallow that cost on our own?'

'I'm not so sure court is the right way to go,' said Emma. 'I feel they didn't offer because there's a good chance we'd lose, and they know it.'

'I've got to clear my name and vindicate the station. John Walters told me yesterday that we're facing order cancellation on a large scale. That advertising will go to the others; that's why they won't back us.'

'There's another problem.' Gerald poured himself a glass of Perrier. 'Pursuing this through the courts will take months, even years. By the time this gets to court we could be out of business anyway.'

'Why don't we string Davies up on the radio?' Emma's question drew silence from the two men. 'No waiting, no verdict, no cost.'

'And no expensive holiday,' added Stuart thoughtfully.

Gerald sat on the sofa, an expression of satisfaction shining from his face. 'That's bloody genius. Why not? Just quote Davies on the radio and let the good old English media do the rest.'

'Exactly.' Emma walked to her desk. 'Jonathan could lead the news with it tomorrow morning.'

'And I can kick the loathsome Mr Davies back to Mile End tonight.' Stuart sounded delighted.

'Not so quickly, old pal.' Gerald took a long drink of water. 'Leave him in the hotel another day. If we work this right he'll arrive home to the biggest press reception of the year.'

The Garmans arrived home shortly after four o'clock. Sir David picked up the large brown envelope from the hallway floor. 'I'll just be a few minutes, dear, something's arrived for me.'

His wife watched him pad down the hall towards his study knowing full well that a few minutes could easily translate into a few hours. She straightened his coat so it hung evenly on the hook and walked into the elegant drawing room, picking up the latest edition of *Vogue* on the way.

Inside the envelope was a small cassette and a hand-written note. Sir David took the note to his desk and turned on the table lamp.

'As you can hear, there's something wrong with our equipment. We must send the telephone man around to service the unit. From what I could gather, they know about Davies, and Salisbury is screaming for legal action. I'll be here 'til eight if you need me – Kevin.'

The tape was almost inaudible; the only clear speech belonged to Stuart when he raised his voice. Sir David heard references to legal action, bloody backstabbing bureaucrats and chasing these bastards to the limit. He smiled to himself as he turned off the machine and phoned Kevin.

'Their telephones definitely need servicing; please see to it as soon as possible.'

Emma answered the phone for the seventh time since arriving back at Ovington Square. This last interruption was particularly annoying as Bill had just reached her lower back with a massage that had started ten minutes earlier at the base of her skull.

'Emma, this is Honey. What's cookin'?'

'I would be if I could stay off the phone.'

'Oh Em, I'm sorry. I'll call back.'

Emma watched Bill wipe the oil from his hands and deposit the paper towel neatly in the waste bin. 'Too late.'

'The reason I'm calling is that it's Saturday night in London and I'm without a gig or a date. You guys up to anything?'

'Stuart's invited us round to dinner and then the Scotch or Cromwellian Club, or maybe a late showing of *Alfie*. Come along; make up a four.'

'An evening with the boss is not exactly what I'd call a night on the tiles.'

Bill turned the radio up and beat out the rhythm of 'Shotgun Wedding' on Emma's bottom. 'Get over here, you old tart!' he shouted. 'And get off the phone!'

'Is he always this crude?' Honey whispered.

'I must agree with him this time. See you in an hour.' Emma replaced the phone and turned over on to her back. 'Now, Mr Mason, in order to have a shotgun wedding I need to be pregnant. In order to be pregnant I need . . .' His mouth curbed all further conversation.

All three arrived at Cheyne Walk just before nine o'clock. Stuart begged their forgiveness, saying he hadn't had time to boil a kettle, let alone cook a meal. He made amends by offering dinner at Trader Vic's.

Trader's manager, Alan Watt, greeted them cordially at the bottom of the red spiral staircase and showed them to the bar. 'We're so busy tonight, Mr Salisbury. Your table will be about fifteen minutes. Please, have a drink on me while you wait.' He signalled to a beautiful Eurasian waitress. 'Try our Scorpion, it's delicious.'

This bowl of fire water had long been a speciality of the house. You could ask, offer bribes or try to guess the recipe; all to no avail. Trader's kept the ingredients top secret. Two things were certain: one, it was rum based; two, if you had more than a couple there was no guarantee you'd walk out in a straight line.

Three Scorpions later the table was ready. Although a year aboard FREE had vastly increased Honey's alcohol tolerance, by the third helping of this knockout cocktail she was beginning to feel very light-headed. She refused wine with the meal but accepted an extra helping of the excellent mangetout and water chestnuts, which she ate with a fork, having given up on chopsticks within thirty seconds.

'I'm thinking of starting an agency,' announced Stuart out of the blue, as the waiter cleared the last remnants from the table. 'A theatrical agency; bring people in from the States and handle a few bright presenters here in London.'

'I'll sign.' Bill cracked open a fortune cookie. 'Be as pissed as you like and have a good day.'

Emma grabbed the slip of paper. 'Be at peace with your mind and live the full day.' She punched him playfully on the arm.

Honey was sure it must be the effect of the Scorpions that gave her this warm feeling when she looked at Stuart. She'd heard all the horror stories about getting involved with the boss and had no desire to become an unemployment statistic, but there was no denying the glow she felt from watching him unfold his new idea. 'How can you be employer and agent?'

'I'd only handle outside work; personal appearances,

voice-overs, that sort of thing. If I can import top American acts, my English clients can compère the shows and the station can promote the concerts.' He reached across the table and held Honey's hand lightly. 'I'd love to have you on my books.'

Honey held on to his hand as he tried to retrieve it. 'Would I get personal attention?' She asked suggestively.

Emma and Bill looked slightly embarrassed; Stuart placed his other hand on top of hers. 'My dear lady, you would always have my personal attention.'

'In that case, Mr Salisbury, please attend to me now and order another of those delicious drinks.'

'Right away.' He removed his hands and signalled to the waiter.

By midnight, Emma and Bill were tucked up in bed. They'd declined the invitation to go dancing in favour of an early night, leaving Stuart and Honey to go boogieing on their own. Emma buried her head in his neck.

'I'd never have imagined Honey would made a play for Stuart like that. When the last Scorpion arrived I thought she'd have him on the table.'

Bill twisted the ends of her hair slowly around his finger. 'Just the booze talking. She was flirting with him; I've seen her do it on the ship.'

She nipped at his neck. 'What else did you see her do on the ship?'

He gently tugged her hair in retaliation. 'Screw seven seamen before breakfast, have intercourse with a visiting Doberman on the galley table, and masturbate the Captain on the quarterdeck.'

Emma slid her hand down his stomach. 'What, like this?'

He responded immediately. They knew each others secret places so well now, seeking out the hidden corners of sensitivity with practised ease, and executing each sensual release with an unhurried touch. The curves of their bodies fitted perfectly together, as if they'd been made two halves of one whole. As Bill slowly entered her, he knew there would never be anything better than this. Emma held him tightly and loved him with all her heart.

> Good evening troops, Prince Mikie here,
> playing sounds to cool your fear.
> It's after midnight and I'm goin' strollin'
> in search of the elusive dude that's holdin'.
> Here's thirty minutes back-to-back
> to give the atmosphere you lack.

Eddie heard the Prince rap over the cabin monitor. 'Shit! I forgot about you.' Beaching into his desk drawer, he pulled out four ready-rolled joints. He lit one, lay back on his bunk and started to count backwards from ten. He'd reached three when the knock came on the door. 'Come on in, Rasta. Eddie's got your dinner in the oven.'

Honey woke in a pint-size bed with a king-size headache. She closed her eyes to stop the piercing arrows of the morning sun penetrating her brain. She remembered leaving the Scotch of St James and holding Stuart's arm very tightly as she tried to navigate around the obstacle-course of big cars unevenly parked in the small mews. She vaguely recalled bumping her head as she tried to climb into the cab, but after that, nothing. She put both hands in front of her face and opened her eyes behind them. Peeking through the gap in her fingers, she scanned the room; it was totally unfamiliar. She dragged herself to her feet and stumbled over to the black Habitat desk that occupied nearly half the space. She picked up an envelope and focused on the address: S. Salisbury Esq, 25 Carlyle Mansions, SW3.

'Feeling a bit rough, Miss Papanicholas?'

Nobody had called her that for nearly a year. She dropped the envelope and turned to face her inquisitor. 'God, Stuart, what happened?'

'You had a good time.' He could see the pained expression on her face and lowered his voice. 'I think the last three Scorpions proved your undoing.'

'Why did you call me Papanicholas?'

'You kept telling me and the cab driver that was your name.'

She felt hot waves of embarrassment rushing up her face. 'Oh, Stuart, I'm so sorry.'

'Don't be. We had a great evening, you just had a few too many. Luckily I was there to take care of you.'

It was then she noticed she was wearing only her panties and bra. She grabbed for the sheet. Stuart averted his eyes.

'Your clothes are folded on the chair,' he said. 'There's a spare toothbrush and towel in the bathroom; you're welcome to take a shower. There's a cooked breakfast if you can face it, or juice and coffee.' He turned and left before she could answer.

Honey stood in the centre of the small room and tried unsuccessfully to recapture the missing hours. She focused on this morning. Why had she been embarrassed in her underwear? He must have undressed her last night. Thank God she wasn't sick; thank God it was him and not some liberty-taking lout. Today was Sunday, day of rest. She smiled to herself. A hot shower and a cooked breakfast with the boss; she could handle that.

Jonathan Gilby also viewed Sunday as a day of rest. He checked the early morning news on the Home Service and was gratefully relieved to find no major upset in world affairs. He strolled on to the deck after the nine o'clock bulletin and inhaled several lungfuls of fresh, salty sea air. The morning was crisp and bracing; a slight swell rocked the boat gently on her moorings, the sun gradually burning off the last of the early mist. His eyes focused on a small, familiar shape a mile off the port bow. 'The bloody tug! What's it doing out on a Sunday?'

'Delivering something to you.'

Jonathan remained facing the bow. 'How come you can sneak up on people like me, Captain, but you can't catch Eddie with his hands on the contraband?'

'Because he's watching out for me and he never does his deals on deck where I can see him. Would you like my binoculars?'

'No, thank you. Do you know what the rustbucket's carrying?'

The Captain moved level with Jonathan's shoulder. 'Mr Salisbury called an hour ago; wouldn't talk about the contents, only that you should act on it as soon as it arrives.'

'In that case I'd better arrange cover for the ten o'clock bulletin.'

Jonathan walked through the main hatch, leaving the Captain alone to enjoy the beauty of this exemplary spring morning.

Emma curled herself into Bill's back and listened to Brian

266

Todd witter on about the good weather and the merits of 'Rainy Day Women' Nos 12 and 35. He sounded either stoned or hungover and to pretend the new Bob Dylan song was anything other than a message that 'everybody must get stoned' constituted an insult to her intelligence. She reached over to the bedside table and turned the radio off, wondering, as she did so, how many thousands of others were doing the same.

'We should keep it on for the eleven o'clock news,' came a muffled voice from under the covers. 'I'd hate to miss the high treason story.'

Emma glanced at the clock. 'That's twenty minutes from now.'

Bill turned to face her. 'I'm sure we can fill in the time.'

'A good massage wouldn't go amiss.' Emma lifted her waist allowing his hand to curl around to her back. He held her against him and pressed his fingers either side of her spine, just below the neck. Exerting pressure evenly, he worked his way down her back until the hand under her could go no further; then slowly up again to her neck. She melted into him as he began the second run and slid slowly on top of him, freeing both his hands. The third run consisted of sweeping downward strokes, stretching Emma's muscles and releasing the tension between her shoulder blades. 'God! You do that so well.'

'I'm so glad to be of service, madam. Is there anything else I can do for you?'

'You could try a mouth massage on my feet. I love it when you lick my big toe.'

Ten minutes later Bill had licked his way to her breasts, caressing her nipples with his tongue while slowly massaging her clitoris with his hand. She'd already orgasmed when he'd explored her delta of venus with consummate skill, licking every crevice with his warm and welcoming mouth before darting his tongue inside her. As his mouth slid up her neck she relaxed her muscles in anticipation of his entry and felt the pangs of lust move through her body a second time.

Eighteen minutes later Emma collapsed on to her back and a bead of perspiration slid down her neck, dispersing on her right breast. 'That was wonderful timing, Mr Mason.'

'I'm renowned for it. Turn the radio on.'

The end of the Coca-Cola advert drifted into the bedroom. Emma turned the volume up as the news jingle began.

'This is FREE news at eleven, I'm Jonathan Gilby. The mystery of the obscenity tape has been solved. Grant Davies, a twenty-five-year-old part-time sound engineer has confessed it was *his* voice on the tape that shocked millions of listeners when it was broadcast on FREE news last Thursday. He also named Sir David Garman, chairman of BHS publishing, as the instigator of the plot. In a written statement to the managing director of FREE Radio, Davies apologised for any embarrassment caused to the station and stated that his motives were purely financial. Other news: the Brady/Hindley case enters its fifth day at the Old Bailey tomorrow. The prosecution will . . .'

Emma switched off the radio and slid out of bed. 'In half an hour the shit's going to hit every fan in Fleet Street.'

'Are you going to the office?'

'WE are going to the office. Now get thee up lest I return with a jug of cold water.' Emma stopped as she reached the door. 'Why don't you phone Stuart, just in case he missed it?'

Right on cue, the small princess phone beside the bed started to chirp. Bill picked it up. 'Good morning, Stuart. We're on our way.'

'You promised me a bloody holiday!' shouted a disgruntled Grant Davies, sitting bolt upright in his hotel bed. 'A deal is a deal!'

'We're not taking legal action so I have no further need to keep you incommunicado. Please ensure you leave the hotel within the next hour.'

'I'll get you, you bastard!' Davies spat down the phone.

'I'm sure you'll try. But for now, good day, Mr Davies.' Stuart hung up and smiled at his three colleagues. 'I think we should make sure our friends in Fleet Street know the Mile End address. Emma, you take the *Express*, *Mirror* and *Sketch*. Bill, *Times* and *Observer*. Honey, you contact the *Melody Maker* and the trades. I'll handle the rest.' He sat back in his chair, a satisfied grin beaming from his face. 'I think our belligerent anarchist is in for the surprise of his life.'

Panic-stricken was the best description of how Grant Davies felt as the cab pulled into Coborn Road and pulled up outside number thirty-five. At least twenty members of the press greeted him with flash cameras and awkward questions. 'How much did you get paid? Is Sir David a relative? Is he your lover? Do you listen to FREE?'

Then for a fleeting moment, he felt like a star. The scenes of media pressure involving the Beatles, Richard Burton, Liz Taylor and even the Kray twins that he'd witnessed so often on the television were now happening to him. He stepped from the cab and held both hands in the air. 'Please, ladies and gentlemen.' The small crowd fell silent, waiting for his next words. This was fabulous; he was king for a day and he wasn't going to let the moment pass without telling the world exactly what he believed in. 'I'm an anarchist and proud of it!' he proclaimed. 'This country, once proud and strong, is now drifting towards obscurity and depression. The only way forward is to abolish the monarchy and the government. To become a society where everyone is free to do as they wish, where the only laws are human rights, the only taxes to build hospitals and schools. We should get rid of the armed forces and curb police powers. We should all co-operate together to build a better world where violence is a thing of the past.'

'Surely, Mr Davies, violence is the end result of anarchy,' came a voice from the back of the crowd.

'That's only because we're selfish and have no consideration for others.'

'Is that why you took money to publicly insult the Queen?'

All the reporters laughed. Grant Davies felt his bubble burst. They didn't want his point of view; they just wanted to ridicule him and distort his words into juicy headlines. 'Fuck you all!' he shouted, pushing his way through the throng and seeking the sanctuary of his cold, damp hallway. He sat cowering on the threadbare carpet next to the front door and listened to them laughing and making jokes at his expense. Within two minutes they'd all gone. A loud knock on the door disturbed his misery. 'I told you, fuck off! I've nothing more to say.'

'You may be a principled arsehole,' shouted a cockney

voice through the letterbox. 'But there's thirteen and six on the meter and it's going up all the time.'

Monday morning dawned full of the joys of spring. The Fab Four, as Stuart had taken to calling them, met at Hayes Mews just before seven o'clock. The main purpose of such an early meeting was to check out the morning papers, but the enthusiasm that prevailed among Bill, Emma and Honey had more to do with Stuart's promise of a breakfast imported from the Ritz and served in front of a roaring fire in Emma's office.

'Look at this!' Honey threw the *Sketch* on to the centre of the table. '"Publishing Chief Hires Nutcase to Discredit Offshore Radio".'

'And this,' said Bill, holding up a copy of *The Times*. '"BHS Chairman Plots to Sink Pirates".'

'I love this One!' laughed Emma, adding the *Express* to the pile. 'Dirty Trick Backfires on Publishing Chairman. Anarchist admits taking money to slander the Queen.'

Stuart picked a hard-boiled quail's egg from the ornate silver platter, bit it delicately in half and washed it down with a mouthful of fresh orange juice. 'I believe we have a result, dear people. You should try the eggs; they're delicious.'

Sir David Garman sat at his breakfast table and screamed abuse down the telephone at his head of public relations. Both men knew this would not be the best day of their lives.

Chapter 14

Thursday, April 28 1966.

'We've been very lucky with this weather.' Stuart stood
on the gently shifting deck of *Offshore One* and inhaled
a lungful of North Sea air. 'We should reach the ship
long before noon.'

Bill watched Radio Caroline loom tall off the port
bow. She was their first stop, to drop off Johnny
Walker and a thousand gallons of fresh water. He
gave Emma a squeeze and walked to the starboard
railing where Johnny was indulging in a quick smoke
and a last look at the coastline. 'Are you coming over
to see us this week for another friendly poker game?'

'Wouldn't miss it. I wish I could live on that ship;
better food, better beds and carpets throughout.' He
took a long drag on the roll-up. 'Too bad your radio
doesn't match your decor.' His face stayed serious
but his eyes smiled. They acted out this little charade
each time they met, a bit like brothers who support
different football teams; the rivalry wasn't nasty but
was nevertheless intense.

'At least we keep our jocks for more than six months,'
replied Bill, referring to Tony Blackburn, who was about
to leave Caroline and join Radio London.

'All part of a master plan. We've got Tom Lodge and

Mike Ahern coming down from the northern ship, so you'll have three heavyweights against you. That should put you in third place, where you belong.'

'In your wildest dreams!' He declined Johnny's offer of the roll-up. 'On the strength of that it seems your programming department is as ineffective as your sales.'

'Jesus, don't talk sales!' Walker took one last puff and threw the butt overboard. 'They've brought in Terry Bate to head up sales. He's bloody brilliant; did fifty-thousand last week. I think your John Walters has put the fear of failure up Ronan's backside, for which my summer bonus thanks you.'

'Don't mention it. I'll be more than happy to relieve you of the extra cash at the poker table.'

'Now who's dreaming?'

'Are you two being schoolboys again?' Emma slipped her arm around Bill's waist.

'Whatever do you see in this Jamaican reject?' Johnny kissed Emma lightly on the cheek. 'He'll never amount to anything.'

She smiled up at Bill. 'I know, but he's so good in bed I can't resist him.'

'No answer to that,' Johnny conceded with a smile. 'You two coming aboard? They'll be at least an hour transferring the water.'

John Walters had more than sales on his mind as he talked to Brian Todd on the ship-to-shore. 'There's this dolly bird from McCann's who's just dying to meet you. I could arrange a little dinner at my place tonight if you're interested. Over.'

'After three weeks on this tub Ena Sharples would look good to me. Where shall we meet? Over.'

'Come to Hayes Mews about six. Over.'

'See you then. Over and out.' Brian couldn't believe his luck.

John replaced the phone and thumbed through his address book. It took three calls to get a result. 'That's fantastic, Julie. If you and Debbie can be at my place by eight we have a deal. Just remember, you both work as secretaries for McCann Erikson.'

He'd met Julie at an advertising function a month ago. From her conversation it was obvious she didn't work in the business. She talked of months cruising the Greek islands, weekends in Las Vagas or Paris, nights in the penthouse at the Dorchester. She was a high-class hooker, and John always had room in his address book for professional people whatever their occupation. Her model figure, angelic face, and micro mini-skirt ensured he wouldn't forget the girl with embossed business cards. If her friend was comparable, tonight should be very pleasant indeed.

At eleven forty-five *Offshore One* moored on FREE's starboard quarter; *Taskforce Two* was already tied up on the port side. Captain Vourner welcomed Stuart and Honey on board with a handshake and a hug respectively and ordered a crewman to help with the luggage. Bill and Emma received the same greeting before all five strolled leisurely across the deck towards the Captain's cabin.

'Is that Mick Tasker's boat?' inquired Stuart.

'It is,' replied the Captain. 'They've been here since ten o'clock. Eddie went on board about an hour ago. With all the activity on deck this morning they're keeping a low profile. I don't expect them to transfer anything today unless Eddie's already taken it with him.'

'Seems likely,' offered Bill. 'Any chance of a hot toddy? I'm freezing.'

Captain Vourner brewed a large pot of coffee and served it with a bottle of Napoleon brandy which he invited his guests to sample according to their tastes. 'To what do I owe the pleasure of so much company?'

'A favour,' said Stuart. 'I think Bill should ask you.'

Bill poured a goodly measure of brandy into his coffee. 'Emma and I are getting married and we'd like you to perform the service,' he said simply.

Jan Vourner's eyes softened as he looked at the couple; Bill cupping his mug with both hands, Emma standing lovingly beside him. 'This is wonderful news. Of course I will – it will be a privilege. When?'

'We thought the end of July,' smiled Emma.

'Good. I'll need some rehearsal time.' He chuckled. 'I haven't married anyone since 1956.'

Bill kissed his bride-to-be lightly on the forehead. 'That's settled, then.'

'I'm afraid the other reason for our visit is less auspicious,' said Stuart. 'The business with Lincoln and Tasker is getting out of hand. If the authorities get them before we do it could signal the end of us.'

'My feelings entirely.' The Captain added a small measure of Napoleon to his drink. 'They're very discreet. Catching them with goods in hand will not be easy.'

'I think I'll pay Mr Tasker a visit, have a little look over his boat.' He addressed the others. 'Why don't you get settled in? I'll meet you all in the mess-room later.'

Stuart walked alone on to the deck. He remembered the first time he'd seen FREE in Galveston harbour, her grey paint peeling, her rigging rusting from lack of use. She was still carrying her guns and mine-sweeping equipment at that time; he wished they were still in place so he could blast *Taskforce* from the water and be done with the troublesome hustler threatening his empire. He looked over the side on to the top deck of the cabin-cruiser. 'Ahoy, *Taskforce*!'

Mick Tasker's round, oily face appeared in the hatchway. 'Stuart, me ol' mate, come aboard; 'ave a drink.'

As the second glass of champagne bubbled in his glass, Stuart cast his eyes around the stateroom in a disguised attempt to find some evidence of contraband. He thought how well the garish decor of baroque furniture and gold-plated fixtures matched Mick's personal preference for loud shirts and vulgar jewellery. He saw nothing that would link Tasker to unlawful activities with the possible exception of bad taste, which Stuart had long regarded as a punishable offence.

'To what do we contribute this unexpected pleasure?' inquired Mick, trying without success to raise his standard of conversation to match his guest.

Stuart decided on a direct approach. 'I've had reports that you're doing more than bringing a few girls out to party.'

'Whatever do you mean?' Mick's look of injured innocence didn't fool Stuart.

'What I mean, Mick, is that I've heard you're running drugs and porn through this ship via Eddie Lincoln, and although I couldn't care less how you make the money to support such a beautiful cruiser, I do object most strongly to you using my radio station as a post office.'

An awkward moment of silence fell on the room. The two bodyguards started to twitch as if waiting for a bell to signal the beginning of the tenth round. Stuart stood his ground and stared directly into Mick's eyes. Before

Mick could retaliate the sounds of an advanced stage of sexual activity could be heard emanating from the next room.

'The only porn's live, and it's going on in the bedroom,' laughed the cockney hustler, then his expression changed to one of controlled malevolence. 'Listen, my ol' son. All I do is bring a few girls out for the lads to get their rocks off with. If your boys decide to give them a little gift for their services, that's up to them.' Suddenly he was back in his customary mode of benevolent buddy, a surly smile twisting on his face. 'All I do is run a friendly whore house. I wouldn't dream of putting your operation in danger. My wife'd kill me, she loves the station.'

Stuart knew a stalemate when he saw one, be it in a boardroom or a boat. There was no way Mick would admit to anything more than international pimping and there was no visible evidence to the contrary. 'I'm not convinced, Mr Tasker, but I'll have to take your word for now.'

'You cut me to the bone, Stuart. I thought we was friends.'

That idea appealed to Stuart as much as another ten years of Labour Government. 'Friendship has little to do with it. I know there's funny business going on here and I think you're involved.'

The bodyguards started twitching again. Mick fiddled with his rings. 'Are you saying you don't want me to come here any more?'

'I'm saying I don't want you running dope here any more.'

Mick refilled his own glass. 'That's all right then, 'cos I'm not running dope through your fuckin' ship. Not now, not ever!'

Stuart noted the mounting viciousness in Mick's voice. His priority now was to get off the boat without provoking violence. 'I'd drink to that . . . if I had one,' he joked, to ease the tension.

Mick signalled to the nearest minder. 'Fill 'im up.' Then to Stuart, 'Why don't you relax? There's two ladies in the next room who can make you forget what day it is. Eddie'll be through in a minute. Have 'em on the house.'

That suggestion rated alongside the offer of Mick's friendship. 'Thank you, no. I don't fancy following Eddie Lincoln.'

Mick and the bodyguards laughed loudly. 'I don't fuckin' blame you,' slobbered Mick.

Blame was busily being discussed in the mess-room aboard FREE as the Captain and the chief engineer squared up to each other over the loss of power to the transmitter.

One generator equals half power!' shouted Stan Beacher. 'I can't pump twenty-five kilowatts to the mast unless both generators are feeding the transmitter. It's simple bloody arithmetic.'

'And I can't run both generators without more fuel. I've got five hundred gallons to last me a week.'

'Gentlemen! Please!' Bill stepped into the room, his hands over his ears. 'Have some respect for courting couples. How can we make love with all this racket going on? Stuart will be here in a few minutes; take it up with him.'

'Did somebody call?' Stuart appeared through the galley entrance.

'Just the man.' Captain Vourner slid a letter across the table.

'I've just heard from Holland. There's a week's delay on refuelling; I'm too low to run both generators for twenty-four hours a day.'

Stuart read the message. 'It says they can send a special ship tomorrow for an extra five hundred pounds.'

'That's beyond my budget.'

'It's a priority,' protested Stan.

Stuart threw the letter back on the table. 'Stan's right. We need the fuel. I suspect the Dutch boys are making a small bonus here, but that's the price one pays, when one is slightly illegal. I want full power at all times.' He winked at the Captain. 'Pay the extra.'

'Very good, sir.' Jan Vourner retrieved the paper and shuffled out of the room. Stuart could see he was less than pleased at having the decision taken out of his hands.

'Everything okay?' inquired Bill.

Stuart walked across the room and put his arm around Bill's shoulder. 'Let's go to your cabin.' Then, turning to Stan, feeling pleased that his visit had at least achieved something. 'You'll always have full power as long as I'm in charge.'

Stan gathered his coffee cup and plate. 'Thanks, boss.'

Eddie Lincoln gathered his clothes from various parts of the master bedroom aboard *Taskforce* and proceeded to dress as slowly as possible. He watched his two lovers caress each other as they lay side by side on the king-size bed. 'Don't you two ever come up for air?' They ignored him completely.

'Eddie, I want a word with you!' Mick Tasker's voice

boomed through the cabin door. 'Get your face off the fanny and your ass in here!'

Within three minutes Eddie stood in front of Mick in the stateroom, his clothes on fairly straight, his hair deshevelled and a half bottle of Old Spice splashed all over.

'God! What a pen and ink!' snarled Tasker.

'Leave it out, Mickey, it's my aftershave.'

Mick Tasker's right fist thundered into Eddie's left cheek and sent him sprawling across the room. 'Mickey's a fuckin' mouse. My name's Mick. Mr Tasker to you!'

Eddie hadn't seen Mick in this sort of temper before and it scared the shit out of him. He pulled himself on to the brocade sofa and gingerly held his jaw. 'What's wrong, Mr Tasker?'

'You're fuckin' wrong, you little burk. While you've been havin' a free fuck at my expense, Salisbury's been giving me grievous ear bashin'.'

'About what?'

'About dope and flicks, and how he's gettin' reports about you stashin' gear on the ship!'

Eddie felt his professional pride, as well as his face, had been dented. 'He can't prove a thing! I only keep my personals in the cabin; the rest is hid so good sometimes I can't find it.' He watched Tasker's face. The look of outraged anger slowly faded to one of weary disappointment. 'He won't find nothin', honest!'

'If he does, the next thing he'll find is you floating face down!' Mick lit a cigarette. 'This is what we do. The next time the Captain goes to Holland you call me. We'll come out and pick up all you've got. Then we close down for a while 'til this blows over.'

'We don't need to do that!' Eddie panicked at the

prospect of losing his main source of income – not to mention the girls.

'I'll be the judge of what we fuckin' do,' Mick's eyes narrowed. 'Now piss off outa my sight!'

Emma expected Bill to return alone. She'd spread herself seductively on the bunk anticipating one last love making session before the tug returned from Radio London. When she heard Stuart's voice resounding down the corridor she sat up, pulling her clothes straight, and silently cursed her managing director.

'And if you can find out where he hides the stuff I'd be most grateful.' Stuart was saying as they entered the cabin. He saw the disappointment on Emma's face immediately. 'I do apologise. You two want to be alone. I'll see you on the tug, Emma.' He left the cabin without further conversation.

Bill locked the door and walked slowly to the bunk. 'Isn't it nice to have a sensitive boss?'

Emma grabbed his jacket and yanked him on to the bed, twisting him around and hauling herself on top of him. His astonished expression amused her. She rubbed her breasts across his chest, his jacket zipper scraping her nipples through the thin silk blouse. She winced with pleasurable pain. 'Not half as nice as having a sensitive fiancé,' she said, reaching down to unbuckle his belt.

'Do me a favour,' said Bill, lifting his bottom so she could remove his trousers. 'Don't make any noise. These walls are very thin. We used to do running commentaries when Honey and Jonathan were together.'

'Bunch of perverts,' whispered Emma, lifting her skirt and rubbing her silk knickers against the top part of his leg. 'I could do it in absolute silence. Could you?'

They half undressed each other, fondled, kissed, coupled and climaxed, with hardly a sound being uttered; just a low, grunting noise from Emma's throat as her body thundered towards orgasm.

The journey back proved pleasant enough, although Emma missed her man from the moment the tug pulled away. It would be two weeks before she'd feel him again. She did notice with some excitement the lingering embrace between Stuart and Honey just before the tug departed. He was a tactile man, but only in short spurts. A fifteen-second hug and a kiss placed lightly on Honey's mouth was very unlike Stuart Salisbury's usual style, and Emma decided to keep an eye firmly peeled for future developments. The only downer of the trip was the unwanted attention of Brian Todd. She knew he'd been on the ship for a good few weeks and was likely to be in need of female company, but if he groped her bottom one more time on the pretence of getting past her, she swore she'd knee him so hard he'd be out of action for a month. Besides, she was sure he'd been a frequent visitor to Mick the Mouth's floating brothel and should, by rights, be wearing a sign warning any future partner about the possibility of contracting the numerous forms of venereal infection to which he'd undoubtedly been exposed.

Emma grabbed her bag and alighted from the Bentley outside seven Ovington Square. London smelled stale and dirty after the bracingly fresh sea air; the flat seemed big and very empty. She wandered from room to room straightening magazines and plumping up cushions, unable to settle. She put the kettle on before going into the bedroom and throwing herself on the floral duvet. As she stretched and twisted on the bed she noticed a piece of paper jutting out under one of the pillows. She flipped on to her back and read the message. 'I love you, I always will – don't forget to take the Pill.' She closed her eyes and hugged the paper to her breast. She wouldn't go back to Bristol House tonight; tonight she'd sleep here so she could smell his musky, masculine scent lingering on the pillow.

Brian accepted a ride to Hayes Mews, arriving shortly after six o'clock. The office was empty save two sales people and Martha the receptionist.

'John left a message to say he's waiting for you in the Coach and Horses,' she said, stuffing her life into her handbag. 'I'm off now. Have a nice evening.'

The Coach and Horses had occupied the corner of Hayes Mews and Hill Street for many years. It was the favourite watering hole for most of the J. Walter Thompson people and therefore attracted a liberal mix of writers, designers, account executives and media salesmen. The long L-shaped bar ran the full length of the pub; small, waist-high walls dissected the room into semi-private areas, perfect for discreet liaisons or discussing forthcoming advertising campaigns.

John Walters sat sipping a half pint of Guinness in a small alcove just to the right of the door. 'Brian!' he shouted above the din of early evening drinkers. 'Over here. What you having?'

'A tequila shot and a lager chaser, mate; that would hit the spot.'

There was something about his Australian accent that grated on John Walters. He knew he had no grounds for disapproval; his own broad New York tones were just as out of place in this very English hostelry, but he kept his voice down or tried to mix in native phrases whenever possible, whereas Brian always spoke at full volume, almost bludgeoning people with his speech. John was also a master salesman and would keep his dislike strictly to himself. 'Only one per customer,' he said, shaking the disc jockey firmly by the hand with every appearance of friendliness. 'We have a long night ahead.'

It took four tequila/lager combinations to persuade Brian to leave the pub. By seven o'clock both men sat in the Victorian lift on the ascent to John's fourth-floor flat.

'This must be handy when you come home pissed,' said Brian, patting the velvet seat covering.

'I believe it was part of Victorian etiquette; always offer a seat to a lady.'

Brian leered. 'Christ! I wonder how many pussies have sat on this very spot!'

John cringed inwardly and wondered if the end result was really going to be worth the crassness he would obviously have to tolerate for the rest of the evening. 'The way Julie was talking, you'll have more pussy than T.S. Eliot by midnight.'

'T.S. who?'

The lift stopped at the fourth floor. John slid open the steel concertina door. 'Eliot. He wrote a book about cats.'

An hour and a bottle of Bollinger later John's entry-phone buzzed three times. Thank God, he thought with relief, hurrying towards the front door. The last hour had seemed like an eternity. Brian's interminable stories of drunken surf parties, outdoor barbies and sordid sex with fifteen-year-old girls in the back of sheep trucks left him not only cold, but also thoroughly disgusted. He hoped he was paying the girls enough to stop them telling him to bugger off, spoiling the entire plan. 'My door release isn't working,' he lied. 'I'll come down and let you in.' On the way back up he explained the situation to Julie and Debbie and offered them an extra twenty if they'd put up with Brian in his inebriated state.

'No problem,' sighed Debbie. 'More drink – less sex.' She ran her fingers through John's close-cropped hair. 'You, on the other hand, should stay *very* sober.'

'We've brought the food like you asked,' said Julie. 'And the smoke.'

The lift stopped once more on the fourth floor. 'In that case, ladies, let's party!'

John had spared no expense. He and Debbie took the food into the kitchen and started placing smoked salmon and pâté de fois gras on plates. Debbie arranged salad Nicoise around the edge of a painted Victorian serving dish, the centre of which was filled to brimming with garlic and mayonnaise dip. They left the glistening Beluga caviar in its Harrods' stoneware pot.

Julie meanwhile walked into the sitting room, expecting to see Brian barfing on the carpet; she was surprised to find the room empty except for a smouldering cigarette in the ashtray. The wall opposite consisted solely of giant French windows leading to a marble and concrete balcony. The windows were shut; no chance he was out there. Her eyes drifted along the fireplace wall with its ornate Victorian surround and large oil portrait of the Duke of Wellington, past the carved double doors that led to the master bedroom, finally settling on the right-hand wall, which was filled with nearly fifty copper on oil prints by George Baxter, depicting scenes from the grossest act of military mismanagement the world had ever witnessed; the Crimean War. She

286

lingered over one of the larger prints showing the battle of Inkerman; then a smaller study of the Light Brigade at Balaclava.

'If you ask me, they could do with a couple of decent Sheilas on that wall instead of all that military palaver.'

Julie turned her attention to the man propped in the doorway, a drink in one hand, his pants in the other. 'You must be Brian Todd.'

'The one and only!' He held his trousers in the air. 'Sorry about this, I just went for a slash and my zip bloody broke.' He placed his glass on the map-top table that occupied most of the space between the two leather Roche-Bobois sofas. 'Are you the darlin' from McCann's?'

'Julie Tufnell at your service.' She performed a small curtsey, playing her part to perfection.

'Well, Julie Tufnell, why don't you come here and we'll discuss the first thing that pops up.' Brian leaned back and opened his legs, revealing a large urine mark next to the small bulge in his Y-fronts.

'Why don't you borrow a pair of my pants?' offered John as he entered the room carrying the platter of smoked salmon and another bottle of Bollinger. He deposited the bottle in the top-hat ice bucket and pointed to the double doors. 'The bedroom's through there.'

As Brian left the room, Julie's smile faded. 'He's dirty. I won't go near him until he's had a bath.'

'That'll have to be part of the game. I've got this new bath gel called Badedas, it's on test in this country for six months. You can say McCann's are handling it.'

Debbie brought another batch of food to the table. 'This is a lovely place you've got here. How many bedrooms?'

'Two, but I use one as a study.'

'What ya study, mate? Playboy mags?' Brian staggered back into the room wearing a pair of John's best suit trousers, with one of his favourite silk ties as a belt. 'Watcha think?'

John's first thought was to throw him out of the window; Julie kept thinking about the stain on his Y-fronts. Debbie spooned some caviar on to a piece of decrusted toast.

'Try some of this, big boy.'

'Ah, fish eggs. My favourite.' He gulped it down in one and looked expectantly for more.

'How about some music?' John walked over to the Chinese chest to the right of the fireplace. Inside, a Quad hi-fi system flashed its readiness. 'Any requests?'

'"Rubber Soul"?' suggested Debbie.

As the beginning of 'Taxman' filled the room Julie extracted a small plastic bag from her purse and tossed it on the table. 'Is anybody good at rolling? I'm hopeless.'

By eleven o'clock all the food was gone, along with most of Brian's brain. John stood in the doorway holding a large green plastic bottle.

'Julie's company is testing this new product and I think Brian should be the first customer.'

'What I gotta do?' asked Brian, spilling the umpteenth glass of champagne on John's trousers.

'Have a bath in it. By all accounts, it's wonderful; says on the blurb it's made with chestnut oil.'

'Only if the lovely Julie will rub my back.'

'I'll rub anything you like.' Julie stood up, making sure the Australian got a good look at her stocking tops. 'You get in the bath and I'll be in shortly with another joint.'

John helped him from the room, making sure he didn't break any of the expensive ornaments on the way. 'There's another new toy I want to try out tonight. I had it sent over from New York.'

'Don't tell me, mate, a twin-pronged vibrator.'

'It's a Polaroid camera. Develops its own pictures in minutes.'

'Christ! You mean we can . . .?'

'We sure can! Anything you want.' Everything was falling perfectly into place.

Brian flung both arms in the air, spraying his drink over the flock wallpaper that covered the top half of the hall. 'Let's bloody party, old mate,' he slobbered, heading unsteadily for the bathroom.

Julie and Debbie left the flat just before three in the morning.

'You've been just great,' whispered John as he pressed the lift button

'And so have you,' replied Debbie. 'I can stay the night if you want.'

'Me too,' said Julie. 'As long as it's with you.'

John kissed them both on the cheek before opening the lift door. Some other time, ladies. I want him to myself in the morning.'

'What are you going to do?'

John smiled as he closed the door. 'Nothing violent, though God knows he deserves it. Press G for ground. Goodnight.'

The darkest hour is on the phone,
the city boys are getting home.
Stay with FREE and hear our song,
we're gonna rock you all night long.

289

Brian returned to the world shortly before ten o'clock. He opened one eye, then the other. Double vision, close one eye. He focused slowly on a Baxter print depicting the battle of the River Alma. 'Bloody war pictures,' he mumbled to himself and closed the other eye.

'They show us the error of our ways.' John's voice cut through his hangover like a blunt saw.

'Show me a picture of Bardot anytime.'

John placed a stack of Polaroids on the table beside him. 'Have a look at these; they're more your style.'

Brian tried to focus on the first picture of himself flanked by Julie and Debbie, his left arm draped over Julie's shoulder, his right hand offering a half-smoked joint to the camera. He spread them across the table; about a dozen snaps in all, each showing our hero doing something he shouldn't. He picked up a shot of him mooning to camera, the two girls kissing the cheeks of his bottom. 'We should send this to Stuart.' he joked. 'No caption necessary.'

'I was thinking of sending them all to Stuart,' said John without a hint of humour in his voice. 'Unless you and I can come to an arrangement.'

It took a few seconds for the implication to register in Brian's stupefied brain. 'Come on, mate, that's not funny.'

John sat down slowly on the settee opposite Brian's makeshift bed. 'I don't like you very much, Mr Todd. You've a crass personality, you're continuously out of your head, and you take money for including records on the playlist which is a shame because you're a good programmer and you're shitting on your talent.' The shock rendered Brian silent. 'I want to know what's going on aboard FREE. I want to know about Eddie, the Captain and Mick Tasker. I want dates and times of drug shipments and the names of people involved.'

'Jesus Christ! What the fuck do . . .'

John slapped his hand on the table next to the photos. 'Just shut up and listen! You'll do as I say, ask no questions and talk to no-one. If you don't, I'll not only show these to Stuart, I'll send them to the *News of the World*.'

The need to buy some thinking time, rather than innocence, triggered Brian's look of injured disbelief. 'I thought we were mates.'

John gathered the pictures and stood up. 'We were never that, Mr Todd. Now, I have a meeting in half an hour and I'd like you out of here.'

The Street twins were jarred from slumber by the tug bumping the side of the ship next to their porthole. A brisk easterly wind made the sea choppy, but the stream of morning sun reflecting around their cabin lent some hope that it could be another 'on-deck' day.

'Mail should be down in half an hour,' said Simon, his enthusiasm for his work undiminished by the early hour. 'And we've got to make the Georgie Fame promo.'

'No rest for the underpaid dear brother. You shower first, I'll get the coffee.'

Their arrival in the mess-room coincided with the mail sack which was thrown on to the table by a leather-clad Dutch sailor. Simon emptied the contents and started to sort the jumble of cards, letters, records and parcels which streamed into the station. He created stacks for all the DJs, and two separate piles for news and commercial production. A large brown envelope near the bottom was addressed to The Twins, FREE Radio, London. 'It always amazes me this stuff gets to us,' he said to Lewis, throwing him the package.

Lewis slid the blade of his Swiss Army knife along the top of the envelope and pulled out a thick sheaf of A4 paper.

'Another manuscript, I s'pose,' said Simon as he put the last of Honey Bogart's mail on the biggest pile.

Lewis didn't answer.

'What, is it?'

'This can't be?' Lewis beckoned his brother to join him. 'It looks like the exam papers for next month's O- and A-levels.'

'Let me see.' Simon took the papers, studied the Department of Education crest on the top of each page, the date and subject index. 'Looks real to me. Where do you think they came from?'

'Who cares!'

'What'll we do?'

An impish grin formed on Simon's mouth. 'Let's do a special Saga show. Danny Braindrip goes to college.'

'Brilliant! Should we tell Stuart?'

Simon tucked the papers under his arm. 'We should . . . but let's not.'

They spent the rest of the day locked in the production studio, breaking only for a roast lamb and two veg lunch, for which they thanked the surprised chef with a chorus of 'For He's a Jolly Good Fellow', delivered at the galley doorway in perfect harmony. It took them less than an hour to write and produce the Georgie Fame promo and a thirty-second commercial for Tropical Fruits, a local retail outlet. The rest of the time was spent meticulously crafting the adventures of Danny Braindrip and his pals Professor Baldtop and Nurse Bridget, who spoke with a French accent. They also made a promotion spot to run every fifteen minutes after three o'clock that afternoon.

Are you tired of swatting six hours a night for a lousy C or D grade? Then tune to the twins tonight for a 'Saga of the Known Universe' special; 'Danny Braindrip Gets Straight As. The answers to every question known to man will be revealed, starting at seven tonight. Help the Post Office profits by phoning a friend now and passing on the news. Win with the twins – tonight on FREE.'

The second promo went to air at three-twenty. Emma listened very carefully, confirming what she'd heard the first time around.

Jeanette appeared in the hatch. 'Lady Heath on line one.'

Feeling apprehensive, Emma picked up her phone. 'Lady Heath, how lovely to hear from you.'

'My dear child. What are those terrible twins up to? I've just had Reggie on the phone saying they're doing a programme on exams.'

Alarm bells started to clang loudly in Emma's head. 'I've heard the trailer. I know they've been trying without much success to do a swat-spot.'

'I hope it's no more sinister than that.'

'Knowing the twins as I do, I'd bet it's nothing to do with exams at all. The Saga is an abstract soap; tonight's episode is probably about finger-painting.' Emma wasn't about to let Lady Heath sense her concern.

There was a slight pause before Lady Heath answered. 'I wish I shared your confidence. Still, on to more pleasant things. Lunch next week?'

Emma thumbed through her diary. 'Tuesday or Thursday is good for me.'

'Tuesday it is, then. The Connaught, at one?'

'Lovely.'

'See you then. I look forward to it. Goodbye.'

'Goodbye, Lady Heath.' Emma put down the phone thoughtfully. She heard Stuart's footsteps clumping down the four steps to her office. He knocked twice on her door. 'Come in.'

'I've got the Essex listening figures; they're fantastic!' He saw the pensive look on Emma's face. 'What's wrong?'

'I've just had Lady Heath on the phone. The twins are up to something tonight.'

'The twins can do whatever they want. They're top by over twenty per cent. John's just put a ten-point premium on *all* their spots.'

Chapter 15

Friday, May 20 1966.

'And I would like to remind the Right Honourable gentleman that it was he who stated some months ago in this House that the pirates would be stopped.'

'Mr Speaker, my Right Honourable friend knows full well that these things take time.'

'How much time, Mr Speaker? Time for another year of students to be encouraged in their exams? Time for another slanderous attack on the monarchy? Time for his friends to make another million pounds from this covert and uncontrolled media?'

A chorus of 'Hear, hear' and 'Resign' rose from both benches.

'Order! Order!!'

Stuart sat in the visitors' gallery and held his head in his hands. In the last three weeks he'd received more flak than 109 squadron. The twins' show had been a riot; fast, funny and spattered with various answers to both levels of national exams. When discussing the Battle of Hastings, Simon suggested that as an arrow in the eye had ended Harold's reign, maybe a few delivered to Downing Street might have the same effect. To date, six thousand arrows had arrived at Number Ten.

The phone calls started the next morning and hadn't

stopped. It seemed everyone wanted a piece of him. Teachers, politicians, failed students who didn't hear the show, his own mother condemned him for what she regarded as a most un-British act. He raised his head to peer over the carved wooden railing and looked with disbelief at the ten rows of grown men and women hurling polite abuse at each other across a gap the length of two gentlemanly swords. As he walked from the gallery and out across Parliament Square he reflected wryly on the up-side. The station had doubled its audience.

He didn't know how much the increase was due to publicity and how much to good programming. With the exception of Brian Todd, whose presentation was increasingly mediocre, the station was flying on the air. The on-shore gigs were always packed, Hayes Mews was struggling to cope with two sackfuls of fan mail a day, and John Walters delivered a monthly sales figure in excess of £200,000.

Tonight, however, would see the beginning of a new adventure for Stuart Salisbury. For over two years he'd eaten, drunk and slept FREE Radio to the point of exhaustion. At the Albert Hall later tonight, the Marvin Gaye Show would signal the birth of Mayfair Promotions and Management. The MC for the evening was also a client of MPM, Honey Bogart.

Thoughts of her filled his mind as he stood in Whitehall looking for a cab. Her face floated into his private moments, disturbing his emotions and desires. Late at night he'd look out over the river and imagine her standing naked beside him. He envisaged her at Calbraith House, running through the maze, with him in hot pursuit; to catch her and tumble into the soft pine branches. Times like now, waiting for a taxi, when he should be concentrating on the next meeting, he couldn't get her out of his mind. He didn't know how to handle either her or his feelings, so he resorted to ground-rule number two: when in doubt, do nothing.

Honey prepared for this historic event by sitting perfectly still, eyes shut, arms folded in front of her, letting Michael work his magic on her beautiful golden hair. His King's Road salon, with its Danish-Modern furnishings and continuous rock music, provided a perfect meeting place for the young and affluent Chelsea set. His flamboyant appearance and outgoing personality attracted not only the wealthy, but also the creative. Pop stars, writers, producers, models, all counted on Michael to work wonders with their hair and fill them in on all the latest gossip.

After careful consultation he'd recommended an off-the-forehead style with a slight centre parting and back-combing on top to accentuate fullness in the harsh spotlights for which the hall was famous. She'd agreed and asked for a half inch off all round to get rid of any split ends. Her mind wandered over the forthcoming night. Choosing a costume had been hell. She'd gone from a straight black Cardin dress to jeans and a funky T-shirt via Biba, Givenchy and even Marks & Spencer. It wasn't until first thing this morning, walking past Harvey Nichols, that she finally made up her mind. She spotted the tailored tuxedo coat over wing-collared white silk blouse with black diamenté-studded bow tie and made an instant decision. Matching skin-tight trousers and black patent stilettos completed the outfit: her only remaining worry was did they have her size? They did; in fact, it felt as if it had been made for her.

She'd declined Stuart's invitation to get ready at Cheyne Walk and ride to the concert in the Bentley in favour of Emma's suggestion of changing at Ovington Square and splitting a cab. She thought Stuart seemed slightly miffed by her refusal and reassured him it was only because she needed another woman to help her dress. She also took the Ovington option to secure the spare bedroom for the night.

Honey had to do something about Stuart. She'd started it all by flirting with him at Trader Vic's and then ran a mile when he followed up her advances. One minute she felt like setting out to discover the real man behind the cool, assured looking managing director. The next minute she'd shun the idea on the grounds it constituted bad business. The upheaval in her own family, the mixed feelings of love and hate for her father all contributed to her state of uncertainty.

Despite several attempts at reconciliation, her father still refused to have anything to do with her, and without his approval the rest of her family remained strangers. She must resolve this whole situation soon; but how? She exhaled a long, deliberate sigh. She hadn't a clue.

'What do you think?' Michael was asking, stepping back to admire his creation.

Having her hair worked on made Honey soporific as well as pensive. She slowly opened her eyes and focused on the mirror, turning her head from side to side inspecting as many angles as possible. 'That looks glorious, Michael.'

'I'm so glad you like it. I think it'll look fabulous with your outfit.' Michael placed one hand on his hip, the other on the side of his face. 'Mind you, in that tuxedo I could fancy you myself.'

Honey spun the chair to face him, a flash of horror in her deep brown eyes. 'Don't tell me I look like a boy!'

Michael changed his hands over. 'With those breasts! Good God, *no!*'

She relaxed. 'Don't scare me like that; I'm nervous enough as it is.'

'Is there any chance of a ticket?' Michael placed both hands on his waist and gave her a pleading gaze.

Due to the popularity of the artist and the frequency of the station promotion tickets had sold out within three days. Rumour had it the black-market price was up to five times face value. Honey looked at the diminutive craftsman with his manicured fingernails and immaculately trimmed beard and thought of a possible solution. She knew it was well worth keeping him happy. She produced her 'all area' back stage pass from her coat pocket.

'You take this. Tell them you're my hairdresser and come to my dressing room. I'll need a touch-up before I go on.'

He took the pass and hugged her shoulders, taking care not to crush a single hair. 'You're so wonderful, Honey.' He turned coy and put both hands to his mouth. 'I might even meet *the* man.'

'You never know.' Honey slipped off the salon gown and wiped a Kleenex lightly around her face. 'I must go, precious. See you tonight.'

'How will you get in?' he shouted after her.

She turned in the doorway, shrugged her shoulders and smiled. 'With the boss!'

This was Honey's first shot at the big time and Emma was glad she'd be there to lend support without having to worry about Bill getting impatient. He'd be on the boat another week, so this was the start of a girls' weekend. Tomorrow, she planned lunch and an afternoon shop with Avril. Sunday she'd see her mother and show off all her bargains.

The cab they'd ordered on the firm's account arrived ten minutes early at six-fifty. Honey inspected herself in the hall mirror. She picked a long blonde hair off the front of her suit. 'This is not a good time to start moulting,' she mumbled to herself.

'You look gorgeous!' exclaimed Emma, emerging from the bedroom. 'The stage-door Johnnie's will be lined up all the way to Battersea.'

'And you,' replied Honey. 'That dress is fabulous.'

'Just a little black St Laurent: every girl should have one.'

They hugged each other, being very careful not to smudge their make-up or disturb a single hair.

Backstage at the Albert Hall bustled with activity as Emma showed her pass to security and vouched for Honey. Stuart found them almost immediately and escorted his two favourite ladies to the green room for champagne and a meeting with the stars.

Why they called it 'the green room' was beyond Emma – it was anything but that. The twenty-foot square area with its high, ornate ceiling was decorated in red flock wallpaper and cream fitted carpets, with gold baroque light fittings dotted at intervals around the walls. A large bar, manned by an equally large barman, dominated the far end of the room.

Stuart introduced them to Marvin, his manager, the music director and two exquisite black women who were described as 'friends of the family'. Marvin had marvellous manners, kissing Honey and Emma lightly on the hand, inquiring about the positions they held within the company, and complimenting them on their 'solid' outfits. Honey forgot her nerves as she sipped champagne and chatted to the Motown star about his life and music. She spotted Michael next to the bar giving her a thumbs-up sign and her stomach refilled with butterflies.

'You must excuse me,' she said, handing her champagne glass to Emma. 'It's final touch-up time.'

At five to eight Honey stood at the stage-right entrance and gripped Emma's hand.

'You'll be fine, Honey. Just don't call him Smokey Robinson.'

Honey dug her friend lightly in the ribs. 'Do I look okay?'

'You look stunning.'

The house lights faded. The announcer's voice resounded through the hall. 'Ladies and gentlemen, would you please welcome your host for this evening – a beautiful young lady who is just as at home under the glittering lights of the Albert Hall as she is fighting force-nine gales at sea to bring you the best music in the universe. The lovely Honey Bogart!'

The thunder of applause erupted in the auditorium. 'Smile,' whispered Emma, placing her hand gently on Honey's shoulder. 'Break a leg!'

As Honey stepped on stage the noise seemed to grow four times louder. Cat-calls and wolf whistles punctuated the intoxicating sound of thunderous applause. Honey walked to centre stage, drinking in every moment. She knew this rapturous reception was not for her tonight; tonight they'd come to see Marvin weave his magic. But this was her reward for all the months of bad weather, sleepless nights and dubious company she'd endured giving them what the BBC couldn't. These were her radio fans and she loved every one of them. The footlights prevented her from seeing anything beyond the second row, but she could feel the warm response roll over her like a giant wave. She would never forget this moment.

'You're beautiful,' came a voice from the centre of the house as the applause died down.

'And you're probably drunk,' she replied. Their laughter gave her confidence. 'Thank you all for that wonderful reception. I shall pass your love to everyone on the ship.' Another burst of applause. 'Tonight we are about to witness the real magic of Motown. Mayfair Promotions and Management, in association with FREE Radio, is proud to present the first UK appearance of one of the truly great soul performers of our time. Ladies and gentlemen, please give a loud, London welcome to Mr Marvin Gaye!!'

As Marvin entered from centre back stage, Honey made her exit to the right and fell into Emma's arms. They hugged each other tightly.

'That was brilliant,' said Emma.

'That was nerve-racking!' Honey could feel herself start to shake. 'I need a very large drink!'

'I'd be more than happy to oblige.' Stuart stood beside them, a broad smile radiating from his face. 'What a great opening! Well done, Miss Papanicholas.'

She didn't mind him calling her by her old name this time. He could've called her anything he liked. 'To the bar, if you please!'

The concert was a massive hit. Marvin did three encores, Honey did three large brandies. Emma chatted politely to everyone, while Stuart negotiated deals for the Supremes and the Four Tops. They all waited patiently for Marvin in the green room and gave him a huge round of applause when he finally arrived.

302

'I've a late table booked at Tiberio,' announced Stuart just before midnight. 'Everyone's welcome.'

Ken East, the managing director of EMI, and his wife Dolly accepted the invitation, as did Marvin's manager and one of the exquisite friends.

'I'm shattered,' whispered Emma in Honey's ear. 'If you want to go I'll leave the key under the first flower pot.'

'I'd like to. I feel wide awake.'

'Then do it. It's been a great evening, go and enjoy yourself. I've got an early start tomorrow.'

The restaurant was packed with its usual mixture of politicians in private parties and pop stars on public show. The diners glided across the white tiled floor between glass-topped tables, greeting business acquaintances like lost friends and competitors like blood relations. Stuart spotted Sir David Garman holding court with three of his juniors and asked the manager for a table on the far side of the room. Sir David glanced up as they passed. Stuart ignored him.

Two courses of noodles with baby clams and swordfish Palermo-style filled the gaping hole in Honey's stomach that resulted from a night of excitement and several large brandies. She enjoyed getting to know Ken and Dolly East. They were both big people; he well over six feet, she well over fifteen stone. They'd emigrated from Sydney last year when Ken accepted a directorship at EMI, and had settled comfortably in a modern fifteenth-floor flat at Porchester Place overlooking Hyde Park.

To date, Brian Todd was the only Australian to have crossed Honey's path. Meeting this warm, amusing and sophisticated couple reaffirmed her belief in judging people, not race or colour. It was a relief to realise that not everyone from Down Under subscribed to the lager-swilling, crude and sexist attitudes that had become Brian's trademark. An invitation to lunch and a tour of the EMI pressing plant was given and accepted during the dessert course of pears in port with whipped cream. After dinner the two American guests made their excuses, leaving the Easts, Stuart and Honey to finish a bottle of Armagnac with ever-increasing levity.

Just after four in the morning Charlie parked the Bentley outside seven Ovington Square. Honey and Stuart sat in the back, reliving the high points of the concert one last time.

'Not only were, you brilliant, but I've got a deal to promote two more big shows.' Stuart shifted slightly in the seat so he could look at her straight on. 'You *will* do them, won't you?'

An impish grin flashed across her face. 'Wild horses couldn't stop me, boss.'

'I wish you wouldn't call me boss.' Stuart seemed to lose enthusiasm.

Honey knew exactly why. There'd been small signs all evening. The attention he'd given her at the concert and restaurant, the way he'd locked into her conversations, his insistence on taking her home. With Charlie in the front seat she felt safe and totally in control. She could tell him to forget it or seduce him there and then. He, on the other hand, would need to remain the perfect gentleman as long as his driver was in attendance. He didn't have the same animal attractiveness that she'd been drawn to in Jonathan; he had far more on offer. Stuart Salisbury was top-drawer.

'What would you like me to call you?'

Stuart thought about her at the oddest times during his day; he'd sat in very important meetings and fantasied about making love to her; he'd walked alone beside the river longing for her company; he'd missed two empty cabs in Whitehall today due to coital daydreaming. But he couldn't speak out.

'Stuart would be fine.' His voice was tense.

She placed a slow kiss on his left cheek. 'Good night, Stuart, and thank you; for everything.'

As he watched her climb the stone steps to the front door of Ovington Square and retrieve the key from under the first flower pot, he reflected ruefully on another lost opportunity. He regretted not being truthful, not telling her how he felt. Fear of rejection seemed the only possible reason for his cowardice and it made him feel ashamed.

Honey slid between satin sheets in the spare bedroom and felt more confused than ever. She'd expected him at least to kiss her goodnight; it would've rounded off a terrific evening. But when she'd placed the kiss on his cheek he'd just sat rigid, looking straight ahead. She felt the brandy chip away at her consciousness. This problem would have to wait until a sober tomorrow.

'Good morning,' Honey whispered from the doorway, one bra strap hanging loose over her arm, the guest towel secured around her waist. 'I didn't get in until past four.'

'I know, I heard you.' Emma was only just awake. 'Would you like a cup of tea or coffee?'

'Coffee, please. Black!'

'Good night?'

'The best.' Honey readjusted the towel. 'Can we talk?'

Emma poured the boiling water into the coffee filter. 'That serious?'

'Yes and no. I'm not sure.'

'Tell me one thing.' Emma filled her tea pot. 'Are you still seeing Jonathan?'

'God, no. That ended months ago.'

'Okay, question two; how do you feel about Stuart?'

'He's wonderful.' She walked slowly over to Emma. 'If he's good in bed he'd be perfect.'

Emma removed the filter and handed Honey a mug of strong black coffee. 'So you haven't?'

Honey took the mug and slumped into the breakfast banquette. 'I could've last night, I think. I ended up kissing his cheek and saying thank you.'

'Good for you.' Emma beamed a reassuring smile across to her friend.

Honey sipped the coffee. 'I know he likes me, I think he wants me; or at least he thinks he does. He's just so polite all the damn time, so bloody proper.'

'How do you feel?'

'Like I'm putting my job on the line.'

Emma poured a cup of tea and sat down at the breakfast table. 'That's irrelevant. How do you feel about him?'

'I don't really know. Sometimes I feel we'd be great together, other times I think I couldn't handle everything that goes with him – the lifestyle, the estate, or the family.'

'In that case, go back to bed and sleep on it. If you wake up in love, go get him: if you don't – don't!' Emma shrugged her shoulders and sipped her tea. 'Easy-peasy.'

Honey sighed, and thanked her friend with a light stroke on the forehead as she shuffled past Emma on the way back to the bedroom.

*   *   *

The phone disturbed John Walters five minutes before his alarm. He hated talking on the ship-to-shore link, but loved what he heard. Brian informed him that six hours after Captain Vourner left for Amsterdam, *Taskforce* had arrived and Mick and Eddie loaded several large crates. There'd been harsh words between them which ended in Eddie being pushed overboard. Brian had rescued him with the aid of a lifebuoy and was rewarded with a juicy snippet of information. Eddie was fed up with working for Tasker, he was going to find another supplier.

'Tell him you can help him, but it will take a few weeks,' John ordered. 'Come and see me when you're next ashore. Over and out.'

This could be better than John had hoped. He formulated his plan of action as he brewed his first cup of coffee of the day. The Captain was obviously not involved, which pleased him as he'd always thought the old boy was straight. Eddie would believe Brian, which made it easier to spring a trap. John had a crucial phone call to make, but it would have to wait until after lunch when New York would be at work.

Honey woke shortly before lunch loathing all men. Whether this was due to her pounding headache or her indecision regarding Stuart was not immediately clear. Her father's bitter words of banishment haunted her first waking thoughts, as they frequently did. The possibility of two or three weeks of sensual bliss with Stuart tailing off into physical and mental mediocrity, as it had with Jonathan, filled her with apprehension. Men, be they relatives, lovers or friends, were not to be trusted. While the thought of becoming Mrs Salisbury, complete with country estate and town house, was extremely appealing, the thought of being stuck with two children and an uncaring husband who took two new lovers every year was not. Anna Papanicholas might have fallen for that; Honey Bogart was going to be a star and she didn't need any man screwing up her plans. She phoned the one person she could trust.

'Hello, Emma. Are you busy?'

'Are the Stones number one?'

'Is Stuart there?'

'He's in a meeting with John Walters.'

'I've decided not to get involved,' blurted Honey.

'Oh, dear,' sighed Emma.

'What's wrong?'

'He's been going around the office all morning saying what a beautiful and talented person you are and how he's got big plans for you.'

'That's fine. I'd like him to manage me, I just don't want it becoming personal.'

'It could be a bit late for that. Let's face it, you made the first move. You were all over him at Trader Vic's.'

'I was drunk.'

'You were stupid!'

Honey's head pounded as she tried to think clearly. 'There must be a way out of this.'

'Why don't you write to him?'

'Saying what?'

'Tell him the truth. He deserves that. He's not your run-of-the-mill tosser with a new dolly bird every week. I've never seen him like this. He really cares for you.' There was a pause in Emma's conversation. Honey could hear garbled voices in the background. 'I must go now, Gerald Copeland's just arrived. Go for a walk, lose the hangover and have a think. I'm sure a letter's the answer. It'll come to you what to say. I'll see you later.'

Honey replaced the phone. After all the euphoria of last night, she now felt plunged into depression. A bath had to be the short-term solution. She wandered into the bathroom and ran the hot water only, adding a squirt of green bath gel from the small sample tube John Walters had given everyone last week.

'It's only a rumour, but the word is BHS are going to sue for non-payment of performing rights.' Gerald sat at the board table and opened his briefcase. 'I've prepared a statement saying we would gladly pay if a deal can be worked out between the stations and the publishers. I think we should press-release this right away before Garman takes legal action. It would take the sting out of his tail.'

Emma glanced over the document. 'How much will it cost?'

'No idea. Based on what the BBC pays, a lot of money. That's not the purpose. It'll take months, maybe years to sort out a deal; we must show willing and show it publicly. If we let Garman make the first move we'll end up making excuses instead of the running.'

'Has Stuart seen this?'

'Yes. So have Caroline and London. We all agree it should go through IRC. We should release today.'

Emma studied the wording closely. She grinned at the part that called on all publishers to 'Negotiate directly with the IRC to establish an ongoing relationship for their mutual benefit'.

'They'll never wear this!'

'I hope not, but they'd look very silly suing us for something we've already offered.' Gerald produced a gold fountain pen from his inside jacket pocket. 'Just sign and I'll get this to *The Times* before they put the first edition to bed.'

Emma signed 'E.M. Saxby' carefully on the bottom of the second page.

Gerald retrieved his pen and placed the papers unfolded into his briefcase. 'What does the "M" stand for?'

'Marie.'

'That's a lovely name.' Not for the first time she felt a little uncertain as to the motives behind Gerald's friendliness.

She smiled a trifle warily at the member for Cheltenham North. 'Thank you.'

Drug-induced smiles were the order of the day in Eddie's cabin. Brian Todd finished off another three-skinner with meticulous care, lit it from the large multi-coloured candle that occupied the front corner of Eddie's desk and took a deep drag.

'Fuckin' great on the ship now wankie Vourner's gone to Holland,' he said, passing the spliff.

'I wish he'd bleedin' stay there,' replied Eddie. 'So who're these people you know in London?'

'There are two or three possibilities,' lied Brian glibly, avoiding eye contact. 'I'd rather not say names 'til I've approached them, same as I wouldn't give them your name 'til they'd signed up.'

'Fair enough.' Eddie inhaled a large lungful of smoke, held his breath and passed the joint to Brian. 'There's a lot of dosh in this,' he boasted as he exhaled, performing an unconscious impersonation of the caterpillar from *Alice in Wonderland*. 'We could make a grand a week from the dope, more if it's cocaine, and another five hundred from the porn.'

'We could make our own porn with some of these tarts that come out to see us. I had one last week, tits the size of footballs.'

'I remember her; the rest of her body was the size of the fuckin' pitch.'

They both collapsed with raucous laughter, confident of their individual wit and collective masculinity.

Chapter 16

Wednesday June 1 1966.

Dear Stuart,

It's taken ten days to write this. Before we meet tonight I must tell you . . .

Honey tore the page from her writing pad, crumpled it quickly with one hand and tossed it with unerring accuracy to join the previous attempts in the wastebin.

Dear Stuart,

That effort received the same treatment.

She'd managed to avoid him so far. This was her first three-week shore leave of the year – there were parties to go to, appearances to make. Life had become extremely busy for Honey Bogart, and she loved every second. Tonight, however, there would be no escape.

Emma's grasp of public relations and marketing techniques astonished even her teacher, John Walters. Tonight was the first airing of her latest idea to give FREE a higher profile at events they didn't promote. Tonight Bob Dylan performed at the Albert Hall. Emma had taken four prominent boxes to the right of stage. Everyone would turn out from the station, plus a smattering of celebrity guests who'd been invited to turn heads and improve photo opportunities. Invitations were also given to friendly press and important clients. Honey was a star of the station; she was expected to attend.

'The daft thing was, she felt sure he knew she was avoiding him. She'd declined his lunch and dinner invitations; her time at the office became more hectic and less frequent. If she'd wanted to be with him, she would've found the time. He wasn't a stupid man, he must have known that. Some small comfort came from the realisation that his upbringing would never allow him to make a public display of his feelings so, really, the letter wasn't necessary.

Honey called tonight's line-up the 'dream ticket'. Brian and Jonathan were on the ship, leaving her, Bill and the twins to fly the flag. Emma had set out the code of conduct at this afternoon's pre-show meeting.

'Stuart – box one; Honey – two; The twins – three; Bill and I – box four. Visit the others' patch at least once during the evening and spend some time mingling in the hall outside the boxes, especially when there's press around. Bill, have a quote ready directly after the show for the *Sunday Mirror*, Honey and the twins for *NME* and *Melody Maker*.' Her voice brooked no argument.

Clothes were not Honey's problem on this occasion. As soon as she'd heard the name Dylan she knew exactly what she'd wear. Last weekend's shopping excursion had produced a full-length floral skirt and a baggy, white muslin top with embroidered flowers and silk tie-ups around the bottom, neck and sleeves. She already owned a chunky amber necklace and a pair of dark brown moccasins. Charlie had just delivered the finishing touch – a three-quarter-length tasselled jacket and matching shoulder bag, made from best-quality leather by a little shop in Hampstead.

She'd borrowed Emma's flat to ensure a little peace and quiet before the stampede of the night ahead. She touched up her lipstick before squeezing out of the small bathroom at Bristol House, carefully locking the flat behind her and joining Charlie in the front seat of the Bentley. They'd all agreed to meet at Ovington Square for a last-minute briefing and the first glass of bubbly.

'I like riding up front – I love the way the doors open the wrong way.'

'Some people say it's the right way.' Charlie grinned cheekily at her from under his cap. 'You look lovely, Miss Bogart. Right lovely.'

'Well thank you, Charlie.' His compliment elated her; she could take on the world. 'Are we picking up the twins?'

'In Sloane Square, miss. Five minutes ago.'

Simon and Lewis scrambled from the shelter of the Midland Bank's doorway and into the back seat. 'Fine time for a shower.' said Simon, trying to mop the rain from his trousers.

'It'll stop by the time we get there,' said Honey optimistically.

Only a slight drizzle greeted them in Ovington Square as they scooted into number seven and up the flight of red-carpeted stairs to Bill's flat. Emma met them at the front door.

'Come in, come in. You all look great, just great. Those T-shirts are wild!'

The twins wore matching tuxedo T-shirts to which they'd added real bow ties. Tight black trousers and white running shoes made them look surreal, like characters from a Magritte painting. Emma wore skin-tight Levi's with small flowers embroidered around the pockets, a plain white T-shirt under a studded leather biker's jacket, and red high-heeled shoes.

'Rock and Roll!' shouted Bill from the sitting room. 'Hot news from Tinseltown!'

'What news, oh, king of the breakfast jokes?'

'That's jocks!' corrected Lewis.

Simon intoned in a WC Fields voice, 'And so it is, my little chickadee. I'm not working well; I've been left out in the rain!'

'Dylan is definitely doing the electric set second half, they've been sound-checking all afternoon,' announced Bill with total authority.

Honey pecked him on the cheek. 'That'll upset a lot of purists.'

'Screw them!' Bill returned the peck. '"Rainy Day Women" is rock 'n' roll. Personally, I think he's boring on his own. I can't wait to hear a full-tilt boogie band behind him.'

Simon raised both arms in the air in prophetic mode. 'You will be afflicted by the wrath of the purists and all your hair will fall out!'

'And your toenails will be extracted and used for gramophone needles,' continued Lewis.

'Playing Woody Guthrie songs,' completed Honey.

Buzzzz.

'Stuart Salisbury, I presume,' said Emma into the entry-phone, pushing the release button simultaneously.

'Adolf Hitler, actually,' crackled Stuart. 'With five of my brutal henchmen.'

'Bring them up. I love a good hench.'

Emma hung up the phone and looked sympathetically at Honey, who'd crept up beside her in the hall suddenly nervous.

'It'll be all right – you'll see.'

Stuart was the epitome of upper-class English charm. In his Savile Row suit and Jermyn Street shirt, he stood among a roomful of rock 'n' roll fashion and managed to look not one stitch out of place; his hair now a little longer, but still neatly combed, his eyes still sparkling and alert. He asked Honey if she was enjoying her time ashore and reminded her about the voice-over she was doing tomorrow afternoon. Not a trace of last week's events pierced his politeness which annoyed her just a little, but banished her fear that there might be awkward moments this evening.

For Bill, the highlight of the concert was 'One Too Many Mornings', with the band at full stretch and full volume. Someone yelled 'Judas' from the third row; Bill shouted 'Bravo' from the box. The press were in a failure frenzy by the end of the show. Booing fans equal many more column inches and a whole host of different adjectives.

'Any chance of an interview?' Bill whispered in Emma's ear amid the din of box four.

'He's not giving any.' She looked around the crowded enclosure. 'Go talk to David Wigg from the *Standard*, he looks lost, poor man.'

'I want to talk to Dylan!'

Emma shot him a look that a school mistress about to reprimand a wayward child would have been proud of.

'Okay, David Wigg it is.' Bill was resigned. 'Where is he?'

Because of Dylan's understandable reluctance to talk to the press, the reptiles gravitated towards the only other free booze in the house. For nearly an hour journalists, columnists, photographers and freelancers mingled with pop stars and FREE staff in the confined space of four theatre boxes and the hall connecting them. They asked what they hoped were probing questions, took dozens of pictures and consumed several crates of champagne.

As the last picture was taken and the photographer closed the door behind him, Honey collapsed onto one of the velvet upholstered chairs and let the smile drain from her face. She had mixed feelings about the show. She'd heard better live bands, but this lot did have a certain raw urgency. The guitarist appealed to her; 'subtle as a brick' she remembered calling out during his solo on 'Leopard-Skin Pill-Box Hat'.

'I think Emma pulls an "A" on this assignment, don't you?'

Stuart's voice wafted over her as she sat eyes closed, enjoying the relative silence of stage de-rigging.

'A major triumph; at least an MBE's worth,' she replied lazily.

'The twins have rounded up a group and are thinking of going to the big Chinese in Leicester Square. Fancy coming?'

Honey didn't open her eyes. 'No thanks, I'm finished.'

'I'll tell them.' Stuart closed the door quietly.

He opened it again two minutes later. 'How about some Meze and a glass or two of Ouzo followed by sea bass in olive oil with oregano and a bottle of Retsina?'

'Sounds wonderful.' She kept her eyes shut. 'Is this a good idea?'

'It's the best food this side of Rhodes.'

Honey wasn't sure if her acceptance stemmed from the exhausting evening or her suppressed desire to be with him; either way, Greek food of that quality could not be lightly passed over. She opened her eyes and allowed a smile to fill her face once more. 'It would be, Stuart. I'd expect nothing less.'

The Parnassus Restaurant, conveniently located behind Harrods, enjoyed the reputation of being a serious food place where the connoisseur was catered for and the prices kept the riff-raff from the door. An airy two-tiered room with a marble tiled floor made up the bulk of the restaurant, while five private alcoves against the back wall catered for customers not wishing to dine in the public gaze. Palm plants in stone pots stood languidly at ease in corners and between tables, rustling slightly with each passing waiter.

Stuart was greeted warmly by the manager and shown the best table in the house, overlooking the glass-roofed patio garden with its tiled murals and shady potted orange trees. It was such a delight to be with him. His manners were impeccable. He seemed to know everybody and if not, they knew him. A stunningly dressed woman whom he introduced as the lovely Anthea from north of Watford, waxed lyrical about the radio station and how she and Bertie listened to nothing else at the farmhouse. She also praised Nureyev and Fonteyn, whom she felt were exquisite this evening in 'Swan Lake'. A Brigadier Hamilton apologised profusely for disturbing them, but would Stuart please thank his mother for the beautiful flowers in the officers' mess.

The biggest surprise came from the young man who introduced himself as a friend of Camilla Bradbury and proceeded to invite Stuart's opinion on the situation presently flaring in the Congo. Although the question seemed out of place and a potential embarrassment, Stuart remained completely unphased. He replied by saying that the great nations had always acted like

319

gangsters, and the small nations like prostitutes. The man was very impressed. Stuart thanked him for his praise but admitted he couldn't really take the credit as Stanley Kubrick had said it first in 1963.

Honey washed the last of her sea bass down with the third glass of Retsina. Being with him was so easy. There was no pressure, no innuendo; he was an entirely pleasant man. She wondered why she hadn't taken her chance; judging by tonight's behaviour, it wouldn't come again. 'Are you going home this weekend?' she asked, in an effort to redirect her thoughts. As he looked up from his food she could almost read his reply. He was going to ask her to go with him.

He took a sip of wine. 'Yes. As a matter of fact we're having a little bash for Peter and his intended.' He took another sip and looked down at his food. 'I expect you're partying flat out?'

'I'm taking my mother to Paris,' she lied instantly, without knowing why.

Stuart looked at her with knowing eyes. 'What a splendid idea. You'll both have a wonderful time.'

Yes it is, thought Honey, suddenly realising how much she'd love to see her mother. I might just do it.

Bill and Emma were the last to leave the Albert Hall. Emma checked all the boxes for major structural damage, counted the chairs and met Bill at the entrance.

'Did you call a cab?'

Bill looked at his watch. 'Five, four . . .' A black cab swung into the courtyard. 'Damn! My timing's rotten tonight.'

In the cab, she held him close and they bounced together as the cab hit the speed bumps at the entrance to the Albert Hall. 'You owe me a massage,' she said, scratching between his shoulder blades.

'Since when?'

'Since this morning. You promised! You said if I . . .'

Bill reached forward and closed the partition. 'Are you trying to embarrass me?'

'Just keeping you honest. Now kiss me.'

The night is young, the song is old,
some rock 'n' roll that's solid gold.
Chuck Berry's about to take a spill
'cos he can't part Mabel from her Coupe de Ville.
This is Prince Mikie keepin' it spiky.

Chapter 17

Wednesday, June 22 1966 dawned sunny and warm over the freshly painted gunwales of M.V. *FREE*. Honey stood on the f'ward deck and let the gentle southerly wind blow away the last cobwebs of a good night's sleep. With Brian on shore, she'd work nine 'til noon. Bill's breakfast show filtered through the galley air-vent; his half-eight weather report promised clear, sunny skies with a high of seventy-seven.

'Thank you, God. That'll do me.' She yawned and stretched both arms above her head, pushing upwards until she felt her vertebrae loosen; she locked her hands and brought them slowly down to her rib-cage and let her shoulders drop. Various small clicks and bumps sounded from her backbone as renegade pieces fell back in line. She dropped her hands and started to jog on the spot; a final loosener before she'd let the morning sun dance on her face.

'No wonder you don't get laid, you never keep fuckin' still.'

Two things she didn't want this morning; a summer storm and Eddie Lincoln. 'This is a big ship, Eddie. Go stand on another part of it!'

'Come to my cabin; you need a shot of protein to

open your throat, make you sound sexy for all those housewives.'

The thought of any kind of sex with Eddie made her feel sick, but the thought of oral sex made her feel angry. Unfortunately, he was beyond slapping range and there was nothing at hand to throw at him. 'I'm on the air in half an hour. I hear it takes you that long to find it.' She turned away and started to climb down the f'ward hatch. 'I'd be better off sucking a straw.' She heard him shout 'crazy bitch' after her and consoled herself with the thought that his wit and member size were probably a well-matched pair.

'Is it really that beautiful out there?' Bill loaded the next commercial break into the cartridge machine.

'It most certainly is.' Honey placed her running order on the Anglepoise clipboard. 'Save me the deckchair next to you. I'll be there at five past twelve.'

Bill opened the microphone. '"Paperback Writer" closing out the breakfast show for today. Honey's here after the news, the news is here after these messages.' He started the Coke commercial and glanced into the production studio. 'Come on, John. Forty seconds to go.'

Jonathan Gilby was in no mood to hurry. All his grand dreams of an independent news service without political barriers were rapidly being washed away on a tide of mediocrity. All his on-shore reporters seemed preoccupied with show-business stories and beauty-contest winners. He was now convinced that Stuart had bowed to pressure from Gerald and was watering down the hard-news input in favour of non-political, local interest stories to appease the rantings of Sir Robin Clarke and company. He hadn't joined FREE to report second-hand news pirated from the BBC spiced up with this year's Miss Ilford winner. He'd spent his spare time last week writing letters to old friends in a frantic search for some real action. In the meantime, he was finding it hard to summon up enthusiasm for his work.

At ten seconds to the hour, Jon slumped on to the stool and rummaged through his sheets of typed paper desperately trying to find his lead story. He found it with two seconds to spare.

'FREE news at nine, I'm Jonathan Gilby. In Australia, opposition leader Arthur Calwell has been wounded in an assassination attempt. So far, no-one has . . .'

Bill flicked his monitor off. 'Are there lots of boats out yet?'

'Not yet.' Honey cued her first record. 'We'll have fifty by lunchtime.' She saw the glint in Bill's eyes. 'You're getting married in a month. You can do without another Catherine incident.'

'I just look and keep my hands in my pockets.'

'So I've been told.'

They both broke into laughter; Bill's tailing away as he closed the soundproof studio door behind him. He dropped his records and paperwork on his cabin desk, changed into his trunks and hastened up on deck. The sun had already started to heat the steel deckplates; it wouldn't be long before shoes were mandatory. He pulled a deckchair from the locker and set it up next to Simon Street's. 'Where's your brother?'

'He always has a pony before a long session in the currant bun.'

'Pardon?'

'He's having a shit!' Simon rubbed sun cream on his shoulders. 'I could do without visitors today. I just want to lie here and not move.'

Bill scanned the coast and counted twenty-three small black dots heading their way. 'No such bloody luck.

Enjoy it while you can, the first one'll be here in an hour.'

By eleven o'clock they were surrounded. Most of the small craft contented themselves with circling the ship, shouting requests and taking photographs. They were all tuned to FREE. On deck, Bill could hear Honey in surround-sound. A forty-foot cruiser with five women aboard bumped sloppily against the side and demanded to see the twins.

'What can I do?' shrugged Simon, following his brother down the rope ladder. 'They want to rub us with oil.'

'Be back by five, I'm not double shifting for you lot.' Bill flopped back into his deckchair and closed his eyes, soaking up the sun. He could hear the hubbub of small boats as they passed among each other, shouting orders at one another and requests at anyone aboard FREE who would listen. He felt a large bump reverberate from the aft quarter, and heard 'Sunny Afternoon' skip from the impact. 'Cowboy sailors!' he shouted across the deck.

'Excuse me.' The gentle voice was right beside him; a shortish girl in a bikini, with a round face, sea-green eyes and soft honey gold hair down to her waist. 'Could you tell me where I'd find Eddie Lincoln?'

'Where'd you come from?'

'The boat alongside.' She pointed lazily at the flying bridge that seemed to rest above the gunwales. 'How else would I get here?'

'Indeed.' Bill began to feel totally pissed off. People who couldn't navigate a bicycle were ramming their marine toys into the side of FREE and making records jump, the twins were cruising with five massage experts, and this beautiful woman appeared out of the blue asking for Eddie Lincoln, of all people. He, meanwhile, was stuck taking requests and hunting the unsavoury supply officer. 'He's most likely in his cabin.' He pointed to the hatch. 'Help yourself.'

The girl looked at Bill with a false modesty that made him think he'd never believe a word she said.

'I couldn't go down there. I'd get lost in a second.'

'Jesus!' Bill stood up reluctantly and offered the girl his deck chair. 'You sit there; I'll go get him.'

Below deck felt refreshingly cool after the heat topside. He knocked once on Eddie's door and pushed it open. The smell of marijuana and body odour combined in a stench to rival bilge water. Bill stayed in the hall. 'There's a lady on deck asking for you.' He walked back towards the fresh air before the cabin smell made him nauseous.

Eddie wasn't expecting anyone; still, a woman is a woman, he'd better have a look. Taking a small amount of grass and cocaine from his private stock just in case, he locked his cabin door and walked slowly into the sunshine. The girl stood next to the hatch, the southerly breeze blowing her long hair behind her like a kite ribbon.

'I'm Helen.'

'And I'm the luckiest man alive.' This was as close as Eddie got to charm. He ogled her body with all the subtlety of a flasher.

She moved as if to kiss him then slid her mouth to his ear. 'Brian says you might be interested in business.'

Eddie nodded.

'Come aboard and meet my friends.' She removed herself from him as quickly as she'd come, walked across the deck, past Bill lounging in his deckchair, and stopped at the gap in the railing.

Eddie watched her slinky walk appreciatively; she was

on the same glide path as the hooker in Amsterdam, and that had ended with sex, drugs and a pair of gold cufflinks. He couldn't see whether Bill was watching him from behind those dark sunglasses, or just lying there with his eyes shut. He blanked the jock from his mind, put his hands in his pockets and started to meander towards Helen. He'd just heard his second favourite phrase next to 'more money' – 'new business'.

The *Lady Zee* was not unlike *Taskforce Two*; a few years older and not the same attention to gaudiness, but, nevertheless, roughly the same shape and size. Helen's friends were the Captain, a heavy-set man in his forties with a substantial beer gut and a battered hat to signify his rank; Thomas the Tank, a mountain on legs with a jovial manner and leather wrist bands; and Frank Horieken, a short Jewish man of Armenian origin who wore expensive suits and cheap aftershave.

Helen completed the introductions and slid, cross-legged, on to one of the white leather banquettes that encircled the stateroom.

'She's not just a beauty,' said Frank, offering the seat next to her. 'Helen's our accountant.' He placed his hand lightly on her forearm. 'What's one plus two?'

'Three million, Frank.' Her voice was totally deadpan.

Frank laughed, the mountain roared, the Captain sat at the wheel and chuckled quietly to himself.

'Now, Mr Lincoln.' Frank's voice softened. 'Who's the bozo on deck?'

'Bill Mason? He's the breakfast jock. Just sunning himself, he's okay.'

'Nevertheless,' he left a slight pause, 'I make it a habit not to talk business within earshot of unconcerned parties.' He nodded his head slowly several times, until Eddie started to mimic his movement. 'I think the Captain should cruise us around this armada of music so we can talk with reasonable security.'

Eddie resembled a nodding dog; Frank's head was now still.

'I'll cast us off,' said the mountain, smiling at Eddie. 'You wanna drink?'

'Hey, sure, anything.' Eddie had decided to go with the flow.

'Helen makes a great cocktail!' Frank raised his voice as the twin engines throbbed into action. 'What's it called?'

'A banana daiquiri,' she said, looking across at Eddie and mouthing the words very slowly. 'I go heavy on the rum.'

Honey popped her head through the f'ward hatch and shouted at Bill. 'Thanks a bundle for saving the deckchair!'

He jumped to his feet, made the deck locker in three strides and had the chair erected within thirty seconds. 'I am a man of my word. Your chair, madam.'

Honey drifted across the deck sipping from her glass of icy lemonade and taking in the extraordinary sight of small craft circling the ship in an anticlockwise direction; their radios blaring out the Rolling Stones and Coke commercials. 'This is seriously weird,' she said, sitting next to him. 'You can't turn it off.'

'The sweet sound of success.' He adjusted his sunglasses. 'Just wave to them every ten minutes.'

She flicked a finger of lemonade at him. 'You're terrible! Who's off?'

'The twins went on a boat with five women and Eddie got picked up by a blonde on a stick.'

'Tasker?!'

'No. Somebody else.' He turned his head to face her. 'Looked just as seedy.'

'That stuff scares me. I don't mind it for personal use.' She saw his expression change to one of concern. 'I had a little puff last time I went ashore with Jilly, you remember, the red-head.' Bill nodded. 'We giggled a lot, that's all.'

'We're not dealing with the little puff, we're dealing with large crates. It seems as soon as Stuart takes Tasker out, there's a queue forming to replace him.'

'I think we should get rid of "vomit mouth" Lincoln.' Honey spread sun cream on her legs, carefully avoiding a shin scrape from last week's encounter with the bridge hatch.

'You should cover that, it'll burn easily.'

'I'll put a flannel over it.'

'And get a striped leg? I've got a transparent Band-Aid in my cabin.'

She shaded her eyes with her hands and looked over to him 'Would you?'

Bill begrudgingly pushed himself to his feet once again.

'While you're up, there's a big jug of lemonade in the galley fridge . . .'

Jugs were uppermost in Eddie's mind as he watched Helen bend over and retrieve a dropped earring. 'The deal I had with Tasker was every time he came out, he brought a couple of ladies with him. Free for me and charge the sailors what you like.'

'I'm sure we can make similar arrangments.' Frank

Horieken glanced briefly towards Helen then back to Eddie. 'On this operation we use limpet containers. No merchandise moves above the water. That way, we are invisible and the temptation for you to go skimming is removed.'

'I wouldn't . . .'

Frank placed both hands on Eddie's shoulders. 'I know you wouldn't, but now it's not an issue.' He stepped back. 'This tug has an underwater hatch; the divers will never be seen. How much did you shift with Tasker?'

'On average, a thousand a week, depending on stock and weather. Do you guys mind if I roll a joint?'

'I do up here!' Frank's voice was jovial, friendly. 'More people with binoculars out here than flies on a shit-heap. Go below. Helen'll show you.'

'Are you Frank's girlfriend?' asked Eddie as he watched her close the cabin door.

'Not for a long time. I'm a working girl.' She sat on the corner of the bed and slid back on to one elbow. 'Got any Charlie?'

'As it happens, I have!' His adrenaline pumped faster. Not only the deal, but also this raving beauty about to get high with him and probably wax his rod. He handed her a small white package from his coat pocket. 'You cut the coke, I'll roll a joint.'

'I'll need a blade from the toilet.' She tucked the package inside her bikini-top and slinked forward until her mouth was inches from his. 'Back soon!' she pouted.

His adrenaline rush reached a climax as he watched her leave the room. He couldn't wait to have a professional sort him out again. These radio groupies were okay, better than a blue flick and his right hand, but nothing compared to a voluptuous, cocaine-high woman who did it for a living. He finished rolling the joint and was about to light it. 'What's the matter? No blades?'

'I've found one!' Helen's voice sounded excited. 'I'm just putting on some stockings. You like that?'

'Take your time!' Eddie lit the spliff and propped some pillows up against the headboard. He thought of her shapely legs covered in black silk; her blonde hair touching the floor as she knelt before him, her ample breasts swinging gently between his legs. He took a deep drag and closed his eyes. He'd soon be in heaven.

'Just a few more seconds!' Helen shouted from the toilet.

'It's okay, baby; when you're ready.' Eddie kept his eyes shut.

'It's done! It's positive!!'

Eddie's eyes snapped open at the same time as the cabin door. The Captain, the mountain and Frank Horieken stepped inside and aimed assorted firearms at Eddie Lincoln. Frank produced a leather wallet from his inside pocket.

'Detective Inspector Horieken, Interpol, at your service. You're under arrest, Mr Lincoln, for being in possession of a controlled drug and for conspiring to transport said drug into Britain.'

Eddie's expression could have been sold to Hammer Horror for a fortune. 'Fuck you! We're in international waters. You can't do this.'

'Oh yes we can!' Helen appeared from the toilet, a brown rubber apron covering her bikini, and definitely no stockings. 'We're less than a mile from the coast and the powder you gave me has just tested sixty per cent cocaine, so spread 'em, you little dirt-bag!'

'Very well put, Sergeant,' said Horieken.

'With such feeling,' grinned Thomas the Tank, effortlessly flipping Eddie over on to his front. 'Do like the lady says!'

Honey Bogart had had enough sun and radio. She felt a bead of perspiration slide off her moist forehead, trickle over her cheek and join the others in a small pool at the front of her neck. 'I'm off for a long, cool shower and a drink to match.'

'Excellent idea.' Bill propped himself on both elbows and looked through the railings. 'Another go on the lilo first?'

'No thanks, and I don't think you should do much more. The back of your legs are turning lobster.'

'I've got some cream for that.'

They folded the chairs, deflated the lilo, gathered their things, and walked arm in arm across the deck.

'And this cream would be in your cabin, would it?'

'Of course.'

'Bill Mason, your chat-up lines are getting worse by the day.'

'MR MASON! MISS BOGART!'

They swung round to face the flying bridge. Bill cupped his hands in front of his mouth. 'CAPTAIN!'

'MY CABIN!'

Bill mimed washing himself, the Captain nodded. 'TEN MINUTES!'

'I wonder what that's about?' quizzed Honey, as she climbed down the steel ladder to the deck below.

'Wants to tell us off for spilling suntan oil on the deck would be my first guess.' Bill followed her down the ladder. 'Right now a shower is all I care about. I'll see you at Vourner's café.'

Captain Vourner's smile was warmer than usual as

he handed Bill and Honey a large jug of lemonade and two glasses. 'Eddie's been arrested by Interpol.'

'Brilliant!' shouted Honey.

'When?' asked Bill. He sounded far more serious than his colleague.

'About an hour ago; he's in Harwich. They're coming back to search the ship.'

'Can they do that?' Honey's mood now matched Bill's as she realised the implications for FREE.

'Only with my permission.'

'Have you talked to Stuart?'

'Of course.' The Captain took a long drink. 'He thinks it's a foreign raid, maybe from Holland. Says we should co-operate.'

'They've got my vote,' said Honey, her cheerful disposition returning. 'Just to have Lincoln off this ship is worth a little inconvenience.'

Bill remained hesitant. 'If they find a quantity of drugs or porn on this ship it could mean serious inconvenience for all of us.'

'I would like to think,' said the Captain, his eyes sparkling, 'that I can persuade them we need a decaying tooth pulled rather than a new set of teeth.'

'I would like to think they're human. Interpol's staffed with the Nazis that got away.'

'I fear you're a bit behind the times, Mr Mason. Sergeant Helen Kowalski seemed very impressed with you; in fact she specifically asked for you to show her the ship.'

Honey gave Bill a slow, exaggerated wink. Bill looked astonished.

'Is she the gorgeous blonde who came on board?'

'I've no idea. She's part of the arresting team, that's all I know.'

Bill rapidly revised his opinions regarding Interpol.

'Shit! Bugger me!! This is not happening!'

Jonathan's shouts from the radio room could be heard through the cabin walls. Bill, Honey and the Captain rushed next door.

'Mr Gilby! Whatever's wrong?'

Jonathan handed the Captain a copy of this morning's *Daily Express* that had just arrived on the service tug. Under the headline 'Pop Pirate Shot Dead', the article read: 'Reg Calvert, 37-year-old owner of pop station Radio City, was shot to death this morning in the hallway of Major Oliver Smedley's home at Wendens Ambo, near Saffron Walden, Essex. Although no charges have, as yet, been laid, it is believed Major Smedley is helping the police with their inquiries.'

All three studied the article with disbelief. It continued by documenting Calvert's career as a cinema operator, TV engineer, hairdresser, ice-cream salesman, fairground impresario and pop-corn maker. It also mentioned that Radio Caroline had taken over the station some months ago, and were themselves in negotiations with Radio London and FREE to establish a stable commercial footing from which the station could operate. In its heyday, under the management of Screaming Lord Sutch, the station boasted a revenue of £5,000 a week, but since Mr Calvert's involvement, the station was said to be operating on a break-even basis.

Bill let the paper drop. 'I was on the tug with Reg a couple of weeks ago. He said he'd got the money situation stabilised.'

'Probably sold the pop-corn franchise,' quipped Honey in an attempt to lighten the mood.

'What worries me,' Jonathan ignored her, 'is why London didn't feed us the story via ship-to-shore this morning. It's twelve hours old now; if the Major doesn't get charged with murder I may as well eat my chips off it.'

The Major had been charged with murder some three hours ago but still London remained silent. Stuart's first reaction had been to sit on the story in the hope it would only make the local papers. As the day progressed it became obvious this would not be the case. He lounged in his office chair and listened to the taped voice-bite from his reporter in Essex with a frown.

'Major William Oliver Smedley, chairman of Project Atlanta, a pop radio company, and former member of the Liberal Party executive, was charged at Saffron Walden Magistrates' Court today with the murder of Mr Pearce Reginald Hartley Calvert, head of Radio City. After a four-minute hearing Lord Braybrooke, the chairman, remanded Smedley in custody until Friday week. This is Brent Coleman for FREE news in Essex.'

'You've got to send it to the ship.' Emma leaned against the office door. 'Jonathan's bound to know by now. It's been on the Home Service, for Christ's sake!'

His private phone rang. 'Stuart Salisbury.'

'Stuart, it's Gerald. We have a serious problem. Have you released the story?'

'I'm sitting on what I can of it, but it's everywhere. The ship must have picked it up on BBC news by now.'

'How about your team?'

'I've got a reporter in Essex. He's just filed some

actuality from the hearing at Saffron Walden; nothing clever, just that Smedley's been charged.'

'Send it all to the ship, run with the story. It's too late to stop it.'

Stuart started drawing triangular doodles on his blotting pad. 'Is that the bad news?'

'I wish, old chap. The bad news is, this is the break Clarke's been waiting for. He's already banging on the Cabinet's door screaming lawlessness, gangsters, security risk and God knows what else. An hour ago I heard him talking to the Ministry of Defence about terrorist threats. He's got a full head of steam up, has our Sir Robin. How's the Eddie Lincoln saga?'

'A blank wall. The only contact I have with them is through the ship. They want to search.'

'Nothing from the Yard or Harwich customs?'

'Not a thing. They all say they've no record of such an arrest being made.'

'What are you thinking of doing?'

'Letting them search and, if they find contraband, dump the blame where it belongs, on Mr Lincoln's backside.'

There was a moment of silence from Gerald. 'We need to keep this story out of the press. If it breaks on top of the Calvert killing you can chop your mast down tomorrow.'

'I should go out to the ship.'

'No! The Captain can handle Interpol, I need you here. Come to the House for tea. I'll gather Slattery, Heath and company; we'll need to plan our response quickly.'

The Captain handled Interpol with the expertise of a seasoned diplomat; Bill handled Sergeant Kowalski as

337

often as protocol would allow. It was an out-and-out flirtation and they both knew it, but somehow it seemed to turn the search into a fun thing, rather than the embarrassing ritual it could have been. Helen had regaled him with the story of Eddie's arrest, and was pleased to find Bill's opinion of him was nearly as low as hers. Bill thought of Emma just long enough to regain his perspective.

Detective Inspector Horieken and the Captain checked over the ship's inventory, noting all the items bearing Eddie's signature; Thomas the Tank and the Captain of the *Lady Zee* systematically searched the crew's quarters.

Bill and Helen were modelling their search of the lower deck and engine room on TV cop shows. Mason & Kowalski or the High Seas, with dialogue like, 'Who's in there?', 'Bernie the bad guy with a Browning Automatic!', 'Well shoot him, partner' delivered in bad American accents. It was all getting very silly. Bill didn't know if it was a sinister ploy to gain his trust before 'doing an Eddie', or some intricate foreplay to a serious sexual pass.

'I hope you don't find anything,' he said, sitting down on the top stair leading to the ship's engines. 'I'm getting married on the tub next month and I don't fancy the ceremony in a customs' lock-up.' He beckoned her to sit beside him. 'I pumped this room out last winter and there's no place to stash anything bigger than a matchbox.'

'Right! You search for the matchbox, I'll cover you from here.'

There was no laughter this time. She put her hand on his shoulder and lowered her head for a moment before snapping it up and catching his eyes with hers.

'I've listened to you for months. I just wondered if you were the same wacko off the air.'

She retrieved her hand and straightened her blouse so that her epaulettes sat squarely on her shoulders. 'We don't want to find anything, Bill. The last thing I want is to see you off the air. We don't even want Eddie Lincoln; he's just bait for the big boys.'

'Then why go through all this?' questioned Bill, becoming increasingly bemused at this seemingly pointless game.

'Because we have to. The report must say "thorough search". What we want are the names in Eddie's little black book. By now Thomas should have extracted it from behind the top drawer of his desk, along with the rest of his personal stash.'

Bill looked surprised. 'He told you that?'

'They all put it there.' She smiled at him. 'Bet you a fiver.'

Horieken and Thomas spread Eddie's life across the mess-room table. Shaving tackle, three half-smoked joints, pornographic magazine, two hairbrushes, a small glass bottle filled with white powder, a toothbrush, a large leather pouch stuffed with marijuana, one slab of hash, six packets of cigarette papers and, taking pride of place, a red leather-bound book with gaffer tape still attached. Bill was glad he'd refused Helen's bet.

'It seems all the contraband found came from Eddie's cabin,' said Horieken in a formal voice. 'It's therefore safe to presume he was acting alone.' He turned and shook the Captain's hand. 'Thank you very much for your co-operation. I can't see any need to trouble you further.' Then to Helen, 'Label the items, Sergeant.' He returned his attention to Captain Vourner, steering him towards the door; his manner changing completely to one of warm cameraderie. 'Tell me, Jan. Is there any way I can get a request played for my wife? Something new and with-it; maybe on Bill's show tomorrow?'

> *It's time to park with Johnny Dark,*
> *and flash those lights in Frinton.*
> *Be careful what you smoke tonight,*
> *you could end up in prison.*

'Be grateful the Lincoln story hasn't broken.' Gerald dunked his croissant in the coffee. 'Where's Emma?'

'Having breakfast with Lady Heath.' Stuart looked at his watch. 'Should be here shortly.'

The loud thud of the garage door signalled Emma's arrival. Breakfast had been traumatic. Emma was shocked and dismayed at Lady Heath's attitude. Gone were the pleasant remarks of encouragement, the verbal ego-stroking. Even the 'So glad to see you' line was replaced with a chilly 'Well, young lady, what a mess!' She informed Emma that the armies of suppression were on the march in the House and gaining support by the hour; that all Emma could do was go home and wait for the axe to fall. She even brought up their first meeting, when she'd expressed her anxieties about anarchy.

'You see,' she concluded, folding her napkin and signalling for her coat. 'One should always trust one's first instincts.' She swept away from the table and the bill.

'I hope you two have good news.' Emma shuffled up the last few steps and deposited her briefcase gloomily on the Sheraton table. 'I thought we were friends. That woman cut me off as if I'd never existed.'

'Come and sit down.' Gerald patted the sofa beside him. 'First lesson in politics, dear lady. Count your friends by the hour.'

'I can't believe she'd be so ghastly.'

'It's nothing personal, just like the friendship.' Gerald smiled at her naivety and took her hand as she sat down beside him. 'You're a new face, someone who might rise in stature, possibly eclipsing her ladyship in the future. She would want to take credit for your status, thereby improving her own. She'll run from failure just as fast.' He could see Emma was about to cry. He cupped her face and looked firmly into her doleful eyes. 'Don't you dare let that bitch of the realm get to you. We are your friends, and we're a long way from losing this ball game!'

'First class,' interjected Stuart, lazily buttering his third croissant. 'Something must have changed her mind since last night. She was the most positive voice at the meeting, I thought.'

'When a politician says you look well, you know you have a week to live.' Gerald squeezed Emma's hand before letting go and sinking back into the sofa. 'When a woman politician says it, you've got an hour.'

Emma forced herself to feel optimistic. 'We don't know this killing wasn't personal. It may have nothing to do with the radio.'

'It doesn't need to.' Gerald clasped his hands together, his face turning serious. 'Because of all the takeover bids, management contracts and equipment deals over the last few months, involving, may I say, *all* the major players, it doesn't matter a monkey's toss if Uncle Reg got popped for a pecker impropriety or for stealing the

341

Crown Jewels. The opposition has you all together in one bag along with one dead body.'

Stuart placed his croissant back on the plate. We were only helping Radio City to keep them afloat. Most of the time we just waived the charges; I don't think Emma's billed them for the last survey yet, have you?' Emma shook her head.

'I'm not getting through to you.' The impatience in Gerald's voice captured their full attention, and he grasped the knife-edge of opportunity. 'I think you should seriously think of getting out.'

Stuart was the first to react. 'Never!'

Emma felt suddenly queasy, and deeply saddened. Since her first day at work she'd never once entertained the thought of quitting, of giving up what she believed was the fight for a generation; her generation. She banished the remark from her mind. 'This will all blow over in a couple of weeks.' She conjured her broadest smile. 'I'm getting married on that station next month, so you can't get out.'

Only their mouths returned her smile; their eyes reflected worry and concern. Stuart went back to his croissant, Gerald poured two cups of coffee.

'There'll be time for that,' reassured Gerald. 'It'll take that long to find a buyer.'

'BUYER!' Stuart nearly choked. 'You mean *sell*, not quit?'

'Of course I mean sell.' Gerald was visibly taken aback by Stuart's innocence. 'My God, boys and girls, we never start and quit anything; we buy and sell.'

'Gerald! How could you?' Emma burned with indignation. 'You're talking about people's lives, careers. This is not some old car you flog before the engine conks out. This is the future of radio!'

The two men looked at each other and then at Emma.

'Don't patronise me! Either of you! This is *my* station as well as yours, and I intend to fight!' She could barely contain her anger. 'Buy and sell? Hell! Stand and fight!'

'Against what?' asked Gerald. 'An act of Parliament?'

'We've been fighting them all along! What's so different now?'

'Until now, we've been a bit of fun; good PR, part of swinging sixties London. Now there's been a bloody murder and most likely a major drug bust, all sitting out there in full view of the whole country. Labour don't want us on principle, my crowd hate disruption of law and order, and the Church has now joined the chorus screaming about morality and American evangelists. We're not fun any more, boys and girls, we're a liability.'

Emma felt tears coming on; it was stupid, unnecessary, and these days very un-her, but there it was. She reached into her bag for a handkerchief.

Stuart jumped to his feet. 'Don't you dare!' His sudden move made them both jump. 'If you cry, I'll sing!'

Emma blurted out a half laugh, half sob, then regained her composure. 'I don't dare say I'm sorry.'

'Definitely not!' Stuart walked over to Emma's desk and perched on the edge. 'I'd be interested to know if you have a plan, Gerald, or are you just spouting bottom lines?'

'I have possibilities. It'll take a month to six weeks for them to table a bill to the House; another year or so to make it law. If you sell before the bill is published, you'll make a fortune; if you sell after publication you'll likely break even. If you go on past the law date, you're pissing into the wind.'

'Point taken.' Stuart walked back to the sofa. 'Any new players on the field?'

A wry smile broke on Gerald's face. 'Right here at home.'

For some inexplicable reason Stuart looked at Emma.

'Not me,' she laughed. 'I couldn't afford a turntable.'

'Bill could. His family has money.'

'Children! Please!' corrected Gerald. 'It's John Walters.'

Stuart and Emma gazed at each other in total amazement. 'Are you sure?'

'His father came over last week for a meeting with Slattery; went on interminably about drugs and corrupt management. Said he had to protect his clients' interests and dropped heavy hints about an offer. I have a feeling John was responsible for Interpol.'

'Makes sense.' Stuart threw his arms in the air and sank back into the sofa, mimicking Gerald's position. 'But Slattery's bound to tell him about the bill; he'll not want to buy then.'

'Slattery is my friend and Walters is American. Apparently, he couldn't stand the man.'

'Like father, like son,' put in Emma. 'I can't see our people taking too kindly to the sales king running the show.'

Stuart sat upright, almost righteous in his bearing. 'We shall ask each one individually. If they don't want to work for him they can come with us.'

Emma laughed her question. 'To what?'

'Mayfair Promotion and Management.'

Gerald joined in her laughter. 'From Marvin Gaye to the Beatles. What an optimist! I love it!'

'What a businessman.' Stuart's face turned serious. 'If this offer's on the cards, I don't want him knowing we know. I think I'll manufacture a rival bid.'

'Bill and I could be some help with that.'

'Bless you, Emma. Give me a day or two of planning; I'll get back to you.'

Chapter 18

Friday, July 22 1966.

On page eight of *The Times*, under the headline 'Pulling Out The Plugs' was a report on a meeting of the Music Publishers Association. It read:

> The M.P.A. is asking its 260 members to sign an agreement pledging themselves not to enter into transactions involving inducements. This is because of worries over 'plug money' which is said to have been requested by employees of pirate radio stations in exchange for playing certain records. The secretary of the M.P.A. said there had been instances of such inducements, but inquiries yesterday suggested the practice of 'plug money' was not widespread. People in pirate radio, usually indiscreet to the point of slander, seemed genuinely unable to recall clear-cut cases of bribery with money. If a disc jockey did take 'plug money' there is no obvious law under which he could be punished. Bribed footballers have been convicted of conspiracy to defraud bookmakers. But Government departments yesterday could not recall any statue or common-law principle that forbids the taking of 'plug money'.

'Are you happy now!' shouted Stuart, throwing a copy of the newspaper across the desk at an exhausted Brian Todd.

'Easy on, mate. Last night was my first ashore. I'm stonko this morning.'

Stuart was unrelenting. 'Who paid for it?'

The thought of reliving the orgiastic evening perked him up a bit. 'There was this lovely Sheila with tits the size of Melbourne. Her friend kept . . .'

'I don't want a re-run! I want a name!'

Brian shrugged his shoulders, unable to believe that anyone would decline a blow-by-blow account of his sexual exploits. 'Manny Sherman took me out.'

'The agent?'

'The very same.'

'Does he want you as a client?'

'Christ, no! He's got this girl singer; she's the one with the tits.'

A feeling of resignation overtook Stuart and he sank wearily into his chair. 'Read the damned article, man. That's just what they're talking about.'

'I've read it!' Brian was as aggressive as his headache would allow. 'It says it's not illegal to take money, so how can it be illegal to get laid?'

'It's morally wrong!'

'So's fuckin' Vietnam!' Brian had taken quite enough lip from someone he considered a rich upper-class poofter. 'If some piece of kangaroo shit stitches me up, it's *me* in court, not you. I'm the best chart man in the UK and you need me. Why don't you balance your books and leave the work to the fucking professionals?'

Stuart reflected wryly that at least he hadn't offered Brian the chance to join Mayfair Promotion and Management. He stood up, walked across to the window and peered into the mews, where he saw John Walters stepping awkwardly out of a black cab. A rakish smile crossed his face. His next meeting, he was sure, would be more productive. 'Thank you, Mr Todd. Good day to you.' He kept his back to the best chartman in the UK.

At Ovington Square Emma hung on to the phone and waited for the airline clerk to confirm her booking. Next she must phone her mother to arrange a meeting place. The only regret Emma had about her wedding day was that her family couldn't – or wouldn't – get to the ship. She'd tried to persuade her mother it was perfectly safe, but received an emphatic 'no'. Her sisters, of course, said they'd stay with the old girl; so that was that. She'd arranged for them to come to Harwich and they'd all travel to Heathrow together – it was the best she could do. It saddened her a little, but not enough to spoil the day.

Bill walked up behind her and slipped his hands under her arms, sliding them firmly on to her breasts. She took one step forward; so did he. She felt her nipples harden at his touch and rested the back of her head on his shoulder, opening her mouth just a little, anticipating his kiss.

'Hello, Mrs Mason, sorry to have kept you.'

She restored her head to an upright position. It was the first time anyone had called her Mrs Mason, and it sounded wonderful. 'Hello, yes. Is everything okay?'

'Two first-class seats to Kingston, Jamaica, on the seventeen twenty-four flight tomorrow for Mr and Mrs Mason. That is confirmed, madam.'

'When do we need to be there?'

'One hour before.'

349

Emma felt so happy that even the conversation seemed in slow motion. 'Thank you.'

'You're welcome. Enjoy your flight and thank you for flying BOAC.'

Emma hung up and turned to face her fiancé. She slipped her arms around his waist and up his back, massaging his muscles with short, deliberate strokes. She pouted and placed a soft, lingering kiss on his lips. 'I love you, Bill Mason.'

'And I love you.' He gripped her bottom and pulled her hard against him. 'Want me to show you how we skewer chickens back home?'

She broke free and danced away. 'You're disgusting! Vile! To the point of perversion!' She lifted her loose floral skirt very quickly, allowing him only the slightest glimpse of thigh. 'I knew there was something about you I liked.'

'I would like to make you an offer you'll find hard to refuse,' said John Walters, dumping his briefcase with a loud thump on to Stuart's desk. 'It's time you and I understood each other.'

Stuart didn't know whether to act surprised, feign displeasure, or laugh. He decided to remain expressionless. 'I'm intrigued; do go on.'

'I find many major flaws in your management strategy. You're spending far too much on creature comforts for the ship. If they want beer, wine and cigarettes, they should buy them from a quartermaster. The news department is costing an arm and a leg financially and politically; it should be scrapped. The overnight shows are not cost-effective; we should close down at nine o'clock.'

Stuart was quite prepared to let him have his say.

He could ridicule the management all he liked, the only statement Stuart waited for with mounting anticipation was 'How much?' But he felt obliged make a show of joining in the rhetoric and decided to take John to task on overnights. 'We're the only people going twenty-four hours, legal or pirate. I think you'll find our audience share would nosedive if we cut back the hours. If listeners go to sleep with us, they wake up with us.'

John continued unrepentantly. 'I don't give a shit about an extra ten thousand. I sell six in the morning 'til nine at night, and that's only when the twins are on; it's six 'til six without them. I have to give away spots after midnight.'

'Heaven forbid you should give anything away,' mocked Stuart. 'We'll be selling the requests next.'

'If I could, I would.' John produced an envelope from his case. 'The bottom line is, I think I can do a better job and so do the backers.' He slid the envelope across the desk. 'A banker's draft for one million dollars in exchange for all your shares and your directorship.'

FREE had so far cost Stuart half that amount. He left the envelope where it lay, his expression unrevealing. 'It all sounds very good, John, and I must say all this rock 'n' roll is making me old before my time, but I'm afraid you're a bit late. I have another offer.' He watched the American try, unsuccessfully, to hide his surprise. 'A few weeks ago, perhaps, but my negotiations have been moving on apace; we should complete by the middle of next week.'

'Wait a minute!' John adjusted his position to one of attack; legs crossed, left arm across his stomach, right hand ready to wag and point. 'You only own a third.

351

Whoever buys you doesn't have control. Who is this Johnny-come-lately?'

'Who it is doesn't concern you.'

'It damn well concerns the American money.'

'No, it doesn't.' Stuart adopted the opposite body position to his sales director, leaning back, hands clasped behind his head. 'I can dispose of my shareholding in any way I see fit; I don't even have to offer them to the Americans first.' He raised his eyebrows. 'At any price.' Time to call time out. 'Tell you what, Mr Walters. Let me think this over today. We'll talk tomorrow at the wedding.' He pushed the envelope back across the table. 'Please excuse me, I'm late for lunch.'

John scooped the bank draft and his case from the desk. 'It's nothing personal, Stuart. The backers see another three years in this, top whack, and they want to maximise profit. Whoever this other party is, we'll buy them out. So why don't you deal with us and cut out the middle man?' He offered his hand. 'Think about it.'

Stuart clasped the sales director's hand in a firm shake. 'Thank you for being honest,' he said, with his most genuine smile.

He waited until he heard the latch click on the front door before phoning Gerald Copeland. 'Game on! I'll need your shares tonight . . . Drinks at my place? Seven o'clock . . .? Good, see you there.'

Honey Bogart contemplated her last voice-over of the morning. Brian seemed to be off the ship so often these days, she felt completely at home in the nine 'til noon slot. More letters were arriving at Hayes Mews for her than for the regular host, mainly from housewives pouring out their unattainable fantasies to a total stranger. Nevertheless, they were women tuning to a woman rather than a man. She had one letter left for today's show. 'Number one on the FREE Forty, Chris Farlow, "Out Of Time". A note here from Jackie Richardson of Dulwich. She wants to say hello to David Percival of Forest Hill and tell him not to be such a, I think that's banker, and call her today.' She started the record. 'She loves you river deep and mountain high. Here's Ike and Tina Turner.'

She loaded the last commercial break as Nigel hurried into the studio, arms full of albums, headphones wrapped around his neck. 'I'm looking forward to the wedding tomorrow, if only for the bridesmaids.'

'It's only me.' Honey signed the commercial log and vacated the chair. 'Do you want to go into the news? Everything's on time.'

'Okay, off you go.' Nigel took the driving seat.

Honey was out of the door before the record ended. She strolled back to her cabin, flipped her door sign to 'No' and turned on the shower. She'd already talked to Stuart about her future career and was inspired by his unbridled optimism. His main goal for Honey was television. He'd said she had the looks, the brains and the boobs; she'd put this last remark down to enthusiasm and forgave his *playboy* mentality. He might bring some good news with him tomorrow. She peeled off her clothes in one flowing movement, stepped into the shower and let the warm jets of water drench her body, washing away the studio grime and lifting her spirits. Tomorrow would be a total one-off. Getting married on a pirate radio ship was not the way your run-of-the-mill couples chose to get spliced; but then, Bill and Emma were definitely not run-of-the-mill. They were friends of Honey Bogart, for a start.

* * *

In Ovington Square lunch was being eaten off two naked stomachs. Bill had shopped at Harrod's food hall and purchased a tub of Beluga caviar as a pre-nuptial treat. They'd decided bed was the only proper 'place' to enjoy this gastronomic delight, and their bodies the only appropriate serving dishes.

'I wonder where Stuart's eating lunch?'

'Off a plate, I imagine,' said Emma, tonguing his navel in search of the last few eggs. 'You're right! It does taste the same.'

Stuart's lunch was indeed on a plate; a paper plate in his office. The phone call he'd stayed in for flashed on line two. It was Detroit, Michigan, confirming the Supremes for August 20 at the Albert Hall. Now he could phone ATV.

'Shit, piss, bugger, bollocks!' Jonathan swore at himself as he tried to untangle the mess of tape on the floor.

'Anyone important?' asked Simon, popping his head round the studio door.

'Mia bloody Farrow! I spent forever getting something with her and Sinatra, and now the little shit-box has unspooled the lot.'

'Just don't step on it. You can wind it back on to a new spool.'

'I shouldn't bloody well have to!' Jonathan was not to be placated. 'If we had a decent machine like a Nagra or Studer, this wouldn't happen. Poxy Revox is always jamming!'

Simon turned Oriental. 'Financial controller say poxy Revox better than no flucking machine at all.'

Jonathan flopped down on to the floor next to the

pile of crumpled tape, a sad look of defeat crossing his rugged features. 'I wanted to do something for Bill and Emma. Mia's married Sinatra, Brigitte Bardot married Guenther Sachs; tomorrow is wedding number three. I wanted a voice-bite from everyone, cut into a thirty-second piece: I'd run it on the air and then give it to them as a memento.'

'That's a lovely idea.' Simon knelt down beside the mess of brown plastic. 'I'll give you a hand. We'll do it!'

Post-luncheon, post-coital and past caring, Emma and Bill lay cosily entwined on the drawing-room sofa planning life after tomorrow. Honeymooning in Jamaica didn't mean staying with Bill's parents. A few days, or maybe a week to get acquainted, then Bill's plan was to tour the island by car, stopping at Ocho Rios and Montego Bay to visit friends, followed by a blissful week in the Blue Mountains visiting no-one.

'When do you want to come back to England?' asked Emma, slipping her hand under his shirt and gently scratching his back just below the right shoulder blade, one of his favourite turn-ons.

Bill mused for a moment before answering. 'I don't care; maybe we'll go somewhere else.'

Emma stopped scratching. 'What about FREE? What about the radio?'

'I'm not that keen to work for John Walters. I signed on with Stuart. If he goes, I'll have to think again.'

Emma disentangled herself from him and sat bolt upright. 'Do you really think he'll sell?'

'From what you told me of Gerald's conversation after Reg got killed, I think he'd be daft not to.'

355

'I've still got the IRC. I can't just turn my back and walk away.'

'If Gerald's scenario is accurate, there'll be no need for an IRC past next summer. We've got a month off for the honeymoon; I'll bet it's settled by then, one way or another.'

'You're right, of course.' Emma sighed, then bent down and kissed his cheek.

'I suppose I'd better check all the press have their start positions for tomorrow morning. I'd hate to screw up what could be my last job.' She flicked the hair from her forehead and adopted an aristocratic pose. 'Would look awfully suspect on one's references.'

They both laughed, then kissed slowly and tenderly, putting John's take-over, the IRC, and the future of British radio into proper perspective.

> *Tonight's the start of celebration,*
> *tonight we're gonna rock the nation.*
> *Bill and Emma tie the knot*
> *at eleven-thirty, on the dot.*
> *Prince Mikie's gonna to play the tune,*
> *to keep you howlin' at the moon.*

Shortly before seven o'clock, as the last wisps of morning mist were clearing from the gardens of Ovington Square, a white James Young Phantom Five Rolls Royce glided to a halt outside number seven. This was Stuart's wedding present; the finest of carriages to take them to Harwich, wait, and then deliver them to Heathrow. He'd drive the office staff in the Bentley and meet the happy couple at the docks, the notable exception to the transport arrangements being John Walters, who said he preferred an early morning train and a British

Rail breakfast. Stuart didn't believe him for a second, but didn't care much either, as long as he still had the bank draft in his pocket.

The bride and groom stood in the hall and gave each other a last look over before departure. Emma had chosen a yellow knee-length silk dress after careful consideration of three vital points – comfort, manoeuvrability and looks, in that order. Her day would be spent climbing on and off boats, negotiating dock-side ladders at low tide, and endeavouring to stand still on a breezy moving deck. The weather forecast was good, but her trust in things meteorological had been severely dented last summer when she'd worn her two-piece sun outfit to Hyde Park on the strength of a sunny forecast, only to be drenched in the most violent downpour of the year. She'd also be faced with numerous photographers and tabloid journos who'd like nothing better than a picture of our heroine disappearing over the side, legs akimbo, to place under their headline 'Wedding has Bride All At Sea'. That horrible vision made her decide on flat, yellow patent-leather rubber-soled shoes, which dear Mr Tombly in Hampstead made for her in just under a week.

Bill saw the wisdom in Emma's thinking and doubled Tombly's order. When his black leather loafers with deck-grip soles arrived at the flat yesterday, he gave a moment's thought to marketing this footwear to the party-giving boat owners of the Miami Yacht Club. He filed the thought in his post-honeymoon memory.

'You look very handsome, Mr Mason.' Emma flicked a small white speck off his jacket.

'And you look stunningly beautiful.'

Emma cupped his face in her hands. 'If this all gets out of hand today as far as the press is concerned, you will

remember that I love you and that's what's important.'
She saw a smile beam through his eyes, his expression
one of languid contentment. She chuckled. 'What?'

'I'm just thinking of life with a public relations director
for a wife.'

'And?'

'Brilliant! Just wear rubber-soled shoes and smile.
What could be easier?'

The door-bell rang.

'Do we have all the luggage?'

'Do we have time for a quick one?'

Emma placed hands on hips. 'Don't wind me up,
you!'

Bill loved that. First sign of aggression – hands on
hips. It was obvious, out of date, silly; but it was
absolutely Emma, and it told him the public relations
expert was about to go to work. 'Two more cases in
the bedroom. I'll get them.'

Emma's secretary, Jeanette, implemented the press
arrangements. She was a pleasant girl of no exceptional
talent, but astute enough to know that, if Emma decided
to leave, she could be in line for promotion – provided
she handled today's events without major problems.
Press packs had been printed, invitations issued and
accepted, arrangements made. She'd covered all the
bases, but in a business that had seen a murder make
front-page news and a drug bust not rate a single
column inch, nothing could be taken as read until it
was in the paper; and then there was no guarantee it
would be the truth.

Jeanette boarded the 08:02 from Liverpool Street
with six journalists, ten photographers, and a sixteen-
millimetre-film crew she'd hired to record the day's
events for the bride and groom and, hopefully, to

produce an end feature for Independent Television News.

Emma had the Rolls Royce stop a mile from Harwich docks.

'Last-minute check,' she said, sliding on to the pile-carpeted floor and opening the cocktail cabinet. 'Pass me my bag, sweetheart.'

'Are we down to stealing the crystal?' Puzzled, Bill did as requested, but held on when she tried to grab it. He looked at her, sitting cross-legged, one hand on her bag, the other clearing the crystal decanters from the cabinet. She tugged at the bag, he held on.

'William!'

'What are you doing?'

'I want to use the mirror behind. They should build these things with a proper vanity instead of these stupid cocktail cabinets.'

Bill took a mental snapshot of his bride-to-be, full decanter of sherry in one hand, clutching her handbag with the other; looking up at him, lipstick slightly smudged, hair a little out of place, eyes alive and sparkling. He let go of the bag and smiled at her.

'I know,' she whispered back. 'I love you, too.'

Fifteen minutes later they stepped out of the limousine on Harwich dock to a volley of flash cameras and questions. They posed beside the car, in front of the car, clasping hands around the Spirit of Ecstasy, and waving from inside the car, pretending to be leaving on honeymoon. From now until they boarded the flight for Jamaica they were public property. The media circus was in town and they were today's ringmasters.

Stuart, Gerald, John Walters, Jeanette, three reporters, three photographers and the film crew joined the bride and groom aboard *Offshore One*. The sea reflected the sun off its flat glassy surface; a warm south-westerly breeze was a welcome antidote to the mid-morning heat, leaving the most pleasant of conditions aboard the crowded tug. Bill and Emma gave two interviews, three photo sessions, and a lot of hugs to each other. Gerald gave a lot of attention to Jeanette, telling her how well the day was going and asking her how long she'd been with the company. Stuart gave no attention at all to John Walters, preferring to discharge his duties as both host and best man exclusively to the principal player and the members of the British press.

As they boarded FREE it became obvious that no expense had been spared to decorate the mine-sweeper for its first wedding. Signal flags stretched from bow to mast-top to stern; red bunting fluttered from the flying bridge, connecting it to the rose-covered wooden arch the Captain had built in the middle of the forward deck. Three wooden rum kegs, sawn in half and planted with fuchsias and shrub-honeysuckle, stood either side of the trellis, filling the air with fresh fragrance. In the centre of the arch, the Captain's card table, covered by the only proper tablecloth on board, supported the ship's best vase, in which stood two dozen long-stemmed red roses.

Honey greeted Emma with an enormous hug; the Captain stood on the flying bridge, a broad grin lighting his usually solemn face, and waved everyone aboard. Jeanette ushered the press and film crew to the mess-room for refreshments and a last-minute briefing.

Emma took in the profusion of flowers and bunting in one gradual sweep. Everything looked so colourful, so beautiful, so *right*. She could barely believe it had all been arranged for her benefit.

She felt so happy, so in love. She tried to think of

a word to fit this heavenly setting; a word that would sum up all her feelings at this exact moment in time, a word she could add to her private dictionary. She felt Bill's arm brush against her; she felt so wonderful, so complete, as if she could burst with joy. Not a single word, real or made up, could aptly describe how she felt today. It was time to jettison her unreal universe, however amusing, and start to live as half of a couple, sharing her secrets, finding out his. The one name she wouldn't change was that of the miniature fern, who now lived on the kitchen windowsill at Ovington Square. She would always call him Giant.

The bride and groom were discreetly separated thanks to the covert schemings of Honey and Simon Street. Honey had volunteered to act as stage-manager as her contribution to the day; an offer accepted wholeheartedly by the Captain, who was none too sure of what to do in the first place. She'd drawn up the floor plan, ordered the flowers, organised the catering and even detailed the timetable to accommodate news requirement, tug arrival time, and press deadlines. She thought it only proper to separate the couple before the ceremony and had arranged for a small spread of hors d'oeuvres and a cold bottle of Bollinger to be delivered to her cabin, ditto the twins'. The bride and groom quickly cottoned on to the evil plan and made mock protests until they were safely in their respective cabins.

Within three minutes of arrival Stuart and John were promenading on a deserted top deck, savouring the warm breeze and brilliant sunshine.

'These are lovely flowers, don't you think?' Stuart thought he'd test the water.

'Are we paying for them?'

Water very cold, thought Stuart. 'You don't want to be here, do you?'

John leaned on the railing. 'Not really.' He smiled at Stuart with a warmth that belied his remark. 'I wish them well, but I really would like to finish our business. New York gets to work in a couple of hours and I want an answer for them.'

Stuart felt the heat of the sun warm his back as he gazed towards the English coastline. So much work, so much soul, so many good intentions had been poured into this ship by so many talented people; now it would only represent maximum profits for a limited time. He knew there was no use fighting it; a vote of no confidence from the shareholders would usurp his power, and he was sure Walters had one securely up his sleeve should it be needed. He would make massive profits; his original investment would be returned, doubled, within eighteen months, he still owned Hayes Mews, for which he would now charge rent, and his director's fees for the previous two years had topped £75,000. But one more goal was yet to be achieved. While he felt no debt of loyalty to the conniving Walters, he did to the people who'd helped him realise his dream.

'I'll accept your deal on one condition. All employees, whether staff, contract, or freelance, are given a choice to sign new agreements with you or leave with two months' pay, no questions asked.'

John's New York brain couldn't fathom why any outgoing director would try to protect his staff rather than negotiate a higher pay-off for himself. 'We'd do that anyway, Stuart. Our company always sweeps clean.'

'Would you offer them the money?'

John protected his eyes from the sun and squinted at the upright Englishman. 'Not unless we had to.'

'Well then: now you do.'

Walters was still not convinced. 'Is that it?'

'That's it.' Stuart shrugged his shoulders. 'I'm happy with your offer. Your business plan is short-term; mine is on dry land.' A wry smile started to curl up the left side of his mouth. 'Tell me one thing. Did you set Interpol on Eddie Lincoln?'

'My father did. I just supplied information.' He tried to impersonate Stuart's voice. 'Couldn't allow that sort of thing, old chap. Just not cricket.'

'Quite right, too. Congratulations.' Inwardly, Stuart admired the attempt at mimicry, he wasn't bad for an American. Outwardly he showed no reaction, save a polite, businesslike smile. 'The paperwork is in my briefcase, duly signed and witnessed.'

John produced from his inside pocket a white envelope, edged in blue, with the initials IWS embossed on the top left-hand corner. He handed it to Stuart. 'Welcome to the millionaires' club.'

They shook hands. Conflicting senses of loss and liberation fought for supremacy over Stuart's emotions, but he was determined not to linger in maudlin afterthoughts. He'd chosen today because of the wedding. This was a day of happiness; he'd cry for his radio station some other time. 'Thank you very much.'

John Walters took the briefcase, checked his watch, excused himself, and strode at a fair pace toward the radio room. Stuart took one last turn around the deck, patting the radio mast affectionately, checking the generator housing was secure, and taking a long, photographic look at the scented altar, so lovingly built by the people for whom he'd negotiated the option.

He was smiling to himself as he knocked on Honey's cabin door.

'Who is it?'

'Stuart.'

Much laughter from behind the door.

'I'll come back later.'

The door flew open. 'You will not!' Honey stood before him, one piece of her 'up' hairstyle hanging decidedly 'down' her face. 'I desperately need help with this and that woman is too much in love to hold a hairgrip.'

Once inside the cabin, Stuart could see the reason for Emma's incapacity. Something had triggered off a crying laugh, and the bride had become blinded by her running make-up. Funny in the office; a problem fifteen minutes before a wedding. 'What started this?'

'This bit of hair!' Honey pulled at the renegade strand. Emma started laughing again.

'Girls! Please! This is a wedding day, not a hen night.'

'You're absolutely right!' Honey controlled her giggles. 'Make us feel serious, Stuart. Show us your willie!'

Both girls dissolved with laughter. Stuart had to get their attention.

'I've sold the ship!'

It worked. Emma and Honey froze mid-laugh and stared at him, aghast.

'And I've got Honey a TV show.'

He watched their expressions transforming from disbelief to joy. Emma was surprised to feel a sense of relief that it was finally over. The sadness she'd endured over the past weeks was more than compensated for by the bliss of loving Bill; and now there'd be no definite end date to the honeymoon.

Honey leaped up and hugged him tightly around the neck. 'Where? When? Who with?'

She felt too wonderful for him to maintain his reserve. He held her close to him, inhaling her sweet fragrance, confident that she'd see him in a more favourable light now he was no longer her boss. Stuart never gave up easily on anything, be it business or pleasure, and he had plans for Ms Papanicholas that would solve her name problem once and for all.

'I thought you two had a business relationship,' chuckled Emma from across the cabin.

'We do,' replied Honey, sliding away from Stuart's embrace. 'And business is very good at the moment.'

Stuart looked at his watch. 'I'll give you details later. My duty now lies with the bridegroom.' He bowed politely to both. 'Ladies.'

'When can I leave here?' asked Honey, as Stuart walked through the door.

'With us. This afternoon, if you like.' He heard their laughter ringing all the way to the twins' cabin.

'A glass of champagne for the best man,' ordered Bill. 'Come and sit with us and tell stories of great courage and adventure, lest I get cold feet and scooteth off to the nearest pub.'

'You'd have to scoot a fair distance, I'll wager.'

'No time, dear comrades,' interrupted Simon. 'The look on yonder boss's face tells me final run-down is afoot.'

'Tell us, oh brain on stilts,' continued Lewis, offering a full glass of bubbly. 'What be our orders for the fray?'

Stuart took the glass and looked at Bill. 'Is no intelligent conversation possible with these two?'

Simon stood up indignantly. 'Objection! Counsel has not yet defined intelligent conversation!'

Stuart decided, once again, on the direct approach. 'I've sold the ship.'

'Of course you have, dear boy.' Simon's impression was spot-on Noël Coward. 'I suspect you've done terribly well.'

'Never mind the money, see,' interjected Lewis's Cagney. 'Just tell me how long, see, how long before we blow this joint?'

Stuart was amazed that his announcement provided such a nonchalant response. He deduced they were ahead of his game and logged a mental memorandum never again to underestimate his staff. 'I think you two should stay a few months. Use the studio time to create new programme ideas that I can take to the BBC. There are no free studios in London.' He looked over at Bill.

'I emptied my cabin last time I went ashore,' said the groom. 'Emma and I will probably take the chance to see a bit of the world before we come back to England.'

'In that case, gentlemen,' Stuart raised his glass, 'drink to future success and happiness and get this reprobate married before he changes his mind.'

Captain Jan Vourner stood in front of his full-length mirror and inspected his number-one uniform for any blemish. Last week he'd received a long and frank letter from Stuart explaining the situation and outlining his options. The Captain needed just one reading to decide; he accepted Stuart's cheque for one thousand pounds and typed his resignation, dated today. Marrying two friends as his last duty made up for some of the more harrowing moments of his captaincy. When he reached Amsterdam tonight he could put his number-one uniform away for good; or at least watch Lisa cut it down to shorts and a waistcoat, which he was sure she would happily tackle at the first available opportunity.

He walked on deck, shoes polished and cap correct. The sun glinted off the gold braid on his jacket. Out the corner of his eye he saw two Dutch seamen loading his trunk on to the tug alongside. Twelve more hours, then Lisa.

'Such a glorious day for it.'

Gerald's voice cut through the Captain's thoughts. He only half-recognised the man before him. 'Mr Copeland?'

'That's right. Friend of Stuart's. We met when you first arrived.'

'And, it seems, when I'm about to leave.' Vourner extended his hand. 'After you.'

The ceremony was simple. The wind stayed light, the sun stayed bright. The Captain didn't fluff his lines; the bride and groom said their words perfectly. As they kissed, oblivious to the clicking of cameras and whirling of movie makers, Jan Vourner slowly removed his cap and relinquished the captaincy of M.V. *FREE*.

That kiss also freed Honey from her ceremonial duties. She rushed to her cabin, crammed all her belongings into her two suitcases, and solicited Mo to carry them on to the tug. Stuart met her on the top deck.

'May I offer you a lift to London?'

'You most certainly may.' She put on her sunglasses. 'What's this TV show all about?'

Stuart saw John Walters emerge on to deck through the f'ward hatch. 'You must excuse me, Honey. I have to speak to John.' He squeezed her arm gently before striding off across the deck. 'Dinner!' he called back to her. 'I'll tell you over dinner!'

Honey watched his back thoughtfully as he walked away, and considered her options.

'A word with you, John.'

The new managing director did not look pleased. 'God damn, Stuart. Everybody's fucking leaving!'

'Let me explain. Honey's quitting the ship. She's due to be off from today for two weeks' shore leave; she's just not coming back. The Captain had always planned to retire with me; his number two will stand in for now and I can give you a list of at least five suitable replacements. The twins are staying, so are Nigel, Peter, Brian, Charlie B and the overnight crew. I'm sure you can pull a twelve-hour operation from that lot.' Stuart watched the rapid calculations flash over John's face. 'I think it best you stay on board for a while and sort things out. It'll be your baby in two minutes.' He saw Walters wince at the thought of staying on board a second longer. 'I'll send the tug back for you around teatime.'

'This is FREE news at noon; I'm Jonathan Gilby. Top story this hour comes from Holland where Interpol have smashed one of the world's biggest drug rings. Working on a tip-off, officers raided a canal club in Amsterdam this morning where they arrested six people and recovered over eighty kilos of top-grade cocaine with a street value of several million pounds. There have been several simultaneous arrests in France, and in England, Michael Edward Tasker of Ilford, Essex, was detained last night and charged with attemting to import controlled drugs into the UK. In America, former film star Ronald Reagan has won the Republican nomination for governor of California; and from Lusaka, confirmation today that Zambia will resume sending copper through Rhodesia, smashing the trade embargo imposed by Whitehall. On the lighter side of life, after Farrow and Sinatra, Bardot and Sachs, come Saxby and Mason. Details of their marriage on board the radio ship following these words about hair care.'

Jonathan started the commercial and finished his letter of resignation.

Once Emma'd changed into jeans and a plain black T-shirt for the journey back, the press seemed to lose interest in both pictures and story. Emma sat on an empty water crate at the stern of the tug and cuddled her husband. She looked at the newspaper men sipping champagne in the midships cabin, through to Stuart and Honey standing at the bow, deep in conversation. 'I hope my family won't tire you too much.'

Bill squeezed her waist. 'It's my family we have to survive.'

'Not exactly.' She looked up at him sheepishly. My mother and sisters are meeting us at Harwich and riding with us to Heathrow.'

'I had plans for that journey, I wanted to ravish you in the back of the Roller.' He adopted a little-boy-hurt expression, his eyes sad and drooping.

Emma spotted a photographer sneaking away from the booze-up and pointing a camera in their direction. She dug Bill gently in the ribs. 'Camera at three o'clock. Smile, sweetheart.'

EPILOGUE

On July 28 1966 the Marine Offences Bill was published by the Wilson Government, forbidding British companies or individuals to supply or advertise on the off-shore stations.

On August 14 1967 that Bill became law.

In defiance of all the opinion polls, in June 1970 the Conservatives won the General Election with a majority of forty-three.

Three and a quarter years later, on September 16 1973, Capital Radio started broadcasting as part of the independent local radio network. Three of its five front-line DJs were ex-pirates.

A Selected List of Fiction Available from Mandarin

☐ 7493 0576 2	**Tandia**	Bryce Courtenay	£
☐ 7493 0122 8	**Power of One**	Bryce Courtenay	£
☐ 7493 0581 9	**Daddy's Girls**	Zoe Fairbairns	£
☐ 7493 0942 3	**Silence of the Lambs**	Thomas Harris	£
☐ 7493 0530 4	**Armalite Maiden**	Jonathan Kebbe	£
☐ 7493 0134 1	**To Kill a Mockingbird**	Harper Lee	£
☐ 7493 1017 0	**War in 2020**	Ralph Peters	£
☐ 7493 0946 6	**Godfather**	Mario Puzo	£
☐ 7493 0381 6	**Loves & Journeys of Revolving Jones**	Leslie Thomas	£
☐ 7493 0381 6	**Rush**	Kim Wozencraft	£